Quelocand:
Land of the Queens

THE GOLDEN REALM CHRONICALS
BOOK ONE

Cadmi Ó'Cléirigh

Book Cover by Cadmi Ó'Cléirigh
Illustrations by Cadmi Ó'Cléirigh
Art work/Paintings by Nancy Davenport

ISBN: PB 979-8-9917834-3-9
ISBN: HB 979-8-9917834-1-5

10 9 8 7 6 5 4 3 2 1
1st edition 2025

Cadhmí Ó Cléirigh

For my Dad
Whose imagination is forever widening,
And whose love of research rivels my own.

&
Alicia S. Rivers who pushed me out of my comfort zone.
Thank you Alicia for the push that gave me
Anene the Witch & Tadhgán the Fairy Warrior.

Preface

Growing up I was so lucky to have a family with a rich Irish heritage, that my brothers and I clung to more than the rest of our lineage. Much to the chagrin of my mother. I love you mom, yes I know you have relatives too. Because of my roots, I've always had a love of wee folk and have a heady respect for them. In 2017 I was given the opportunity to visit the Emerald Isle, and it was everything I'd thought it would be. The Irish hospitality certainly lived up to the hype. I had a wonderful time everywhere I went. The conversations, the food (Best damn ribeye and fish ever), the drinks, the music, everything was exemplary. It was on that trip I first saw Beltany Circle on the outskirts of Raphoe, County Donegal.

The path leading to the mammoth circle in the middle of a cow field was almost as magickal as the circle itself. I walked through a tree covered tunnel that must have been touched by fairies. As I spied the circle peeking through the flowers, a joy and wonder filled me that I couldn't explain. It was when I approached the circle that I felt more than the wind whipping through my hair or the thrashing of my coat this way and that. I'm not sure why I felt I needed to, but I touched the outlying stone before entering the circle. Now, some may call me crazy, nuts, or just plain silly, but I know better. I *felt* what that circle had to offer. It was in the ground where I stood, in the view, the air, and in the stones. Power. Old and waiting. For what, I did not know.

There's a picture my father took of me while I was in the circle. The utter joy that was on my face was unmistakable. What wasn't caught were the tears stinging my eyes or the fact that I let a few of them fall. I walked the entirety of the circle touching every stone. Two years later another trip took us to Ireland, and I insisted we go back to what had now been deemed, My Circle, for it hadn't left my mind once since I'd stepped foot on that ground. They say you can't go home again, and I had a genuine fear that the sentiment would be correct. I was nervous I wouldn't have the same feeling as the first time. As it turns out, I had nothing to worry about. And if the feeling is true, you can go home again.

While on that last visit to my circle something flashed into my brain. A witch, there was no doubt she was just that, standing in the heart of her circle. For the circle was hers as much as it was mine. Yet the witch was not alone, with her stood the most gorgeous Irish Dane both guardian and companion. However, it was what was on the *outside* that tugged at my mind. A man, with a feeling of *other* about him, stood waiting for her. Clad in leather armor and armed to the teeth, yet there was no fear or worry on the witches face. I wondered what their story was. Was I seeing the past, having been standing in the middle of that powerful place, it was possible. Or as a writer, was my mind simply turning? If it was the first, then, cool. If it was the latter however, as I was a contemporary romance author I knew the idea would never leave the confines of my mind. Or so I thought.

In the summer of 2024 an opportunity to write a short story presented itself. Of course the rub was I had never written a short story and it had to be fantasy. "I don't write fantasy!" I would say. Alicia S. Rivers wouldn't take no for an answer. She was crafty let me tell you. Once I was voluntold, I used my love of Ireland and the wee folk for the basis of the short story. A memory, from when I was standing at the heart of Beltany Circle, of the witch and her waiting warrior flooded my brain. This was the perfect opportunity to delve into their story. And Naturally I was going to use our circle, the witches and mine.

I did something that I'd never done before while writing. I am what is known as a pantser, generally. I might have a vague idea of what the story will be about, but for the most I just write and let the chips fall where they may. Yet for this short story I sat down and plotted! I decided about the story, where I wanted it to go. Characters and so on. It was really bizarre. I had so much written down; it was questioned if I would be able to make it fit in the short story. I maintained that I didn't know what I was doing and wanted to cover all the bases.

I realized; rather quickly, how much I really *didn't* know about fairies. So research and more research. After reading the short story, my father, who had been researching right along with me, was appalled than my fairies were the same size as the humans in the story. "They aren't supposed to be more than 3 inches tall!" he would say. And my retort, "This is fantasy, I can do whatever I want." It was that realization that I loved the most. In fantasy, I had the freedom to do whatever I wanted. However when the 1200 word short story was finished, it hit me. It wasn't enough, I hadn't even scratched the surface of what I wanted to tell. I needed their beginning, middle and end.

Before I knew what was happening, I began to write. And Quelocand: Land of the Queens; the first book of the Golden Realms Chronicles was written. While doing research on certain elements I began to mesh Mythology from many cultures, Fandom, and reality together. Once again my father would say, "That isn't what the myth says." or "You have the timelines wrong." or my favorite, "And you still have the fairies too tall." I would just smile and once again I found myself saying "This is fantasy, I can do whatever I want." And I did precisely that. I allowed that freedom to wash over me and I wrote whatever I wanted.

So why am I telling you all this? Mainly so I can say this. I researched bits and pieces from Irish, Celtic, Norse, and Roman Mythology, and the Tuatha de Danann. I've taken the information I compiled, threw it all in a mixing bowl with my own thoughts and created my own world, with Goddess, Gods, villains, and heroes. If in reading you think "huh that's cool." and decide to do your own snooping(as I tend to do when reading *anything*), wondering if the God or Goddess is real or made up, the places mentioned are fact or fiction, or if you want more information on witches, fairies or the Tuatha de Danann. Then YAY! I did my job well.

I hope you enjoy reading Quelocand: Land of the Queens, my first fantasy. Just remember, this is a fantasy, and I can do whatever I want. Enjoy.

Cadmi O'Cléirigh

Irish/Norse Phrases, Names and Translations

Phrases

saighdiúir brutish (sighja brood-ish) = brute soldier

Suíochán an Ard-Shargert = Seat of the High Priestess

Mo ghrá duit a banphrionsa (Mo garra di a bon-free-on-sa)= My love to you my princess

Is breá liom túmo Rí (iss brah lum too muh ree)= I love you my King

Is breá liom tú mo Bhanríon (ihs-bra-lum tu mo ban-ree-un) = I love you my Queen

heimskr (hame-sker) = fool

Shop

Búistéir (boost-ee-y-air) = Butcher

Grósaer (Gro-say-er) = Grocer

Bácús (bak-ciss) = Bakery

Names

*Brigid_* (bri-gid) Irish Goddess of Fire and Water

Cailleach (KAH-lee-ack) Irish Goddess of Winter and the First Witch

Caoimhe (Kwee-vah) Gypsy Vanner

Cathal (CAH-tal) Shire Horse

Ciarán (Keer-awn) Father and King of the Fairies

Meili (MAY-lee) Norse God of Travel

Póg na Díoltas (POG-ah-DEEL-tus) Kiss of Revenge – Flann's Sword

Rí (ree) = King – Irish Drought

Scáth Chiaráin (SKAH-kahn KEE-uh-reen) The Guardian summoned for Miranda

Siobhan (SHIV-awn) Witch From Witrotean

Tadhg (Tie-g) Connemara Pony

Tadhgán (Teegan) Right Hand of the King/ Warrior

Places in Both Realms

Ireland - Co. Donegal- Raphoe

The village is just outside the city limit- made up

Locbroalm(Loc-bra-lum)- Fairy Realms

Eldcolary (Eld-Col-ary)- Sanctuary of the Elders

Elvkinles (Elv-kin-alls)- Isle of the Elves

Quelocand(Quee-loc-land)- Mortal Realm- Land of the Queen

Witrotean(Wit-rote-e-in)- Ocean of the Witches

Trigger Warnings

This book contains mentions and descriptions of dismemberment, as well as mentions of the slaying of an animal.

One

"You have to go!" Ciarán urged his Right Hand. "Flann just informed me of the new decree to ensure there are no claims to the throne."

"How is that possible sire?" Tadhgán's shadow wafted around the cell that the King had been thrown into years ago. Yet, thanks to the aid of some spellcasters, Tadhgán was able to reach his king. "You have a daughter who is about to come of age."

"Flann has heard whispers of her, and the rumblings of war to free me and unseat him as the ruler." Tadhgán watched as his king dropped his head in his hands, his long cascading silver hair slipping gently over his broad shoulders. The large silver and black wings on his back shimmered with hints of green in the waning light as they drooped, mimicking the despair that had lodged itself into his heart the moment Flann had brought the news to him of the decree. It didn't happen often, but he was always taken aback when his steadfast King, the true ruler of Locbroalm, showed any emotion regarding his incarceration. No matter how long Ciarán had been imprisoned, with his realm being ruled over by the usurper Flann, he never allowed the passage of time to dull the regalness of his true stature. "Tadhgán, I haven't seen my wife and daughter since the war broke out. Anene was only eight years old when I was taken. To ensure the safety of my child, steps were taken so she wouldn't remember much about me, or anything of our realm. Miranda, the love and light of my life, my mate will remember. She will do all that is right in protecting our daughter from harm." Ciarán's deep green eyes flashed with pride, love, and despair at the mention of his mate and only child. Not since the time of the Gods had there been a mating bond as strong as Ciarán and his Miranda. The separation should have killed them both. Yet, because of the child, Tadhgán knew his King and Queen wouldn't perish due to their separation. "Miranda, my mate," her name was like a prayer on his lips. "Is the most powerful witch to ever walk in this realm or any other. If she knows about the threat, if she knows the true danger Flann now poses, she will do everything in her power to ensure Anene's protected." The fierceness in his voice vibrated quietly off the dark stone walls of his cell. Ciaran's eyes flitted to the sound of the approaching footsteps. Tadhgán moved needlessly to the darkest corner of the King's confinement.

"Well, *your majesty*," the guard sneered. "Have you heard the news? Your half-breed abomination will be hunted down, tortured, and sent to the chambers." He paused for the euphoric high he received when Ciarán's normally neutral face paled at the mention of the chambers. The entire realm was aware of those torturous rooms and what took place in them. Stories of dark sadistic acts and the horrors that befell all who entered, females in particular, were those in which nightmares were born of. "Then, after she has been used up," his black tongue darted over his lips. "Your spawn will be slaughtered like the animal she is. Just like all other half-breeds in the realm."

The chuckle that spewed from his jailer was unnatural in sound and carried with it a rotten sulfuric odor. Ciarán could only guess the putrid smell was that of the decaying soul within. It was his odor that served as a reminder of the true dangers in his midst. Feeling, rather than seeing Tadhgán in the corners of the room, Ciarán was so grateful to the legions of spellcasters loyal to the true King. Thanks to the casters, this, and every conversation he and Tadhgán held over the years have been in the confines of his mind. Thus, protecting the contents from the enemy. Ciarán knew the shadow of Tadhgán seethed with anger. But there was something else happening to the realm, something Flann, the usurper himself, had boasted to his prisoner. Something that Ciarán would keep to himself until it was the right time to reveal. "What? Nothing to say?"

"Only that I would like to have my dinner please." Ciarán smiled and looked at the food in the guard's hands. Flann had decided that keeping the king alive and well, was the best way to keep the realm in line. He was a prisoner; however, his surroundings were comfortable. There was a serviceable bed, books to read, paper and quills to write, and a lavatory for bathing and other needs. Because he was never allowed out of the cell he now occupied, a single window had been added in which he could have an, albeit small, view of the realm that was his by right. Ciarán looked into the guard's hateful, soulless eyes and sighed as he took the tray that was thrust at him through the slot in his prison door.

"Eat, you blood traitor." His jailer spat. "After your spawn has been executed it won't be long before Flann orders you to be next." With that he turned on his heel and retreated, taking the stench of decay down the corridor with him.

Ciarán set the tray on his desk and gave his attention to the phantom of Tadhgán who was now in the center of the room. His heart hardened with his new resolve. Straightening and pulling his shoulders back he became the King he knew in his heart he still was.

"Go through the doorway." His voice took on the authority of the office he held. "Find Miranda and my daughter Anene. With the help of my mate, I have every confidence that you can keep what is precious to me and the realm safe until the time is right." He could see the objection on Tadhgán's stony face. "I will be fine; Flann knows better than to kill me until he's sure there can't be another claim." A stiff nod was the only answer Ciarán received. "Good, now go and--" gone was the king and in its place was that of a father, husband and mate. "Tell them that I love them and give my mate this message." Closing his eyes, he wrapped the message still in his thoughts in a cloaking binding spell. Through the magick that was granted to the true King of the realm, Ciarán inserted his missive to his mate into Tadhgán's mind. Thus protecting the words the King was sending to his long absent mate.

"I will do as you command." Tadhgán bowed his head and with the words given him by the casters, he broke the connection to his King.

Tadhgán stood in the center of the Spellcaster's circle. Head bowed in sorrow for his King and the realm. Knowing what needed to be done, he took a deep breath and raised his eyes to the casters that surrounded him.

"Flann beat us to it. That bastard usurper gleefully told the King that his daughter was to be hunted down, and slaughtered." He unclenched his hands to run them through his long Auburn hair. Fire mixed with grief shown from his eyes of the same color. "I've been ordered to seek out the Queen and protect the heir until it is time for her to claim the throne." Shaking out his long muscular arms Tadhgán stepped from the circle and faced Fintan. His lifelong friend, confidant, and head of the Spellcaster's Order. "While I am gone you will have to prepare for the coming war. Keep the Fae talking of the heir and give them hope that we can retake the realm."

"How long do you foresee we have until war finally takes hold?" Fintan asked while handing Tadhgán his bow, quiver, and sword.

"I don't know. Our time moves so much faster than the mortal realm. The queen could have moved from where they settled. Hell the heir could have left." His large black feathered wings fluttered as he added his weapons over his leather armor. He knew once he went through the doorway to the human realm, he was going to have to pull his massive wings back into himself. He was used to it. Having to hide his wings was something he'd had to contend with over the course of his long life. "But when the daughter is ready, we will come back through."

"Here, this is for your safe travel through the doorway." Fintan handed Tadhgán a small vial containing silver swirling liquid.

"And what might this be?" Tadhgán inspected the vial. He trusted the head of the Spellcaster Order with his life, but he wasn't made Right Hand of the King by taking everything at face value. There were always questions that needed asking.

"Have no fear, you great olf." Fintan chuckled at his friend's suspicious nature. "This will render you undetectable while you make your way to the doorway. But keep to the high clouds for as long as you can. This will only work for a short time. Glug down the whole of the contents before you make the descent to the doorway." Fintan watched as Tadhgán peered closely into the silver swirls. "Do you doubt me brother?"

"Indeed, I do not." Placing the vial in his satchel Tadhgán gave Fintan his full attention, "I was only wondering if you have mastered the ability to add a pleasant flavor to your concoctions." He smirked.

"You have only to taste to find the answer to that my friend." Fintan held out his hand and the two clasped forearms in farewell. "Be safe, be well, be ready." Fintan said in the way when a journey is on the horizon.

"You as well." Tadhgán bid Fintan and the order farewell, unleashed his black wings and vaulted in the air. Tadhgán's powerful wings gave him the ability to fly higher and faster than the rest of the Fae in the realm. This meant that he could travel, mostly, without being detected by Flann and his armies.

As he flew toward the hidden doorway to the human realm, he thought about the Queen and the daughter he was going to protect. He remembered when the king brought Miranda, a human witch, to the realm. There were few who took a human as their mate, and for a ruler of the realm to do so was unheard of. But when seeing how happy and suited the couple were, the majority of the realm applauded the King's choice. However, there was a small, uncharacteristic to the realm, group that felt for the King to choose a human was an insult to the Fae. It took some time, but soon the small group quieted. It was thought that the unrest had been won over by the King and his now crowned Queen. For years, Locbroalm lived up to its name of The Golden Realm. There was joy, love, and harmony.

When the royal couple announced there would be an heir to the throne, there were celebrations throughout the realm. Locbroalm was overjoyed at the prospect of a babe in the palace. Soon, the small group thought to have been won over, had instead, in secret, become a small but fierce faction. When the news of the child hit the ears of the intolerant and malcontent, words that had never been spoken were suddenly running rampant. Halfbreed, blood traitor, and abomination. For the first time in memory, there was a true threat of war. Not wanting to have the realm fall to war, Ciarán decided it was time to protect his mate and their unborn child. It was decreed that Tadhgán would be the only one to help his King move the Queen to the safety of Ireland. A little cottage, just outside of Raphoe, County Donegal was created. The hope was that it would only be temporary. Miranda, determined not to be separated from Ciarán long, went to the basement and created a doorway that Ciaran, Miranda and Tadhgán could use to travel between the two realms. Tadhgán smiled at the memory of the three of them deciding where the doorway in his realm would be. For the castle was eliminated as a choice immediately.

While still high in the clouds, Tadhgán, needing to keep his wits about him, took the vial given by Fintan from his satchel. The crafty Fae had given him the ability to cloak himself as he made his journey to the doorway.

For, as of a few days ago, Tadhgán was the only Fae who knew where the doorway was. When the rumblings of the heir came to Flann's ears, Ciarán had used the spell his mate had given him all those years ago to remove the knowledge of its placement.

He hovered, using the clouds as cover, Tadhgán looked at the little glass vial that held a silver liquid and shivered. Fintan never made anything that didn't taste like shit. Uncorking the stopper, taking a deep breath he threw back his head and swallowed the substance down.

"Fucking hell!" Tadhgán coughed and wheezed as Fintan's brew worked its way down his throat and into his body. Placing the now empty vial back in his satchel, Tadhgán watched as he disappeared. It was unsettling to witness his own body vanish before his eyes. "You are one crafty Fae Fintan." Remembering the cloaking would only last so long, he dove through the clouds making his way to the doorway, Queen Miranda, and the heir to the throne.

Two

"Time to lock up luv." Anene Wilkinson called from the back of the shop. Looking at her watch told her that the clock tower would soon be sounding four. And on a Saturday evening, with a single young girl working the register, Anene knew there was nothing worse than having to be at work.

"But," the teenager, who was fresh out of school and on holiday before going off to university, called back. "We don't close for another two hours." The girl padded to the back where Anene stood sorting the stock for the next sale days. Summer days meant lots of sales thanks to the height of the tourist season.

"I know Patty, but if I am not mistaken, don't you have a date with the O'Brian lad from the village?" Anene smiled as the young girl blushed. "Aye that's what I thought. You go on. The shop is slow, and this will give me the chance to go through the stock in peace."

"Are ya sure then?" At Anene's arched brow Patty practically bounced. "Oh, I thank you. Ye have no idea how excited I am, I thought Sean would never get the nerve to ask me on a date."

"And why not ask the lad yourself?" leaving the box she was rifling through, Anene sat on the edge of her desk and listened as Patty prattled on about how no respecting woman would lower herself to ask a man out. "Och, that's silly. But you are wastin' time luv, go off with ya and have a good time."

"Thank you Anene!" Patty sailed out the front door, but not before flipping the sign to close and locking the door. Waving, she ran to her car to ready herself for the date of a lifetime, as she put it.

Anene sat for a moment smiling after her employee and the excitement of a most wanted date. She tried to remember what it was like to be that age and readying yourself for 'the date of a lifetime' while on summer holiday before going off to university. She smiled to herself and nodded, *Aye, I remember the feeling alright.* she thought. Anene would be lying if she said she didn't miss it. And she never lied, especially to herself.

"Oh well," She sighed and stood at her full five-foot six height and stretched her back. "Enough of the pity party, me lass. Time to take advantage of having an empty shop for once."

Thankful for not donning a dress that morning, Anene picked up the box of trinkets, placed it on the desk and set to unwrap the contents. At twenty-five years old, Anene was always driven, and was the youngest shop owner in her village. No one was surprised, mind you, that she would be so successful and at such a young age. When she decided to open Cailleach's Nook, she couldn't wait to fill it with all manner of witchy things. She had candles, crystals, incense, herbs, and books. She also carried some clothes, scarfs, hats, and blankets. All of this she sourced locally. The candles and herbs were all made and grown by a woman from her own coven. The crystals and books were the only thing she had to scour for. There was a witch down south that had a connection for the crystals and the books Anene traveled for. She was excited to unpack the crystals from the clever witch in Ardmore. Every crystal was prettier than the last. Most customers who came in the shop had no idea what they were, other than that they were pretty and would be a good souvenir from the trip to Ireland. She knew that it was also a boon to buy from a supposed witch as well.

Now there were also just as many who came in and knew what every candle, crystal, herb and so on was for. It was for that reason that Anene wanted to make sure that she had the best quality in her shop.

"Oh, you clever witch!" Anene laughed as she pulled a small wooden box wrapped in white silk. She carefully unwrapped the silk to reveal an intricate carved Rowan tree on the lid of the box. "What have you done Deirdre?" Anene gently lifted the brass latch securing the lid. "Oh, my Goddess." She whispered.

Inside nestled in the box were ten individually wrapped wands, each of a different wood, carved to perfection and tipped with a crystal. She pulled the wands out and laid them gently on the white silk that wrapped the box. The wands were stunning and with each one tipped with amethyst, blue, green, yellow, and red aventurine, along with lapis lazuli, red jasper, clear quartz, and black tourmaline. Each one would have its own purpose. Running her fingertips softly over each one, she could feel the small amount of magick that had been used to create them. Not so much that a novice or someone wanting nothing more than a souvenir would be able to do anything with. But enough that if a true witch were to pick it up, they could add to what was there and use the wand as it was intended. Picking up her cell phone, she called Deirdre.

"You are an artist!" Anene exclaimed when the other witch answered on the second ring.

"I was waitin fer yer call, luv." Deirdre's sweet singing lilt chuckled over the airwaves.

"Why the bloody hell didn't you tell me you could make these? I would have bought you out monthly."

"Well to be honest, I wasn't sure they would be to yer taste."

"Not to my tastes! Don't be an eejit. Of course, they are to taste. Deir, they are magnificent. How quickly can you make them?"

"Well, those ten took me two months, but that was fast. Normally ten would take me more like six months because of work and coven duties." She cleared her throat. "Are the wands something you would like to carry? I mean I wouldn't be able to give a ton of them, but they could be a special item." She sounded hopeful.

"Are you daft? Aye I want them! And I will work with whatever timeline you want. Because of the time I can price them higher which might make them less appealing to the less magically inclined, but the rest would know the worth. Let's work on the cost and the commission now."

"Oh, I don't need a commission. Ye're already going to give me more than what I spent making them anyway."

"As I said before, don't be an eejit. This is fine craftsmanship, and you will receive commission on them. Not to worry about me making the money on them, they will be priced so we both benefit I can tell you."

The two women haggled over the price and commission. After the call was finished, Anene priced the wands twice the amount she agreed to on the phone. That made the wands at roughly three-hundred Euros, and to be honest that might still be too low. This way both she and Deirdre would make a *very* nice profit. Taking the wands and giving them a prominent spot on the round oak table in front of the register. This way they were front and center, but someone would always have their eye on them. They looked stunning. Even though they weren't in direct sunlight, the light that filtered through windows at the front of the shop made the crystals simply sparkle and catch the eye.

"Perfect. Now, time to get down to work." She pulled her raven hair in a twist and secured it with a clip from her desk drawer, she inherited the raven from her mother, but it was the sparkling silver throughout that got the most looks. In the sun her hair just shimmered. She asked her mother once where it came from, all Miranda would say was it came from her father. Anene found this odd, the only people who had silver hair were, well, old people. She mused over this as she began to unpack the rest of the box. This shipment was loaded with restock for her crystals and some new books to add to the bookshelves around the store. Anene moved around her shop placing books, and crystals here and there. Noting things around the shop that needed to be marked down or taken away for a later date. Rotating stock was something others hated, but she found it most enjoyable. She looked through the shawls and caps she received from local weavers moving them to better locations and grabbing some things to drape on the mannequin for customer inspiration.

By the time Anene was satisfied with how the shop was looking, it was well past time for her to head home. Shutting down the lights and locking the back door she started on her way. Knowing it was a risk to walk, not because of danger, it was the rain you had to watch for. However, seeing as she lived just over the hill, Anene decided to take the risk of getting wet for a good stretch of the legs. She loved walking, and if it weren't for the need to leave the village from time to time, she wouldn't even have a car. But as her mother pointed out, no matter what, everyone should have one. Now to be honest there were people who didn't, but her mother was an American. She moved to Ireland before Anene was born. It was during a visit to the Emerald Isle that Miranda had met, fell in love and married Anene's father. A father Anene hasn't seen or heard from since she was almost eight years old. And even then, she didn't have many memories of him. Happily, the ones she did have were wonderful ones.

Those happy few memories from when they lived in the little cottage on the outside of the village in Raphoe, Co. Donegal. It wasn't a very large cottage, but Anene knew that they were happy there. Sometimes she would swing by and look at the old place. Her mother still owned it, but couldn't bring herself to go by the old place, let alone go inside. *Too many memories* her mother would say. Anene asked one time if the memories were so good why wouldn't she want to go back and visit them. When she thought of that conversation, Anene could still remember with amazing clarity the sorrow and grief that shown in her mothers eyes as she explained.

"Because those wonderful memories would make me want to stay in the cottage. To live in the past instead of living for the here and now, my love. I miss your father terribly and I know that one day we will have him back. But if I went back to the cottage, it would break me."

This old conversation played through Anene's head every time she passed the now dull and barren cottage. It was strange, in all the years since they left, it was never overtaken by weeds or brush. The paint never peeled, windows never broke, and the roof stayed solid. It was the *color* of the building that showed it's abandonment. The white held neither luster nor life, with windows that were dull and vacant. That was what Anene thought when she walked up to it that evening. The place looked forlorn, depressed. It was a sad sight, for she knew that place could just stand up and shimmer with pride.

Houses and cottages live and breathe just like everything else. It was when the homes were neglected and abandoned that made them become sad and home to spirits. It was true that not all homes that have spirits are like the old cottage, sad and abandoned. Some homes have families that just don't want to leave, or a spirit with no family, just wanting to have the feeling of one in their afterlife. It was when a *home* changed to a house, building or shack that drew malcontent and the haunting began. Anene was always surprised that no matter how sad and abandoned the old cottage became, it still had the air of a home. But something was different as she approached the place. She could feel a presence. It was not a witch, but there was no mistaking the magick that was battering against her senses.

Putting up her guard she slowed her pace. Suddenly, she saw the source of the essence.

There he was, standing just outside the front door of the cottage. A door that was still open, as if he were coming out from the dwelling. But that was impossible, for her mother and later she herself had spelled the place so none may enter. How was this possible? There was also no mistaking that, this giant of a man, was where the power she felt was coming from. Anene stopped and stared at him. He certainly didn't look like he belonged here in Ireland, hell or even in this century. *Is that armor he's wearing?* She wondered. *Aye, it is! Leather armor! With a sword on his hip and bow and arrows on his back!* Once the realization hit her that he was armed to the teeth, she sent out her magick to freeze him in place. Friend or foe she wasn't sure yet, but she wasn't going to give him the chance to attack before she could figure out what the hell was going on. The expression on his extremely handsome face was pure shock at the immobilization. Under other circumstances, it might have made her chuckle.

"You're going to stay right there until I know who and *what* you are," she told him as she straightened her stance to better observe him. *Aye, he is certainly gorgeous,* she thought. He had a mane of auburn hair that was pin straight and hung well past his shoulders. The hair, which looked like fire, had small braids threaded throughout with glints of gold and silver catching the setting sunlight. A few other things caught her attention as she looked him over. First were his ears, they were not those of a human. His ears were long and pointed at the tops. Then she noticed the large black wings ghosted on his back, she could tell he had them, but were somehow pulled into his body and hidden from view. *Goddess, why would he hide those?* She wondered. *They're breathtaking.* Anene caught herself and she started toward the unnamed man. With no words or hand motions, Anene lifted her spell on his body, but still blocked him from moving from the front porch. "Who the bloody hell are you, where did you come from, and how did you get inside the cottage?"

Even though he was no longer held in place, he still didn't move a muscle. He just stood staring at the woman before him. Her long raven hair with silver throughout would have been enough to convince him of who she was. But it was the power that nearly knocked him back through the door of the cottage that told him. This was the heir to the throne. The King and Queen's daughter. This was the little girl he had known all those years ago. It took Tadhgán all of three seconds to figure out that what that woman didn't need was protection. He stood, roving his eyes over her body, it was a fantastic one, toned, and well maintained. She looked like she was in shape for most purposes, but not war. He could help with that. Then he moved his gaze to her face. Here she was the perfect balance of the King and Queen. She was stunning. Knowing he had better speak before she put the lock back on him, but still, Tadhgán was at a loss for words. He came to protect and instead he was stunned, literally. For a myriad of reasons, that he didn't have the time to think about at the present-time.

"It's you." Was all he could come to say. "I can't believe it, it's you." He took one step forward and was lost to darkness.

Three

Anene figured if she'd been watching a movie, seeing the big man crumple to the ground, would have been one of those shocking/funny points in the film. However, seeing it in real life, well, it was still a shock, and funny. She supposed she could have warned him that there was a barrier still around him, but why? The only thing she might've felt a little guilty about, was the hit to his head on the door going down. Anene took a few steps closer to get a better look, and determined he was fine. No blood, no foul. Once again, she was captivated by the phantom wings on his back. Who was this man? Where did he come from? And what the hell was he? He couldn't be a fairy. *Could he?* She wondered, *Nay surely not.* She had seen them, and their wings were more like butterflies or dragonflies. He had black wings like a giant eagle or raven. And to be able to hide them away, was another give away in her mind. Fairies could spell their wings so the mortal world wouldn't see them, as she was able to, but they couldn't pull them back in their bodies like this.

Upon closer inspection of his face, Anene had some watery memory trying to break through her mind, yet there was some barrier keeping it at bay. Something that has happened to her many times in the past, and it was a source of great annoyance. It was as if her mind was playing a farce and trying to withhold memories that should be simple to recall. *Focus, Anene!* She shook her head to bring her back to the present. She jumped back when the man in question began to stir.

"Bloody hell," Tadhgán sat up, rubbing his now throbbing head. "What the fuck was that?" he couldn't talk too loud for the split in his head that the pixies were now hammering in was screaming. He looked back at Anene. "Did you do that?" *It couldn't have been her,* he thought. He looked around. Maybe Queen Miranda was somewhere he didn't see.

"Of course, it was me!" *What a silly question to be asking.* She scoffed. "But I think I'll be asking the questions here. For instance, how in the feck did you get in our old cottage?"

"But you didn't say a spell, words, or move your hands." Gingerly he got back to his feet, being extra careful not to move forward should he get zapped a second time.

"I don't need words or to move my hands. Now once again, how did—"

"There has never been a spellcaster to not use words, tools, or have a circle about."

"I'm not a spellcaster I'm a witch—"

"Same thing." Tadhgán cut her off once again.

"Stop interrupting me." Taking a deep breath "Now I'll ask again. How did—"

"I came through the doorway." Cutting her off yet again. This time however, he had done so on purpose. She was a good-looking lass, and he liked a little mad once and a while. But seeing the change in her eyes and smelling the power rolling off her, he decided he had better back off before she smites him, or worse. "I apologize." He bowed slightly. "It shall not happen again."

"So help me, it had better not." She warned. Her anger was something that she prided herself never to lose. If she lost control, horrible things could happen. "What doorway? You couldn't have gotten in through the front door. My mother and myself made sure of that."

"I didn't say I came through the front door, but the doorway." Seeing her frustration Tadhgán held up his hands. "It might be a good idea to ask Queen Miranda about the doorway."

"Who the hell is Queen Miranda?!" She stopped short, "No, *fecking* way are you referring to *my* mother." At the man's nod "You, you're…" she took a quick second to settle. "Where did you come from?" She would circle back to her mother later.

"Locbroalm." When there was no recognition from the name, he clarified, "The Golden Realm." Once again he was met with no recognition. "The Fairy Realm." He stated. "Where else?"

"I'm sorry, what?"

"You heard me plain enough, Princess." Deciding that he had better call her accordingly since that is what she was, even if she didn't seem to know her heritage. *Strange*, he thought. *Ciarán said she wouldn't remember, but why would the queen not have told her daughter that she was heir to the throne of the realm? Or inform her of other realms at the very least.*

"Do you think I am stupid or something?" Not waiting for an answer, she plowed on. "I know what fairies look like, and you…" She looked him over once more. He was certainly good looking enough to be a fairy, that was for sure. But it was the wings that she was having issues with. The large ghosted black wings. Anene wanted to ask about them, but there was something inside that told her not to. So instead, she focused on the weaponry he had strapped to himself. "You don't fit the bill of any fairy I've met."

"Have you met many fairies?" He went on high alert instantly. Standing to his full height, his right hand on the pommel of his sword on his left hip while the left hand grasped the sheath. She watched as his eyes scanned the surrounding area, ready to draw that blade at any moment.

Ok, wow! She allowed her eyes to scan more slowly over the form of him. *That's hot. Oh my god girl, what is the matter with you!* Anene mentally smacked the back of her own head. "Ok, you need to go back," she gestured with her hands, "To wherever you came from." She was tired, and didn't have it in her to figure out what this nut job was going on about. Plus, she needed to get away from him. "So go back through whatever doorway you came from." And with that, Anene rifted away.

"What the—" Tadhgán's jaw dropped as the witch just vanished before his eyes. "How the hell did she do that?" Picking up a stone from the small landing he was standing on, he tossed it forward. "Seems she lifted the barrier. It's time to find the Queen." Taking a tentative step forward. Relieved at not being put down a second time, he unleashed his wings and took to the sky to better sense where the Queen was.

"Mother!" Anene called out as she came through the kitchen door. "I have need to talk with you." Anene looked at the kitchen of the majority of her childhood. Not much had changed over the years. The stone floor, warm worn cabinets and countertops felt like home to her. As did the old hearth and set of stuffed chairs that invited a nice sit down for a chat or just to enjoy the roaring fire. The one thing that had changed over the years were the appliances. Where Anene had what you might call a chef's kitchen of sorts, her mother had what Miranda called *serviceable appliances. 'I am not a fancy cook, so why use the fancy to cook with,'* she would say. But as something would peter out Miranda would replace it.

Sighing Anene dropped her purse on the kitchen table as she sailed on through to the front rooms. Looking in the laundry room, the office and small living room as she went. It was in the parlor that she finally spied her mother. And she was not alone.

"What the hell are you doing here?" The wind had been knocked out of her. Here stood the man from the cottage. "I told you to leave! And how the hell did you get here before me?"

"Anene," her mother's voice took her gaze from the man in question, "I have some things I need to tell you." Miranda positioned herself between Tadhgán and her daughter. Wringing her small delicate hands, she's been dreading this conversation. She'd known it was coming, felt it in her bones. When The Right Hand arrived mere seconds ahead of her daughter, Miranda knew her time was up, and it was time to come clean about who she really was. Who her father was, and why he had been absent.

"What the hell is going on?" Anene threw up her guards while looking at her mother.

"Sit down baby."

"No, I think I'll stand." She looked at the giant behind her mother. "Since you seem to know him. Who is he? And how did he get into the cottage?"

"My name is Tadhgán Ultan, and the rest, the Queen will fill in." He knew he needed to be here for the explanation, but he didn't want to be the one to fill in the missing blanks. He didn't envy his Queen in her task.

"You know, years and years ago when I was much younger, I came to Ireland, met and fell in love with your father." Miranda's heart squeezed at the mention of her absent husband. She missed him more than words could say.

"Well give or take twenty-five years." Anene added, but her skin was starting to tingle with nerves.

"Not exactly. But more on that later." Sitting on the sofa, she took a steadying breath. "What I haven't told you was where your father was from."

"Ireland." Anene put in as she leaned against the wingback chair. "That's what you said anyway."

"No, I only said I met him here. I left out where he was from," lifting her dark blue eyes to Tadhgán for some assistance. At his go ahead, she knew she was the one that needed to explain, not him. "Ok, I met your father while I was on vacation here; Ciarán is from, Locbroalm." She raised her hand to stop her daughter from speaking. "Please let me get this out, baby. Your father and I were drawn to each other at first because of the magick. However, it didn't take long for us to fall in love. As soon as the coven found out about our relationship, they demanded that I renounce it and go back to America. Refusing, I was banished from the coven and forbidden from coming back. Ciarán asked me to come to the realm with him to live. It was after I said yes that he told me what he was to the realm."

"I don't really know what to say here." Anene confessed. "Are you telling me that my father is a fairy?" She was astounded that she was taking this so well.

"Yes, but... He was more than just a fairy. Your father was, is, King. When we entered Locbroalm, he wasn't sure how the realm would take to their King mating with a human. Witch or not." Miranda smiled for the first time since she started to tell her story. "Your father and I were overjoyed at how the realm, with the exception of a small few, reacted to me and their King's happiness. After we had been there for what would have been a year here in the mortal realm Ciarán crowned me, Queen. We were happy for. . ." Miranda hedged. She wasn't sure how much her daughter was going to be able to manage at once

"Go on." Sensing her mother's hesitation, Anene sat in the chair she was leaning against. "Don't leave anything out."

"Even though I knew that being a human and that we would face some difficulties, I accepted your father and entered the realm. The thing is, when a human enters the realm and mates with a fairy, your lifespan is extended." In her peripheral Miranda saw Tadhgán, shifting with unease.

"Explain." Was all Anene said.

Miranda took a very deep breath and continued more quickly than she had planned, but felt if she didn't get it all out fast, she might not be able to say what she needed to say. "I was born in America, but I was born in," Miranda cleared her throat, "1702 in what is now Massachusetts." She sat and watched her stunned daughter. Miranda and Tadhgán both braced themselves for what Anene's reaction to this new information would be.

"Are you trying to tell me that you are over three-hundred years old?" Her quiet lilted voice filled the room. "Because if that is what you are saying, then I think the next step is to have you seen by an analyst."

"Baby please—"

"*Don't* you *baby* me!" She rocketed from the chair. "If you expect me to believe this, you are out of your fecking mind."

"Don't speak to the Queen in that manner." Tadhgán warned.

"Kiss my ass!" She fired back at him, then looked back to her mother. Her mother, who, for all she knew, was crazier than a sheep playing the bagpipes.

"No Tadhgán, she has that right." Miranda reached up and laid her hand on Tadhgan's wrist. "Although I would prefer to keep the conversation curse free," she added as an afterthought. "Anene, I speak the truth." Miranda stood and stepped to her daughter. "You have the ability to see the truth, use it now, and settle your mind so we can finish telling you what you need to hear."

"I am not looking in your mind!" She whispered to her mother. "Not only is it an invasion of your privacy, but I also don't need to. I can see by your aura that what you speak is truth."

"How is this possible?" Tadhgán asked as he moved from his stance in front of the fireplace. "How is she able to wield magick without the aid of words, tools, or herbs? Not only shifting from one place to another. I know of no spellcaster who has that power."

"I told you once before, I am a witch, *not* a spellcaster." Anene said through gritted teeth.

"She has the powers of the High Priestess twice over and that of the King coursing through her veins. She is the most powerful witch to exist."

"What do you mean twice over?" Anene questioned.

"I was the most powerful witch in my country and High Priestess of my coven before I was banished. When I created the coven here in Ireland in 1845, I was once again High Priestess. Not to mention your grandmother, my mother was High Priestess before I took her place. You have been thrice blessed. To be honest you should have taken over the coven as its High Priestess years ago, but you weren't ready." Miranda allowed that to hang in the air for a short minute.

"We'll get back to that later." Retaking her seat in the chair. "Why, if everything was so fantastic, why are you here and my father is not?"

"As I said before, there was a small group that were angry at the King for taking a human to be his bride, then, to make her *Queen*." Miranda shuddered. "But after a while they died away as the realm became quiet and happy for nearly three hundred mortal years."

"Then what?" Anene crossed her arms. Waiting to make up her mind until she heard the rest of the story.

"Twenty-six years ago, I became pregnant. As before, the majority of the realm was overjoyed that your father and I were finally to be blessed with a child. However, over the years the small group who objected to me as mate to the King, had quietly grown in numbers. After the announcement, they were now calling for my head and by extension yours. Ciarán didn't want a war in his realm. So, he and I decided the best way to calm things down was for me to leave for a while." A disapproving grunt came for the mostly silent man. "I know you, and the rest of the council didn't agree with his decision. But it was for Ciarán and I to make the choice, as Anene was *our* child that we were protecting." She reminded him.

"So, you came back here to the *mortal realm* to live." Briefly in the back of her mind she wondered, if the fairy realm had a name, what was the name of the mortal one. *Now isn't the time for that question girl.* She reminded herself. "Why didn't my father come with?"

"The King needed to stay in the realm to quiet the unrest." Tadhgán's deep voice answered, earning a glare from Anene.

"When I was settled in the old cottage on the outskirts of the village, I created a doorway so your father could come and visit as often as possible. But within four years, Tadhgán came through the doorway to inform me that the unrest had grown to an even larger faction and there was a true threat of war. Then, after another four years, Ciaran's visits stopped. Tadhgán came back through to tell me that the faction leader, Flann, had taken over the realm and imprisoned Ciaran."

"What!" Anene once again shot to her feet. "Is he dead?" She looked to Tadhgán.

"Nay, he is still being held. To ensure the realm does not retaliate, Flann has kept him alive, well, and cared for." His words were delivered in a calming manner. But Anene could see in his clenched fists and the vein pulsing on his forehead that he was fighting to keep calm.

"Why haven't you tried to get this Flann guy and his band of minions out?"

"Because my King and Queen ordered us not to until it was time." The answer was clipped and not nearly as calm as before. He was coming close to losing the battle with his temper. "I am here now because the heir has come of age and the realm is preparing for war."

"There's more to that, isn't there?" Anene narrowed her eyes. "Spill it."

"Please tell me." Miranda pleaded. She stood and faced Tadhgán's. "What has happened to my mate?"

"Nothing, my Queen. The King is as he was when you saw him last." Taking a deep breath. "Rumblings of the heir coming of age has, once again, started the whispers of war. Flann will do anything to ensure he keeps the seat of ruler, no matter the cost. When the threats of imprisonment or death didn't quell the murmurs and instead had them getting louder, Flann decided to take a final action." Looking to Miranda, he tried to figure a way to soften the words that needed to be spoken. When no solution came to him, Tadhgán decided it was better to tell her out right. Knowing she would demand it of him in any case. He took a deep breath and continued, "He has decreed the false Queen and the abomination be put to death. To be followed by the King, thus securing his claim to the throne." A heart wrenching cry came from Miranda as she collapsed on the floor at his feet.

Both Anene and Tadhgán reached for her. Miranda was inconsolable as she was on all fours. "No, no, no, this can't be happening." She clawed at the warrior's leather armor. "You can't let this happen! I can't. I can't lose him!"

"Ma, stop." Anene gathered her weeping mother in her arms. If there was still any doubt as to the validity of her mother's and this Tadhgán's story, this cleared them. "What can we do?" She asked the man over her mother's head.

"My orders were to come here and protect you and the Queen. Until it was time for you to go and claim the throne for yourself."

"To *what* now?" She almost forgot her broken mother at his words, then shook her head. "I do *not* need protecting."

"I agree," Tadhgán saw the power rising in her multi-colored eyes. He would reflect later that her eyes were yet another marrying of her mother and father. With the dark blue centers and the iridescent green on the outside. "There very well may be no one who can out match you in magick, but I doubt you can manage a bow or sword in battle. Let alone fight in hand-to-hand combat."

"Well, laddie there hasn't been a lot of call for that sort of thing here of late." The statement was positively dripping with sarcasm, as she glared at him again.

"You will train her." Miranda decreed as she pulled from her daughter's embrace. "You will show her how to wield a sword. Use a bow. You will train her like you have trained countless soldiers in the past."

"Now wait just a minute." But before Anene could protest any further her mother went on as if her daughter hadn't spoken.

"You will do this so that when it is time, she can go, claim the throne, release her father, my mate, and finally fucking annihilate Flann and his followers."

"My Queen," Tadhgán bowed his head at her command, then looked to Anene. "We will start in the morning." With that he stood, turned to leave only to be stopped when a hand took a strong hold of his arm by a furious female.

"Now both of you wait just a goddamn minute. If you think you can just give me orders after the bomb you just dropped, you're both completely insane!" She told her mother. "And you!" Releasing his arm, she moved to block his path. "If you think I am going to do anything with you, you're acting the maggot! I don't know you; I don't know where you come from and to be honest," she crossed her arms over her chest and simply sparkled with power, "I don't like you."

"Anene!" Miranda scolded.

"Nay!" throwing her hands in the air, Anene had reached her limit. She couldn't take anymore information. Putting her hands on the side of her head to keep it from exploding. "I can't take any more." And she disappeared from where she stood.

"How does she do that?" It was still a shock to see a spellcaster shift as she did. "A spell—"

"If you want to keep from being turned into a toad, you had better stop calling her a spellcaster. She is a witch." Miranda warned as she stared at the spot her daughter had occupied only seconds before.

"My apologies, my Queen. You never objected to the term." He pointed out.

"Yes, well I am not my daughter, and she objects, so mind yourself." She sagged into the sofa hanging her head. "I should never have kept the truth from her. She should have known where she came from at the start." She didn't miss the slight arch of his brow before he caught himself and normalized his expression. "I know you don't approve, but when Ciarán was taken, you gave me a letter. In that letter he told me that she would be safer not knowing. He is also the reason I left the cottage and sealed it." She looked at him standing in her parlor. "I thought."

"It was sealed from others entering it. Not from those of us who can, from coming through." He informed her. "You made the doorway so the King, you or I could come and go through it. You closed off the cottage but not the doorway within."

"Does Flann, or his followers, know how to find it?" She worried.

"Nay," he assured her. "None know of the doorway." He glanced out the window and wondered where the Spe—*witch* had gone. Not wanting to be turned into a toad, he decided to curb his language. "Will she bend to your will?"

"Oh, Tadhgán, you have a lot to learn about my daughter." She chuckled. "Anene bends to no one. Leave her be for now, so she may take in all she has learned today." She stood slowly, "Wait down here while I get you some of Ciaran's old things to wear, then we can see about getting you a place to stay."

Tadhgán watched as his queen slowly walked from the room and made her way to the second floor. He took the time he was alone to look at the pictures that were on the wall and the mantle of the fireplace. There were pictures of her and Ciarán on his visits to see his mate and child. There were a few that held Anene and Ciarán laughing as he spun her in the air. But most were of Anene as she grew throughout the years.

He remembered when Anene was born. She was a pretty babe, he supposed. He never understood the fascination with wee ones. In the time he spent with Ciarán and Miranda, while Anene was a babe, all he observed was that the little creature ate, slept, and made the most pungent unpleasant smells. On the occasions he came when she was a toddler, now there he could see the appeal. She was precocious, wily and kept her parents, and at times himself, running after her.

When he had to come and tell Miranda that Ciarán had been taken, it broke his heart to hear that she was going to leave the cottage and seal it. He knew that there was a possibility that he might not ever see the Queen, or the little girl again. Tadhgán knew Anene wouldn't remember, but when he told her she might not ever see him again, the little girl she was then, clung to him and wept. Before her mother took the weeping girl from his arms, Anene whispered in his ear. It had been too many years to count since he thought of what that sweet girl had said.

"Donna worry Teeeegen you belong to me. We will be togever again." Her sweet soft lilty voice nearly broke him that day. A shiver worked its way down his spine as the long forgotten memory worked its way back in his brain.

"Here we go." Miranda's voice filled the room as she returned, dragging Tadhgán back from his thoughts. "These should work until we get you things of your own." She handed him a pair of faded jeans and a white t-shirt.

"My Queen," he started.

"Please I'm just Miranda here." Waving her hand to stop the title that caused her pain.

"You will always be my Queen, but I will bow to your wishes." Bowing his head to her. "Before I left Ciarán gave me a message for you and you alone."

"Where is it?" Heart racing along with butterflies in her stomach at the prospect of a message from her mate. "What is the message?"

"He placed it in my mind, sealed. I unfortunately have no way to retrieve it."

"Unfortunately, neither do I." she sighed. "The Coven should be able to manage it, or if not, Anene *certainly* can." Resettling herself she smiled at the man before her. "Well for now, change into these and we'll go to the village and see about lodgings." She told him while directing him to the spare room to change his clothing. Once he was finished and his things were stored, they set off to the village.

Four

Anene could have rifted to her stone circle, but chose her home instead. Knowing that along with the solitude to mull things over, she also needed food. Solitude her circle had, but food, it did not. Muscle memory had her placing her purse on the kitchen table. However, in her haste to disappear from the situation, Anene realized she left her belongings at her mother's cottage.

"Damnit." Anene knew that her mother would bring the forgotten items to her, but not ready to see her mother just yet, in an act of self-preservation, she decided to call for them instead. Within a few seconds her purse and keys appeared on her less scarred kitchen table. "Seamus laddie, where are you?" Smiling as the black and gray Irish Dane made his sleepy way to greet his owner. "There you are me boy. How was your day then? Did you chase many rabbits, or did you pass the day lazing about on the bed?" She scratched his large sleek head and scruffy muzzle. "How was my day you'd be askin? Well, I'll be tellin ya. But first," Anene straightened. "I'll be makin us our dinner." Then went about and collected the fixings for hers and Seamus's meals.

Like her mother's kitchen, Anene had stone floors, and a large hearth with seating. But that was where the major similarities stopped. Anene's kitchen was *fancier* as her mother would call it. Because Anene loved to cook and bake she indulged herself in her appliances. Did she need the fancy to cook the way she did? Certainly not. But did she *want* the fancy to cook and bake with? Hell yes! So, her pride and joy, the first big ticket item she purchased, was her oven. She searched for and finally decided on the ILVE Nostalgia II 48' range in black and gold. Black and gold was an odd choice for her, she tended to go more toward the blues and greens. But when she was researching the range, saw that one and the colors grabbed her. The rest of her appliances were far less fancy, for now anyway. She did add a small dishwasher next to her stone sunken apron sink, but to be honest, it didn't get used often. She also had a small under-mounted microwave in her walk-in pantry, but like the dishwasher, it was hardly ever used.

Deciding to have the stew she made the night before, it was placed on the hob to heat through while she scooped up Seamus's food. Adding a little rice and stock to his bowl, she mixed the meal and placed it on the raised stand next to his water bowl. Stirring her stew until slightly bubbling, cutting the heat, and transferring the thick homey stew to a large wide bowl. After adding a couple slices of buttered bread, Anene finally sat at her kitchen table to eat and think. Up until now, she had the ordinary mundane tasks to keep her mind occupied, but now she had to face the music and go over the events of the evening.

Once again, Anene was surprised at how well she took to most of the information that was thrown at her. She knew fairies existed; she'd seen them with her own two eyes. Being raised in Ireland, she was taught about the wee folk, the dos and don'ts, should you encounter them. Never eat or drink anything should you be taken to the otherworld and so on. But to hear that your own father was one of the Tuatha dé Danann, and the ruler no less. Well, that was a bit much to *fully* take in. But the revelation about her mother, now that was a harder pill to swallow.

If Anene did her math right, and she was certain she did, her mother was three-hundred and twenty-two years old. Now that was something Anene just couldn't wrap her head around. Then, there was that she herself, had been kept in the dark about her own lineage. This was something she wasn't sure she was going to be able to forgive. In the back of her mind, there was a small voice that was reminding her it was for her own protection. Anene decided to hit that voice over the head with her cast iron skillet. A whimper took her from her inner thoughts to her pup resting his head on the kitchen table.

"Now, my lad, are you supposed to have your head on my table?" She smiled as he kept his head where it was plopped, but his massive body swayed as his tail wagged back and forth. "What can I do for you handsome?" His eyes just radiated with love. Before she could dodge his huge tongue, he lapped the side of her face. "Och, you silly hound, go on with you." Anene laughed, temporarily driving the melancholy feelings away, which was the desired effect the dog was going for. Chuckling to herself, as he sat at her hip, leaning against her. Draping her arm around the perceptive animal, she told him about her day prior to the walk to the cottage, while finishing up her own dinner.

Dishes finished, dog and owner left by the kitchen door for their nightly walk. With the sun set and twilight taking hold, Anene was in her element. When looking for a place of her own, it didn't take her long. As a child, she would always run to the land and the circle that sat there. The place simply called to her all her life. As a historical site, the sixty-four stone circle was protected, and when Anene took over ownership, she added her own magickal protection to the circle and the surrounding land.

For many years preceding Anene's ownership, the land had been owned by a sheep farmer. Fortunately for Anene, when he passed and there were no children to take over the farm, it was put up for sale and Anene snatched it up. Knowing that the sheep and the dairy cows would be good for her economically, she kept the farm going. But not knowing anything about sheep farming, she offered the running of it to the former manager. The older man told her that he was too old to run it, but he had the perfect man for the job. That was how she met Colm O'Cleary. The thirty-year-old was perfect for the running of the farm. The only thing Anene wanted to change was to add a sheep and cow free walkway from her door to the circle. However, when the quote for the lumber and labor was placed in her hand, and after she was peeled from the ceiling, Anene scrapped the request immediately. Deciding, instead, it was cheaper and far easier to spell hers and the dog's feet. This way they may walk through the fields and not be plagued by the sheep and cow shit that was littering the land.

Finally, reaching the site of her stone circle, Anene took a satisfying cleansing breath. Touching the outlying stone as she passed was her way of letting the circle feel her before entering. Like homes, this circle was a living being. And like a home, the circle could be temperamental. If one were to enter without the circle knowing them—or liking their intentions— it can, and will, keep them out. Thankfully, Anene had never had an issue, but she felt the need to be respectful. The circle has always felt like home to her, and she liked to think that the circle felt the same.

This historical site was one of the largest stone circles in Ireland. Anene smiled as she thought about what the history said about the site. Dating back to 700BC with what they think, was about eighty stones, now it had only had sixty-four. As Anene reached the center of the circle or as some prefer, the dance, she marveled at how much history can be wrong. For this circle, her circle was far older than any modern historian would be able to date. As for the stones. Sixty-four was what most people saw when they came to visit the place. On her eighteenth birthday, which fell on a full moon, Anene restored the circle to its full eighty-three stones. When she restored the stones, she also restored the chamber that was below the circle as well. History would say that this chamber was more than likely a tomb or a prep room for a body before cremation. But once again history was proven wrong. What Anene found when she entered the lower stone room with a ledge that could be used to hold herbs and all manner of magickal tools. There was no question that the chamber was used for preparation, but it was for magickal means, not the handling of the dead to their afterlife.

There was one thing in the chamber that was a matter of great interest to Anene, however. At one end of the chamber was a round topped door of ancient Rowan wood held together with black iron straps, and a braided iron handle hanging. Along with the iron straps and braided handle, the ancient door was also adorned with an intricate carving of what Anene could only deduce was of the Rowen tree the door was made from. However, for all the beauty of the door, it lacked any discernible locks. This was a matter of frustration for her, because whenever Anene would come down into the chamber she would try to open the door to no avail. Something else that was strange, even to her, was that only she could enter the chamber. Anene even tried to bring her mother Miranda inside. But not only could her mother not enter the chamber, she also could not see that the chamber had been restored. Deciding that it was meant for her, and her alone, was something that Anene would ponder from time to time.

Standing at the center of the circle, Anene's gaze flitted to the entrance of the chamber and the door that it held.

"Ok, well might as well go and do the daily pull huh?" She looked to her faithful companion who for some odd reason was able to go into the chamber with her. *Go figure.* She thought to herself as she made her descent down the wide stone steps to the inside of the chamber. Once again, she stood in front of the door, grabbed the handle, and pulled. Nothing. "What did I expect?" She asked the dog, who was looking at her with an expression that can only be described as exasperation at the annoyance wafting off her. "Oh, be quiet you." She smiled and ruffled the big dog's ears.

She went to the other end of the chamber where the stone ledges held numerous spell books. She took down one of the bound books that she sourced on one of her buying trips. This one was thankfully bound in leather. With some of the others, she might not be so lucky. Most books she encountered on her buying trips, Anene placed in her shop, as they were harmless. But there were times a book, like the one she held in her hands, was simply too dangerous for the shelves of her shop. The reason she came across such books was usually because the witch or clerk in a book shop knew the book was wrong in some way. When a book that held a power too great and could be disastrous in the wrong hands, the chamber was where she would take them. Having a place she could store them where unskilled hands were safe from them, and where the books themselves were safe from misuse was a Godsend. In her travels, Anene was hopeful to find something about the door in one of the books. But so far, there has been nothing found. The books did offer some good information though.

"Just not today." Sighing, she placed the book back in its spot with the others. "Come on luv, let's go back up, you can run, and I can get centered." Seamus bolted from the chamber and was gone from view by the time Anene crested the opening. Smiling, she was once again in the center of the circle. From there, she could draw from the earth to recharge and the moon to cleanse her mind and body. Kicking off her shoes so her feet were grounded, she shook out her hands, then raised them to the moon. Closing her eyes, Anene took a deep breath to fill her lungs with the crisp cool night air. While she expelled the air from her lungs, she could feel the troubled pieces of her heart and mind shift, move about, and settle.

This was one of the most relaxing things she could do for herself. And after all the information she had been given, she needed to calm her mind and recharge. Anene didn't know how long she stood in the heart of the stone circle. When she finally finished, Seamus, was sitting next to the King Stone on the outside waiting for his mistress to finish wielding her magick.

"I think it's time to lay down, take in the night sky and enjoy the show she is putting on, don't you?" Anene called for a blanket to cover the dew fallen grass. "Come in." She told him as she laid down on the blanket. Seamus settled next to her while placing his mammoth head on her middle. "You know, I *should* be furious with her for keeping me in the dark all my life." She decided to talk it out to herself and her trusty companion. "And I am to be sure but, if the reason was because of this Flann. Aye, I can understand her wanting to keep me safe."

She was quiet for a few moments while she mulled the threat of Flann over in her mind. She thought about how her childhood would have been affected had she'd known. Would she have gone outdoors and played in the sunshine, rain, or snow? Would she have ever stayed at a friend's house after school? Hell, would she have even gone to school like the other children in her village. And, what about the other children? If she had known about the threat that was at her back, would she have even had any friends? Not to mention dating. Would she have ever gone on a date if she had known?

As Anene asked the questions, one after another, she concluded. The answer to all her questions was met with a resounding, "No." she sighed. "Not knowing the truth has given me a childhood," she admitted. "I can see that now, and I can be grateful for the childhood I was able to have. But growing up I always felt that my father had abandoned us." To this Seamus lifted his head, blinking at her. "I know that ma said he didn't, but I never really believed her. Now I know, he *really* didn't. So, that's on me, I guess." She sighed and stroked the dog's large head. "But can you blame me? And that's another thing. If he wasn't captured until I was eight years old and until then he came to the cottage, why do I have so little memories of him? At eight years old I should have memories."

Then the realization hit her. She knew why her memories were either murky or non-existent. Her mother had spelled her memories. *Now* she was really pissed. She now knew that her father *was* a part of her young life, and she couldn't remember him! As her anger swiftly grew at the thought, it faded just as fast. Realizing her memories were tampered with for the same reason her lineage was kept secret, her safety. "Will they come back?" wondering aloud, Anene pondered the rest. Miranda was over three-hundred years old. Her father was the King. Her mother was the Queen. Which made her a. . . "Nay, I'm not going there. I am many things, but I am *not* a princess."

Then there was the other bit of information that was glossed over. There was a war gearing up in the Fairy Realm. "What did he call it?" She looked to her sleeping dog. "Locbroalm? I wonder what that even means." She knew that Tadhgán had told her, but at the time she simply didn't care. Only that there is about to be a war in said realm, and she was expected to be a part of it? "Not, *would* you, or *can* you? Nay, it's train her and send her off." Even to her own ears she sounded like a petulant child. But feck it, this was war they were talking about. "I should have a say in whether or not I will put my life on the line for a realm and its people who I know nothing about." And speaking of people. Tadhgán, what was his story? How the hell did he fit in? Gorgeous wings or not, he had some explaining to do. "Going to have to tread lightly with that one though." Anene noted. After observing him with her mother, Anene could conclude that he was not a threat to her, or anyone else for that matter. But there was something off there. "I'll have to think on that for a while more." Yawning into her hand. "It's time for bed my lad." Patting his head before she rose, "I'm too tired to walk back." When he leaned against her side, nearly knocking her back to the ground. "You too?" chuckling Anene, with Seamus in tow, and rifted back to her cottage.

Deciding that it was better to sleep and let her subconscious workout the onslaught of information. Anene banked the fire in her room before slipping her pjs on and climbing into bed, which was the perfect size for both her and Seamus. Thankfully, the room was large enough to handle the king bed, her dressers and whatnot. She was thankful that she didn't have to take down the wall to the bedroom next to hers to make room for the large bed. Not that she had many guests, but she wanted to be able to keep the option open. Settling down under the covers, Seamus waited until she finished before hopping up and cuddling next to his mistress. Anene smiled, rested her hand on his paw and allowed her body to relax, and soon sleep found her.

Her dreams were not the restful sort she was hoping for. Anene was accosted with visions of a fairy with white hair and red batlike wings pointing an arrow at her chest. There was another, with once gleaming silver hair, which was now dulled by the lack of sunlight in his cell as he sat writing at a desk. Another flash of a circle, like her own, where she was surrounded by armed soldiers ready to kill her. There was a field, once the site of love and golden peace, which was now bathed in the blood of the dead. On the highest point of the field stood a Fairy with black hair wearing a crown fashioned with the bones of the slaughtered King and the false Queen.

Five

Tadhgán walked around the kitchen of the little cottage that Miranda was able to find for him. Thankfully, a member of her coven had a small cottage that was used for her sister when she came to visit. The little building was currently vacant as the sister was on holiday in America. Tadhgán couldn't be sure, but he got the distinct feeling that the witch was thrilled at the prospect of being sister free for the time being. Being an only child himself, it wasn't a feeling he had any experience with. Unless, he counted Fintan in that regard. The two Fae grew in each other's pockets so that most, including them, considered the two brothers. He smiled at the thought. *Aye, Fintan is a brother to me to be sure. Blood or no.* He decided. Miranda's voice pulled from his thoughts.

"The old cottage really would be the better place for you," she told him. "But thanks to the spells myself and Anene cast, once you stepped over the barrier and left the grounds the cottage stood on," she shrugged her shoulders, "you wouldn't be able to access the grounds again. It will take both of us to lift the magick that was wielded to block entry." Miranda fussed over the kitchen and the state of the pantry, while she worried over her daughter.

"Just how powerful is she?" Tadhgán asked while he stood, not sure what to do with himself as he watched his Queen clean and fuss.

"I'm not really sure, to be honest. She's the most powerful witch I've ever encountered. When I was growing up my mother was the strongest.

41

Then, when I came into my power, I surpassed her. I guess that pattern holds true as Anene surpassed me long ago. As you saw, unlike myself, or any other witch for that matter, Anene has no need to use words, tools, and herbs to have the magick bend to her will. And, she has the ability to rift from one spot to the next."

"Rift?" Not being able to stand it any longer, he took the cloth from her and guided her to the small table in the corner of the kitchen. "Please stop fussing." He would have sat at the small table with her, but the table and chair looked so small. Tadhgán feared he'd shatter it to toothpicks if he so much as *breathed* on them. So, he kept his stance leaning against the countertop, slightly hunched, as the ceiling was not meant for a six foot six inch Fae to stand in.

"I can't help it." A genuine smile graced her delicate features for the first time since he found her that evening. "And rifting, which is what we call it when Anene disappears and arrives somewhere else." She closed her eyes briefly and sighed. "At least that's what Ciarán called it the first time it happened when she was three years old."

"Ciarán called it? So, it is not a spell—" he cleared his throat at her raised brow. "Witches power?" he corrected.

"No, it was passed to her by her father. Ciarán said that the Kings and Queens of old used to have that ability, but for some reason the power was lost." Running her hand through her pixie cut raven hair, "Until now that is."

"Kings and Queens of old?" Why had he never heard of them? It seemed silly that he had not. "Did he know who they were? The Kings and Queens?"

"If he did, it never occurred to me to ask him. I was more concerned about my toddler, who could up and disappear with a single thought." Miranda found herself smiling at the memories the conversation invoked.

"Boy did it keep he and I on our toes." She chuckled thinking the King of Fairies being outwitted by his three-year-old daughter. "God I miss him." Standing, she went to the pantry to see what he would need for food. There was plenty of canned and boxed food for him to eat until they made other arrangements. Suddenly, something occurred to her. "How long has it been since you were here?"

"When I came to tell you about Ciaran's capture. So, by your time, seventeen years, by mine roughly two-hundred years." Leaving his spot at the counter he joined her at the pantry door. "Why do you ask?" His eyes roved over the shelves simply filled with boxes and colorful little round tins. *What the bloody hell is all of this?* Tadhgán hoped this wasn't what passed for food in Quelocand. If it was, he was for sure going to starve while in the mortal realm.

"Well, do you know how to cook?" The dubious look on his face told her all she needed to know. "Ok, this will be a learning experience for you then. Here." Taking a can of stew from the shelf and handing it to him, "Follow me, you're about to get a crash course in cooking. Mind you, I've got nothing on my daughter's skills, but I can show you how not to starve."

"Not bloody likely," he mumbled under his breath. "Is this the best fare you have here in Quelocand?"

"Oh my," Miranda stopped in her tracks, hand on her chest and eyes the size of saucers. "It has been years since I have heard the name of this realm spoken." Tears threatened to fall as she thought of the name Ciarán had told her. "Quelocand, Land of the Queens." She cleared her clogged throat and moved to the hob. "And no, this is not the best fare we here have to offer. But I am tired and worn out." She looked back at The Right Hand of the King and glared. "So, this is what you're going to get tonight. So, pay attention."

"Aye, milady," Tadhgán bowed, joined her at the hob, and took the instruction like a good soldier.

For the next half hour, Miranda showed him how to use the can opener, the hob, and other essential items in the room. Afterward she took him through the small cottage to show him the toilet and explain about the plumbing. It wasn't that he didn't have indoor plumbing in Locbroalm, but this was quite a bit different to what he was used to. However, he was overjoyed to see there was a fireplace in every room for heat. In one area, thankfully, Tadhgán didn't feel hopeless. At least she didn't have to worry about showing him the tricks to the fireplace.

"Do you think you have everything you need for the night?" She didn't want to abandon him, but she desperately wanted her bed.

"I will be fine. Thank you for seeing to my needs. Should I. . ." His words trailed off. No matter what, he was sent on a mission. And that mission was to protect the Queen and heir.

"I wouldn't if I were you," she warned. "Anene was given a bomb today, and she'll need time to sort it all out. When she is ready, she will seek us out to talk about it." Sighing, it hurt her heart to know that her daughter felt betrayed by her. But if Miranda was being honest with herself, betrayed is precisely how Anene should feel. "I want nothing more than to go to her and try to explain, but that'll do more harm than good." Patting his arm, she turned for the front door. "It would be best if you stayed here. Tomorrow I'll come for you to give you a better lay of the land." At his small bow, Miranda left him to his solitude.

Tadhgán had immense respect for his Queen, and no matter what she said, Miranda was still his Queen. Yet, he was relieved to have his solitude. The moment the door closed, he released his wings. It wasn't that he was in pain when his wings were hidden, but he felt... cramped. Releasing his wings from their concealment was like a giant satisfying stretch after too long in one place. Tadhgán stood in the kitchen for a moment deciding what he wanted to do first. He was tired, to be sure, and longed for sleep to come, but his need to soothe his bones in hot water won out. Going back into the washroom, then after knocking and hitting every surface in the small room, Tadhgán relented and pulled his wings back into his back. The black tattoo created was an exquisitely detailed replica of his feathered wings. Because his wings are so large, the tattoo covered his entire back, down the backs of his arms, and legs.

Once his wings were again concealed, Tadhgán was able to navigate the small toilet without much fuss. He had to admit, the shower here was not as nice as in Locbroalm. Needing to manually adjust the temperature until finding the right spot was an actual hazard. He scalded and froze himself more than once while trying to get clean. Not to mention the number of times he slammed his head on the shower head. Which was going to become a welt. The witch said the cottage was for her sister when she came to stay. As Tadhgán stooped to get the suds out of his hair, he wondered if the sister was part brownie or leprechaun. Surely that was the only reason for the accommodation to be so petite.

Finally able to leave the claustrophobic space, Tadhgán wrapped a towel around his waist. It was not lost on him that the cottage was miniscule in its size, yet the towels could wrap around him in triplicate. Donned in his towel kilt he moved to the bedchamber. There he stood and surveyed the ridiculously small single bed and wondered if it might be better to sleep on the floor rather than try to squeeze on a doll sized bed.

"Stop complaining, you ungrateful sod, and be happy the lady found you somewhere to lay your head," he chastised. Tadhgán pulled back the covers and tried to fold his six-foot six-inch warrior frame into a bed that was meant for a child sized human. It would have been laughable had it been happening to anyone other than himself. "This is going to be a very long night."

After he had lost all feeling in his legs, he pulled one of the overstuffed chairs from the corner of the room so he could attempt to extend the length of the bed. Now being able to lay on his back, he stretched his legs, so his feet were now resting on the overstuffed chair. Was he comfortable? Not a chance. Was this better than the floor? Debatable. Soon, because of pure exhaustion, he finally fell asleep. His dreams, much like Anene's, were filled with hints of war, death, and the downfall of his beloved realm.

Anene stood in the door of the bedroom staring at the Fae and the creative solution he erected for the small bed. Once again, at his expense, she found a sick humor and slight satisfaction in the situation he was in. She supposed it wasn't really his fault. He was only following the orders that his King, her father, had given him. As she stood mulling over whether or not to give the man in question a break, she allowed her eyes to roam over the man's exquisite and mostly naked body. Save for the towel that wrapped his waist. And that was another thing, *could she refer to him as a man?* She wondered. While her eyes took in the sight of him, she decided it was a question that needed asking. But for now, she had to admit that he was quite a delicious specimen. *Aye it would be hard to find one to match his equal.*

"Are you done looking me over? Or should I stay here a while longer?" Tadhgán's groggy deep voice jolted her from her examination of his body.

"For now, aye, I'm finished," she answered nonchalantly, not caring one iota at being caught at her ogling. "Get dressed and come with me." She turned to leave but stopped at his voice.

"Might I ask where we are going?" Anene turned and winced as she watched him try to move from his position and fail. "This would go a lot easier if you would leave."

"Hey now, wait a sec there bub." Hands on hips she glared. "I was on my way out the door. *You* called me back in here." Anene crossed her arms over her chest. "To answer the question, we are going to my mother's. I know she was going to come and get you, but I decided to do the fetching. Now, what would be easier if I weren't here?"

"My getting out of this fucking torture chamber." At her frown he continued, "In case you haven't noticed, and I bloody well know you have, all I have on, at the moment, is a towel wrapped around my middle." Holy Gods his back was killing him. "It might have been better to sleep on the floor," he grumbled to himself, or so he thought.

"You considered sleeping on the floor?" Looking at him, this giant of a fairy, sleeping on doll-like furniture. "Yeah, it might have been better. Would you like some help?" Deciding that there was no reason to treat him like the enemy, because he simply wasn't. She figured he was, however, going to be a pain in her ass, for the foreseeable future.

"To be honest with you lass, I think my back might be broken." He groaned as he tried to adjust.

"Where are your clothes?" she looked where he pointed at them, thrown in the corner on the floor. "Typical." Apparently, all men are the same, no matter where they come from, or what realm. "Ok, are you ready to stand?"

"I don't think—" his words cut off as he was laying down in agony one second and standing fully clothed the next. The pale stupefied look on his face was enough to make Anene burst out laughing. "Don't do that again." Was all he said.

"What, no 'thank you'? Or 'Wow, how did you do that?'" She sobered a little as he looked at her. It was not a look of anger or gratitude. What she read was fear. "You're afraid of me." This was not a question. It was an accusation.

"You are misreading." He cleared his throat. "It is not fear you see, but you have to understand. I have never encountered a spell—" at the flash in her eye he adjusted his words. "Witch, who..." He trailed off.

"Who had no need of words or tools for magick." Anene supplied. "Well laddie, you've met one now, so get used to it." She nodded as if to make her point. "Now, how is the back feeling?" She smiled watching him realize she had done more than get him vertical and clothed.

"It's," he marveled at the loss of pain from his back, neck, and everything in between. All the pain was gone, just gone. Twisting slightly at the waist and rolling his shoulders was easier than it has been for years. She had taken not only what was brought on by the tortures of the following night's sleep, but also the tension of the last two hundred plus years. "Perfect." He bowed to her slightly. "I thank you for that as well." He looked back to the makeshift bed and grimaced. "I'll sleep on the floor tonight."

"When you saw how small the bed was, why didn't you do that last night?" Looking at the bed again, Anene decided, if it had been her, she would have chosen the floor. Or maybe the couch downstairs.

"Because I was doing enough complaining about the shower, the size of the washroom—"

"What's wrong with the shower?" She pulled the shower in the small cottage to her mind. It was small, but if her memory was correct it worked very well.

"I don't want to be ungrateful to the lass for allowing me to stay here. But the plumbing here is different from in Locbroalm."

"Well, you can explain that as we head to my mother's so we can all talk." Without another word Anene turned and left the room. "The plumbing is different?" she mimicked in her best interpretation of him. She was in the kitchen before Anene noticed he was not behind her. "Where the hell did he go?" She decided to give him time. Hell, she *had* just woken him up. "Let the man pee, Anene." She told herself. Ten minutes later Tadhgán walked into the kitchen. His long auburn hair was damp around his face and there were water droplets on his black t-shirt. A shirt that was about half a size too small. It looked delicious to a woman's eye. Showing off his extremely well-defined chest and arms, but it had to be uncomfortable for him. Same goes for the jeans he had on. They left *nothing* to the imagination. "Are you comfortable in those clothes?"

"To be honest, no. Do the men here not care about the blood circulation to their... limbs?" He was doing everything he could not to adjust himself while she was staring at him.

"Aye they care. But these were meant for a... smaller man." Anene couldn't help but smirk. "We will get you some proper fitting clothes later today, but for now." Remembering what he had said earlier about being unsettled about her magick. "Would you like me to adjust the sizing of those now?"

"Gods, aye please." And just like that, his jeans were cut to fit him perfectly, and he could take a solid breath without wanting to cry out in pain. But when his shirt didn't change, he arched his brow.

"What?" she said sweetly. "Oh fine." She relented and adjusted the shirt as well, slightly. "Sorry, but you gotta give the ladies *something* to drool over." She loosened the collar, and arm sleeves so they weren't cutting off the circulation. Made the length longer so the shirt hung to mid hip. But as far as the cut went, she kept that a little more fitted. Not so much that the fabric stretched but enough that it hugged his muscles beautifully.

"I am a warrior and the King's Right Hand. I am not a thing to be ogled." His voice took on authority and annoyance.

"Huh, well that was a nice speech, and I respect that." She stood, picked up her purse and headed for the door. "But you are in a small village and built like a Greek God. So, get used to being ogled. Now, let's head to my mother's."

Tadhgán followed her out the front door grumbling to himself. The pair walked together in silence for a few minutes giving him a chance to look at the village. He was trying to remember the last time he was there. Granted it was roughly two hundred years for him, but the village didn't seem to have changed much.

"The village seems the same. I would have thought it would have grown."

"Well, Raphoe has grown, but our little village sits just outside the town's limits, so we have managed to keep it—"

"The fact that the coven is here might have something to do with that," he cut in. "If memory serves, your people don't take kindly to magick and have persecuted those who use it."

"You're not wrong on both counts. Now those that are aware, as it were, tend to band together. The rest look at magick as a fun, I don't know, parlor game." Stopping, she looked at the village that, for the whole of her life, was unchanged. He was correct in that the coven residing within or close to the village was the reason for the lack of industrial progress. Instead, it was filled with small shops for every need of which you could think. Tourists would come to Raphoe to shop and see the sights. Most often on the way to see the stone circle in the middle of nowhere, it became a must to come through the little village that has been reputed to be run by witches. It was also a boon that they were the largest coven in the Republic of Ireland. A novelty that could be dismissed at or forbidden depending on where they were from. But in the picturesque village, visitors could revel in the varieties of shops and eateries the village offered. It was for this reason that the people of the small village kept it as it was. "But having the town of Raphoe has been good for us in many ways."

"I suppose. It seems to be a good place to live." He wasn't entirely sure he would want to spend his days here. Though it was quiet and there was no threat of war, unlike in Locbroalm.

"But?" Anene was able to read his face enough to know that there was more to his statement. When he glanced at her, she knew. "You wouldn't want to live here." *Well, you can go feck yourself then!* She thought and wanted to say. But kept her tongue, for now.

"I mean no offense to you or your village." Tadhgán noticed her change in body language and his misstep instantly. "This is a lovely village, and it's filled with generous people. The few times I have come through the doorway I have never had any cause to find fault with Quelocand, or her people. But..." he trailed off knowing that he was only making matters worse by speaking. If there was one lesson his mother taught him, it was better to stay quiet when dealing with an angry female. Particularly if you were the reason she was ticked.

"Nay, I get it, you prefer Locbroalm. I have to admit, it sounds like a wonderful place. Your King is in prison. The guy that is sitting on the throne is threatening to kill not only the imprisoned King and his child, but his wife, the Queen. The rest of the realm is essentially being held hostage while they wait for war to break out. And this is all because the King fell in love and married a human witch." Anene nodded her head in mock consideration of the facts as she laid them out. "Aye, that really does sound like the better of the two places to be." Stopping, she looked him dead in the eyes. "I envy you your choice." The look she gave him was one of indifference. On the inside however, she was seething and was doing everything she could to control her anger. Anene did give credit where credit was due though, at least he had the forbearance to hang his head in shame.

"My apologies." He normally would've gone to his knee to beg forgiveness for the poorly chosen words, but he figured that would anger the witch further. "I truly meant no offense. And the words you have spoken are the truth. Locbroalm is not what it once was nor what it should be since Ciarán met and married Miranda. It should've been a time of celebration. The realm has always been one of tolerance and acceptance. The intolerance that spiked had never been there in the past. Mostly." Thinking of the taunts he would receive as a child because of the wings he possessed. When he became a man and Ciarán took him as his Right Hand the jeers stopped. It wasn't until the King mated with a human witch that the realm took a dark turn. "I was only speaking of some of the mechanics Locbroalm offers." Still seeing her anger, he remembered another lesson of his mother's. *'No matter what, you always say you're sorry. An honest apology will take you much further than fancy words that make excuses.'* "Truly, I am sorry."

"There it is." She pointed to him and finally smiled. "An honest 'I'm sorry' is sometimes the best way to say it. And I accept your apology." Anene relaxed her shoulders. "You say that Locbroalm was always a realm of peace and lived in harmony. If that is true, then why did you have soldiers?"

"That is a story for another time." With a slight bow he hoped to be able to stop the questions he knew she would ask next. Questions that Tadhgán only knew some of answers to. As to the others, Anene was going to have to wait for Fintan to fill in. When Tadhgán had asked questions, Fintan had been cagey and said the answers were for the heir and the heir only. "There are things I can't tell you, not because I won't, but because I don't know the answers." He cleared his throat and looking more closely at the village.

It truly was a fantastic little place. There, at the village center stood a massive ancient Hawthorn tree. At the base of the tree were picnic tables and little benches for villagers and tourists to sit and rest, or just to take in the beauty of the tree that offered shade. The stone and wooden buildings that encircled the perimeter where the village's shops and places to eat. The variety of shops was amazing to Tadhgán. Several different shops for clothing, a butcher for meat, a small grocer, gifts, apothecary, and some other shops that Tadhgán didn't understand the names of. There was something about how the village was laid out that made him want to unleash his wings and get an aerial view. He also noted that there was not one vehicle in the village heart. Not that he was disappointed at the loss mind you. As he said, his visits to Quelocand were far and few in between, but on those short visits, it was the vehicles that Tadhgán detested more than most. They were loud clunks of metal that made the air around them almost as pungent and certainly as foul as a babe's dirty diaper. He was about to ask Anene why there were, thankfully, no motorized modes of transportation, when a small child came running up to her, taking her focus. Seizing the opportunity to explore alone, Tadhgán walked further into the village. Upon closer inspection he realized the 'road' would have only afforded enough room for two horses at best to ride side by side.

"When you refer to the village, are you meaning the place as a whole or this?" Tadhgán asked as Anene, who had finished chatting with the happy child, was once again by his side.

"The village itself is small with only a population of five hundred at the most. Suíochán an Ard-Shargert is at the center where the shops are and the surrounding homes." She gestured at their current surroundings. "In other words when we talk of the village, mostly we are speaking of the entirety of the place, shops, and homes. But on the maps, if you're looking for Suíochán an Ard-Shargert, it will guide you here to the shops."

"What does that mean? Suíochán an Ard-Shargert?" He felt it was a phrase he should know, and he might have at one point. But in two hundred years some information had been lost.

"Seat of the High Priestess." She smiled "Speaking of which, it's time to head to my mother's. Shall we?" She held out her hand and waited. He eyed it with mistrust but finally took the hand she offered. "Don't let go, understand?" At his nod, she rifted them to her mother's.

Six

Miranda sat in her kitchen with a mug of strong black tea in one hand and the latest Nora Weirich romance in the other. She found the author by accident several years ago when she was looking for a Nora Roberts book online one day. When the book arrived and she noticed the different last name she nearly sent it back but, decided to give it a few chapters first. The following morning, sleepy from staying up all night to finish the book, she gleefully put the rest of Nora Weirich's catalog in her amazon shopping cart. Miranda decided then and there that she had a new favorite author. Since then, she scooped up everything the American wrote.

"Well, that'll show the bastard." Miranda said, took a sip of her tea as she turned the page, knowing she needed to put the book down and make her breakfast. Reluctantly she placed the bookmark, went to the fridge for eggs, bacon, and butter for the toast. She cracked the eggs, whisked them into oblivion, then threw butter in the cast iron skillet to melt. While the butter melted her memories and heart drifted to Ciarán and the blissfully happy life they had together. Both suffered when she left Locbroalm for Ireland. It wasn't natural for mates to separate in that way. After being together for over several millennia, and suddenly needing to live apart, especially after Anene was born. It felt as though their souls were being torn from their bodies during the separation. Soon Miranda came to resent the realm and its intolerance. Then when Ciarán came to her on the night the war was coming to a head, Miranda wanted to go back with him and help. It was the first time they had ever disagreed since becoming mates.

"Let me come back with you!" Miranda pleaded with her mate. It had been three weeks since he had been back to their little cottage, and she was desperate to not be parted again. She observed him now, his 6-foot 4-inch frame now clad in battle armor instead of the breeches and tunics he wore when he came through the doorway. He had removed his weapons leaving them in the basement before coming to his mate. "You know that I can help you." Miranda watched his bright green eyes close, and Ciaran's molten silver head bowed in defeat.

"My Luv, you can't come back." He cupped the sides of her face and crushed his lips to hers. Gods, he missed her. When they were apart it was as if he was missing a piece of himself. And now he knew that they would be parted for the foreseeable future. Ciarán wanted to tell her all he had learned during his visit to the Elder Temple in Eldcolary where he learned about Flann. However, the Elders had warned him that he needed to keep silent, or all would be lost. For the first time in over four thousand years, he needed to keep the truth from his mate. The knowledge did not sit well with him. Breaking the kiss Ciarán rested his forehead to hers, tears slipping from his closed eyes as he spoke. "You need to be here with Anene Luv, she will need you." He kissed her eyes, cheeks, nose and finally he kissed her lips softly. "I don't know when I will be able to come back here." His voice broke on his words.

"There is something you are not telling me isn't there?" She knew her man. They had never kept anything from each other since becoming mates. But she could feel there was something he wanted to say but wasn't. "My love, tell me." Miranda whispered, her dark blue eyes shimmering with tears she was trying not to shed.

"If I could tell you Luv, you know I would. I can tell you that things will get worse before they get better. I can tell you that there is a reason for all of this. I can tell you that you and Anene are more precious to me than even the realm." Taking a steading breath Ciarán smoothed his hands down her long raven hair. She had said that she might chop it off one day and asked if he would mind. He just smiled and said that whatever she wished he would love. Though he secretly wished she never cut the glossy locks. So much like their daughter's, save for the silver strands he had given her that shimmered throughout. "I wish I could stay with you tonight my Luv," Gods he hated this. Knowing this was likely the last time he would ever see his mate. He wanted to see Anene, hold her and tell her how much he loved her. Warn her. But if he saw that sweet face he wasn't sure he would be able to do what was needed of him. "I'm sorry I can't stay and see Anene. Please tell her I love her."

"Let me wake her and you can tell her." Anything to get him to stay with her. At the shake of his head Miranda knew, she looked at her broken mate, and his shattered eyes. This strong warrior, yet gentle King, loving father, and mate. Ciarán was standing there a husk of her man and the troubled King of Locbroalm. Miranda knew that this could be the last time she would ever see him. She nearly broke herself as the realization hit her. But seeing him she knew she needed to stay as solid as she could. For him. "Come here my love." Pulling him into a fierce hug. "Remember that you have my love and the love of that little girl asleep upstairs. Not to mention the love of most of the realm. Anene and I will wait right here for your return to us. Be strong in your deeds and never falter." There was so much more that she wanted to say but could feel her breaking point rising to the service.

"Gods, I love you, Miranda." He crushed his mouth to hers, kissed her as deeply and as passionately as he could. If this was their last kiss, he wanted to make sure it stayed with him for a millennia if need be. Breaking the kiss Ciarán brought his hands to cup the sides of her face and drank in the dark blue pools of her eyes. The blue eyes now shimmering with the tears she refused to let fall, making him smile slightly. Knowing she was trying to be as strong for him as she could, filled him with pride in his woman. In his way, he kissed both eyes, cheeks, nose, and her lips softly before resting his forehead on hers. Eyes closed with tears now streaming down his cheeks "My Luv, my mate, my Queen. Mother of my child and the other half of my soul, I love you more than words can say."

"Ciarán," Miranda's wobbled voice was all he needed to hear to know she was losing her own battle on her strong will to hold it together. "I know you are trying to tell me goodbye. I know you can't tell me why. I know this will likely be the last time I have you in my arms." Eyes closed and tears now betraying her by falling on her cheeks she kissed her man. "My love. My mate. My King. Father of my child and the other half of my soul. I love you more than words can say. Please be safe and come back to us." Kissing his eyes, cheeks, nose, and finally ending on his lips for one final joining.

Two days later Tadhgán came to her and told her that Ciarán had been captured, and the realm was now under the control of Flann. But before he was taken Ciarán had given Tadhgán a letter to give to Miranda. In the letter Ciarán told Miranda that she and Anene needed to leave the cottage, but to leave the doorway intact. Ciarán also told her that she needed to keep the knowledge of Anene's heritage from her until it was time, and to put blocks on her memory regarding him and others. These blocks would remain intact until it was time for them to fall on their own as she needed them to. Miranda agreed with moving, but she hated needing to hide the truth from her daughter. Not to mention playing with her memory. Tadhgán had disagreed with the orders of the King. Keeping Anene in the dark about who she was, was cruel and in his mind put the girl at a major disadvantage. But in the end Miranda had adhered to all of Ciaran's orders. A week later Miranda and Anene had moved to a cottage closer to the village. Anene's memories had been altered and the cottage the little family had lived in for the past eight years had been closed and spelled so no one but Miranda could enter.

"Mother, your eggs are scorching to death." Anene's voice brought her out of her memory and into the present.

"Oh Christ!" Miranda pulled the skillet from the burner, burning her hand in the process. "Shit!" Miranda shook her hand and cursed herself for being so careless. "I forgot the fecking pad."

"Here, give me your hand," taking her mother's hand in hers, Anene healed the burn and roamed her eyes over her mother's face. "Are you alright?"

"Aye, I was just being careless and not paying attention to what I was doing." Looking at her now healed hand still resting in Anene's, "Thank you for that." Miranda looked at the now brown eggs stuck to the pan and sighed. "I was looking forward to those too damnit." She eyed her daughter. "You know Tadhgán, my daughter, is one hell of a cook."

"Uh," not sure what to say Tadhgán stood and tried to stay out of the way.

"I came here to talk to you, not make breakfast." Anene told her mother.

"Well, have you eaten yet?" Miranda sweetened her voice like honey.

"Nay," Anene sighed. "I have not and neither has he since I woke him up to bring him here to talk to you." Smiling at her mother's shamefully bad attempt at *suggesting* she cook. "If you want me to cook, just ask woman." Smiling Anene chuckled. No matter what, she was never able to stay mad at her mother for long.

"Anene, my love, would you make breakfast?" Miranda even went so far as to bat her eyes.

"Oh, go sit down." Anene set to work at scraping out the burned eggs, re-oiling the pan and placing it on the fire to heat back up. "Now while I do this, we all need to talk. First, Tadhgán can't stay at Mary's cottage. It's meant for her sister, a tiny woman, not a giant."

"I needed a place for him, and Mary was willing to lend it. But you're right. It's too small. Where would you suggest?" Miranda winked at Tadhgán while Anene's back was turned.

"Well, he could stay here." She smiled as her mother protested. "Then where?"

"I have no issue with staying in the woods." Tadhgán offered.

"You will not stay in the woods." Anene placed the bread slices she cut from the brown loaf and placed them in the buttered pan to crisp before the eggs. "Where do you want to put him mother? The old cottage?" Knowing that it made the most sense didn't change the fact that it was going to be hard on her mother to have someone living in the cottage after all these years.

"It seems the best choice. And since Ciarán had created the place, it will certainly accommodate Tadhgán." Her heart cracked a little at the memory that flashed through her mind.

"Created it?" *Aye that made sense. Why had I never realized it? That was why the place never looked neglected over the years.* Anene nodded her head. "Settled then. Now about the rest." Scooping out the bread, adding more butter to the pan Anene cracked the eggs and threw the shells in the bin for the compost. "I am going to have some conversations with you about the blocks you put on my memory. But for now, let's talk about the reason Tadhgán is here." Flipping the eggs briefly then scooping them onto the waiting plates her mother provided. Adding the fried bread, Anene handed one to her mother and Tadhgán before taking the third and sitting at the table to eat. "You are here because the current King—"

"He is not King." Tadhgán's voice boomed in anger at her words. "He is the usurper and the one who has imprisoned the King, your father." His chest was heaving as he tried to rein in his temper.

"Don't speak to me that way." Anene warned, but she knew that she had misstepped in her words and felt sorry for them. "I'm sorry, but here the one who sits on the throne, whether liked or not, is the King or Queen. But I will respect your feelings on the matter." At Tadhgán's nod she continued. "You are here because Flann is on the throne and is now threatening to kill my father, my mother and me, correct?"

"Aye, but you have a claim that he can't take away, and we need you to claim it." Tadhgán took a bite of the eggs and bread.

"Why is my claim any stronger or better than that of my father's? The true King?"

"Because you are the heir." Miranda answered. "And because you have come of age, you're eligible to take the throne. In Locbroalm the sitting King or Queen may hand the realm to the next in line if they wish or they may keep it until death." Her mother was struggling to explain. "There are things that I don't know about, Anene. When your father came to me a few days before he was taken, I knew that there were things he was holding back. Things that he knew, that for whatever reason he either wouldn't or couldn't tell me. I am inclined to believe it was the latter because we never kept things from each other. Then there was the letter that Tadhgán gave me after Ciarán was taken. In it he laid out what needed to be done. It was at your father's behest that we leave the cottage, that your memories be altered and that your lineage be kept from you until the time was right. The only thing he told me was that there was a reason for his capture, the unrest, and that when the time was right you would need to lead the war and claim your place as the rightful Queen of Locbroalm."

"Lead a war and become Queen?" Anene sat back in her chair as she tried to absorb the information. "I have to lead a war? How the hell do you suppose I do that?"

"You will need to be trained in combat, weaponry and—"

"Combat and weaponry!" Anene cut him off. "Are you out of your fecking mind?" She chuckled. "You want to put, what, a gun in my hand and send me off to war?"

"What is a gun?" Tadhgán's eyebrows drew together as the foreign word rolled around his tongue.

"Locbroalm does not have those kinds of weapons, Anene." Miranda put in. "They have swords, bows, magick and so on. In many ways they are far more advanced than we are but are not in other ways. Warfare is one of the latter."

"You want to put a *sword* in my hand?" At Tadhgán's and her mother's nod she scraped back her chair and began to stalk around the room. "Do you have any idea how asinine that is?"

"Why? I know how to handle a sword, and how quite well, I might add." Miranda quipped.

"Aye, well you have been using them since you were a girl, in the 1700's." Anene still couldn't wrap her head around that little tidbit of information. Stopping in front of the cold fireplace, a sudden feeling of foreboding chilled her to the bone. Her eyes held the reflection of flames as they danced to life in the hearth. Feeling the eyes of her mother and Tadhgán as they bored into her back. It wasn't *her* realm that was in danger. They weren't *her* people that needed help. But it was her father's realm, and his people that needed help.

Turning she looked at the two sitting at the table. Her mother, whom she loved and respected more than any other. Who had lost the love of her life, and whose life had been forever altered by that loss. Then there was Tadhgán, a man she didn't know. With stunning wings, he shouldn't have to keep hidden, but for whatever reason felt he needed to. She wanted to know about the wings. What was his parentage that allowed him to have the majestic black wings? How was he able to pull them completely inside himself? This was something, Anene was sure, that was not a typical fairy trait. But these questions had to wait, there were other, more important questions that needed to be answered first.

There was a feeling that she was forgetting something every time she looked at the man. It was infuriating to know that there were things she should know, *did* know, but couldn't bring them to the forefront of her mind. All because a spell had been worked on her memories. It was such an invasion of one's mind. Mind spells weren't forbidden, but they were discouraged and looked down on for that very reason. *Maybe this is why I have been so against mind work.* She pondered. *Subconsciously I knew firsthand the true invasion of mind spells.* Anene decided that could just ask the questions that were plaguing her do to the holes in her memory.

"Why do I have a feeling that there is something I should know whenever I look at you?"

"Because Tadhgán is part of the memories that have been blocked to you." Miranda supplied. She positively hated what she and Ciarán had done to their daughter. No child should have a part of themselves ripped away. And in taking her memories, that is what they have done. Miranda hoped that Anene could forgive them as time passed and she retrieved the memories that were blocked.

"And when will these memories be returned to me?" There was anger in her tone. She was doing everything in her power not to let her temper loose.

"They have not been taken from you, my love." Miranda's voice was small, but filled with love she hoped her daughter could hear through the well-deserved anger. "You still have them, and they will return in time, as you have need of them."

"It seems that it might be a good idea for her to have them now so she can make her decision about whether she will help the realm." Tadhgán added. He could feel the anger and betrayal battering off his senses like ice shards in a blizzard.

"No, she needs to make the decision on her own without any coercion from the past. That was how her father said it needed to be." Miranda stood and went to her daughter. "I am so sorry for all this, my girl." She could also feel the icy anger from her daughter. "I never wanted this for you and neither did your father. And I wish I could tell you more, but this is all he told me." Taking Anene's hands in hers Miranda brought them to her heart. "All we can do now is help you to train until you are ready to travel to Locbroalm. If that is your wish." Kissing her forehead. "The choice is yours."

"I know." She looked at the man still sitting at the table. "Why do I need to know how to handle a sword and bow when I have magick?" Walking back to sit at the table and finish her, now cold, breakfast. She could reheat the eggs and bread, but that seemed not only a waste of power, but a misuse of it as well. So, she ate what she had. Cold eggs sucked, but the fried bread, was good no matter what the temperature.

"You need to be able to defend yourself from a physical attack." Tadhgán's deep voice filled the room. She didn't know if it was because of the manner in which she'd met him, why he was there, or just because. But every time the guy opened his mouth, she wanted to slap it off his face. "You can bend magick to your will this is true. However, I assume, you still need to think about it to wield it." At her reluctant nod, he continued. "When on that field you must have your mind honed to what is in front of you. When to duck, when your opponent has left an opening for an attack, or parry a move that could, if you're too distracted by casting, separate your pretty head from your shoulders. It is not a question of *if.* You *will* have training in *all* manner of weaponry." He knew he was pissing her off, but this wasn't the time to bother with kind words, or coddling. She needed to know what the stakes were. She also needed to understand that no matter what her magickal abilities were, she would be required to have battle training. "The battlefield is not the place for you to ponder what manner of spell to wield." There was fire lighting her eyes, and once again, he didn't care. "You are the heir to the throne, it is my job to keep you safe, which I will, even at the cost of my life." He watched the fire in her remarkable deep blue eyes dim. "However, in that field you *will* know how to handle yourself beyond the wielding of your magicks. My soldiers will be busy enough. We can't protect you all the time because you're ignorant on how to use the proper weapons."

"Watch it buddy." His words might be correct, but his tone was beginning to border on that of a highborn looking down their nose at a servant. "You may be right, but don't forget that *you* are here for *my* help, not the other way round."

"My apologies, but—"

"Stop apologizing." Cutting him off she looked to her mother. "Did you know this was going to happen? That he was going to come here? That I was going to have to, I don't even know what to call it, go to war?"

"No," Miranda hedged, "but if I am being honest, I was afraid this was going to be the way of it."

The three of them sat in silence, absorbed in their own thoughts. Tadhgán worrying that he was going to fail his King, Queen and ultimately his realm. Miranda was concerned for her daughter's safety, not to mention the safety of Ciarán. She needed to behave like the Queen she was, but she couldn't bury the mother she always would be. Anene had so many things running through her mind, she was never one to run from her problems. No matter what she always faces hard decisions head on. But this, this was too much. What was she supposed to do? *Well, you know what to do girl,* she scolded herself, *the question is what are you* going *to do?* She sighed.

"Ok, here's what's going to happen." Anene crossed her arms. "Tadhgán will move into the old cottage, and tomorrow he can start to work with me on the sword and the bow. I'll hold my decision until I have more time to think about it. By the way, where are you going to get the sword and bow anyway?"

"All the weapons you will need are in the basement of the cottage." Miranda said while she began to clear the table and clean up the dishes. "When we lived at the cottage your father worked with them in the backyard. Before he was taken, he started to work with you. If memory serves, even as a child of seven your aim with the bow was almost perfect. I don't know about the sword. I couldn't watch you with that in your hand. Even if it was just a small 12-inch blade. It was spelled so you wouldn't hurt yourself or your father, but I just couldn't watch."

"Your bowmanship was remarkable at that age, and for one so young you handled the small blade well." Tadhgán saw no reason to hide the fact that he was around enough to know the skills taught to her by her father. Even though the woman before him was nothing like the child he knew. "Aye, I was here from time to time when you were a child. Nay, I have not seen you since you were around eight. I helped you and your mother move from the cottage, and that was the last I saw of either of you until yesterday."

"I assume this is some of the memories that have been altered?" She looked at her mother for confirmation. "Well, we need to work on breaking the spell you used."

"I... I can't break it. I may have said the spell," Miranda cringed at what her daughter's reaction was going to be. "But I was not its creator. The spell was in the letter that your father sent to me. I don't know who its creator was."

"You," Anene stared, dumbfounded, at her mother. "You used a spell, on your eight-year-old daughter, not knowing where it came from!" She couldn't believe it. "How could you have known that it was safe? Or that I will get the memories back!?"

"Baby I trusted your father."

"Well, I'm glad you trusted the guy who kept secrets from you." Anene cut in.

"Careful," she warned her daughter. "I might not know all the reasons for what he did," Miranda continued, "but I know there were reasons. Just like when he asked for a spell for himself to remove knowledge of where the doorway was. He didn't want there to be any way for Flann to learn how to travel from one realm to the other." Miranda's eyes turned to Tadhgán's asking a silent question.

"Aye, he used the spell before I left to come here. There is no longer anyone in Locbroalm who knows where the doorway is located. When I left the knowledge came with me. I am—"

"I swear to the Goddess," Anene interjected, "if you say you're sorry one more time I will turn you into a toad and throw you in the fire." It had been many years since she had been this angry and she could feel her magick bubbling to the surface. "I've got to head to the shop and open for the day. Why don't you get him settled in the cottage?" When her mother paled at the thought of going back Anene's anger softened. "It might be a good thing for you to go back. Feel closer to him somehow." She hugged her mother. "I really wish the memories of him would return. It might get rid of some of the resentment I have felt all these years for him leaving. I know now that it was misplaced resentment. But I have it all the same."

"Maybe that's why the spell is the way it is." Tadhgán offered. "So, you can make up your own mind without the feeling of loyalty and love getting in the way or at least clouding the choice."

"Maybe, but it fecking sucks." Anene was already exhausted, and the day hadn't officially started yet. "I'm leaving, I love you mother." She kissed her cheek, and looked at Tadhgán, "I'll see you later. I'd suggest getting to the village." Turning for the handle of the kitchen door she paused, "It might be a good idea to introduce him to the coven and explain what is going on and where he's from, before Colleen does." Referring to the coven's seer. And with that Anene sailed out the door.

Seven

Anene entered her quiet, dark shop and reveled in the solitude. Of course, she knew it would be short lived as Patty would be in later that morning. She walked through the storage area to the retail portion of the shop where her desk sat. The sight of the new stock and movement of other items gave the place a new charge in energy. It also brought a much-needed smile to her face as she scanned the new layout.

"Has it only been one night?" She asked herself. Anene felt like she had been run over by a lorry and hung on the line to dry. "Interesting combination my girl." Chuckling, as she opened the bottom drawer of the desk to store her purse. But not before slipping her cell phone into the pocket of her long dark blue maxi dress. Figuring she wouldn't have to climb, crawl or any other manner of things that made wearing a dress ill-advised, she chose to wear one of her favorites. Anene was not a wearer of dresses on the normal, but when she was at the shop; a shop that was reputed to be run by a witch, a dress was usually part of the uniform. She sat on the corner of her desk, a desk that most thought, should have been placed in the storage area. Thus, making it so she could work and not be seen or disturbed by the patrons. However, Anene wanted to be seen by the people who came in. What was the point of coming to a shop owned and run by a witch, if you never *saw* the witch? Besides, she enjoyed the customers, and it also gave her a firsthand view of what the flow was, what drew the customers in, what called to them, and what didn't.

Looking at her smartwatch, she walked to the front turning on lights as she went, unlocked, and flipped the sign from closed to open. It was officially the start of the workday, and as if on cue, Patty sailed in.

"Good morning Anene." Patty was simply brimming with excitement. "How was your night?"

Anene smiled and sighed, "Never mind how my night was." The entire village might know that she was a witch, and that the coven was at the heart of the small village of Suíochán an Ard-Shargert. But Anene felt there was no reason to air out the newest revelations of the coven's High Priestess and her daughter. "You were the one with the, what was it you said? Ah, Aye, the biggest date of a lifetime. So how was your date with the O'Brian lad?"

As Anene expected it would, that gave Patty the window to fill the morning with all the details about her night. The clothes she wore, how she did her hair, makeup. Where they went, how the food was and so on. Anene's ears felt like they were going to start to bleed after a while and wondered if the girl was ever going to draw a breath. *Did the lad get to talk on their date?* She wondered. *Or did she carry the whole of the conversations?* Thankfully, the bell hanging over the front door chimed announcing a customer. "It's time for work then." As she watched the young lass bound off to meet the new face in the shop. Anene was cursing herself for not going over the new stock and placements of some of the items. In particular the wands from Dierdre. As if by magick that's where the customer was headed. *Well, go do your duty and explain what they are Anene.* Chiding herself as she moved to help Patty.

"Mornin," Smiling at the woman. As Anene drew closer there was something about the woman that seemed off. She was by no means a witch; however, there was no question that magick had been simply jammed into her very pores. Anene called out to her mother's mind, *Mother, I need you at the shop. Come now and bring the Fairy Warrior.* She might not like mind magick, but there were times, like now, it was a blessing from the Goddess.

The woman before her had most definitely been human, and yet she reeked of *other*. Her eyes were an eerie vacant shell, with a slight film obscuring the irises. As the woman stretched her hand for one of the wands, Anene froze her in place, like she had with Tadhgán. *Oh, no you don't.* She thought. "Patty, would you please flip the sign on the door to closed. Then luv, take the rest of the day for yourself." Anene never took her eyes off the puppet, for that was what this poor woman was, a puppet on a very tenuous string.

"Anene?" Patty was at a loss for words. "I don't understand. What's wrong?" Because Patty, not being a witch, was blind to what was standing before her. But she could feel that there was something of the *other* happening and knew to heed to what Anene was telling her.

"Nothing that I can't deal with." She wanted the girl to leave, "But if you can ask around and find out where she is from, that would be wonderful." She reached to squeeze the girl's arm. "Don't worry me girl, all will be fine." The door opened and in sailed her mother with Tadhgán trailing behind. "Welcome, and thank you for coming." *Wow they got here fast, did he fly her here?* Anene wondered briefly. "Patty," Drawing the girl's wide eyes back to her. "Please do as I ask." The girl nodded and followed Anene's orders, leaving the four alone. "Now," She started out conversationally. "Who are you and what have you done to this woman?"

"I am your death, abomination." The guttural and grovel voice that most certainly did not belong to the woman answered.

"I see," with eyes locked on the woman's, Anene felt her mother step to one side of her with Tadhgán to the other. "Where do you hail from? Locbroalm?"

"After a fashion." it chuckled darkly, making the hair on Anene's neck raise. "That is where we are now."

"We?" Wanting to get as much from it as possible before expelling it from the woman. "If you do not hail from Locbroalm, then where?" What she received was another gargled dark chuckle. "What have you done to this woman?"

"The human spawn is nothing more than a husk for us to use." The use of *us* and *we* were not lost on Anene or the other two. "We used it for our bidding. When we are finished with you, this sack will be of no use to us. It will go where all abominations should be put," a sickening smile slid across the woman's face and slowly morphed to something that was not her own. "To death and given to the hounds for food."

"You bloody bastard." Tadhgán growled but was silenced by Anene's hand on his chest.

"You cannot protect the spawn, warrior," eyes that were no longer human scraped over to Tadhgán's. "She will die like all her kind, but not before we use her as our plaything." It flicked its now black tongue in Anene's direction. The act churned her stomach.

"Well, this has been simply thrilling," Anene's voice hid the nerves that were jumping underneath. "But I think it is time you left and give this woman back to herself."

"Oh," A laugh, wet with a pungently rotten odor slithered from its mouth. "it's been gone from the moment we took it." The shock of the information caused Anene to lose her focus. The freeze that had immobilized the woman was now gone. "Were you planning on saving it from us, abomination?" The longer it spoke the more the woman it was wearing melted away. The deformation from the woman to the grotesque figure that was now in her place, was both sickening and terrifying. Anene was known to on occasion watch horror movies from time to time. But the education she received from those films did not prepare her for what was before her. What stood before them was a tall, hulking gray humanoid figure. The wide face held black eyes void of life, with slits where the nose ought to be. Its long thin mouth revealed rows of razor-sharp teeth that any apex predator would slink from. Its body was covered in ropelike tendrils that were slicked with some sort of oily substance while smelling of sea rot and sulfur. "We and our marionette will finally take back what is ours. Our victory will reign when the land has been rid of your stench. We will dance on the bones of your dead while the living shall be put back in the chains you once wore."

"Enough!" Miranda spoke in a manner fitted for a Queen. "You will answer the question put before you. Who are you?"

"You have gotten all you will get from us, false Queen." The venom spewing from the black hole that was its mouth was almost palpable. On the floor where the creature stood were the shed remains of the woman's body that now oozed and bubbled on the floor. "Go to your Elders warrior, your memories need reminding."

"I agree with my mother, enough!" Anene clapped her hands, and the creature was blinked from existence along with what was left of the unnamed woman. "We need to find out who she was and where she encountered the creature." Anene shivered, whether it was out of fear or anger, she wasn't sure. "I don't want any more visits like this, and I certainly don't want anyone else to be harmed." She turned to her mother. "Can you and the rest of the coven try to glean who she was and where she came from?"

"Of course. What do you think it meant by 'your memories need reminding?'" Miranda asked Tadhgán as she squeezed her daughter's hand.

"I'm not sure, I know there are Elders. But the King of Locbroalm is the only one who knows where they are. The Elder's Temple, where the old scrolls and histories are held, is the most guarded secret in the realm."

"Can I ask *why* you would keep the history of your own realm locked up?" Anene rounded on the warrior. "It seems to me that might be something everyone *should* have access to. Especially now." There were many things she believed in, keeping histories, *all* histories out in the open was one of them. Nothing should be hidden or glossed over. No matter how good, bad, or despicable the history may be. It is in fact history and should never be forgotten. Or rewritten.

"It is not my place to question the decisions of the King." He answered with steel to match her fire.

"Oh, for feck's sake! It is everyone's job to question those in charge! It is how you make sure that you're not being taken advantage of!"

"Maybe here, *witch*. But not in Locbroalm." It was not lost on anyone that his use of *witch* wasn't meant to be kind.

"Maybe if you had asked some questions, saighdiúir brutish you might have been able to avoid all this trouble!" She was closer to losing her temper than she had been in years.

"Alright both of you stop." Miranda stepped between the two hoping to halt the yelling. Besides that, she was beginning to see a slight blue-green glow around her daughter that she had never seen before. "Anene you need to understand that in Locbroalm the ruling King or Queen has the final say in the land. Just as it was here hundreds of years ago. You both need to take a breath and calm down." Looking once more to the spot where the creature was no longer. "I think for now we need to find who she was, where she was from, and how she was taken. Leave that to me and the rest of the coven." Running her small delicate hands over her face and taking a deep breath. Miranda knew what needed to be done now, and Anene wasn't going to like it. "You daughter, you need to start your training." The look Anene threw at her was withering to be sure. "I'm sorry, but you lost focus, and that thing was able to move. If its goal was to kill you rather than scare…" she sighed. "You need to be able to defend against a physical attack. If nothing else this proved that."

"I know you're right." Anene focused on Tadhgán who still held his, she wasn't sure, warrior stance? Not knowing him she had nothing to compare it to. But there was no question, should anyone walk in the shop now he was likely to kill first and ask questions later. "How do you suppose you're going to train me?"

"First, I want to put the blade and bow in your hands to see what your body remembers, even if the mind doesn't. Then we can go from there. Also, we need to work on your strength and endurance." He wasn't mincing his words that was for sure.

"Did you just call me weak?" Given her heightened state, Anene just about sparked. *Prick!*

"Nay," Tadhgán held up his hands in surrender. "I am saying nothing of the kind. However, you lack the fitness to wield the weapons required of you. And the same could be said of anyone in this realm." Lowering his hands, relief washed over him as her sparking stopped. *Last thing I need is to be zapped.* He thought to himself.

"Ok, fine." She shook her hands and looked around her shop. Her place of business, besides her circle and home, was her sanctuary. As her eyes passed over the walls and then the spot where the creature had been, the feeling that her shop now felt violated and tainted sunk in. "But now I need to cleanse this place, then go check on Patty. She was confused and I want to make sure she's alright."

"Why don't you go with Tadhgán, the coven and I can see to the cleansing of the shop." Miranda rubbed her hand on her daughter's arm.

"The two of you can find Patty then head over to the cottage. I was about to lift the final spells on the place when you told me to come to you here. So you will have to lift them. I have no doubt that you can." Normally another witch would not be able to lift a fellow practitioner's spells, but Anene was no ordinary witch.

"Grand." Anene shivered and turned to Tadhgán. "I guess you're with me boyo. And mother," She hugged Miranda close. "Please make sure not to use *too* much sage. I'm not overly fond of the lingering scent." Anene smiled as she released her mother.

"I never use too much of anything." Miranda's mock insulted voice rang out.

"You may not, but there are members of the coven that feel that if the room isn't thick with smoke, it's not enough." Anene retrieved her purse from the desk drawer.

"Edith hasn't been a practicing member of the coven for years. For feck's sake the woman is nearly one hundred years old." Miranda placed her hands on her hips and scowled.

"Just so, her daughter and granddaughter are members, and they tend to follow her lead in many things." Anene kissed her mother's cheek "Be careful please. Especially if you are going to investigate where the woman was taken."

"I don't think you're going to find her family here." Tadhgán's deep voice was delicious to the ear, and it irritated Anene to admit it, even if it was only to herself.

"And pray tell, why do you think that?" The irritated tenor of her voice was not lost in him.

"I can see there is another thing you will need training on is your power of observation and detecting the details." He said to Anene, loving the haughty look on her gorgeous face and the straightening of her spine in agitation.

"Watch it, soldier boy." At his arched brow she knew she had found a word that he didn't know. "What was it that we didn't notice?"

"Her clothing, what does that word mean?"

"What about her clothes? And the word is not the point right now."

"Her clothes were more like the Queen's when she and the King met," he told them. "What does it mean? The word." Anene smirked but ignored his question.

"My god you're right." Miranda drew her hand to her mouth, "Not quite the same, but no more than a few years or more." As she was trying to pinpoint the woman's era there was a small inkling in her brain that wasn't ready to surface yet. "It's something to think about. There is something there, but it won't come until it's ready." She gave her head a small shake. "You two go on and I'll start here while I wait for the others." Her fingers were flying on the phone she now held in her hands. "There are times when modern technology truly is marvelous.

"Aye, take care mother." One final kiss on the cheek and Anene and Tadhgán left the shop through the back door and headed to Patty's, then to the cottage. Anene supposed now was as good a time as any to start her training.

Eight

With the shop cleansed; with minimal sage used, Miranda and two of the coven members went to the small library to investigate missing person reports. Miranda didn't feel the need, as of yet, to tell Bridget and Katherine about the woman's supposed origins. She had a strong suspicion the missing persons would be a dead end. Miranda only hoped the reports would jog her memory to whatever it was that was trying to break through her mental barrier.

Every time she walked in the small stone building that held the library and archives, she felt a great sense of pride. Miranda established the library a few years after she created the coven. Whenever she traced her fingers over the stone plaque etched with Est. 1860, as always, it filled her with such joy. For the majority of Miranda and Ciarán's relationship the couple lived in Locbroalm. But, she made sure to come back to Ireland as often as she could, which, as it happens, was quite often. She was Locbroalm's Queen, that was true, but Miranda had her duties to her coven as High Priestess as well. As it turned out, it was a good thing she did as much as she did with the coven and the village. Even though the coven was overjoyed to have their High Priestess with them at all times, they recognized the sorrow that came over their head of coven.

Over the years the contents of the library increased, as they should of, however, it was the archive of which she was most proud. In its beginnings it was Miranda who wrote down the histories. Adding books and journals to the archive, so when memories faded the knowledge could and would be there should the need arise. There were the histories of Ireland, the village, coven and even a small amount of Locbroalm. During the passage of time and getting the world's histories became possible, they were added as well. The fairy archives, however, were looked over by Ciarán and herself. *I need to have Tadhgán come down here to fill in the years I can't.* Miranda decided as she and the other women descended the curved stone stairs to the 'basement' where the archives were located. Normally the lower levels would be damp and would be detrimental to scrolls of parchment, linen pamphlets and later to the modern paper of today. Thanks to Miranda and the coven, the archives were kept perfectly dry to preserve all the knowledge that it held.

"Do you know where you want to start Miranda?" Kathrine was the oldest active member of the coven at seventy-seven. Although there wasn't an age limit of the coven, there was a time when members weren't stable on their feet to attend to their duties. When that was the case, those members were moved to Elder status and their knowledge was coveted. Most would see being an Elder as a high honor. Katherine, however, saw it as being put to pasture, and flatly refused to be an old cow set to graze in the fields to live out her days in peace.

"Aye, let's start in the seventies, her dress was not of today." Miranda didn't want to hold back, but she was hoping that Tadhgán was wrong, and the poor woman wasn't taken in the 1700's. Roughly three hundred years is a long time to be kept in limbo.

"What did she look like?" Bridget was a wiz at research. She was the coven's scholar, and at thirty-three her knowledge was better than most anyone in the village.

"She was tall, dark wavy hair, light tanned skin, I'm not sure about her eyes, they might have been brown." She shuddered at the memory of the woman's filmy dead vacant eyes. "I think she might have been around twenty." But if Tadhgán was correct in his timing, she might have looked much older than she was. Times were hard then and people aged much faster.

The three of them set to work looking for the missing woman. While Katherine and Bridget worked in the newer area, Miranda went back to the older section of the archives. The first histories Miranda wrote in small diaries, then to larger manuscripts and kept them in the palace in Locbroalm. As time went on, she and Ciarán moved all the histories to the library, thus creating the archives. Miranda stood at the entrance of the older section and decided to start with the oldest diaries first. Although she has never forbidden the reading of the older histories, she often felt a twinge of invasion of privacy. The oldest histories held hers and Ciaran's histories after all. Most of what was written was personal, but Miranda knew that knowledge was more important than privacy. Pulling the first journal off the original polished oak bookshelf. Miranda stood looking at the old leather-bound book that was in her own hand. A small sigh escaped as she moved to one of the overstuffed chairs in the corner and sat down to read her own words. In these words she would read her beginnings in Ireland and the beginnings of her and Ciarán.

Anene stood facing the old cottage that held watery and fuzzy memories from her childhood. Memories that were blocked from her. It was harder than she thought it was going to be to remove the spells she and her mother had placed on the building. Not because of the magick that was required, but because this was a memory she wasn't sure she wanted to share with anyone. And whether she has full memories or not this was the place she and her parents lived, where they were happy.

"I will be fine at the little cottage." Tadhgán sensed her unease. "It really isn't that small." His back and head would say otherwise.

"Nay, you can't, and aye, it is too small." Taking a breath, closing her eyes. She could see the spells of blocking, barring, and protecting woven around the cottage. Anene was impressed in the intricacy of her mother's spells. She could feel how difficult it was for her mother to close the place off. Miranda's grief and sorrow filtered through her spell work. Anene's heart wept at the emotions that her mother wove into the spells. There was sorrow, aye, but there was also love, strength, hope, and anger. Anene could feel Miranda's anger, but mostly it was her loss of Ciarán, that loss and love hit Anene the hardest. The love was so strong she thought her heart would burst. To have a love like that only to have it ripped from you. How was her mother able to survive? Would Anene be lucky enough to have that kind of love? If she was lucky enough, would she then survive the loss if it were stripped away like her mother's had been? Anene wasn't sure she would, and now held a newfound respect for her mother that she didn't have before.

Tadhgán stood rooted to the ground while he observed Anene. There she stood, without words or movement for what seemed a full ten minutes. He was about to speak when he noticed a single tear falling down her tanned cheek.

"Are you hurt?" He touched her arm and got a slight zap for his trouble "Fucking hell?" Snatching back his hand and shaking it in hopes of bringing back the feeling to his fingers.

"Don't you know not to touch someone when they are in the middle of weaving magick?" Anene smiled. She kept her eyes closed while she worked to take the last of the spells off the cottage, save one. She decided it was best to not only keep the spell that prevented anyone with ill intent from entering the premises, she also decided that a boost in power was warranted.

"How the hell am I supposed to know you are in the throes of wielding power, *witch,* when you make not a sound from your lips?" He all but growled out.

"Can't you smell the magick on the air?" She turned to face him; she was starting to miss being called a spellcaster. He's only done it twice, but when he uses, *witch,* it sounds like a derogatory slap.

"I am not a dog;" he bit out, "I don't sniff the air for magick making."

"Too bad, because magick has a distinct scent to it. It might be useful to familiarize yourself with it so you can detect it in the future. Maybe it is something *you* should be *trained* in." Before he could answer she turned on her heel and headed for the front door leaving him where he stood, seething. "Are you coming?" Anene called over her shoulder before slipping through the door, disappearing inside.

"Irritating witch." He grumbled but made his way to the door and the woman beyond.

"I tend to find you *equally* irritating." She murmured as she looked around the main room of her old childhood home. Anene hadn't been in since she was eight years old, absolutely nothing had changed. Hell, the teacup and saucer were still sitting on the mantle. Along with a plate that held, what looked to be, the remains of her mother's lunch the day they left. "Why would I remember what she was eating that day and not the rest of the time here?" she asked herself. "Do you want a tour of the place, or have you been here enough that you know where everything is?" Anene couldn't keep the sadness and unease from her voice as she spoke.

"Why don't we both look at the place?" Sensing her unease.

"Grand." After looking around the living room they moved through the doorway that led to the very outdated kitchen. "Well, given the place hasn't been touched in seventeen years, tis` not a surprise that this is out of date." Anene looked back to Tadhgán, her silent specter, following her from room to room. "Not that you will be using it much, I imagine."

"I do know how to cook, you know." Insulted at the insinuation.

"Do you know how to use these appliances?" Arched brow and pursed lips told him that she already knew the answer. "Didn't think so. Well, boyo you had better get some *training* on that, if you intend to eat while you are with us." She chuckled at the growl that followed her out of the kitchen to the first of two bedrooms on the first floor. Anene spied the door at the end of the hallway. "I remember that the attic was made into my playroom, then when I was older, six or seven, it was made into my bedroom. I was so excited to be up there. I felt like a princess or queen being so high up."

"Do you want to go up and look about the room?" He couldn't help to notice the joy that crossed her features when recounting the fractured memories. And once again he was angered at the King and Queen for removing the knowledge of her own past from her.

"Aye, we can go have a look." Opening the door, the scent of her childhood wafted down the stairs. She smiled at the joy and love the scents triggered in her memory. Anene might not have the memories of her childhood, but she had the impressions and for now that was going to have to be enough. Her old bedroom took most of the attic space. While she walked around in her childhood, Tadhgán took notice of a door at the far end of the long room. As he opened the door, he found that the last bit of the attic was still usable storage space.

There he saw something was in the back of the small storage area, but he couldn't get to it. "There might be something back here, but I can't seem to move toward it." He drew his brows together in a scowl. "Strange since there doesn't seem to be anything that would block my path."

"Ahh," Anene joined Tadhgán at the door, peering into the dark space. She could feel the magick used, she could easily break it and get to whatever was there. Except there was this feeling coming from, she knew not where, that said, *Aye, you can break me if you choose, but it isn't time for you to have me. Please wait and return to me when it's time. Mo ghrá duit a Banpnrionsa.* "Oh," resting her hand on her heart, "I think this was my father's doing." It was so difficult for her not to race in and see what he had left for her. "There is something there. And it was left for me, but it's not time for me to retrieve it." She needed to resettle her racing heat. "I could break the spell he weaved, but I won't."

Taking a step back she slowly closed the door. The feeling of leaving her father locked away in that closet was so palpable Anene wasn't sure she could do it. But do it she must, so the door was closed so as not to tempt fate. "Let's head back down and get you settled in a room." Without another word, she headed back to leave the room and the gift from her father.

Tadhgán wanted to choose the larger of the two rooms, but he figured that was where Ciarán and Miranda had slept. The idea of sleeping in the bed his King and Queen had shared and made love in made him feel like a voyeur. Instead, he went for the smaller spare room. He froze in the doorway as he watched in awe as his belongings materialized in the corner. Belongings that were, originally, stored in the spare room of Miranda's home.

"That's handy," clearing his throat, "and a little unnerving."

"Huh?" Anene saw his things and chuckled. "That wasn't me. Mother must have sent them." She took some pleasure at seeing the warrior off kilter. "Now you said there was a basement here?"

"Aye?" Shoulders square he took them to the back hallway and gestured to the coat closet.

"Well it has been established that my memories are blocked. But even if they weren't," she opened the closest door, not sure what she was supposed to find. "I have no memories of this." Pointing to a door, hidden back of the closet. "Odd placement, which tells me the cottage didn't always have a basement. This was a creative way to conceal it." Opening the door, they descended down the spiral stone stairs to a basement that was *much* larger than it had any right to be.

"You have the right to it, mostly." Tadhgán walked around the ballroom sized space. "The entirety of the cottage was created by Miranda and Ciaran. They wanted a place that would fit any need that might come up. Children, guests, training and planning for war." The sorrow in the latter explanation was not lost on Anene. "When Ciarán came here it was to see his mate and child, but it was also to train. To be ready for what, I think, he knew was coming."

"How could he have known?"

"I don't know all the knowledge the King held at his fingertips. However, given what he has here, and the things he put in motion even before Flann took over. I'm beginning to think he had some advanced knowledge of what was needed for the future."

"Can you use this for training me?" It still grated her that she needed to be trained in anything. She was quite capable of handling herself.

"No one is doubting your skills in magick." Reading the resentment of her face. *Ciarán was never able to hide much either,* then he considered recent events. *At least that's what I used to think.* Tadhgán thought. *What have you been hiding, my King?* "It is the skills you have without the aid of magick that need honing." Walking over he took a wooden sword off the wall and beckoned her to join him.

"I'm not exactly dressed for sword play here laddie." She motioned to her dress as she joined him at the rack that held all manner of wooden and steel swords.

"This is waster," he informed her while holding the wooden replica. "I use this for training in the blade. I only want you to get a feel for it." He was all business as they say, when he handed her the implement. "The weight will not be the same as when you are holding steel, but this will give you a good reference."

The beechwood handle was smooth from wear. It was heavy and felt foreign in her hands. Holding a weapon of any kind, wood or no, felt wrong. The wooden handle was long enough for two hands stacked on one another. A small plain pommel decorated the bottom, ensuring the hands would not slip off during use. The cross-like guard at the top of the handle protected the hands from slipping forward over the blade.

As she placed both hands on the hilt of the waster, there was a tickling feeling in the back of Anene's mind. *This is right,* it seemed to say. At Tadhgán's go ahead, she moved to the center of the room and began to wave the sword around. She felt quite silly in the process, like a child. A small giggle bubbled up as her movements became more fluid.

Tadhgán stood back and watched her wave the beechwood waster back and forth. He grew concerned that the block on her memories also blocked all the muscle memories her body should have. She looked like a child swinging at a fragile pot to get the sweet treats at a celebration. However, soon her play started to take a different tenor.

The playful choppiness of her swings slowly turned to a smooth arcing dance. There was no doubt muscle memory from the childhood instructions Anene received from her father, and on occasion Tadhgán, were beginning to resurface. Tadhgán was pulled from his reminisces when the swift movement caught his attention.

Anene's movements sped to almost Fae speed. No longer leaning against the wall, Tadhgán stood in full attention as Anene spun the sword with deadly precision. In front of her, behind her, to block from an attack at her back. Her movements with the blade were that of a seasoned warrior, but her footwork was a mix of old teachings and that of which he had never seen. He wasn't sure if he liked it or not. It looked fancy, but time would tell if it offered the stability that was required to defend an attack. Suddenly the sword in her hands glowed blue-green. When she hit the stand in the dummy it burst into matching flames; in her shock the waster clattered to the floor. Tadhgán rushed to put the flames out, but the towel he used to smother it, lit in the same blue-green flames. Looking around the room, he saw there was a bucket and a small sink. Filling the bucket with water he rushed back.

"I wouldn't do that." Anene's voice croaked out as she warned him to stop. "I have a feeling the water will make the flames spread." She walked over to get a better look at the blue green flames she created. "I have never made a flame like this before." She reached out her hand, but Tadhgán snagged her wrist before she touched the flames. "Don't worry, they won't harm me. They're of my own making." To prove her point, with her other hand she reached into the flames that were making quick work of the dummy. While the flames licked at her hand, she could feel the gratitude at finally being released. Closing her eyes, she listened to them.

Thank you, mistress, for finally releasing me from my confines. A soft distinctly female voice filled her mind. The voice was sweet yes, but Anene knew instantly that the sweet was also a fierce ally.

"How long have you been closed off?" she asked aloud. Tadhgán still held her wrist while her other was still in the flames.

It has been sixteen years since I was with you.

"Why were you locked away?"

He said it was time to sleep, and you would wake me when it was time. It has been a very long sleep.

"I guess it has been. I'm not sure but I think it was my father who closed us off." She wasn't sure how to feel at knowing there was yet one more thing that had been closed off to her by one of her parents. But for now, Anene needed to focus on what was '*in front*' of her. "Can you tell me how I am to use you?"

I am yours to use as you wish. As you see I will give you no harm. I can't be extinguished by normal means, and I can destroy anything you wish me to. I can also lend you light and warmth when needed.

"Do you have a name?"

My name is Brigid.

"Means Fire." Anene smiled, "It is nice to meet you again Brigid."

It's grand to be back with you Anene. Anene?

"Aye."

There are more of us that have been sleeping and waiting for you to wake them. But don't worry; the rest will wake when it's time.

Brigid's voice went silent and Anene was given the knowledge of how to douse the flames. As they flickered out, she was left with the feeling of being just a little more complete than before. Oddly enough, other than the spots in her memories, she never felt like pieces of herself were missing. But when the flames awoke, and Brigid came back to her, she fit in like a missing puzzle piece. Even now, Anene didn't feel like other pieces were missing, but thanks to Brigid, she knew otherwise.

"Thank you, father." Anene realized her father had closed off her powers while making sure she didn't feel their loss. What she can feel is the rightness of their return.

"Would you tell me what the bloody hell just happened?" Tadhgán demanded. "First your swordsmanship goes from child's play to master. Then you light the bloody sword aflame and burn up the stand-in dummy. *Then* with your hand *in* the flame, you're having a conversation with a phantom!"

"First, let go of my wrist." Anene eyed the massive hand gripping her. "Thank you, second I have no idea what happened with the practice sword." She shrugged her shoulders at his frustrated expression. "Honestly, I felt like a child swinging it around. I started to think about being one and suddenly I was moving differently and...well, you saw what happened there." She looked down at her hands, arms, and feet simply dumbfounded. "You said yourself, 'there was going to be muscle memory.'"

"Can you repeat the event?" Crossing his arms over his chest.

"I don't know." She looked at the wooden sword on the floor where she dropped it, unharmed from the flames. Anene figured she could, in fact she *knew* that she could. But the idea of doing so made her uneasy somehow. "But I don't want to try today."

"Very well." He could understand her aversion to going again. "What about the flames? Where did that come from?"

"Well, the flames..." How could she explain the flames? *Should* she explain them? If she did, should she tell him they have a name she wondered.

It is your choice what information you share with the warrior. To be honest I have no objection. He is quite attractive. She purred.

"Brigid!" Anene snickered at the playfulness of her flames. She looked back at Tadhgán and had to agree, he was very attractive. "The flames are something that were made dormant by my father." She blurted out. "Apparently, he put them to sleep, along with some others, until I was ready for them to wake." She wanted to be angry but just couldn't manifest the feeling. *Interesting,* she thought.

"Odd, I don't recall you having flames as a child." Arms still crossed over his massive chest Tadhgán began to rack his brain to when she was a child. "Who is Brigid?"

"The flames. Brigid is the flames." There it was again, a joy in her voice that simply radiated from her. "And I would be willing to bet that no one knew about them. Not even my mother." *Right?* She asked.

You are correct. When you were seven years old, I was released for the first time. We played for a while, you and I. Then one day, he came to say that I needed to put to sleep.

"My father didn't tell anyone about the flames. They came to me when I was seven years old." She began pacing the large space in her agitation. With every turn she made, the light caught the silver in her raven hair. Tadhgán liked the way the light sparkled off the raven locks. "We only had a short time to get acquainted then they were, as Brigid puts it, put to sleep. My father said she would have to sleep until I was ready and woke her up." She came to a stop in front of Tadhgán. "You now know as much as I do."

"The flames have a name?" she nodded, and he went on. "And you can *speak* to them? A power, you can speak to a power?"

"Is that not normal?" She was so ill-informed that she felt like a child at school once again.

It used to be very common, Brigid's soothing voice brushed her mind, *but as the passage of time went so did the sentient powers and the relationship to them. Until you, that is.*

"Sentient powers? You are a sentient power?" Anene didn't need Brigid to confirm, she knew the answer in her bones. And she had more of them waiting for her to wake them. "Well, I guess it used to be," Anene filled Tadhgán in on the conversations she had with Brigid. It was a lot to take in, for both of them.

"Any idea what the others are?" It was all he could think to ask. Sentient powers? He hadn't heard of there being a Sentient power in his lifetime. *I bet Fintan would know more about it.* The thought ground his nerves. At the moment he was cut off from Fintan and the rest of Locbroalm.

"Nay," Anene suddenly felt drained. "I think that's all I can take today. And I am exhausted."

"That is the endurance I was referring to," she shot him a ball-shrinking look. "But I think you're right." He affirmed.

"That's what I thought." Taking a millisecond to gather herself. "Look, I'm not going to shirk my duties. I will train with you as I said, but after the day I've had, and it's not even midday yet. I think I've earned a respite."

"Just know, it won't get any easier. Flann knows about you, and it would appear others do as well." He warned her. "This is going to get much harder and taxing." He held up his hands at the fire in her eyes. "But you're right. You're not outfitted in the proper clothing for this." She turned to go but stopped as he spoke again. "Just as an aside. What is your normal maintenance routine?" Picking up the discarded wooden sword he missed her dropped jaw.

"Maintenance routine? Maintenance?" she growled. "What the hell do you think I am? Some kind of lorry that needs tuning once and a while! Do you think I need to have my oil changed!" Not waiting for his answer, she stormed up the stairs.

Do you want to throw a little flame his way, burn his ass a little? Brigid asked with a chuckle.

Tadhgán stood dumbfounded, sword in his hand.

"What the fucking hell was that about?" Above him he heard the front door slam.

N.M. Davenport

Nine

The following morning, Tadhgán laid in bed marveling in the perfect cradling of his body it offered. With a mattress that formed perfectly to his body, offering a level of luxury he not only wanted, but needed. It was probably the best night sleep he'd had in years. Finally, convincing himself to leave the confines of the warmth and comfort, Tadhgán rose and padded to the adjoining bathing chamber.

"That's not what she called it." Mumbling to himself as he turned on the spray of the shower and rejoiced. For it operated like the ones in Locbroalm. Instantly to the right temperature and water pressure. The shower head had adjusted to his height, which meant that he wouldn't have another lump like the one he received from the little cottage. Stepping under the spray his tensed muscles the bed had not taken care of, sighed into a glorious, relaxed state. "What was the term used when she showed this room?" Taking the soap, he lathered his body while simultaneously trying to remember what Anene had called the chamber. Finishing with his shower his need for the, well, the toilet called. "That was it!" Flushing and washing his hands. "Toilet, she called it a toilet." Wrapping the towel around his waist he walked back in the bedroom and looked to the closet as instructed.

There hanging, were an assortment of shirts and pants that, he only had to assume, would also conform to his needs. "What an interesting name to use for the room where you bathe." Deciding to opt for the stretchier material for his bottoms. As he pulled them on, he couldn't help how strange they felt to him. "But very comfortable." He moved his hips, brought his knees to his chest, and finally bending his six-foot six-inch frame to touch the floor without bending his knees. "Aye, these will allow for more ease of movement." Fingering the soft gray fabric, he wondered what they were called and the fabric they were made of. "I will have to ask her that."

"Ask who what?" Anene asked from the doorway of his room. She was enjoying the show he put on while dressing in the sweatpants.

"Do you never *knock,* woman?" Tadhgán didn't jump, years of training honed his body to never reveal when he had been caught unaware. But that didn't stop his heart from jumping every time she popped up out of nowhere.

"I did knock on the front door; you didn't answer." At his arched brow she shrugged her shoulders. "What? How was I to know that you hadn't slipped and fallen in the shower?" She feigned concern.

"The shower would never have allowed me to slip." Tugging on the knit pants he was wearing. "What are these?"

"On this side of the pond they are joggers." She informed him. "However, if you're from across the pond, they would be sweatpants." The term felt strange to her tongue. "Nice, aren't they?"

"Aye, that they are." Tadhgán examined her attire. Her legs were covered in a knit that formed to every curve of her lower limbs, showcasing the magnificent shape they had. *Don't think about her legs, man.* He mentally smacked the back of his head to refocus his attention to safer ground. "Will your lower limbs get the blood they need?" At her questioning look he went on. "The knit is so tight how is the blood able to flow?" *Not the way to not think about her legs.* He scolded. "What are those called? And will you be able to move in them?"

"These are leggings." Anene supplied with a small chuckle. "And aye, I will be able to move in them. They are the least constricting pants I own, unless you want me to be skyclad?" At his glare she turned and walked to the kitchen and stopped in her tracks. "What the bloody hell happened in here?" The room looked like a culinary bomb exploded all over the floor, walls, and ceiling. "The ceiling? How…"

"Hmm, the room doesn't right itself?" He looked thoroughly confused at the state of the room.

"Of course it doesn't *'right itself'*, you eejit!" Staring at the confounded look on his face had her dropping her head in her hands. "You must clean up after yourself." She didn't know whether to laugh, scream, or cry at the situation that was before her. Anene walked to the center of the small kitchen. There wasn't a spot that wasn't covered in something. "What did you do to this room?"

"I tried to make a meal." He at least had the sense to be embarrassed by the state of the room.

"Where did the food come from?" Putting the room aside, Anene felt horrible, that in her anger at his words the night before, she left him without a scrap of food. It was one of the reasons she came back so early that morning. After waking she realized her blunder, dressed, packed a hamper of food, and hightailed it over.

"Miranda stopped over not long after you left." He cleared his throat. "I will admit that I don't understand how these things work." He gestured to the appliances throughout the room. "And," clearing his throat of distaste of what he was about to say. "I could use some assistance." Tadhgán, to his credit, didn't shuffle his feet at admitting that he was inept. But he couldn't hide the discomfort of the acknowledgment either.

"I see, well," She could have made him grovel a little, but felt that was petty, and beneath her. "First, we need to clean up this disaster, then we can work on the basics of cooking." She gave him a warm smile which he returned in kind. "But first let me get the hamper I left at the door, there are things that need the fridge."

After storing the cold items in the fridge, Anene and Tadhgán set to work on cleaning the room. The job was done mostly in silence with him asking the odd question here and there. Soon it was time for Anene to give her first lesson in kitchen safety and cooking. After a few failed attempts, and needing to clean the microwave, twice, she decided it was better for him to limit his talent to the hob. He seemed to have the grasp of cooking over a fire, just needed to remember to turn *off* the fire when he was finished. She could spell the hob, but decided he needed to remember on his own. To be on the safe side however, she did work a spell. After thirty minutes of being unattended, the knob would turn, cutting the fire and gas. But Anene didn't tell him that, for fear that Tadhgán would just wait for the flame to extinguish on its own if he knew.

Breakfast fixed, consumed and the dishes cleaned, it was time to start with the training. This was, in Anene's mind, the best time to lay down some ground rules.

"I have a shop to run and a coven to see to." She began while leaning against the counter with her arms crossed.

"Aye?" Not sure where she was going and since he seemed to step his foot in it every time he opened his mouth, he decided to wait.

"The shop opens at nine-thirty every morning, except on Sunday's. It closes at six in the evening. I am in the shop every day. I will not allow this to interfere with my business." She paused, "I have my own livelihood and that of the others who work for me to worry about. Is that understood?" At his nod she went on. "I can be here at six every morning and give you two hours. That will give me time to shower, change, and be at the shop on time. I can also give you from six-thirty until seven-thirty in the evening.

I don't go in on Saturday's unless there is an issue, so you may also have the weekend as well. If this proves to be too much, the training will take a backseat."

"May I speak?" He smirked at her arched brow. "First, I understand that you have a business, and those who work for you to tend. I know your shop is important to you and those whom you employ." He wanted to be sure that he conveyed, he understood the sacrifices that she was going to have to make. "But do you understand that this war in Locbroalm will happen? And it requires you? Your father, my King, requires you. We need *you*. We need you there, trained and trained *well*. So that you not only survive, but defeat those who have held our realm prisoner for over two hundred years." He paused to control his emotions. "I know that you didn't ask for this, and I know you don't *want* it. But there is nothing for it. This has been put in motion, and it cannot be stopped." He took a deep breath and continued. "I don't know why this has happened, and I am sorry this has been laid at your feet and placed on your shoulders. If it had been up to me, you and your mother would never have left the realm. But that can't be undone. I am sorry that your memories have been blocked from you." He ran his hands over his face in frustration. "It would be much easier for you *and* me if you remembered." Tadhgán left his stance in the doorway to the kitchen and moved to stand before Anene.

"I don't want to take over your life. But you need to understand that your life is not the only one that has been and will be altered by this. I can't force you, that is true. And if what you laid out is all you are willing to give, then I will endeavor to work with it. But I promise you, it will only lead to you being ill-prepared and will only lead to your death," he paused, "and the death of your father, mother, and Locbroalm." He could see the tears and fire threatening to surface in her eyes and felt sorry for them both. He knew what he was laying before her was unfair, but Tadhgán also knew that she needed to hear it.

"This is not fair." Her quiet voice wobbled with emotion.

"Nay it's not." He nodded and itched to reach out and take her hand in comfort. "But neither is the King and Queen having to separate. Or the King being a prisoner in his own realm for over two hundred years. Neither are the horrors we have had to face in those years. Or the Fae who are being put to death at the whim of the man who now sits on the throne." Taking a breath, he continued to speak "None of this is fair. And only one thing will end it."

"A war that I am supposed to lead?" Anene saw the concern and pity in his eyes. She didn't want his pity but knew that it was meant to show he understood how she was feeling. "I am not a commander of men and women. I am a human, a witch. I am not a general to lead troops to the battlefield."

"You are more fit for the role than you know." He corrected. "Aye, from your perspective you are a human, a witch and not fit for battle. But you are also the daughter of the King and Queen of Locbroalm, The Golden Realm of the fairies. You, my lass may be human, that is true, but never forget that you are also half Fae. You are your father's half. In that half lies the ability to lead. Have you ever considered why you have the wherewithal to run your business?"

"You're telling me that I need to fix my priorities." It wasn't a question she was asking. Anene made a blanket statement. While he spoke, she listened and listened hard to his words. "I don't know your realm. And to be honest I don't know your King. I barely remember the man who was my father, and they are not the same thing." She took a deep breath and closed her eyes.

What he speaks is truth, Anene. Brigid spoke softly. *The choice laid before you is not fair, but...* she trailed off.

"But no one said life was fair." Anene finished what Brigid wouldn't. "I don't want to lose my life and business." She whispered then looked back at Tadhgán, still standing before her waiting for her decision. "And you don't want to lose your realm, world." She corrected. "Ok, ok," taking a breath to steady herself, "today and tomorrow will have to be as I said." She raised her hand to stop him from interrupting. "Give me some time to work out the logistics. I need to ensure the shop is taken care of first, then I can give you more time for the training." She watched as Tadhgán closed his auburn-colored eyes and his body relaxed slightly with relief. She hadn't noticed he was more tense than normal.

"Thank you Anene." He allowed his body to relax and was grateful for it. Opening his eyes Tadhgán settled on hers. *Her eyes are the perfect mix of her parents, dark blue of her mother in the middle and the bright green of her father on the edges,* he said to himself. "Same as the flames."

"What?" with her eyes locked on his she could see that they held more than just the auburn that matched his hair. There were also flecks of gold here and there. *Interesting,* she thought.

"Sorry, your eyes, they are the same colors as your flames." He felt a warmth spread over his chest followed by a powerful need. Clearing his throat, he took a few steps backwards. Tadhgán needed to move to more comfortable ground. For him in any case. "Shall we start?" Not waiting for her answer, he turned and headed toward the back door that led to an open manicured field behind the house. "I was thinking that in the mornings we would start with endurance and strength training."

"This sounds like PE class." She grumbled. "I hated PE class."

"I don't know what that means." He found himself using that term over and over again since coming through the door. He didn't like it.

"Physical Education." When he still didn't understand she clarified. "Running, pushups, sit-ups and so forth."

"Ahh." He considered this. "Then aye, that is what it is." Smiling. "Shall we?" Not waiting for her to answer he took off in a slow jog, Anene reluctantly followed.

An hour and a half later Anene, on her back gasping for air while the bane of her existence had barely broken a sweat. *Damn him, the gobshite.* She struggled to look at her watch, *thank the Goddess it's time to leave.* If she'd had the energy she would have jumped for joy but couldn't muster up the body power to move. *I thought I was in good shape for Christ sakes!* She whined inwardly. She went to the gym; she did yoga and the occasional jog here and there.

"How can I really be *this* out of shape?" Anene struggled to a sitting position. "All we did was..." She lolled her head in his direction "What did we do?"

"We ran, some light leg and arm strengthening." Tadhgán stood over her, hands on hips with barely a sweat broken on his brow and auburn eyes twinkling with mirth at Anene's state.

"We ran," She looked at her smartwatch. "Three miles, and the *strength* as you call it was pushups, planking and scissor kicks until I thought my limbs were going to fall off."

"Mmm, well this was just an introduction so to speak. This evening, we will work on your footwork for the blade."

"I hate you." Eyes narrowed, Anene grouched.

"Just so." He smiled but suppressed the laugh that was bubbling to the surface.

"I've gotta go home, shower and change so I can go to the shop." She held out her hand. "Help me up please." With hands gripped, Tadhgán hoisted her up with enough umph Anene had to grip his arm with her other hand to keep from falling on her face. "Show off." With that she limped a few steps and stopped. "Och feck it." And just like that she disappeared.

"I will never get used to that." Tadhgán walked back inside, deciding it was time he made proper use of the training area. "What was the term she used? Ah aye, basement." He sniffed at the word. "She may call it as she wishes, I will call it as I see fit." So he made his way down to the lower level of the cottage. He would truly like to know why she seems to have more power than any being he had ever heard of. The King didn't have the ability to throw flame, or rift from one place to the next. He knew that the Queen didn't have them either. "So, where the bloody hell did it come from?" He considered heading back to Locbroalm, but he didn't want to risk tipping Flann's spies as to where the doorway was. If only he could find a way to reach out to Fintan and get him to investigate. But without the use of the Spellcaster Order there was no way for communication. "Put it from your mind for now and get some real training in." Picking up a long sword he began to work on his own foot and handwork.

Anene stood under that spray of her shower and just about cried as the warm water soothed the over worked muscles. If nothing else this proved to her that she was, in fact, *not* as fit as she thought she was. The last two days had been very humbling for her. She was very powerful, that was true, but to lose her focus in the shop? Thankfully, the creature was there for no other reason than to scare and make threats. If it had been there to do real harm, it would have been able to do so in that moment. Then to be proven an utter failure with Tadhgán's physical training. *Aye, I have been humbled.* She decided as she suds up her hair.

Not having the energy to deal with pants and a shirt, Anene went with another of her long maxi dresses. She could make a tonic to take the soreness away, but chose to feel the muscles instead. Slipping her feet in sandals, Anene stood and stared at the keys to her Mini on the hook and sighed. Would it be easier to take the car? Aye. Would her muscles thank her for not taxing them more by driving as opposed to walking? Aye. Was she going to drive and be kind to herself? Nope. She was going to walk to the shop and feel every muscle as it screamed at her. This was her penance for thinking that she was better than everyone else and not needing to improve her own assets to their best potential.

In the shop, lights were on, and the open sign was flipped on the door. Anene stood in the middle of the space to get a feel for it. The coven had done a fabulous job in cleansing the space after the smudge left by the creature. There was no trace left behind of the event. Anene was grateful to the coven for taking care of that while she and Tadhgán looked in on Patty. The girl was confused by the event but not shaken. The tinkling from the bell over the door announcing Patty's arrival was a welcome sound.

"Good morning, Patty." Anene wound her way behind the register to fire up the Point of Sales System. "Did you enjoy your day off then?"

"It was nice aye, as it turns out it was good to have the day. I helped ma in the garden. Da needed some help down in the Apothecary and then I went to dinner with Shawn O'Brian." As the name of the lad passed her lips a rosy blush filled her cheeks.

"Oh? And how is the lad?" With the register turned on, Anene walked gingerly back to her desk and contemplated sitting behind if for the day.

If you sit you might not get back up. Brigid chimed in.

"Aye, you have the right of it there." Anene grinned.

"Pardon?" Patty observed her boss closer. "Anene, why are you walking like my grandmother?"

"I started a new workout program this morning and I found out that I am not as fit as I thought." Leaning on her desk. "I should tell you about the new items we have in the shop." Desperately wanting to take the focus off the pain in her body.

"Like the wands?" Patty laid her hand on the table displaying the hand-crafted wands. "They're, gorgeous." There was no hiding the awe in her voice as she gazed over the magnificent craftsmanship displayed on the table. "Did they come from Deirdre?" She wanted to touch, but knowing who she worked for and the items that Cailleach's Nook stocked, Patty felt it was better to ask permission first. "May I?"

"Of course." Anene waved her hand toward the items. "Aye they are of Deirdre's making. And I have already asked her to make us more."

"They're works of art. What are we marking them as?" Picking up the wand of ash and tipped with onyx.

"That they are. And for now, we are pricing them at three hundred euros." *I have to sit down. My legs are killing me.* Anene's muscles were still screaming, but she refused, so far, to wink them away.

"Three Hundred? Really?" Patty rolled the wand between her fingers. She was not a practicing witch, that talent had passed her by, but she could feel the small traces that resided in the wands.

"Too high?"

"I was thinking it was too low. You know these are going to walk out of here, especially in the village." Placing the wand back she turned to face Anene. "Why don't you sit down?"

"If I sit, I won't get back up." Stretching out her back and arms. "Let's make some coffee for me and tea for you, and get the day started. Since we were closed yesterday, I'm sure there is double the amount to finish today."

Both women went to the back of the shop, Anene to the coffee and Patty to the kettle. Once brewed and mugged the woman set out to begin their tasks. Anene decided it was a good idea to look over the online orders for the last couple of days. She'd been slacking on that, truth be told. But it had been a rough forty-eight hours. Opening the order portion of the website she saw that she had over two hundred orders to fill.

"Holy fecking hell, how the hell did I fall this far behind?" shaking her head. "Don't answer that. I know how." She said to herself. "Well, time to settle down and get to it."

For the rest of the day Anene worked on fulfilling the backlog of orders, while Patty looked after the front of the shop. There were a couple of ladies who came in that were perusing the wands. After some debate they both purchased a wand for themselves. Anene did stop filling orders long enough to help Patty with the sale. The two were practicing witches and Anene wanted to make sure they had the wands that fit them the best. One was a kitchen witch and the other a green witch. Where Anene didn't need the wand to help hone her skills, most either did need the aide, or just liked the boost the wand was able to provide if charged correctly. After a longer than anticipated conversation it was time to close the shop for the lunch hour. Patty chose to run home and Anene chose the same, but by rifting. She didn't like to misuse her gifts for petty things, like going home for her lunch break. But today, she felt it was ok.

Of course it's ok, you heimskr, came a gruff, male voice from inside her head.

"What the bloody hell was that?" Anene stood in the middle of her kitchen with Seamus leaning against her for comfort.

I was told that you were ready to hear from some of us. Was Brigid wrong, girl?

"Nay, she wasn't wrong, but I'm just a little taken back when a male voice or any voice for that matter starts to talk to me within my mind."

Ja, well you had better get used to it there girly, for this is goin' to happen more than you think. Unlike Brigid's smooth soft lilt, this one was gravely and had a much different accent. One she couldn't quite place it.

"I need to sit down." And with that Anene just plopped in her chair and buried her face in the neck of her dog. "What is your name?"

Meili, and I am the reason you can move from one place and time to another at whim.

"Meili? I'm unfamiliar with the name. What does it mean?"

Unfamiliar! Meili the God of Travel.

"We don't have an Irish God of Travel."

You're right you don't. But there is a Norse God of Travel, named Meili. Doesn't know about Meili, that's insulting. Meili griped and grumbled.

"I am sorry." She giggled. "There has never been a reason for me to study the Norse Gods. I mean, I know the basics, but beyond that...I am sorry if I have offended you."

Well, I guess I can't blame you. But you might want to start getting acquainted with something other than your Irish Gods.

"I see, well," Rising to gather fixing for a sandwich. As she built the sandwich something snapped. "Wait. I didn't meet Brigid until yesterday when I used her flames."

Ja.

"I'll assume that means yes." Not waiting for an answer, she went on. "I have been rifting all my life. Why am I just now hearing you?"

You are correct, that means yes. And like Brigid, you did hear me when you were a little, but he came and said we needed to sleep, and that meant all of us. He wanted you to have use of me, but I needed to keep silent until you began to unlock the rest. You are not ready for the others yet, but since you now have Brigid, I wanted to be fully rejoined with you. I have missed the conversations we had. Granted you were no more than a child, but you had a good mind, and a petition for mischief. Anene could hear and feel the mirth he felt in his words to her. *You still have a good mind, but your mischief could use a little jump.*

"You think my mischief could use a little jump?" She scooped out some kibble for Seamus, then sat at the table with her own lunch. "Have you ever heard that too much information too fast isn't good?" There was no need for Brigid and Meili to respond 'verbally' as Anene could feel their answer. "Well, it is. Too much too fast can overload, and right now, I am becoming increasingly overloaded. The number of new things I've learned about myself and my family in the last few days is staggering. I honestly don't think I'm going to be able to take much more before I blow." There was a knock on her door, with her mother on the other side. "Hi ma."

"Hi luv." She hugged her daughter then closed the kitchen door. "How you doing?" Miranda could see the wear in her girl's eyes and the soreness in her movements. During her visit with Tadhgán that morning, Miranda had been given an update on the training.

"Well," a weary groan escaped her lip,. "not well to be honest. You know," not wanting to sit anymore, Anene, feeling a little fired up and needed to blow a little. "I have spent my life being fairly levelheaded."

You didn't used to be. Meili grumbled

"Quiet," She told him.

"I didn't say anything." Miranda pointed out.

"Nay not you mother, Meili."

"Who is Meili? Oh! Did you get Seamus a new little friend after all?" Her mother's voice took on a higher octave as she looked for the puppy that didn't exist.

"What? Nay there is no puppy here mother."

"Then who is Meili?" covering her mouth with her hand Miranda smothered a laugh. "Anene honey, do you have a man here?"

"I'm getting a headache." Anene dropped her head in her hands. Using her fingers, she tried to massage the pain in her temples and forehead.

Um, you could just move the pain away. Brigid suggested tentatively

I don't know how to do that. Anene sighed.

Me either. Brigid answered sheepishly

"Then why the bloody hell would you suggest it?" Throwing her hand and casting her eyes to the ceiling.

"Honey, I didn't suggest anything." Standing Miranda moved to her daughter. "What's going on?"

"Ok, how do you want it? Sugar coated or right between the eyes?" Anene quoting her mother's favored movies.

"You choose, baby." Miranda smiled.

"I am half fairy; my father is the King, and he has been a prisoner since I was eight years old." Ticking off on her fingers as she goes. "My mother is over three hundred years old, there is a war happening in the very near future that I am supposed to be a part of, I have a warrior here that is supposed to train me in *combat*. I find out that my father has closed off some of my powers only to come back 'when I'm ready'. Oh, and I had some creature in my shop to issue a threat that was apparently from a different camp than the one that has imprisoned my father. So now there are two camps that want me dead for no other reason than the fact that I exist. And to top it off I find out that I am completely out of shape and made a fool of myself this morning with Tadhgán."

Way to hit her between the eyes, girl. Meili chortled *But you left out a few things.*

"Is it too late to get it sugar coated?"

"Oh mother," Anene sighed as she rubbed her hands over her face "That was sugar coated. I omitted some things."

"Ok, well, since there is more, let's have it. What do you mean your father closed off some of your powers?"

What do I tell her? Anene wondered. *She doesn't know what he did.*

She is your mother and the mate of the King. I think Meili will agree that what you tell her is your choice, but I would exercise caution. Not everyone will rejoice in the joining of sentient and Fae as they once did.

If you have their trust, tell who you feel may need to know for now. As the passage of time moves forward it might be that the joining will be celebrated as it once was. Meili's gruff Norwegian voice chimed in.

"When I was a little girl some of my powers came to light and after I had time to get acquainted with them, my father decided they needed to be put to sleep until I was ready. Since they haven't started to wake before now, my guess is that they are needed for what's coming." Sitting back down and looking at her watch. "I only have thirty minutes before I need to be back at the shop. What do you know about sentient joinings?"

"I've never heard of them, why?" Miranda's thoughts were jumping into overdrive.

"Sentient joinings are when a sentient power joins with a Fae and they become one. They have a voice that the one they have joined with can hear. They have names and, as I am learning, have very distinct personalities." Anene smiled for the first time since her mother arrived.

"You've discovered." Miranda narrowed her eyes.

"Yesterday, while I was with Tadhgán in the basement of the cottage, I threw blue-green flames. It was then that I met Brigid. She is the sentient that has joined with me and gives me the flames. It was through her I learned there are more that will emerge in time. Then today I met Meili. He is the sentient that gives me the power to rift."

"And your father cut you *off* from these gifts?" There was a definite edge to Miranda's voice that wasn't there before. She stood and moved around the room.

"Well, it would seem so, but—"

"He took your powers away!" her voice, normally quiet and even was booming and bordering on shrill. "He blocked off our child from herself!"

"Um,"

"Powers I didn't know that you had! He did this without discussing it with me!"

"Well,"

"That son of a bitch!" Miranda stormed out of the cottage leaving the door ajar in her wake.

"Bye." Anene stood dumbfounded as she watched a wrathful witch storm off. Putting her hand on Seamus's head. "You should probably go with her." With his large eyes staring at her with complete understanding. One blue, one green he seemed to nod the massive head and start for the door. "Wait," Seamus stopped, turned, and sat facing her. "Why do I get the feeling that I am missing something here with you?" Walking to her companion and placing her hand on his cheeks she looked into his eyes, there Anene saw the subtle movement of colors that was gone almost as fast as they came. "Would you be another piece that I might not yet be ready for?" The thumping of his tail told her she was on the right track. "So, you can't tell me yet?" A genuine laugh felt wonderful as her face was slathered by his laps. "Alright, I'll wait. But go now and look after me ma." A booming woof and out the door he sailed to find her mother.

With another glance at her watch Anene picked up her sandwich, took a bite and rifted back to the shop to finish out the business end of her day. She was already dreading the training portion of her evening yet to come.

Ten

Miranda stormed through the fields, with a red haze over her eyes. How *dare* he make decisions about *their* daughter without discussing it with her first. As she neared the edge of Anene's property her anger rose to the boiling point. Miranda knew she needed to stop and cool down before she blasted an unsuspecting person. Feeling pressure on her side, Miranda looked down at Seamus, making her lips twitch slightly.

"Sent you after me, did she?" Miranda was shorter than her daughter thus bringing the dog's head to just about even with her elbows. Wrapping her arm around his neck, she could feel her temper begin to tamp down. "I'll say this for you," kissing the top of Seamus's head. "You sure know how to calm a person down." With her forehead to the dogs, she took a ragged breath. "I am so mad at Ciarán." It was the sound of his name crossing her lips that brought her tears to the surface. Sad tears yes but fueled by anger. She needed to lash out at something, someone. But who, Ciarán was in Locbroalm. "Who can I tear apart Seamus?" He answered with a soft bark and took off in a run.

"Hey, what are you about? Come back here!" It didn't take Miranda long to figure out where the dog was heading. "Oh, you very clever dog! Perfect!" Miranda followed in a much slower pace. Soon the destination could be seen over the ridge. There, nestled in the small valley on the outside of the village was the cottage she and Ciarán had shared. Now occupied by the next best thing to lash out at. Tadhgán. Picking up a stick on the way, "Look I have a stick to beat the luvly' man." she told Seamus and followed him down the hill to the cottage and Tadhgán. If she couldn't lash at her mate and King, then she would make do with the Right Hand and be satisfied. That is until she had her mate in front of her, then she and Ciarán were going to have a go. He will wish to be back in prison when she is done with him.

From the sky, Tadhgán had taken advantage of not having Anene to train and unleashed his wings to take a much-needed flight. It felt glorious to have his wings free and moving after being closed up for so long. To soar up high in the clouds, and to feel wind tickle the tips of the feathered wings filled him with a joy that has yet to be unmatched. After some time in giving his wings a much-needed flight, he decided it was time to have a look about. Tadhgán remembered while he was in the village with Anene, there was something about the way it was set up that made him want to see it from the air. He was not disappointed in what he saw. Miranda was a very clever witch to be sure. From the air Tadhgán was able to see that she had arranged the village and the surrounding cottages to create the Irish Shield Knot for protection with a distinct sword running through the center and two arrows crossing over each other. The hilt of the sword, and the main source of protection, was Anene's stone circle. At the tip of the sword sat the old cottage. He had to assume the coven members lived in the cottages that held the points of the arrows. The design was truly masterful. He wondered how long it took for the design to come to the full fruition that was before him.

While he was trying to decide what the first element that was added, he spied Miranda storm across the field. Even from the air and with the clouds filtering his view, he could see the red anger pumping off the Queen in waves.

"God's help the poor sod that she goes after." His chuckle lodged in his throat as he watched her march over the hill to the cottage. "Oh, shite. What the bloody hell did I do?"

"Tadhgán!" Miranda bellowed from the ground.

"Do you suppose I could stay here and wait for her to leave?" He asked the pretty hawk who had come to check him out. A soft answer from the female told him what he already knew. "Nay I didn't think so." Huffing he pulled his wings close and swooped down. Once he was roughly twenty feet from the ground, Tadhgán opened his massive black wings, slowing his descent and allowing a soft landing on his feet. Bowing his head, "My Queen."

"Did you know?" She wanted to shout but was very proud of herself for keeping her voice at a low murmur. For the moment.

"Did I know what, my Queen?" Brows drawn together.

"Did you know that Ciarán had blocked off Anene's powers?" The effort to *not* shout was beginning to cause her to shake. Seamus sauntered over and leaned against her in the hopes of the calming comfort that usually came with the pup.

"My Queen, I swear I did not know about the flames until Anene used them yesterday." With his hand over his heart Tadhgán bent at the waist slightly.

"Don't you *dare* bow to me Tadhgán." Miranda ground out through her teeth. "I have *never* wanted you to bow to me and sure as shit don't want it now!" She waited for him to stand to his full height before going on. "How could you, The Right Hand of the King, not know what he did to my daughter!" No longer able to keep from shouting. Seamus decided the better and safer choice was to back away and inspect the nearby bush for rabbits.

"The last years before his capture, the King made a lot of decisions without the aid of council. Making trips within Locbroalm, and he wouldn't reveal where he had gone. The King had become quite adept at moving about the realm without the protection of his guard. When he would resurface all he would just say he needed to keep some things to himself for now."

"How could he do this!" Stick in hand, Miranda whipped it around like a Louisville Slugger smashing a nearby clay pot to smithereens. Turning her infuriated gaze to Tadhgán, with the stick still poised for another bout of smashing, Miranda changed her stance and planted her feet. "I think it's time you give me the message my dear *mate* gave you." The quiet in her voice was more dangerous and ball-shrinking than the shouting.

"My Queen, I have no way of giving you the message." Keeping an eye on the weapon in her hands because at this point there was no other word for it , Tadhgán took a tentative step back.

"I *want* the message, *now*." Tightening the grip she had on her makeshift bat.

"I can't give it to you without the aid of a spell—a witch." He stated.

Three things happened at once. Miranda finally screamed out her anger and frustrations, Seamus snatched the stick from her hands in mid swing and a loud force of thunder cracked, followed by a blinding lightning strike. The circle, the highest point in the village, was blanketed in a powerful filled white glow. Inside the circle Miranda could swear she saw a figure silhouetted in the glow. There was no question what she saw was something divine. However, as soon as the thought flitted through her mind, it was gone in a flash. Something wasn't ready to be known just yet. Looking down at her now empty hands she was mortified to realize that in her anger at Ciarán, she quite literally tried to lash out at someone else.

"That was my stick." She told the dog as the stick was still clamped in his large jaws. "But I thank you for taking it from me." Scrubbing Seamus's head before he trotted off, spat the stick in the bushes, only to return back to sit by her side. "I am sorry for attempting to hit you with the stick." She told Tadhgán with a bow of her own head. "It's Ciarán I am angry with, and I tried to use you as a placeholder and that was inexcusable of me. Please forgive me."

"You have no need to ask for my forgiveness," he told her while still holding his stance. She may have been stripped of her physical weapon, but she still had her magick. And Tadhgán wanted to be on guard should her temper rise once more. "But if you wish it, you have it fully and freely."

"Thank you. I also apologize for yelling at you. I know you told me you needed a witch to remove the message." Her aura that had been pulsing a deep red in her anger was calming to her happy sunny yellow.

"I'm thinking that it might be time to try and retrieve the message. It might hold some of the answers you seek." Relaxing the stance he had been holding since he arrived on the ground, Tadhgán rolled his shoulders and fluttered the wings that had also been tensed up. "But I'm thinking that it might be a good idea to get another to try."

"And why is that?" Her calmer voice took on a sweet tenor that meant anything but sweet.

"Well, forgive me, but given your agitated state I'm not sure I want you poking about in my head." Tadhgán spoke the truth and hoped that she would take it well.

"You're right, I'm sure." She sighed and had to give him credit for not holding back or placated her. "However, if I know my mate, I have the feeling that only myself or Anene will be able to release you of the burden. So, for now, I think I will try..." The look of doubt on the warrior's face would have been comical, but in her state, Miranda found it insulting and infuriating. Which told her that he was right, and she was not the witch to be poking in his head. "Ok, fine. We will wait for Anene to finish at the shop." With a nod she turned to leave.

"May I ask you a question?" Tadhgán stopped her in her retreat.

"Of course." She was wary and wanted to be alone with her thoughts. But given her actions she figured to give him her time.

"The layout of the village?" he started.

A knowing small smile formed on her delicate features and waited.

"Yes." Anticipating the question. "I laid it out that way as a form of protection." Taking a calming breath, Miranda walked over to the little patio and sat in one of the two chairs. "As you know my old coven excommunicated me and forbade me from returning home. I was afraid they would come and try to cause trouble for Ciarán and I. So, when I started the village, I wanted to ensure the safety of the people from any type of attack."

"Thus, using the Shield Knot. But the sword and arrows?" Tadhgán took the other chair, pulling his wings back into himself first. He had learned the hard way that not all the chairs in the cottage were fitted for wings.

"Later, when the unrest started in Locbroalm, I added the sword for added protection. Using the stone circle as the tip of the hilt, then later placing the cottage at the point of the blade. When the war started..."

"You added the arrows, placing coven members in the cottages to add more protection." Tadhgán added.

"Correct, only I was no longer worried about the former coven, now I was worried about rogues in Locbroalm loyal to Flann."

"Have you ever had to defend against your old coven?" He often wondered at the hierarchy and politics of the human witches and their orders. In the old days of Locbroalm spellcasters and the orders they formed were formed for love, not for power. If there was one who wanted to leave their order, for whatever reason, it wasn't something that caused pain or as Miranda called it, excommunication.

"There was a small group in the 1860's that needed to be dealt with. Apparently, they had a seer who said I was consorting with the Devil, and I'd set my sights on them. A hunting war party was formed to kill me and the coven I'd created."

"I don't remember this." Racking his brain trying to bring the memory from his banks.

"You wouldn't." She told him in her most nonchalant voice. "It was during a time when I came here for a while and Ciarán stayed in Locbroalm." She waited for a moment for him to put the timeline together then went on. "He needed to deal with matters there and I was needed here." Miranda shrugged her shoulders. "I handled it on my own with the aid of my coven."

"If there was an attack why the bloody hell didn't you call for the aid of your mate and his armies?"

"For the same reason Ciarán never asked for the aid of the coven for his troubles." She defended. "We wanted to keep the worlds separate. It needed to be known that the two realms would handle their own issues and not interfere in each other's troubles."

"Well, that was doltish." He mumbled under his breath.

"Beg pardon?"

"Well given the state of Locbroalm, it seems to me that there should have been a joining of the two realms to stop Flann and his followers." He was bitter at the current state of his realm. Not to mention the fact that his hands had been tied by the King, to not intervene until the right time.

"I had offered him the aid of myself and the coven, but he said it wasn't time yet. I wonder now if he was waiting for Anene." Thinking it over she decided the King might have known how things were going to play out and he was planning. "Do you think that when Ciarán went out on his own, he was somehow getting knowledge for the future?"

"I have no way of knowing. To my knowledge the only seer we have is Fintan and even he can't glean that far into the coming." Gods! He wished he could talk to Fintan now. Maybe he could see if there was a way to know what the King had been up to. "Circling back to the protection of the village." He wanted to get the conversation back on track. "Have you added another kind of protection?"

"Believe me if I could put a dome of protection around the village I would. To be able to protect them from a physical and magickal attack has been my fondest wish. But I am not knowledgeable or powerful enough to make that happen. I've laid the village in a way to offer protection, placed amulets at the five points of the pentacle, and added what spells I can. That is all I can do."

"Mmm, that's something to think about. Especially after the visit the other day. Had there been some sort of barrier the creature might not have been able to get through."

"True, but if it had been blocked, we wouldn't have known there was another threat." Standing Miranda looked down at the warrior who was dwarfing the lawn chair he was occupying. "Speaking of which, I need to get back to the archives. I would like to identify the woman or see if there is anything in that section that Ciarán had created about what might have taken her." It was then that she remembered about the missing entries of the Locbroalm archives. "When you have a moment, I would like you to go and fill in the years that Ciarán has been unable to."

"Anene is to come to me here for her evening training after she is finished at the shop." He couldn't keep the irritation about her splitting her time and focus for training.

"I know you aren't happy about her splitting her time between your training and her work at the shop, but Tadhgán, you need to give her the time to work this all out in her mind. You won't get anywhere with my daughter if you push her too far. You try to get her to go your way, whether it is the right way or not, whether she knows it's right or not. You push her, and she will go the other way just for spite."

"This is you telling me that she is stubborn."

"No, this I tell you because she is the daughter of the King and Queen and a witch. Not to mention she was born and raised among strong Irish women." She patted him on the shoulder. "Good luck and try to be patient with her. This was a huge amount for her to accept and work out in her mind in a very small amount of time. And I have a feeling she is going to continue to get more information than she wants."

"So, tread lightly. Not my strong suit I'm afraid." Standing himself and allowing his wings to be free for a little while longer. "How much longer before she is finished?"

"The shop closes at six-thirty, so you have a few more hours yet."

Miranda smiled and with Seamus in tow she left the cottage to head back to the archives. It was nagging at her that she should know more about the woman, but like her daughter there seemed to be a block on her mind. At the halfway point the dog took off to do what dogs do while Miranda continued to the village and the archives.

Eleven

Anene contacted her other employees to inform them of a meeting at the end of the day. It ground her nerves to admit it, but Tadhgán was right. After the morning's calisthenics and her epic failure at them, Anene knew she was going to have to put more time and effort in if she was going to be of any use to anyone. She moved throughout the shop gathering what she needed to finish filling the last of the online orders. While she was in constant movement her body was beginning to relax and not scream at her for the morning workout with the taskmaster from Hell. Anene sighed, knowing that when she went home, changed, and went to the cottage, that bastard was going to make her body scream all over again.

"And not in a good way." Anene stopped mid stride and grimaced while she considered her words. Did she want him to make her body scream in a good way? Pausing for a moment longer to think. True he was gorgeous, and he *looked* like he would be able to properly rock her in the bedroom. And she *definitely* had the talent to destroy him in that department. It might be fun to see if her assessment was true. But "Nay, he looks good aye, but he's an arrogant, pushy, gobshite."

"Who is?" Sam, one of her employees asked as he came in through the back of the shop.

"Och, no one really." She looked at her watch. "It's only half past five. You're early?"

"Well, I thought I'd come in to help out before the meeting." He was talking to Anene, but Sam's eyes were on Mary in the front of the shop. It never escaped her notice when there was unrequited love in her midst.

"Oh, for the love of…" Anene gazed at Mary then back at Sam and shook her head. "You came in to help huh?" She smiled. "Perfect. You can help me here." She handed Sam the clipboard containing the rest of the online orders. "You can finish packing these up and take them down to the post." She nearly lost her composure at the look of utter devastation on his face. "And be quick about it. They close the same time we do." She snapped her fingers to snap him to attention and get to work.

Anene was impressed. By the time Cailleach's Nook closed for the day, Sam had packed and taken all the online orders to the post. The ladies in front had straightened up and replaced the stock that was missing, and the rest of the staff had arrived for the meeting. In total Anene had six employees and in counting her, she had the magickal number of seven. There were three non magickal; Sam, Patty, and Mary as well as two coven members, Edith, and Patrick. Sharon, the Assistant Manager, was an American who'd come in a few years back, fell in love with the village and Cailleach's Nook. And, as luck would have it, she was a kitchen witch, so she was a great help when it came to sourcing items for the shop. And her being an American was a boon because she could give insight on what people across the water would like to see.

"Thank you all for coming in tonight. I know this was a last-minute meeting. It has been a long time, too long really, since we have all been here together." She looked around the shop and chuckled. "I really need to come up with a room that will allow us all to sit down. But for now, I'll keep this brief." She turned to face Sharon. "I'm going to need you to be in the shop more for a while. As you know, Patty will be going off to University soon." Everyone clapped and congratulated Patty, making the girl blush.

"Aye, congratulations, luv. I'm so happy for you. As for us," Looking to the rest of the staff. "There will have to be some moving of schedules to fill in and cover her shifts." There was some slight jockeying for the better time slots and Anene needed to fill them in on the rest first.

"Now hold on here, I think you need to hear the rest before you start claiming her shifts." Taking a deep breath, she went on. "As some of you are already aware, my mother and I have had a visitor arrive. Because of this, I'm going to need to step back from the shop for a while. I don't know for how long." It hurt her heart more than she knew it would to say those words. This shop was her pride and joy.

"Wait." Sharon waved her hands in front of her to stop the conversation. "Are you telling us that you are leaving the shop?" There was a real edge of panic in her voice. "Please tell me that you're not handing the place over." She loved the place and her job, but she really had no intention of ever wanting to run it on her own. She was the manager, not an owner.

"Sharon, take a breath." Anene could see the girl begin to hyperventilate. "Nay, I'm not handing the shop over and I'm not leaving. I just need to step back a little." She looked to the rest of the staff, "I'll still be around, and I'll still be in the shop, but it won't be as regular as it has been. I'll need to work with all of you so we can fill the schedule."

"Wha aboot gettin stock?" Patrick's gruff Scottish brogue was always a delight to listen to.

"We do have recurring orders that fill automatically, but for the most part, I will still be handling ordering of the stock." Anene watched as the entire staff relaxed and couldn't help but to laugh. "I see that was a worry for all of you."

"Weeelll," Patrick scratched at his red salt and pepper beard. "To be honest we're not sure where you get all yer stock, and none of us want to bugger it up."

"I see." Anene smiled. She really did love him. "Not to worry. As for the rest, can I count on you all to pick up and fill in for me?" There was a collective yes.

Grateful for the people she had surrounded herself with, they set to work to come up with a schedule that worked for everybody. By the end of it Anene was coming into the shop for two full days a week and small snippets the rest of the time to make sure all was running smoothly. She was mostly concerned about Sharon. Anene had every confidence that the girl was capable of the job and doing it wonderfully well. But it was Sharon's confidence that *she* couldn't do the job that worried her. Anene had no doubt that after a few weeks, Sharon's nerves would settle, and she would be perfectly fine.

Tadhgán, longsword in hand, took the opportunity to go through his own training with the sword, bow and mace. For once, he was pleased that he was alone, which meant that he could release his wings. Keeping them locked up so to speak for so long was, uncomfortable. He wasn't sure why he felt the need to hide them from Anene, it just felt necessary. But being able to have them out while he was training alone was essential. His balance and center of gravity was very different with and without them. Tadhgán had in the past chosen to train with them hidden away so he could get the feel of it. As an adult he has kept up training with and without his wings. Noting that there would be times when he might need to keep them in for more flexibility in tight spaces.

Now he once again, could hone the ability to fight and train without the aid of his wings to give him balance and ease of escape. Looking at the time piece on the wall Tadhgán noticed that Anene was late. This was something she needed to understand was unacceptable. The woman simply couldn't be late for his lessons. She needed to take them seriously and her lack of attendance or the ability to be on time was intolerable. The more he thought about what he *supposed* was her lack of interest, the more ferocious his movements with the sword became. In the back of his mind, he heard the door above him open. Sensing Anene's presence two things happened at once. His wings disappeared, and the head of the dummy was lopped off in one powerful slice.

This was the scene that greeted Anene as she made it to the bottom of the winding staircase. Tadhgán, in a t-shirt dark with sweat, the cotton fabric clung to the muscles of his arms and chest. Black intricate tattoos running down the backs of his arms, sword in hand and the head of the dummy flying through the air. The man looked like a god and gladiator in one. Legs in the perfect stance, both hands on the hilt of the longsword and the muscles in his arms rippled with the tension of holding the sword in the killing blow.

Wow! Brigid's voice was simply dripping with awe, and if Anene didn't know better, drooling at the sight of the man. *How do you feel about him letting your body scream now?*

Before Anene had the opportunity to answer, Tadhgán stood to his full height and without turning to face her he growled, "You're *late*."

Not on your life. Anene answered Brigid finally.

"I beg your pardon?" She stood on the bottom step, jaw dropped at not his words, but the manner in which the two words were flung at her. The sheer malice that was used was simply astonishing.

"You're late." Tadhgán walked over and placed the sword he was using on the rack with the other weapons. "This might not be important enough for you to take seriously, but my realm is—"

"Hold it, right there!" With her wits back in place she took that final step off the stairs, marched across the room, slapped both hands on his chest and gave him a solid shove. She could have used her power to boost the shove, but she never ever reached for her power in anger. "You haven't a fecking *clue* what is important to me or what's not." She gave him another shove. "You don't *know* me!" Another shove, this one with enough force his balance to slip. "You don't care about me other than as a weapon for your precious realm!" Another shove. "You fecking gobshite! You have *no* idea what I have had to do today!" Another shove, only this time she used her fists to shove him. "And do you want to know why you don't know?" She dropped her hands by her sides. "Because you didn't ask me!" She stood seething, fists balled up. "You just *assume* I was shirking my duties." It was now when her voice went calm that had Tadhgán worried that he used the wrong tactic. He wanted her mad, wanted to see what she would do and how she could and would handle herself.

"Well," *in for a penny*, he thought. "Weren't you?" *in for a pound.*

Oh, that was the wrong thing to say there, laddie. Brigid cooed.

"Was I?" That was the final straw. First, she slammed the heel of her shoe as hard as she could on the top of his foot, making him bend slightly with a grimace. Taking full advantage, she took her fisted hand, the way she was taught, and punched him square in the nose. Followed by a satisfying crack.

"Fuck!" Tadhgán brought both hands up to his bleeding nose.

"Shirking my duties is right!" Since he was preoccupied with his now bleeding nose, he wasn't able to brace for the blow she delivered to his stomach and knocking the wind from his lungs. "I had to basically quit my job, you fucking bloody *bastard*!" On the last word, her final blow was to kick him square in the balls. Standing over the giant of a man brought to his knees, bleeding and in pain, Anene knew she should feel good or even proud to have dropped him. But she didn't. She squatted down to be at his level. "I was late because I called a meeting to hand my shop," pressing her hand to her chest, "*my* hard-earned shop over to the staff. Now, that might not mean much to you but," Using his own words, "I did this so I can devote more time to the training that *you* and my *mother* want me to participate in." The anger wasn't exactly spent, but it had lost some of its luster. Anene stood and turned to leave.

"I wanted to get you angry." Tadhgán, whose balls ached and nose still bleeding, but thankfully not broken, slowly got to his feet. "That was a good punch by the way, but it needs some more power behind it."

"What the bloody hell do you mean you wanted me angry?" She took a step toward him, and he, smartly, took one back. "You... you baited me? Deliberately?!" she ground out.

"Aye I did, and to be honest you did well." When he saw the sparking in her eyes, he prepared himself for another strike. "You need work, but you're not half as hopeless as I figured you'd be." The second bait worked, and this time she did for the first time reach for her power and blasted him with wind. But he had some power of his own. Bringing his arm in front of himself, hand fisted, he created a shield. The long oval iridescent shape caused the wind she sent to cut around him, instead of blasting him off his feet, like she intended. It was a surprise to Anene that he had the ability to create a shield, and it threw her off.

"How did you do that?" She was dumbfounded. Not even *she* can make a shield. At least she didn't think so, there had never been a need for one before.

"It's one of the things I can teach and train you to use." Tadhgán dropped the shield and stood to his full height. The blood, no longer flowing from his nose, had dried on his face and covered his shirt. "It needs to be said, you might not like the way I do things. In fact, I can guarantee that generally, you will hate the way I do things and myself along with it."

"That's an understatement at this point, laddie." Anene snarked, but she sighed as she looked at the blood on his face and shirt. "Let me fix that." Before he could say yea or nay, she cupped her hand over his nose while her other, hovered over the areas on his shirt where there was blood. When she was finished the blood was gone and the damage to his nose was fixed. Anene might not have broken his nose, but there was already bruising. "For future reference, it might not be the best course of action to deliberately provoke my anger."

"I wanted to see what your reaction would be to anger, and how you are when you lose control." He gingerly touched his nose, found it unharmed and his shirt clean once more. "Thank you for the fix."

"Tadhgán, I was mad and maybe angry, but that was not me losing control. I don't lose control. With the amount of power I have, to lose control, is to lose myself. I refuse to do either, bad things could happen to me or those around me if I lost the control I have." Stepping back from him. "And you're welcome. I caused the pain; it was mine to fix."

"Well, you caused more than just the nose." He shifted slightly to relieve the pressure on his screaming balls.

"Och, I am not fixing that, you deserved that and the nose to be sure. But I don't like the sight of blood, and it would pain me to see the bruise. But I'm not fixing those, my lad." Pointing to his groin. "I walked around all day sore and in pain from this morning. You can spend the night in the same pain." She smiled.

"Cold, that's bloody cold, witch." His smirk was disarming. His eyes seemed to bore into hers. It was then that he allowed himself to acknowledge her attire. In the same coverings as the morning, leggings she called them. She was also clad in a top that fit like a second skin, showcasing her mouthwatering curves. He didn't want to notice the way she looked, but it was beyond his control. Now his balls hurt for a whole bloody different reason.

"Just so." It was impossible not to feel his eyes on her. All over her. She should find it intrusive, and like a piece of meat he wanted to gobble up, but she couldn't find it in her to do so. She couldn't explain it, his eyes on her warmed the skin and her insides in a way that no one had before. Quietly clearing her throat. "Now, show me the shield."

"Nay, we are going to work on your blade work." He handed her the wooden sword. "No fire this time." He warned.

Spoil sport. Brigid grouched

"Fine," snickering at Brigid, she took the offered waster. "This one is different from the other." Noting that there was only room for one hand on the hilt, the blade was wider and was 'sharp' only on one side instead of the two like the other one.

"This is a broad sword. These tend to be heavier and are for cutting down your opponent." He instructed as she got a feel for the wooden weapon. "You see that there is only one side that has an edge." Taking the sword from her to demonstrate. Sword in one hand Tadhgán slices it in a downward motion. "This is useful in close combat. You use this when you don't have the space for a long sword."

"Given the magick I have, is it really going to matter? Wouldn't I just use Brigid for flame or Meili to leave the area?" hands on her hips.

"You need to be versed in the weapons for a number of reasons. First, because there may come a time when you can't or won't be able to rely on your magick. Who is Meili?"

"I can't see a point where I would ever be cut off from my power." Anene cut in.

"Second, the realm won't accept a ruler who can't use the weapons we use to defend ourselves. And again who is Meili?" Tadhgán continued.

"You guys use magick, and I am sure there are those who don't pick up blade or bow." Anene challenged while ignoring his question. Not because she wasn't going to answer, but because she could see his annoyance.

"Aye, we use spells and such, aye, there are those who don't use blade or bow—"

"See, so why must I—"

"Dammit, witch, who is Meili!" Tadhgán shouted in his frustration. He had never dealt with someone who got under his skin the way she seemed to.

"Well, you're not going to get it out of me by shouting. That's for sure." Brigid and Meili both were laughing at her ability to throw the warrior off his game. As it happens, she was enjoying herself as well. Particularly when he growled.

"You're trying my patience, witch. Who is Meili?"

"Meili is the rifting power I have." She smiled. "He is the reason I can move from place to place." She answered sweetly. "See, all you had to do was ask me nicely." With a wide grin plastered on her face.

Not to correct you my dear, but what I said was I am the reason you can move through time *and space.* Meili put in.

"I know, that's what I said." Anene waved her hand. "May I have that back?" Pointing to the wooden sword in his hand, "Thank you."

Getting a feel for the training tool she tried swinging it about. "I don't think I have ever handled a sword like this. I feel completely off balance." She swung the waster about. She desperately wanted to use her other hand to give her the needed balance. "I know this is a one-handed blade and all I want to do is put my other hand on the hilt." Deciding to move on before the big man blew a gasket.

"I don't think your father ever showed you the broad sword." Tadhgán grouched. *Gods, she can be so...* he couldn't even figure out a word to describe her. "The balance is something that you will need to get used to. The stance in your body and feet will be different when using this one as opposed to the long sword. There are those who would say to just train you on one, and there is no reason for you to know both. I disagree." He watched as she tried to find her feet and balance of the upper body while swinging the sword. He figured he'd let her move about for a while and see if she can find her center without help from him. It would be better all-around if she found it on her own without his interference.

"Why do I need both?" She looked over her shoulder as he stood watching her fumble about. "And why aren't you helping me?" Anene felt ridiculous. Swinging wildly, tripping over her own feet and nearly toppling over more than once.

"I want you versed in everything so that you are more prepared and can defend yourself no matter what." *I need you strong and able, I need you capable of deadly force at a whim. I need you...* his thoughts trailed off. "I don't want you killed because you don't know how to handle a weapon that was placed in your hand." *Focus you bloody sod.* He told himself. "And I *am* helping you. I want to see if you can find your own center and balance. It is better if you find it yourself."

"Ok," She stopped and faced him. "I will concede that being well versed in all weapons makes sense. But why is it better not to help me with the balance stuff?"

"Because, if you find your center, on your own, there will never be a time when you can't find it again. It will become second nature. However, if I find your center for you, all you will learn is *balance* and that is not the same. Learning one without the other will place you in a major disadvantage." Taking a breath, he spoke slowly and carefully so as not to show his frustrations. "I want you to stay alive, I want you to defend yourself, I want you to be formidable. There are those who want you dead, I *will* do everything I can to make sure that doesn't happen. As will the realm, but we need you to do the same for us."

With a nod Anene went back to work. It took most of the night and she felt like her arms were going to fall off, but she did eventually find her center. The balance however was not quite there. But Tadhgán was pleased with her. And Anene was pleased with herself as well.

"My arms are jelly. I have to call it for today." She handed him the wooden sword and started for the stairs. Anene sighed and trudged up the winding stone stairs only to find her mother sitting in the front room with a cup of tea. "Mother?"

"Here, have some tea, it will help the soreness." Handing her the tea and waiting for Tadhgán to join them. "Baby I know that you're tired, but there is something that I need you to do for me."

"What do you need?" The tea was working its magick on her arms and the leftover soreness from the morning's exploits.

"There is a message from your father in Tadhgán's mind and I would like for you to retrieve it." Miranda was wringing her hands. She was still angry at her man for what he did, but moreover she was hurt that he didn't trust her enough. Didn't trust her enough to explain about their daughter and what he was going to do.

"He gave you a message for her, why can't you just tell her?" Anene asked Tadhgán as she finished the last of the tea. She was always impressed how her mother could make teas for healing and have them taste good. Something the rest of the coven couldn't seem to grasp.

"He used a spell to shield the message. I don't know what it says. He said that it would need to be magickly removed." He really didn't like the idea of someone poking about in his head, particularly Anene, but there was nothing for it.

"And you can't remove it?" She asked her mother in surprise.

"I didn't think it was the best idea for your mother to be poking around in my head for a message from the man who has angered her." Tadhgán coughed.

"Hmm, good point there." Putting the empty teacup on the mantle Anene turned to face the keeper of the message. "Ok are you ready?"

"Aye." Once more his amber eyes locked on hers.

"Here we go then."

Twelve

I t was elegant magick, Tadhgán would think later. Anene stood at his front, her hands in his. Eyes locked, Tadhgán was witness to the pure beauty of Anene when she was full in her power. Her eyes sparkled, the blue centers went impossibly deep and the bright green rims almost glowed swirled with power. Her phantom hands felt gently around in his head. Truth be told he was not looking forward to anyone fiddling around in his brain. There have been times, in the past, when the Order needed to extract information. Tadhgán always felt like it was hot fingers scratching and scraping around. It didn't hurt, but it was definitely uncomfortable. Yet, with Anene, it felt soft and comforting. There was no pain, no hot scratching or icy picking. This was a careful caress and soothing with a hint of warm sensuality.

Miranda stood and watched as Anene worked her way through the spell that Ciarán used to send his message to her. Every time she thought about her mate, she was filled with love and longing, but now there was an anger that had never been present before. And she hated it. As she observed the magick weaving in front of her, Miranda knew it was right for Anene to retrieve the message. There was no danger of her daughter hurting or damaging Tadhgán like there would have been had Miranda gone after the message.

As Anene unraveled the spell she decided that instead of transferring the mental message from Tadhgán to her mother it would be better for her mother to have a letter her father would have written out, in his own hand. Above Tadhgán's head parchment with the handwriting of her father appeared. While her eyes still held his, her third eye, her witch's eye, watched as the letter took form and filled not only one page, but three pages of parchment. Ciarán's handwriting was so small and flowing that Anene wondered if her mother would be able to read it. Then she remembered, her mother was born in 1702 and probably wrote in the elegant script. Finally, the spell was complete. Laying on top of Anene and Tadhgán's still joined hands sat Ciarán's letter to Miranda. What surprised her was that on top of the three-page letter to her mother was on for Anene. Once the magick's closed, they released each other's hands, while the letters stayed suspended in the air, waiting for their recipient to take them.

The women took their letters, "Mother, there was something not in the letter. Father left a verbal message." It was strange, she was hearing the voice of a man she knew was her father. Yet her memories were void of the sound of his voice. "To me, it seems he knew I was the one who would get the message. He said that after you read the letter, you needed to burn it." She chuckled under her breath. *He knew I will turn the message into letters.* "Also, you are not to show it or speak to anyone about the letter or what it says, not even me as it turns out." Anene watched as her mother gently ran her fingers over the handwriting and her daughter's heart broke for her mother.

"It has been so long since I've seen his handwriting. Even when we met, in 1722 his form of writing was an art." Miranda gave a watery chuckle. "He would leave me notes almost every day. You might call them love notes." She flicked a stray tear away. "He had such a way with words. If he hadn't become King, he would have been a wordsmith." At her daughter's questioning look she clarified. "An author, my love. He could have been a writer." She folded the letter and slipped it in her purse for reading later.

Miranda knew that no matter what, she was going to be a blubbering mess when she read Ciarán's words to her. Even if they upset her, these were his words, and she wanted them to herself. "What about yours, baby?"

Anene looked at the letter from her father that read:

My Precious daughter,

Please forgive me for not being there for you. I wanted nothing more than to see you become the woman I know you are. Believe me when I say leaving you and your mother was the hardest thing I will ever do in my whole existence.

I know you must be angry at me for not allowing you to grow up with all your amazing gifts. Even though I can't tell you why now, please know that there were reasons they needed to sleep until you were ready for them. By now you should have become reacquainted with Brigid and Meili.

You also, by now, should be acquainted with Tadhgán Ultan. I sent him to you, this is true. He will think it is to protect, but I know that you do not require protection, only training in the ways of combat. There shall be things your body will remember in time during your work with him. However, I have every confidence that he will teach you things I did not. You were so little, and I did not want to overtake your childhood with the ways of weapons and battle. My Right Hand will be a challenge for you at times, and there will be times when all you want to do is kick him in the balls and bloody his nose. As a man, I plead with you not to do so. As your father, I demand that you do. But remember that his job is to make sure you can not only defend you and yours, but to also lead men and women in battle. He is a very good man; I trust him with my life and the lives of those who are more precious to me than that of my realm.

I am so sorry that this has been laid at your feet. I would have had it otherwise. I love you my girl and I can't wait to see you again when you come to Lochroalm. I want you to be aware, I have given your mother more of an explanation for my actions. I am sorry she will not be able to relay any of it. I wouldn't have told her, but keeping things from your mate will burn a hole in your soul. I need you to remember that, to keep things from your mate is painful in more than one way. This being said, I knew actions needed to be kept secret until the right time for them to be revealed. Your mother will know there was things kept from her, by now she is hurt and ready to kick me in the balls for doing this when she was not consulted. Don't be upset my girl, you will know all when you need to. Mo ghrá duit a banphrionsa.

Your Father

After reading the letter to herself first then aloud, Anene set her gaze to her mother then landed on Tadhgán.

"How is it that he seemed to know what was going to happen beforehand? What I mean is, he knew that I would already have Brigid back and know about Meili. How is that possible?" She asked Tadhgán.

"I know not." Tadhgán was stunned. The king never intended him to protect the heir, but to train her, as he already had begun. "Why not just tell me what he wanted instead of setting me off on a farce?"

"It would seem that he was doing a lot of things without informing anyone." Miranda interjected. "I would be willing to bet that it was for Anene's protection as well as the realms." Miranda added. She was itching to be at her own home so she could read the words Ciarán had written to her.

"Wait, why would he risk putting his words to paper." Tadhgán was muttering to himself while pacing the room. "Flann had the guards read everything he wrote. Then burn it."

"He didn't write the letters." Anene whispered as she reread her letter. "They were written in his mind. When I was unweaving the spell, I was able to turn his thoughts to written words." Tracing the script on the parchment. "Because they were his own thoughts, they transcribed in his script. But whoever gave him the spell," she was still marveling at the perfectly woven magick that surrounded the spell-work, "knew what they were doing, for I couldn't read what was transcribed while in the spell." She chuckled, "A very clever witch indeed."

"We don't have witches in Locbroalm. We have spellcasters, and they can't create a spell like the one you're describing." Tadhgán was getting a very unsettling feeling in the pit of his stomach.

"That may be why it was a spell of witchcraft, but not by a *human* witch." Miranda was rubbing her fingertips to get a better feel for the spell that was woven in Tadhgán's mind. Something was niggling at her. "Are there other realms, beside yours and mine I mean?" Miranda asked him with some urgency that Anene didn't really understand.

"Aye, I don't know how many there are though." At her look, Tadhgán continued "There is Elvkinles, Isle of the Elves, Witrotean, Ocean of the Witches—"

"Stop there, right there." Miranda was aghast. "There is a realm that means Ocean of the Witches?"

"Aye, but we don't have any contact with them. They have been cut off from the realms for too many millennia to count. And before you ask, I know not why."

"I don't think it was them anyway." Anene cut in. "But what do you know about Elvkinles?

"Not much—"

"Is there anything that you *do* know about?" Her exasperation was getting the better of her.

"*But*," He went on as if Anene hadn't spoken. "They are our closest kin, and they have witches." He rubbed his hand over his face and sighed. "I suppose it is possible that he got the spell from them. When Ciarán was a boy, his mother had sent him to the Isle for a number of years to live."

"He never told me about that. I wonder why." Miranda spoke softly to herself.

"Mother," Anene saw the way her mother was cradling her purse containing the letter. "Why don't you head home, I know you want to read your letter. But remember, after you read it…"

"I know, I have to destroy it." She turned to go and stopped. "You know no one can enter the chamber in your circle, do you think we can just…"

"I'm sorry," it broke her heart that her mother had to destroy the first tangible link to her mate in decades. "I don't think it is something that we can risk. He was very clear, after you read the letter, it needs to be destroyed." She rested her hand on her mother's shoulder, "If it's too painful for you to do, I can take care of it after you read it." pausing, "But he did say, *you* needed to do it."

"I know, I was just hoping there was a way I could keep it." Sighing, Miranda left the cottage and went home to read the first communication she'd had from her man in seventeen years.

"What time should I expect you in the morning and for how long?" Tadhgán had a lot to think about and wanted to do it from the air.

"I'll be here in the early morning, if you had been paying attention when I first got here you would know that I will be here all day for the foreseeable future." Her smile was strained and forced. "I handed Cailleach Nook over to my staff so that I could concentrate on the training. There will be days however, that I will need to work in the shop." She wanted to see if he would object. When he smartly kept silent she went on. "I didn't want to hand the ordering of stock over. That will always be my responsibility."

"You named your shop Witch's Nook?" He smiled "Isn't that a little on the nose?"

"Aye I did and aye it is. The non magickal get a kick out of the name and the magickal get a kick out of them." Anene turned to leave but stopped and turned to face him. "By the way, have you had a proper tour of the village yet? Not including the run through we did the other day with the creature in my shop?"

"Nay, it is something I will need to do. As well as see your home and this circle of yours." Of course, he had seen both from the air, but he wanted to get a lay of the land from the, well, land.

"Alright, why don't you give a little time in the morning and meet me in the village before the mornings torture session."

"Where do you want to meet? And training is not torture." He defended.

"Actually, why not meet me in the circle. I'm sure you can find it, in your own way." She smirked and walked out. Anene was fully aware that he'd been flying about while she was in the shop that day. She wasn't sure why he was keeping the wings under wraps, but figured he had his reasons. She was sure he would unleash them when he was ready. In the meantime, Anene would behave as if she weren't aware of them, for now. It had been a long day for everyone, and she couldn't have been the only one who wanted to have her supper and head to bed.

Thirteen

Miranda sat in her bed with tears running down her cheeks, just like she knew she would. To read Ciarán's words to her, something she wasn't sure would ever happen again, filled her heart with joy and love. It was true her man had started the three-page letter to his mate with words of love and devotion. Words he hadn't been able to say for, in his time, over two hundred years. And to think, Miranda only had to endure seventeen years of separation. Knowing that two hundred had passed for Ciarán and the rest of Locbroalm was something that Miranda still had difficulty comprehending. She knew Anene was having a difficult time dealing with the knowledge of her mother's birth in 1702. Miranda wasn't sure her daughter had done the math that told her that she and Ciarán had been together for over three thousand years. One of the points Ciarán had made in the letter. Goddess, she missed him.

As Miranda read on, she learned about his time in Elvkinles-Isle of the Elves and what he knew about Witrotean-Ocean of the Witches. What she learned from his letter was both chilling and hopeful. There were other places that he told her about; it made her smile, as he sounded like he did when he was schooling her in the ways of Locbroalm in the beginning. It wasn't until he started talking about Anene and her gifts that her tears stopped, and her ire took over. Once again, she was met with the feeling of hurt and disbelief at the audacity of her man to make those decisions about their daughter without her. Even if she would have agreed to the choices he made. And after reading the letter, Miranda had to admit that she did in fact agree with what Ciarán had done. She might even understand his need to conceal it from his mate.

"I understand, but dammit I am still so pissed at you for doing it." She told the empty room.

The deeper she read in the letter, the more vague he got. He told her that Anene and Tadhgán, when she was ready, would need to come to Locbroalm. Miranda read more and sat up in her bed. The hair on her neck stood up.

"Oh my God!" she whispered in shock and horror. Now she knew, and she was terrified. Miranda now understood the need to burn the letter. If it should fall into the wrong hands? All would be lost, and not just in Locbroalm, but every realm. "Ciarán, how did this happen?" On the last page her question was answered and all the warmth within her body and room seemed to be sucked out. In the last paragraph Miranda was again brought to tears.

My luv, there are some things that I cannot tell you yet. It hurts me deeply having to keep anything from you. I truly hope you can forgive me concerning the moves that I have taken without your knowledge. But it needed to happen in this way. I have given you all the knowledge that I can. I've provided you with a spell to remove the knowledge I have laid at your door. I know the burden of knowledge and not being able to share it with others. If you feel that you can't hold it in, please use the spell. But I know as my mate, my soul, my Luv, you will burn the spell along with the letter. I have never known a stronger being in my life than you.

my mate. And since I know you, go to the archives, search and learn. I can't tell you what to search for, but my clever mate, you will know what it is when you find it. I miss you my Luv, I can't wait for the day when I can hold you in my arms and kiss your lips. Be safe, be well, be ready. Aye, be ready Luv, for when I have you again, and I will have you, we will make up for the last years apart. Is breá liom tú mo Bhanríon.

Ciarán

It was the last line that did Miranda in at the end. Is breá liom tú mo Bhanríon, I love you my Queen.

"Is breá liom tú mo Rí." Miranda reread the letter once more before heading to the kitchen. Placing the parchment in her cast iron pan and saying the spell Ciarán provided to destroy the letter. Miranda watched as the heavy paper disintegrated leaving no trace behind, ash or smell. It was eerie to know that the letter was gone, and it was as if it never existed.

Ciarán was correct, she would not use the spell to remove the knowledge he had given her. It would be hard not to share the information with Anene. But she understood what was at stake should Anene and others learn before it was time. Miranda looked at her watch and groaned.

"Damn, it's too late for the archive tonight." She should eat something, but the idea of food at the moment turned her stomach. "Crackers, I can have crackers," she had a chill run over her body that made the hair rise on end. "Take a bath and go to bed." This was the first time in years that she wished she had a dog with her. There was something to be said for the comfort they give when you feel uneasy in your own home.

Like magick there was a scratch at her kitchen door. "Well, hello there." On the other side was a small black dog. "Aren't you a handsome lad." Miranda knelt to have a better look at the little dog. "You have the look of a Newfie my boy. But you're not a puppy." She rubbed his Newfoundlandesk head and smiled. "Did someone put you in the dryer and shrink you?" She chuckled as the unnamed pup slathered her hands and face in loving kisses. Even in the moonlight his coat just gleamed. Running her hand over the silky soft fur and gently looking at his teeth. "I'd say you're about five years old. Have I got that right?"

"Woof." said the smiling pup.

"Would you like to come in?" And just like that, the pup raced in and began to explore the kitchen making Miranda smile, chasing some of the dark dread that the letter's information had caused. "You can stay here tonight, but I'm sure you must belong to someone in the village." She poured some of Seamus's kibble in the bowl. Miranda watched as the black dog devoured it. "I guess you were hungry huh?" Filling the water bowl then going to get herself some food. "It's a good thing I keep some of Seamus's food here for when he comes to visit." She added a little more as the pup was licking the empty bowl.

Deciding that instead of the crackers, she would make an omelet with diced ham, that she shared with the dog, and cheese that was also shared. Along with some mushrooms and tomatoes which were not shared. "These aren't good for you, my boy." She told him while he sat at her side with sad pleading eyes. "That won't work on me, boyo." Miranda chuckled as she placed bread in the toaster. Her timing was perfect, the egg was slid from the pan onto her plate as the toaster ejected the bread. Toast buttered and added to the plate. Miranda decided that she had earned the right to watch *The Big Bang Theory* while eating her late-night dinner. Dog in tow, she headed to the living room, sat on the sofa, and pushed play on the Blu-ray player. She loved how the four scientists dealt with the women in their lives. Her favorite character on the show was also the most irritating one of the bunch, yet when he showed personal emotional growth, it always made her smile. Then, of course, he would say or do something that made her and the others in his life want to slap him silly. "You can come up with me if you want." She told the waiting pup. "I really should give you a name," she told him as he came up on the sofa. "But if you have a home, I don't want to confuse you." She scratched his head. When he finally accepted that he wasn't going to share her dinner, he laid his head on her lap dozing off while she ate.

"I am secretly hoping that you don't have a home, so I can keep you." Miranda admitted. "Olivia has Newfoundlands I love them, but unlike my daughter, I don't want a dog that size. Now, you, you're the perfect size." Running her fingertips down between his eyes. "I'm guessing you are about forty-five pounds. And if I'm right about your age, you won't get any bigger."

The pair sat on the sofa while Miranda finished her dinner. After three episodes, it was time for bed. As Miranda moved about the house, cleaning her dinner dishes, turning out lights, the black shadow followed in her wake.

"You should probably go out before I head to bed." Opening the front door, the dog ran out, did what he needed to do and ran back to her side. "Ok, to bed." The pair climbed the stairs to Miranda's bedroom. "Go ahead." She watched as her shadow hopped on the bed, circled three times, and curled into a ball with his head facing her. It was as if he didn't want to let her from his sight. Miranda would think about that later she decided as she headed into her ensuite bathroom. After she donned her pj's, brushed her hair and teeth along with other bathroom needs she joined the ever-watchful pup in bed. She slid beneath the covers and sighed as the dog, once again using his soulful eyes, lifted the cover to let him snuggle under them. "If I end up with a bed full of fur, I will have no one to blame but myself." However, as the dog curled up in the crook of her arm and he laid his head on her shoulder she couldn't have cared less about the fur that would be in the bed. "I really hope I get to keep you." She whispered, and kissed the pup on the nose, earning one in return before drifting off to sleep.

While Miranda slept, Tadhgán flew through the skies trying to clear his head. The news that his King had never intended for him to protect, but train his daughter for war? This was more than wanting her to be able to defend herself. He really was training her for battle. Tadhgán wasn't sure how he felt about that. He knew he had said as much, but until that moment he never really believed Anene would have to *physically* head into the fray of battle. So, he flew through the night to work his pent-up wings and get his thoughts in order. Things were changing right before him, and he couldn't get his bearings. During his first pass over he watched as a Guardian materialized in front of Miranda's cottage. He would have gone down, but knew if the Guardian came it was for a good reason.

"There could have been a summoning spell on the letter." Tadhgán told the night sky. "I wonder if she'd burned the letter then?" He shook his head. "Of course she did, you imbecile." He watched as the queen opened her door and the Guardian pranced into her home. "One less charge to worry about then." Without realizing it, his whole body turned to the direction of Anene's cottage. "Do it my lad or you will never find sleep." And with that he flew off to clear his mind, before heading to his bed.

Fourteen

The following morning Anene and Seamus made their way to the circle. She really needed to recharge and reconnect with herself and her magick. Feeling a bit off kilter of late and knowing the visit would help, she was practically running to the circle.

Why not just rift if you're in that much of a hurry girl?

"Because Meili, not everything needs to be done magickly. There are times when it is better to use good old muscle power. Besides, if I am to build up my endurance, walking is better than rifting."

The early morning was covered with white swirls of fog and crawling mist. It was a scene that lent to a frightening witch, spirit, Banshee, or any manner of terrifying creatures to go on the prowl. The idea that a witch *was* on the prowl, so to speak, made Anene laugh a little bit. Her favored times were the early mornings with the fog and mists and the nights when the moon and stars were awake.

Like always Anene touched the outlying stone before entering her circle. There was a familiar charge and tingle as she entered the sacred place. Something that she hadn't noticed until just then was that when Seamus entered, he shivered like he had the same charge and tingle. Standing in the heart, Anene slipped out of her shoes and planted her feet. She stretched her arms to the sky and took several deep cleansing breaths. It had been a long time since she'd been to welcome the dawn, and she was going to take full advantage. A smile spread across Anene's lips as she could feel the man with massive wings high above her. It took all the willpower she had to keep her eyes closed, including her third eye. Closing off her ability to see what she's sure would be a gorgeous sight. His wings full and spread open as well as the sight of the warrior who possessed them in the air.

"You know," she told her dog, "sometimes having scruples and morals, really suck."

Woof

Would you like me to tell you what you're missing? Brigid sounded like she was in awe.

"Aye I would, but please don't. And you shouldn't look either." she lightly scolded her flames. "It's rude and an invasion of his privacy to do so without his permission."

Spoil sport. Came Brigid's grumbled lilt.

Women. Meli grumbled

"Would both of you shush please? I'm trying to concentrate." Anene giggled as the sentients bickered back and forth. She supposed she was going to have to work on tuning them out. "No better time than now to start on that." She said as she cleared her mind and tuned out the still bickering sentients.

Tadhgán landed behind Anene's house and followed the route he saw her take on the way to her circle. Not sure why she felt it necessary to meet there, it was her space and to be honest he didn't really want to be near her witchcraft. He knew in his heart that there was nothing sinister in hers or any of the other's powers. But they were not of his realm and therefore he felt them, not wrong, just unknown. Anene was the first being he'd ever met who could wield power without the implements to make it so. And the amount of power Anene had was staggering.

"And there is still more to come." Tadhgán said to the little female hawk he had met the other day. Holding out his arm so she could perch for a moment. "You know, you're a bonny lass, but you need to be chasing after the male I saw flitting about. He has his eye on you." She tilted her head slightly to where the male in question had perched in a nearby tree. She ruffled her feathers and gave a soft coo. "Oh, I see this is your mating dance, make the lad jealous and have him chase *you* instead." His chuckle was warm as was his touch while he rubbed under her chin. "I think you have made your point, my girl. Fly now and he will be yours. Be safe, be well, be ready." Lifting his arm, the hawk took flight and as predicted the male was in hot pursuit.

What Tadhgán didn't know was that Anene, who was high above him in her circle, was able to see the exchange of man and hawk. It gave her a different perspective of the warrior that had not been shown before. It was a good side, and one that he kept well hidden. Turning her back so he wouldn't know she had a new view into his makeup.

Seamus went bounding off to do whatever it is he does when he leaves her. Oddly though he took off in the direction of her mother's place. *Odd,* she thought.

"Morning." Tadhgán called from the outlying stone. "May I enter?"

"Please do, and I thank you for asking first." Anene slipped her shoes back on her feet and turned toward her chamber. "I'll be right back."

"My gods." His shocked whisper stopped her.

"What is it?" Anene stood while he made the circuit around the inside edge of the stone circle. He stopped in front of her, yet his eyes were trained to the chamber that, until now, only Anene could see. Her mother knew it was there, and Seamus was able to enter, but that was it. "You can see the chamber below?"

"How..." deciding at the last second to hold his tongue. Feeling in his bones that he *needed* to keep silent. Tadhgán chose a different course. "How could I not see the chamber?"

"Well," Anene narrowed her eyes. There was something that he was holding back. *I am getting pretty damn sick of these fecking secrets!* She thought to herself. What she really wanted to do was throw those words at him, if she was being honest. "When I restored the stones the chamber was revealed. Yet no one, besides myself and oddly enough Seamus, were able to see it. Until you, that is. Can you go in it?" She waved her arm in a way that told him to head in. "What the bloody hell is happening!" Anene wasn't sure if she was pissed, or in awe as he could, in fact, enter the chamber.

"Where does this door lead?" Came his voice from below.

"I don't know. It has been there since the circle was restored, but I can't open it." She whipped her head to him. "Don't touch it." She warned.

"Your circle, your chamber, and your door." Hands up in defense and a smirk at the corner of his mouth. "I see you have books here, what are they?" He wanted to touch but instead gripped his wrists behind his back to stop the temptation.

"They're books and grimoires that are too powerful or dangerous for use. When I go on buying trips for the shop, and I come across a volume I scoop it up. I don't want them to go into the wrong hands. Also, I was hoping that there might be something in one of them that might explain the chamber and the door. But alas I've had no such luck in that regard."

"If they don't hold what you need and you won't allow others to have them, why not destroy them?" He asked absently while he was examining the old bound volumes.

"We do not destroy books here." The words were like ice. "Is that what you do in your realm? Just destroy what is of no use to you?" Along with the ice in her words the room began taking on a much colder temperature, and Tadhgán was able to see his own breath.

"Take it easy, witch," Tadhgán wanted to back out of the small chamber that was quickly becoming frigid, but Anene was blocking his way. And when he looked at her, he noticed her lips were moving but the cold voice was not hers. "I meant nothing of the kind. I only wondered that if the books are far too dangerous, would there be a better option than storing them. Instead of in a chamber where it might be stolen." Tadhgán said while he watched the ice start to climb up the walls. He wasn't sure what was happening, but he knew it was coming from Anene, and it needed to stop. He approached the witch, regardless of what she looked like, Tadhgán knew the witch before him was not Anene. "Whatever it is you're doing you need to stop before you kill us both." He warned, not only was he freezing, but her own lips were turning blue, and she was shivering. Going with instinct Tadhgán placed his hand on her arms.

"You seem to think it is best to remove or destroy what doesn't fit into your perfect view." The voice was stronger now and not like Anene's lilt. This was older, ancient, full of rage and pain.

"I know not where you hail from or what you have endured," Tadhgán spoke in calm, even tones. It also did not escape his notice that Seamus and the little black dog from Miranda's were also in the chamber. The growl coming from Seamus was one that would stop any threat. But it was the black dog that nearly took Tadhgán's focus from the freezing witch. "But heed me when I say, this is not the way to make your point. Anene would never forgive you or herself if you kill me or the dogs here."

"The Familiar and The Guardian," she sneered at the dogs. "Where were you when we needed you? Why do you protect her?" She stopped and looked down at herself. "What is happening?" There was a blue green glow around her, giving back the warm color that was stolen. Around the room, the ice that had overtaken the walls and ceiling had begun to melt. Tadhgán who still held her upper arms was grateful that not only was the room warming up, Anene was as well.

"I have an issue with those who try to hijack my body." Anene's voice was a welcome sound to hear. "I don't know who you are, or *what* you are," her eyes came back to her, and she kept them trained on Tadhgán while she spoke to the force within her. "But if you *ever* try that again, I will make it my mission to not only expel you but, ensure that you never join with another again." Her lovely lilt took on one of might and great authority. One higher than that of King or Queen. "Do you understand me?"

Aye, I understand. The harsh cold voice came.

"Grand, now stay down until I call you." Anene waited until the cold feel of the sentient left her before she sagged. She would have gone to her knees had it not been the warrior's hands on her arms and was grateful for them. "I would like to sit down please, but not here." Without a word she was scooped up in his arms and carried out of the chamber into the warm sun. "Damnit."

"What is it?" Still holding her, Tadhgán looked for another threat.

"I missed the sunrise." Anene burst out laughing at the look on his face. "Put me down please."

"She missed the sunrise." He griped as he placed her feet on the ground. He still held her shoulders should she fall. However, she was steady enough and she had The Familiar and The Guardian on either side of her. Both took notice as Miranda charged up the hill.

Fifteen

"Anene! What happened?" She collided with her daughter and gathered her in a fierce hug. "Seamus came charging out of the woods barking like a dervish. Norman shot out of the house like a bat out of hell when I opened the door, and the two of them lit out like a flame was chasing them." She looked down at the dogs. "I ran after, but when I hit the base of the hill, I was blocked by a cold that took my breath away." She could still feel the chill that seeped into her bones from the barrier. "It wasn't until I saw Tadhgán carrying you out that I was able to make it up the hill." Miranda released Anene but held her at arm's length. She looked over her daughter with a fine-tooth comb.

"Norman?" Tadhgán couldn't hold back the chuckle, earning a glare from the black dog. "You named him Norman?"

"I haven't named him anything, yet." Miranda waved her hands to clear the thoughts. "Don't take me off task, what the hell happened?"

"Well to put it bluntly," Anene placed her hand on Seamus's head. "I believe that I just met another sentient. Although I'm not really sure what brought her out." She turned to Tadhgán. "What were we talking about? I mean I remember that we were in the chamber and discussing the books. But what did you ask me?"

"You don't remember?" at her shake he cleared his throat. "Well, to be honest I'm not sure I want to repeat it. If I ask again, will she come back?"

"Nay. Besides now that I know she's there I have to figure a way to, if not control her, at least to tamp her down somewhat." She reassured him. "What was the question?"

"I asked why if the books didn't contain what you need and you won't allow others to have them, why not destroy them?" He braced himself for the ice that came before.

"That's it? That was the question you asked?" Cocking her head to the side she looked at his stance. Which was ready for an attack. "Tadhgán, that's a perfectly logical, and frankly normal question to ask. And the answer is simple. What I deem too powerful and dangerous now, might not be in the years to come. Also, some books *can't* be broken." She instructed. "Besides, what is of no use to *me* doesn't mean that it won't be useful later. Why would she react to that?"

"Do you remember any of what happened?" Miranda didn't like this; she hated not being able to explain what she knew. And knowing didn't make it any less scary.

"Nay, I only remember I was pushed aside for her. I knew she had control, and I couldn't stop her." Never in her life has she felt that total loss of self as she did when she was pushed aside. The freezing blackness that covered her and stole her control was something that she would never allow to happen again. She would never again go back to that frigid abyss. She locked eyes with Tadhgán. "It wasn't until I felt warmth on my arms that I remembered Brigid. I called on her to help me. With her, I warmed my frozen body and broke out of the ice cage this new sentient slammed me in. Once out, I was able to take control back." Anene shivered. "She is so angry, vengeful even, and I don't know why. But somehow, I feel like she is justified."

"What did she say?" Her mother asked Tadhgán.

Tadhgán replayed the event, then looked back to the chamber. The ice seemed like a dead giveaway as to who the sentient could be but how was that possible. The old or rather ancient feel of the voice and power that came with it. *It couldn't be.* He thought.

"Did you say, "Familiar and Guardian?" Miranda smiled at the dogs who were now sitting at attention. "What does that mean?"

"I *think* it means Seamus is my Familiar." Anene nuzzled the large dog's head. "But what's a Guardian?"

"They are beings who are summoned by one to protect another." Tadhgán informed the pair of them then looked to Miranda. "Did you burn the letter last night by fire or spell?" Tadhgán asked absently.

"Spell." Miranda answered thoughtfully, then looked down at the little black dog. "A few seconds later there was a scratch at the door and there he was." Miranda knelt down to look into the black dog's eyes. "Is that what you are? Not a lost pup but a guard dog?"

"Guardians are not guard dogs." Tadhgán corrected. "They are very powerful and *respected* beings. Shapeshifters. They take the shape of that which is most pleasing or needed by whom they guard. You apparently wanted a small dog." He felt sorry for the mighty guardian to be in such a small unassuming form. "But remember, no matter the form he has taken, he is of a mighty race of warriors and is to be respected, not cooed over."

"He begged for food while I made my omelet and slept under the covers of my bed." Miranda snickered. "Wait, what does the letter and the, I don't know what to call him," she ruffled the Guardian's ears, "have to do with one another?"

"Obviously when father used the spell for his letter there was a summoning spell attached for when you destroyed it." At the unsettling nod from the black dog, Anene shifted on her feet. "Does he have a name?"

"Aye, but their true names are not known to us. So, if you must name him, please make sure it fits his station."

"So not Norman then?" Miranda asked. She looked that the bright green eyes that somehow reminded her of Ciarán and sighed. "Scáth Chiaráin, his name is Scáth Chiaráin."

"Ciaran's Shadow." Anene supplied. It seemed perfect; it was her father that summoned the guardian to be her mother's shadow after all. "I think that is perfect." She arched her brow to Tadhgán to see if he would have the balls to object to the name. He did not.

"Seems to fit. Although I do not think it would be wise to inform the King that the guardian has shared your bed." Both dog and Miranda whipped their heads in his direction causing him to release a true laugh.

"So that's why they could get in the chamber, Seamus a Familiar; a type of guard and helpmate and Scáth Chiaráin; a Guardian." Anene smiled and was relieved to have *that* mystery at least explained. "But you are neither. Why is it you can not only see, but enter the chamber?"

"A question for another day perhaps." Miranda stood. *It truly is a bitch to have information and not share it.* Miranda grumbled to herself. "I have to get to the archives, and you need to have a look around the village and meet the coven members." She pointed to Tadhgán.

"I thought you did that already? The coven members." Anene's hands on her hips.

"Yes, well I didn't. So now *you* can." Miranda smiled. "I'm off." She looked in awe as Scáth Chiaráin bowed his head to Seamus before going to her side. "What the bloody hell was that?"

"I'm not sure, but I have a feeling that Seamus might have the command here amongst the two of them." Tadhgán put in.

"Ok, now I've had enough information. I'm going to the archives. You two go to the village and the coven members." And with that Miranda sailed back the way she came. "For Christ's sake I'm not even dressed yet!" Came her voice over the hill making Anene and Tadhgán laugh at her expense.

"What do you intend to do about your new friend?" Tadhgán asked in regard to the freezing sentient.

"For now, she is in a time out, I guess you could call it." Anene looked back at her chamber, a place that until that moment had always been a haven for her. But now felt tainted.

"Don't let the actions of this being change the way you feel about your place." He told her gently. "No matter what, unless you relinquish it, it is yours. Go and reclaim what you feel has been taken."

"You know, you could just say, 'don't let her ruin it, go and prove it's still yours'." She told him as she went back into the chamber.

"That is what I said." Brows drawn, and scowling he followed behind her.

"No, you came out all old worldlike. Don't get me wrong," she said as she descended the stairs. Anene ran her hands over the wall ledges that held the books as a way to reclaim through touch . "I happen to like the way you speak." Tracing the stone walls with her fingertips. "Kinda makes me feel like I am in the middle of a good book." She did her daily pull on the door. "Still won't open. It's just not the way we speak any more. It's kind of a shame, but if your goal is to blend in..."

"Is it necessary to change my speech pattern to be welcome in the village?" He asked while running his hand over his ears. She watched as his ears changed from long pointed, to that of round human ears.

"Please don't do that." Without asking she reversed the magick. "I know that they aren't the same as ours, but they are yours and I won't have you changing them." She didn't mean to sound demanding, but she was emphatically against him changing to conform. "And the same goes for your speech. Forget what I said about fitting in. If there was ever a place where you could be yourself, your *whole* self, it is here and in this village."

Anene moved to stand before him and without asking, tucked his long auburn hair behind his ears. She had long admired the braids and adornments throughout. "I wanted to ask, what do the gold and silver pieces fitted around the braids mean?"

"They have been earned for accomplishments in battle, training and in life." Her close proximity was almost too much for him to handle. His fingers itched to touch her, but years of training had him standing motionless. "Do the men here not get rewarded?" Keeping his eyes on her as she wound her fingers through his hair to examine the cuffs that had been placed.

"Och Aye, they get rewarded alright." Anene scoffed. Not something she did often. "Sometimes they get rewarded a bit too much if you ask me. Most deserve the reward, others do not." She dropped her hands and stepped back. "Do you have women in your forces?" Stepping around him to go back up. Being so close to him, in a confined space was proving to be a bit much. Her heart would not slow its rapid rate, no matter what she did.

"Why wouldn't we have women in our forces?" He rounded on her with disbelief and a little anger on his handsome face. "Do you tell me that you do not!"

"Nay we do, but women in the military have been a relatively new thing in the human world, I am sad to say." She smiled at his reaction and wished that there were more men like him in power.

"Ridiculous." Hands on his narrow hips, Anene was once again floored at what a really good-looking man he was. Standing there with a little mad on his face, long auburn hair blowing in the breeze. His shirt, which she had to say fit him perfectly, even if he thought it was a little tight, showcased the muscles in his chest and arms to perfection. And the tattoos on the backs of his arms made him look a little dangerous. *I guess that is a little true, he is dangerous.* She had to admit. She wanted to ask about the tattoos but, again felt that it was better left until he volunteered the information.

You're drooling there lass, again I might add. Brigid added with a chuckle.

"Right, so, umm, we should head to the village and have a look about." Anene chuckled. As they walked to the village, she was given a lesson on all the ways women are better than most men in his realm. To hold one back from whatever she wanted was to take your life in your hands. She wondered if she could take him all over the world to educate today's world of men on the true value of women.

Sixteen

nene had a good time showing Tadhgán around the village. It was nice to see him when he wasn't training or acting like her protector. Even though they both knew that she didn't need his protection.

"Do you have places like this? You know, shops, bunched altogether?" Anene was very curious about the realm her father was from.

"We have villages, cities of sorts and marketplaces. But," *How the hell can I say this without the witch taking offense?* "all of which are much larger than what you see here." He side eyed her to gauge her reaction. "Not to say that this is—"

"I get it." She loved that he was trying not to step wrong with her. "How big is Locbroalm?" She was envisioning this small little place no bigger than, say the state of Texas.

"I am not sure, but I believe your realm is considerably smaller than that of mine." He thought for a moment. "That is a good question that I don't have an answer for. When I return, I'll ask the scholars."

"How the bloody hell is that possible? The doorway is in the basement of the cottage? How can the realm be bigger than, well, everything?" By now they were under the tree in the center of the village. She wanted to let him get his bearings before she took him to all the shops. Knowing that he needed to be introduced to the coven members, taking him on the tour of the shops was perfect. As most of the shops were owned and operated by members of the coven.

"You must remember that Locbroalm is another realm, another world. We aren't in the same space or time as you." He shifted like he was holding something back. But she wasn't going to push. "I think you have the notion that we live in the cellar of your Ireland, with no sky, sun, moon or stars."

"Nay not really, at least, I *know* that isn't the case. But I can't seem to wrap my brain around it." She looked at her village and had another thought. "Are the realms running parallel to each other? I mean are we occupying the same space but can't see or feel the other?"

"Nay, not precisely. Think of it as going to another place in your world." To watch a six-foot six-inch man fidget was like watching a gorilla try to be stealthy. It was both as amusing as you would think but irritating. "So, what are the shops you have here?"

"Nice subject change, very subtle." Crossing her arms and arching her brow.

"My apolo—"

"Don't you dare. For the love of Pete stop apologizing all the time."

"There are things that I feel are better not explained until you are in Locbroalm. Nay I have not been told to keep the information from you. It is something I feel in my bones."

"OK, fine."

"I think that phrase is a universal one." He smiled. It was a nice smile. "As for the apologies, it is, where I hail from, customary to beg pardon when there has been an offense made. Something that I seem to do often with you." He added with a smirk.

"Well, it's annoying."

"I can see that for you it is but, bear in mind that I also find it tiresome to have to feel the need to do so." His smile became a big toothy grin, "Ad nauseum."

"Oh, aye, that was good boyo, Aye that was good." Anene laughed. "Let's take a walk around so you can get acquainted with the shops and the coven members."

"Shall we." Tadhgán bowed at the waist and held out his arm. "If you would please lead the way."

"Oh, knock it off you eejit." She snickered as she smacked him on the arm as she passed by.

Tadhgán was enthralled with the little village. They had everything you could possibly need and more. The Búistéir carried all the meat you could want. The little witch that ran the place was not a woman you would want to tangle with.

"She seems a little scary." Tadhgán told Anene quietly after they left.

"Mary Kate?" She could understand the feeling. "I can see that, but she really is very sweet when you get to know her. But..."

"Don't make her cross?"

"Aye, don't piss off the Búistéir."

Next were the Apothecary, Táilliúa, Grósaer, Bácús, and the Tea shop. Which Tadhgán was surprised to learn, didn't sell tea, but it was a place to sit and be served food. There were other places to sit and eat as well as gift shops and specialty shops like Cailleach's Nook. Tadhgán was both amused and a bundle of nerves in Anene's choice of naming her shop after the Goddess of Winter as well as a very powerful witch. He decided not to ask the question for now. He had been in her shop before, but given the circumstances he didn't have the opportunity to look around.

It really was a nice space. Light, airy with lots of things to look at. She had a variety of items placed artistically all over the shop that Tadhgán had to admit had no idea what they were for. She had books, candles, rocks of some kind, he'd overheard one of the workers call them crystals. Upon closer inspection, shaking his head. *I still wouldn't have known.* He decided. While Anene was talking to the girl behind the counter about an online order, *whatever the bloody hell that is,* Tadhgán noticed the wands on the nice-looking round oak table. Now these, he did know something about. He knew that in the wrong hands they were dangerous. However, as he hovered his hand over the items, he was pleased to find that they held little power.

"Do you know something of wands?" Anene asked as she stepped to his side. She'd watched him move about her shop and was amused by what she saw. Hands clasped behind his back, so he won't be tempted to touch what's on the shelves. Even as he approached the wands, she noticed he hovered over them instead of picking them up.

"Aye, I do. And it's pleased I am, that these hold so little power." At her go ahead he finally picked one up to examine it closely. "They truly are fine craftsmanship. Do you make them?" His Amber eyes roved over the intricate carvings on the Hawthorn tipped with Red Jasper. His massive warrior hands gently traced the ins and outs of the craftsmanship.

"Nay. There is a witch in Ardmore, I get my crystals and some of the books I stock from her. In the most recent shipment, she sent these. Up until now I didn't know that she made wands. But now that I know..."

"You will stock them on the regular." He had moved on to another wand by this point. "I can honestly say that she might be as skilled if not more so than some of the wand makers we have in Locbroalm." Placing the wand back and giving her his full attention. "She has a true talent. As do you for noticing it." Before she could say anything, he moved on to look at something on the shelves nearby.

Tadhgán stood in front of a shelf staring but not seeing what was in front of him. Throughout the morning and early afternoon, he had been watching her interact with the villagers and the people who came to buy their goods. He was seeing a different side of her. This side was warm, giving, and the type that one could, and it would appear did, come to her for advice and assistance. It also seemed she was the one that her coven looked to, even though her mother was the High Priestess. He was seeing all of this, and he hated it. He didn't want to think of her as warm, giving, and so on. He didn't want to have warm feelings toward her. He was here for one reason and that was to train her, not have feelings for her. True, she was a beauty, there's no denying that fact. Even though he could see it, it was something he would overlook. It was her duty to lead, and his obligation to make her a better warrior for the war.

"My Gods, could you be a bigger prick?"

"I'm sorry?" Came a male voice next to him.

"My apologies, I was speaking to myself." Tadhgán offered a smile and moved away from the male patron before he lost Anene a sale because of his inability to keep his thoughts in his head. *Where they bloody well belonged.* He spied Anene deep in conversation with one of her people, Patty, maybe. Not wanting to disturb, he decided to take a walk around the village on his own.

Because of the way Miranda had laid the village out there was virtually no way for him to lose his way. He liked what he saw. The shops all had their doors open inviting you to enter. The proprietors for the most part didn't hide in the back counting their coppers but came out to see and speak with the people. Another thing that was like his home.

As he wandered around, there was a delectable scent drifting on the breeze. His mouth began to water, and he had to know where it was coming from. Across the square at bácús there was the clever witch putting her newest baked goods in the case for the people to buy. He had met her briefly with Anene on his tour. Tadhgán was only hoping he would remember her name.

"Well, are you back so soon then?" Came her husky voice. She was not of Ireland that was for sure, but Tadhgán had no way of knowing where she hailed from. But there was something *other* about her. He didn't get the sense that she was intending any harm to the ones around her, but she was different than the others about. "And what is it I can get for you?"

"What are those that you brought out? They smell delectable."

"Well thank you for that, there're bagels." She watched him lean down and draw in the scent of the fresh baked bread. "Have you never had a bagel?" she narrowed her eyes

"Where I hail from, we don't have bagels." The strange word felt odd on his tongue. He looked back at the witch. "Anene has introduced me to so many today and I am afraid that I don't remember your name."

"Siobhan, and you are Tadhgán." A cold feeling was marching up her spine. "Where do you hail from that you don't have the pleasure of bagels?" Siobhan opened her third eye to get a better look at him. Something that she never would've done with Anene or Miranda about. They are the most powerful witches she had ever encountered, and she didn't want to bring more attention to herself. As Siobhan looked him over with her third eye she gasped. "Locbroalmlaim!" She bungled the tray she held in her hands and if Tadhgán hadn't been so fast, she would have lost the bagels to the floor. "Please," she had gone ghostly pale as her knees gave out.

Seventeen

"Siobhan," Tadhgán caught her around the waist with one arm while he placed the tray on the counter behind her. "Excuse me," with both hands now free he got a better grip on the dazed witch. He got the attention of the other baker in the shop. "Can you look after that please," indicating the tray of baked goods he dropped on the counter. "I think Siobhan might need a little air." Not waiting for an answer, he took her elbow and all but carried her to the bench under the tree in the heart of the village. Once they were both seated, he let go of her and took a deep breath.

"Now," he started quietly and gently, "how did you know where I hail from and why does that frighten you to the point of fainting?"

"It frightens me because your kind kills or imprisons mine." Her voice was quiet and meek, but there was an edge of anger mixed in. She was starting to get her feet under her so to speak.

"I have no knowledge of my realm doing such a thing." Brows drawn, the amount of information he didn't know about his realm was mounting up. And he didn't like it one bit. "But I can assure you that I have no ill intent toward you or your kind." He waited for his words to sink in. "Unless that is, you have dark plans when it comes to Anene and hers." He had gone from the gentle concerned to the cold commanding warrior in a snap. If it hadn't been directed to her, she would have found it impressive. However in that moment, Siobhan just found it frightening.

"I have no ill will towards Anene or any of hers." The small edge of footing she had was gone and what was left was the witch who was frightened. She needed him to know that she was not a threat. "I love it here and I want to belong. Please, don't...don't out me." She begged.

"I cannot out what I do not know." Tadhgán was not a seer or one who could peer into someone to see their true intent. However, he was a very good judge of character, and he felt that she was what she said. A witch who wanted nothing more than to belong. "Why have you not told your coven head, at the very least, your story?" Tadhgán knew Miranda and now Anene to be fair. He could see no reason or that to change regardless of this witch's origins. "You are not of this realm, of that I am sure, or mine. Would you tell me where you hail from?" At her hesitation he shook his head. "I mean you no harm, and I will not press the issue. However, if I feel that you—"

"I swear," she pressed. "I mean them no harm." Siobhan looked around her at the village and the people she loved. "I love it here; I've loved it even *before* I came." She swiped at the tears falling down her narrow face. "When I gleaned it three years ago it became my mission to find a way to reside in this place with her people. Anene and Miranda were my salvation when I was in darkness," She brought her watery eyes back to his. But instead of the normal green he was met with eyes of black storms raging in a green sea. "A darkness that your people placed us in." Closing her eyes and giving her head a little shake. "I know it was not you," Her eyes once again the light watery green they were before. "But it *was* your realm, and not the realm of today, but the one from the ancient times when we all wanted the same thing."

"And what was that?" Tadhgán was getting an eerie feeling.

"Domination." Her voice took on a darker, older, and more sinister tenor.

"I am going to ask a question that a man should never ask a woman." It was the way she spoke of his realm and the ancient times.

"And what's that?" She smiled, for she knew the question, and he was right.

"How old are you?"

"You're right, a man should never ask that of a woman." She was silent for a time and decided that she didn't want to say where she was from but felt that to prove her point she could answer the question, kind of. "I am far older than you, boy, and that of your King and Queen." She smiled and was relieved that he returned it with his own.

"I know not where you are from, although I have my suspicions. There is a lot about my home that I am not privy to, and this is a failing on us." He had a small feeling picking at his psyche. "I have a feeling that you may be the beginning of correcting that. The holes in the history that we are going to need uncovered." He narrowed his amber eyes in a thoughtful manner. "Are you aware of the coming war in Locbroalm?"

"This war has been foretold since almost the beginning." She stopped short. She had more but wasn't prepared to disclose it. Not yet anyway. "Will you truly not give me away?"

"I will not." He leaned back into the bench and gave the look of a man lounging. "But I will say that you should at the very least go to Miranda and give her the knowledge."

"Not Anene?"

"I feel she has enough for now, and I may not like it." He closed his eyes and ground his teeth in frustration. "Actually, I hate it." And yes, if he was going to be honest, he hated that so many things had been and still were kept from her "The one person who should know all that she can, has been and still will be denied the knowledge required. Aye I hate it." Scrubbing his hands over his face he looked over to see Anene emerge from her shop, searching until her eyes, those fantastic eyes landed on his. "Aye," His heart jumped as their eyes locked. "Tell Miranda, but have no fear, I will not share your story." He stood as Anene stepped on the green that surrounded the center tree.

"Here you are." Hands on her hips and a scowl on her face. "I turn around and you're gone." She looked at the witch still on the bench. "Siobhan are you unwell?" Scowl gone, and concern took its place.

"Since you were needed," Tadhgán spoke up, "I looked about the village. I caught a delicious smell coming from the bácús and decided to head in that direction. Siobhan, here needed a breath of fresh air and asked me to join her." Tadhgán supplied. "Never being one to deny a beautiful lass, I obliged." He looked back to Siobhan and smiled. "But I would still like to try the bagel." Holding out his hand to hers. "Shall we?"

"We shall." Her grin was wide and genuine. *Thank you.* She told him in his head. His eyes widened slightly in surprise, but it cleared instantly. "Anene, can you believe this man has never had a bagel?"

The trio walked back to the bácús and Tadhgán was over the moon with his first, and vowed it would not be his last, bagel.

On the walk back to the old cottage Anene was treated to silence for the first leg of the walk. Something that she was grateful for, being that her own mind was full. It was the first time she'd not put a full day of work in since she opened Cailleach's Nook. And she hated it. Even if she knew it was necessary, she hated it.

"I have noticed that you use coin and paper for the goods that you give and take." Tadhgán's deep voice seemed to boom in the quiet they'd created since leaving the village.

"Aye, it's called money. That's what we use to buy and sell the items that we need and want." She stopped short. "Don't you?"

"Nay," *Money,* he rolled the word around in his mind, "we trade for our goods. We have no money in Locbroalm. I do not have the coin and paper that you use." He stopped and placed his hands on his hips. "This will be a problem I think."

"Hmm, I never thought of that. Yeah, you're right." *Well shite now what?* "Well, this'll take some thought. It's not like you can go and get a job." She had visions of him behind the counter of a fast-food restaurant in full armor and weapons asking if they wanted fries with their order. The image had her burst out in laughter.

"May I ask what is so funny?" His scowl only made her laugh harder. "I don't see what the bloody joke is." He waited until she collected herself and went on. "I will not take charity, so without the money what can I offer in trade?"

"We'll work something out, don't worry." He was right. She couldn't allow the village to just hand out their goods to him. He wouldn't take the charity, and she didn't want the shop owners to lose money either. "I'll talk to my mother, we'll come up with a solution." Placing her hand on his arm. "It will not be charity. And I will not allow the owners to lose sales. Not to worry, mother and I'll will come up with something."

"Fine." He didn't like the way her eyes lit from within with her mirth, and he certainly didn't like the feel of her hand on his arm. "We have wasted enough time today. Time to get to work." At least, that was what he was telling himself as he turned and marched the rest of the way to the cottage. He knew that he'd pissed her off and that was fine. If she was pissed at him, she wasn't laughing at him.

"You're a real bastard, you know that!" She shot his way.

"Aye, I have been told that from the day I was born. Now let's start with the slow run and move up from there." Not waiting for her he started to jog off to the large field behind the cottage.

"I have no doubt that you were." She grumbled, but she went after him to do what she had committed to, and that was to be trained. Even if it was by someone who both confused and infuriated her to no end. She knew that this was the man that her father had chosen, to ensure that she was ready when the time came. But did he have to be such a prig?

Eighteen

Over the next few weeks Anene and Tadhgán's lives were training, sniping, sleeping, sniping, eating followed by more sniping. Whenever Anene had to go into the shop for ordering stock or just needed to get the hell away from her tormentor under the guise of a trainer, Tadhgán would go to the village to talk with Siobhan, or any of the other shop owners. He did however avoid the witch MaryKate, búistér or not she made him nervous. He'd been told she was a very nice woman, but nope, he stayed clear. It wasn't that he thought the witch was evil or had bad intentions, she just simply made his balls shrivel.

However, over the course of the weeks on his treks into the village, he had developed a solid reputation for being willing to help. He enjoyed it, and it gave him something more to do. And he liked having his hands busy with other tasks besides training. There were a few times he was able to go to the Archives and fill in the missing years from Locbroalm. It felt strange to him to write in the pages that Ciarán had started. He wished what he was writing was happier, but since the time of Ciarán's imprisonment, the realm had fallen darker and oppressive. He wanted to write things would get better and everything was going to go back to the ways of old. When the Golden Realm was as its name sake told. Shinning of light, warmth, and love. He desperately wanted to write about how the palace gleamed in the sunlight. Or how the fields swayed with the blue grass in the gentle breeze. How the waters of the lakes rippled with diamonds. Children flocking around the villages and markets testing their wings. But this was about writing the history not the assumed future. On those days when he visited the archives, he always left feeling a little heavier and melancholy.

One glorious day he was able to sit on the bench under the large tree in the village and just watch the world go by. After a while, a little girl with her new puppy wandered over to him. The girl was about seven or so and the pup was almost as large as she was. He looked like Miranda's Scáth Chiaráin, only this one was a pup.

"Hello." She said in the sweet young lilt. Much stronger than those in the village and maybe a little different.

"Hello there." He bowed his head slightly and looked around for her parents. Even in his realm, young ones don't walk up to strangers on their own. "Where are your parents young one?"

"Me mam is in the witches shop." She pointed to Anene's Cailleach Nook making Tadhgán smile. This is why she was alone; she was a wee witch herself. "Where are you from?" The way she was watching him was slightly unnerving. Like she was looking *in*, not *at* him.

"I am from far away." A non-answer. "And where might you be from young one?"

"We came here from Scotland when I was four." She tilted her head, making her long bright red hair slide off her shoulder. "I'm six now." She narrowed her eyes. "Why do you hide them?"

"Hide what?" Not wanting to seem alarmed, he kept his lounging state on the bench. His long legs stretched out before him crossed at the ankles while his arms rested on the back of the bench.

"You don't need to worry," She smiled and leaned forward cupping her hand around her mouth and whispered. "I can keep a secret."

"You can, can you?" He couldn't help himself. He had to smile. She was enchanting. Small, pale skin, hazel eyes, and bright, bright red hair. "Well then." He reached his hand out for the pup to sniff, when he was gifted a kiss on the knuckle, Tadhgán took that as a sign that he could pet the pup. "Why do you think I hide them?" There was no reason to outright lie to the girl, he didn't think he could even if he wanted to. She was disarming and sweet. He watched her look him over, a scowl covered her face, and he knew she was considering her answer carefully.

"Weelll, I think you hide them because no one here has them and they might be jealous?" She shook her head, "No that's not it." She looked again and her eyes opened wide. "Who could hurt you! You're so big." *A child's view of the world. The bigger you are the safer you are.* Tadhgán thought and smiled at the pretty little girl. He changed his position resting his forearms on his knees bringing his face closer to the girl.

"Big men get hurt too, you know." He told her somberly.

"Really?" She was in awe. "But there's more." He could see that she was getting frustrated as her little seer power wouldn't give her all the information she wanted.

"Aye, there is, but that is enough for now." He chuckled as the pup leaned against his legs "So what is this one's name?"

"This is Angus." She smiled and ran her hands down the pup's sides. "He is six months old, and I think he would like to have a house all to himself."

"Really only six months!" he looked at Angus and whistled. "He will be a massive dog for you. And that would be a very large house to build."

"But" She looked at him through her lashes and blushed, "you're so big." Tadhgán's laugh boomed out of his chest.

"Aye, that I am lass, that I am."

"Do you hide your ears for the same reason?" She whispered.

"Among other things." He sat still as she reached for his hair and played with the metal adornments.

"How do you get these in?"

"Magick." He winked.

"Who does your braids?" Giggling she traced her little fingers over the braids that started at his temple.

"I do of course."

"Can you do my hair like that?" Gone was the young seer only for the girl of six to emerge, making him chuckle again.

"What's your name, young one?"

"Sonya, and you're Tadhgán the fairy from another place." She said absently as she removed her hand from his braids and placed it back on the pup between them.

"Aye, but Sonya, that can be kept just between us, right?" He figured all the young ones were the same and just spoke whatever that came to the head.

"Oh Aye, you don't need to worry, I won't tell about you. I also won't tell about—"

"Sonya! There ye are, pet." The older version of the little girl walked over with Anene in tow. "I hope she wasn't a bother."

"No bother at all, we were just talking about her Angus, here." He winked at the girl, making her giggle and blush. "I hear he needs a house of his own?"

"Och, please tell me she wasn't blatherin to ye aboot that?" She gave an exasperated look at her daughter. "From the moment she saw ye, she has been talkin about how Angus was goin to love the house that ye were goin ta build for him."

"And he will." The little girl was three seconds from stomping her feet trying to get her mother to believe her.

"Aye he will." Tadhgán ruffled the pup's ears and stood to his full height. Simply towering over all of them. Anene would think later about how her heart melted a little when the girl grabbed his fingers only to get a little squeeze in return from him and a wink.

"You will make him the house?" Sonya jumped and looked at her mother. "I told you he would build it." Her mother closed her eyes and looked a little deflated.

"Aye, that you did, luv."

"You have nothing to fear," Tadhgán said to the sad and worried mother. "You, my girl, will be a very talented seer. Even now she has a wonderful grasp on her gift."

"Aye but at her age how can she know what should be spoken or not?" her mother worried.

"I think she knows more about that than you think." Tadhgán soothed. "As long as she knows that some things are better left secret, I think she will be fine."

"I agree with Tadhgán." Anene put in as she placed her hand on the mother's shoulder. "Besides Amara, is this not why you came here? So Sonya could be trained by the coven's own seer, Colleen?"

"Aye, ye're right. I know ye're right, but..."

"She is your daughter, and you worry, as you should." Tadhgán added and looked down at the girl who was trying to climb up his leg. Glancing at Amara for permission, at her nod, he picked up the little girl and rested her on his hip. "But I feel that you are in good hands with Anene and the coven here." At Sonya's tap on his face, he brought his ear to her mouth. Anene watched a barrage of emotions play over the warrior's face, surprise, worry, anger and embarrassment. All of this was over the course of one maybe two seconds. Anene wanted to know what Sonya had said to him in secret, but she knew she shouldn't ask. It didn't mean she wouldn't. Just that she *shouldn't*.

"Can you make his house now?" Before her mother could object Tadhgán answered his little companion.

"I cannot today, my lass," he touched his forehead to hers and smiled. "But if you gather what is needed and what you think your Angus will like. Then I can come by in a few days to build Angus a fine house."

"Thank you Tadhgán!" Sonya threw her arms around his neck and squeezed. "I promise to keep it all to myself." She whispered in his ear.

"Thank you, Sonya." He visibly relaxed, making the women wonder more about the interaction between them. "You need not worry," He told her mother and Anene. "We had a conversation before you arrived." He put Sonya back on the ground and glanced back at the two women. "You have a very talented seer here like I said." He nodded to Sonya and her mother before walking off the green and out of the village. He waited until he was out of eyesight, unleashed his wings and vaulted in the air.

Anene was a natural with the bow there was no denying it. When Tadhgán placed the Horse Bow in her hands, she felt the same awkwardness she had when the waster was placed in her hands for the first time. Silly and like a child. However, like the sword it only took getting her in the right stance for her muscle memory to take over. Soon she was knocking arrow after arrow and hitting center mass every time. Tadhgán wanted to get her on a horse to see if her aim had the same accuracy. Now that was something that he didn't see here in the village. Horses. He supposed that might have to wait until they got to Locbroalm and said as much at the end of the training that night.

"If it's a horse you'll be wanting, I have some over at the farm stables." Anene told him as she retrieved the last of the arrows from the dummy target.

"You have horses here?" He wanted to be annoyed that she hadn't disclosed this earlier, but he knew that would just be plain prickish of him. How the hell was she to know that he wanted horses?

"Aye, I have horses. I might even have one that will hold you up." With bow and quiver in hand Anene, followed closely by Tadhgán, made her way back inside to stow all the equipment in the training area of the cottage. "I had no idea you wanted to have horses around, you should've said something. I can have them brought over here if you like. There are four of them and they need to be kept together."

"Aye I would like them here. Why must they be kept together?" He didn't really care. Tadhgán missed the feel of a horse, and the sight of them would be welcomed.

"Well, three are a bonded trio and when I added to Rí they became a quartet."

"Why must they be brought? Why not just retrieve them?"

"I wasn't aware that you had more than one ass on ya." She chuckled and looked around him. "As for me, I only have the one ass, so I can only ride one horse at a time."

"You have a donkey as well?" His arched brow which made her laugh. "Why not ride and lead the others to follow?"

"Because I've never done that, and I have no idea how good of a seat you have."

"I have been astride a horse long before you were born, witch." Her barb was well placed. And he knew he had fallen to the bait.

"We still have plenty of light if you want to head out now. Or you can meet me there in the morning."

"The morning will suffice." He told her as he picked up a long sword off the rack. Her night might be over, but he was going to continue for a while longer.

"Fine." She turned to leave and stopped. "By the way they are in the back red barn. Go past the white one for the cows and you'll see the horse barn is next." Seeing the look in his eyes when he learned about them, Anene knew that he would not wait until morning to have a look. She decided it would be best if she phoned over and let the staff know that they would most likely have a visitor that night. And to let them know she would be relocating the horses for a little while. "Have a good night and I'll see you in the morning." Leaving him where he stood Anene made her way back upstairs, grabbed her things by the door and rifted home.

Nineteen

Anene was correct in her assessment of how Tadhgán would spend his early evening. After waiting for her to be out of sight, he unfurled his wings and set off through the clouds to the red barn. He set down in the wooded gravel lane outside of the farm perimeter. Tadhgán stood and knew that if he went forward that would take him into the farm, but if he turned right. He would enjoy the same trek visitors took when they came to see Anene's circle. It really was a very pleasant looking walk, with a magickal feel to it. The gravel walkway seemed to be carved through a tunnel of trees where sunlight peeked through branches giving a soft ethereal glow. Enchanted, Tadhgán decided to let the red barn with its horses wait and follow the path that looked magickly blessed by the Sidhe.

Tadhgán wandered up the gentle rising path, taking in all the beauty that surrounded him. One side of the gravel trail was a wall lined with flowers of every color and variety. On the other side sat a pine forest that had somewhat of an eerie feel, even to Tadhgán. He came to a spot that looked like there might have been some ruins, deciding to investigate, he stepped off the path into the wooded area. The rocks that might have belonged to a ruin were covered in bright green moss, while small flowers were trying to take a stab at life. But as Tadhgán turned to look directly behind him the difference was staggering. Where there was greens and small pokes of life on the rocks and the trees in one direction, there was dark grays, almost death at his back. The trees in their regimented straight lines with bare branches that stabbed from their trunks. The polar opposites were unsettling there was no question. Tadhgán knew that the pine tree canopy wouldn't allow the light to penetrate, thus creating the look and feel of death on the forest floor. But knowing why this was happening didn't make it any less eerie. Deciding to leave the area Tadhgán went back onto the path to the circle.

As he neared the top of the incline, the canopy of trees began to open. The walled side of the graveled trail naturally lowered the higher up he went. Slowly as the canopy overhead opened up, small peeks of the field and the circle it contained teased the eyes. From his vantage point he was impressed, as he assumed all would be, by the massive stone circle sitting alone at the highest point in the middle of the field. Tadhgán stood at the gate entrance, looked back down at where he started and then back at the circle.

"Aye, I can see why this is such a popular spot. Stunningly beautiful." Looking at the round cage-like gate with its door that only swung in one direction. Going through, he figured that the odd-looking gate was to ensure that visitors didn't leave the gate open and let stock out. As he approached the circle something was odd. He only saw sixty-four stones. He knew when Anene restored the missing stones, it returned the circle to its original eighty-eight. Tadhgán remembered she'd spelled the circle so only a few would see it for what it truly was. He'd only seen the circle for what it was and now to see it like this, unrestored, made him feel a little off kilter. He walked to the heart of the circle, where the entrance of the lower chamber should be, instead there was unlevel green ground that dipped slightly. Looking around he spied the outlying stone. Wanting to test a theory, Tadhgán walked over, and placed his hand on the outlying stone as before. He might not know this kind of magick, it may make him uneasy while it was being wielded. But what he felt when the veil had been lifted was indescribable. The area simply shimmered with iridescent blues and greens while the magick revealed the missing stones one by one. The lumpy green ground smoothed and dipped to showcase the chamber below. The circle that was now before him was fully restored and magnificent. There was no doubt the outlying stone was the key. To touch it filled him with a charge that he wasn't expecting, but the result was truly magickal.

Not wanting to call attention to himself, Tadhgán went back the way he came. The magnificent tunnel was now full of reds and oranges making it feel as if you were walking through fire thanks to the setting sun. He might want to come this way more often. It was almost as fantastical as the circle itself.

Tadhgán walked past barn after barn until he found the red one that held the horses. He did find it a little odd that no one stopped him from walking about the place. As he made his way inside, he no longer cared about being stopped. Here, this is what he came to see. There standing in the stalls, were four of the best-looking horses he had ever seen.

"Good evening there, and might you be Tadhgán then?" Tadhgán looked over his shoulder at the man who was walking over.

"Aye, I am that." Reaching his hand out to clasp the other's, and smiled as it dawned on him at last. "Anene called you and said I might come by."

"Aye, she did that," the man let go of Tadhgán's hand and chuckled. "She knows a horse lover, that one. I'm Colm O'Cleary a pleasure it is to be meetin ya. And I see ya found the horses."

"Beautiful, what are they?" Tadhgán walked over to the first and held out his hand before touching the horse's head.

"Well, this one here is Rí. He's an Irish Drought." Colm ran his hand down the dappled greys neck. "His breed is the National Horse, and unfortunately, endangered, this lucky lad is a registered stud for hire."

"He's a tall fellow." Tadhgán noted as he patted the long graceful dappled gray neck.

"Aye he stands at roughly 16.3 hands. He truly is a nice horse. Well-tempered and easy to ride." He chuckled. "You would think he was a gelding instead of a stud rearing to go. Do ye ride much then?" Colm gave the stranger a once over. He may have been given a pass by the boss lady, but that still didn't warrant him a pass to put his butt in the saddle as far as Colm was concerned. This Tadhgán was a big man to be sure. He towered over Colm's 5-foot 9-inch frame and definitely outmuscled him. But when it came to the farm and the horses, no one intimidated Colm O'Cleary.

"I have not since coming here a month ago, but I have been riding since I was a very young lad." Tadhgán knew when he was being evaluated and couldn't find fault in it. He would and had done the same in the past. "You are a handsome beast." He told the dappled gray before moving to the next stall. "Who have we here?" Inside was a black and white beauty.

"This is Caoimhe, our Gypsy Vanner, she stands at 16.3 hands. about the same as our Rí here, but as you can see, she is a bigger horse in stature." When speaking of the Vanner, Colm's voice took a much smoother, gentler tone. "She is in foal right now." He told Tadhgán while rubbing her head. "One night the farm a few miles down, their stud got loose and paid Miss Caoimhe a visit." He laughed, but the mirth didn't ring true.

"What will you do with the foal?" *Nothing nefarious, I hope?*

"Och the boss will keep whatever it is no doubt. But she is charging the owner of the stud for the vet fees until and after the birth. Thankfully, it's another Gypsy Vanner like our miss here."

"You're not riding this one here now?" Tadhgán liked the look of her. She was a good size and seemed to be a sweet kind of mare.

"We could for a while yet, but nay. We don't want to cause any stress to her. This is her first foal you see, and she is a little younger than we would like."

"How old?" Tadhgán smiled as Caoimhe nickered and nudged at his named for more attention.

"She's two. But I would have preferred her to be a year or two more before a foal was planted in her."

"And this one?" The next horse was considerably smaller than the other two. "It looks like someone made a smaller version of Caoimhe here."

"This one is Tadhg, our Connemara Pony. His coloring isn't accepted, so he was sent to auction. Anene found the poor lad and scooped him up. He was just off his mother at that point and not properly weaned. It took some time, but he's become a very distinguished gentleman. He's great with the kids when they come for rides."

"And the last one," Tadhgán stopped in his tracks when the large black head popped out of the stall. "What the bloody hell is that?" He was in awe of the animal's sheer size and all he had seen thus far was the head.

"This here is Anene's pride and joy, and the beast knows it too." Colm walked over to the stall. "This here is a Shire. And a giant he is that's for sure." Both stood and eyed the massive animal that was before them. "Now, the largest in the world measured at 21.2 hands. Cathal here is 21 hands even at the withers. Do ya want to know the scary part?" At Tadhgán's nod Colm went on. "This beast is only two years old." When Tadhgán stepped forward to get a closer look, he was halted by Colm's hand. "Be careful and don't get too close to that one." He warned. "He's a beauty to be sure; a true black as they say, but he'll tear the piss out o' ya before ya can call out." To prove that point Cathal let loose what could only be described as a battle cry and kicked at his stall, making both men take a solid two steps back.

"He is a good-looking horse like you said, But I think I'll leave him be. Can anyone ride him?"

"Oh, Aye, Anene takes him out all the time." Colm shakes his head. "I wish she wouldn't, but the moment I say that, she'll be taken that beast and start jumping fences to prove that there is nothing to fear."

The two men stood and talked horse for a while before Colm announced it was time for him to have his supper. Tadhgán bid him good night and watched as the farm manager walked off. Before leaving himself, Tadhgán gave each horse another pat before stopping at Cathal's stall.

"I agree with Colm. You, my spirited lad, seem too wild for the princess to ride." He nodded at the low nicker from the stall. "But for Anene, and as you know, she is two different women, I think you might be properly suited for her." Tadhgán found it a little disconcerting to be towered over by a horse. But Cathal was doing just that, towering over him. With an air of royalty, it was true, but this horse, he was fit for war as well. "Oh Aye, you would be perfectly suited to take her into battle." Cathal stood higher, and Tadhgán wasn't sure it was possible for him to get taller. But the stance said all it needed to say, *You bet your sweet ass.* "Aye, that you would. I will leave you now." Tadhgán wasn't sure why, but he bowed slightly before leaving the barn.

Twenty

In the morning Anene stood at the entrance of the barn with Colm when Tadhgán arrived. It did not escape his notice that the two of them looked very comfortable with each other. He gritted his teeth when Colm said something that made her laugh. She looked so light and free standing there with the man and Tadhgán wanted nothing more than to bash him over the head with the hilt of his sword. But the instant those thoughts entered his mind, they were immediately dismissed. He had no right to feel the way he did about the young man, or Anene for that matter. Tadhgán swallowed the irritation and tamped down the need to drown the unsuspecting sod who was making her smile.

"Good morning." Tadhgán smiled and held his hand out to Colm in greeting.

"And here is himself now, it's a good mornin to ya." Colm's kind brown eyes smiled in mirth over the conversation he'd had with Anene.

"Good morning." Anene nodded to Tadhgán. She needed to slow her heart a beat. When she saw him walking toward her and Colm, she had a vision that nearly took her to her knees. Tadhgán in his full armor, a massive sword in his hand dripping with blood. A mixture of blood and dirt smeared on his face and armor. His wings behind him on full display, but they were still murky to her. The face he wore was that of pure hatred and anguish. Anene never wanted to see that look on his face ever again. It was both heartbreaking and terrifying. There was another thought that passed through her mind. He was incredibly sexy. The whole thing only lasted a few seconds, but it was enough for her to know that she was going to be in trouble if she wasn't careful. He was an arrogant, judgmental, brute that she had no business fawning over.

He is also caring, sweet and steadfast. Brigid interjected. *Whether you want to admit it or not, when you are not training, he is a very good man.*

Shh Anene told her.

"I want to thank you for giving me access to the horses last night. It was very kind of you." Tadhgán told her while briefly looking her over. She was clad in leg hugging pants, boots, and a bulky top with a hood.

"Riding breeches, boots, and a hoodie." She told him as she saw the question on his face that she knew he would ask. She looked at his blue jeans, boots, shirt, and flannel and needed to remind herself, again, that she was not to fawn over the man. Regardless of how he looked. "Shall we?"

Anene turned and walked briskly to the barn. She made sure to stop at every stall, checking on her babies, as she called them. "Tadhgán I want you on Rí," gesturing to the Grey Dappled Irish Draught. "and lead Tadgh behind you." She said as she took the Connemara Pony's nose in her hands and kissed him. The pony whinnied and danced with pleasure. "Aye luv, you are a handsome boy." She looked back at Tadhgán. "They are a good pair, and neither will have an issue with you." She gave the pony another peck on the nose. "I'll ride Cathal and lead Caoimhe. I don't want her ridden and Cathal will look after her. Won't you, my boy." The massive Shire dropped his head and nuzzled her like an oversized puppy.

"I don't know how you do it Anene." Colm put in. "That beast won't let anyone near him. We have a hell of a time cleaning the stall because of it." He told Tadhgán.

"He knows who the queen is and will only serve her." Tadhgán's voice seemed to be off in the distance as he spoke.

"You're a queen, are ya?" Colm chuckled "Well then your majesty shall I saddle up the horses for you?"

"Aye, luv, why don't you do that and while you're about it fetch me an ale and the coffers so I may count my riches." She mocked and noticed the hard look from Tadhgán. She wasn't sure where that was coming from.

"As you wish." He bowed.

"Get on with you now." Anene shoved his shoulder playfully.

"Would you like me to saddle them?" Colm asked.

"Nay, I'll saddle Cathal and I'm sure Tadhgán can saddle Rí." She looked to him for confirmation and at Tadhgán's nod she went on. "But if you could grab all the feed, bedding and whatnot, load up the trailer and take it to the old cottage that would be helpful."

"Aye, we can do that for ya. Do you want us to set up the small barn and lean-to while we are there?"

"That would be wonderful, thanks luv." Anene patted his shoulder and went to the tack room, but not before seeing the hard look from Tadhgán, again. She was going to have to ask him about that on the ride. "We have a number of saddles for you to choose from. I can tell you that the ones on the far left are fitted for Rí so take your pick."

"Why are there so many different styles?" He wondered as he looked for one that seemed familiar.

"I have traveled a great deal and when I went somewhere new, I rode, thus the choices you have before you. Different saddles for different types of rides." She chose a saddle for the ride and began to prepare Cathal in his stall.

"I see." Tadhgán made his choice and began. "Easy there Rí." He murmured to the horse. "I know you don't know me, but I assure you that I mean you no harm and will be gentle with you."

Anene listened to Tadhgán as he spoke softly to the horse as was Cathal. "Good boy," she nuzzled the big black's neck and smiled. "Let me get a halter on Caoimhe and Tadgh." She went to both stalls and haltered the pony and the Gypsy Vanner and clipped on the lead ropes. Gently, Anene led them from the barn and handed them to one of the stable hands. On the way back to Cathal she saw that Tadhgán and Rí were ready to go and were on their way out.

"Alright my lad," she told the black Shire, "let's put on a small show." Instead of mounting him outside, Anene chose to get in the saddle and ride him out of the barn. And she was not disappointed in her decision. She and Cathal got the looks she wanted. Cathal knew it too and stood tall and regal. She knew who the show was for. Cathal walked right up to the biggest male stopped and snorted to prove *he* was the biggest and best, not Tadhgán.

Tadhgán knew it too. There was no more impressive sight than Anene on top of that massive black beast. He was glorious to be sure. Black from head to feathered hoof, there was not one ounce of color on his glistening coat. Tadhgán decided then and there that Cathal's name was well suited, Battle Rule. For the horse and his mistress were a perfect pair for battle and he had no doubt that they would rule that field. At that thought there was a pinch in his heart that he wasn't ready to deal with.

"We aren't quite ready to head over yet." Colm told her as he walked over. "But you go on and we'll meet you there." He ran his hands down Caoimhe's neck while he spoke, and the pretty Gypsy Vanner simply preened at the attention.

"Sounds good." Knowing that Colm had a soft spot for Caoimhe, Anene wanted to assure him. "Don't worry about her, she will be just fine."

"Och, I know that. It's just..." He trailed off as he nuzzled her.

"You have a soft spot. Aye, I know." She smiled at the pair of them. They had bonded, there was no question. She had given serious thought to gifting her to him. "Whenever you have an urge to see her, just go over." She took the lead rope from the young stable hand. "Thanks, luv," glancing at Tadhgán, then back to Colm. "See you there." She wrapped the end of the lead rope around the pommel of her saddle, then gave her attention back to Tadhgán, who was carrying the look of confusion rather than the hard one he'd been sporting. *What the feck is his problem.* She wondered as she gave Cathal the subtle order to move along.

Thankful that the farm, her property, and the old cottage's land all touched, for it meant that they could move the four horses without having to go over other's land. Not that it would have bothered anyone, but it made things simpler and faster. Otherwise, if they crossed paths with someone she would need to stop and chat for a spell. Once they had been out a few minutes Anene decided to figure out Tadhgán's problem, however he beat her to the punch.

"How long have you and Colm been mated?" The words felt like acid on his tongue, but he had to ask.

"I beg your pardon?" she gasped out a laugh. "Mated? What the bloody hell is that?"

"Have I asked a question I shouldn't have? Are things that different here that you cannot ask about a mated pair?" He couldn't understand the dynamics of this realm. "I must say that he can't be that good of a mate." He grumbled not so under his breath. "Where the bloody hell has he been all these weeks?"

"OK, just stop." Anene halted Cathal, turned so she was facing Tadhgán. It struck her then, she was looking down on *him* for a change. "Am I to understand that you are asking me if Colm and I are seeing each other?"

"I don't see him here now." Tadhgán scanned the area for the man in question.

"Nay," Anene dropped her head in her hand in brief exasperation. "What I mean is, are you asking if he is my boyfriend?"

"I do not know this term." Eyes narrowed on her.

"Jaysus, Mary and Joseph." Anene began to laugh while gazing at the sky. "So '*mated*' means what? Married? An item? Together? In love?"

"Is this not what you have here?" At her shake he sighed. "To be mated means that you and your mate are each other's one and only." His deep voice softly explained. "You will do anything for each other, do anything to keep each other safe, happy, sated." He smirked slightly while his voice took a sexy turn on the last word. Anene might not like the insinuation that brought on the conversation, but if it meant listening to his deep tenor that could turn her legs to jelly, then so be it. "Your life starts and ends with your mate. There is no separation other than death, and even then, most never find another." His auburn eyes simply smoldered. There was a slight color shift happening in the rims of the eyes, but Anene couldn't catch the shift fast enough. She was lost in them for a, she didn't know how long. When Cathal snorted, she shook her head and cleared her throat.

"Well, we don't have that here. We fall in love, get married, have babies, and hope to hell that it doesn't end in divorce. But nay, Colm and I aren't mated. We are not a couple." When he still looked like he needed more convincing she added what she hoped would be the driving point. "I think his wife would have issue with it." She rubbed Cathal's neck while her words mulled around in Tadhgán's head. "We should go on."

They spent the rest of the short trek in silence. Anene was still annoyed that Tadhgán had the audacity to ask her about her dating life. Also, why in the fecking hell did he think she and Colm were dating?

Do any of you have any input? She wondered why Meili, and Brigid had been so quiet. Actually, they had been unusually quiet since that day in the chamber when a new sentient tried to take over her body. *Hello? Where are you?*

We are still here, but since the other day we wanted to give you space. Meili answered.

But now you mention it, came Brigid's soft lilty voice, *you might want to deal with…her before long. It won't be a good idea to keep her tamped down for long.*

I'll bring her up when I am certain she understands who's in charge, and it won't be her. Anene still felt a nugget of violation and it angered her. *She tried to hijack my body and doing so she nearly killed Tadhgán. Not to mention the dogs. I won't allow her to do it again.* She took a calming breath. *So, until I know that I can control her to insure it won't happen a second time, she'll stay where she is.* Anene was firm and resolute.

We understand, girl. Meili assured her. *But keep in mind, one of the reasons she was able to take over was because she has been kept locked up longer than the rest of us.*

What do you mean? Anene stopped the horses again "What the hell do you mean locked up longer than the rest of us?"

"I didn't say anything." Tadhgán said, surprised by the sudden stop and the outburst that followed.

"Nay, not you." She dismissed him with a quick wave. "Meili answer me, what the feck do you mean?"

I cannot answer for her, Anene. You will have to have her story from her. Just as you did with Brigid, myself and the others as they come. Their stories are their own and deserve to be told as such.

"This is bullshite!" All the secrets were getting to more than she could bear. For once she wished that all the information were laid out for her, instead of being doled out a little at a time.

"I do not know what has caused this anger, witch, but it might be better served to wait until you are no longer around the nervous herd to have your fit." Tadhgán was being condescending, and he knew it. But that didn't make him any less right. Her anger was making the horses jittery.

"My *fit*." She gritted her teeth hard enough that it wasn't any wonder her jaw didn't crack. She would have truly had a go at him; Cathal was steady under her; however, the rest were unsettled and nervous. The last thing she wanted was to make it worse. Closing her eyes to calm down her emotions and get herself back to a regulated state. "We will discuss this later." She told both Tadhgán and Meili.

"Good. Let's go Rí." Tadhgán took his horses ahead of her and avoided eye contact. "Steady on there my little lad." He told Tadgh the little Connemara Pony. "Not to worry there, for she can be fierce when she needs to be, but she loves you and will do all that needs doing to keep you safe and happy." He leaned over to gently tug on the pony's ear, making Tadgh whinny and rub his cheek on Tadhgán's leg.

It was a sweet scene and had she not been pissed off, she might have loved seeing it. But now all she wanted to do was pick up the nearest rock and smash him over the head with it. First, the question of her dating life, then, he refers to her as having a fit, now, he takes the lead and loves up to her pony! She could feel her temper again and had to tamp it down. *What the hell is wrong with me? These things might be irritating aye, but not worth the anger I'm experiencing.* She thought about it, *Aye I need to figure what is causing the spike in anger.* When the cottage came in to view Cathal called out making the rest answer in return. Whether Tadhgán wanted it or not, Cathal and Anene would lead the way in. Rí halted and nothing his rider did could make the Irish Draught move until Cathal and Anene passed. Rí may be named King, but Cathal was head of the herd.

Anene reached down and unlocked the fence around the paddock. Thankfully, the fencing had been built high enough that she only had to reach down to open them. It was nice not having to dismount. Once everyone was in the paddock the gate was closed, and the leads and halters were removed from Tadgh and Caoimhe. She stayed on Cathal's back and Tadhgán stayed on Rí.

"Before the others arrive with the horses' things I want something answered." Addressing Tadhgán.

"If I am able to answer, I will." he told her.

"What was it that made you think that Colm and I were, as you put it, mated? And why did you have that look on your face?"

"You called him 'Luv'." His answer was short, and it still didn't answer the question.

"What?" she didn't know what else to say. His response was ridiculous.

"Where I hail from the term 'Luv' is only for those who are mated." He wanted to know why she should look so perplexed; it was perfectly normal to him.

"Are you having a go at me?" She started to laugh. "Nay, really you're telling me that the term that we use on the regular is the one and only term of endearment for Locbroalm?" She sobered when she saw that he was in fact '*not*' having a go at her. "Tadhgán, I'm sorry, but understand that here, we use 'luv' as a kind of 'place holder' for someone's name. It can also be used as a term of endearment. But..." she shrugged her shoulders.

"I see." And he did. But not wanting to call more attention on the subject, he opted to move on, before she noticed that he hadn't answered her other question. "We should get started with the bow on horseback.

Then we can go to your circle and have it out with your sentients." Anene agreed, reluctantly, and they got to work on the daily training.

Twenty-One

"I must admit," Tadhgán told her as they walked to the circle. "I have a feeling that your aim with a bow is better on horseback than on foot." It was amazing to see. He didn't know of anyone who had better aim than himself in the saddle or on the ground, until he saw Anene in action.

"Thank you." Anene was stunned at how well she and Cathal did. He seemed to have a better time than she did. Running, cantering, doing loops around the fields so she could shoot from every speed, and scenarios that Tadhgán could think of. However as much as she enjoyed riding horses, Cathal especially, she was thrilled to be out of the saddle. Walking felt odd, like she was bow legged from the hips down. But she refused to show her discomfort, Goddess, she hoped she was walking normal.

Mother, she sang out, mind to mind. *We are heading to the circle to deal with the new sentient. I think it might be a good idea to come and bring the coven in case I can't control her and need to expel her.* "I should warn you," she told Tadhgán after she contacted her mother. "my mother and the entirety of the coven will be arriving at the circle as well."

"I think that is wise." Tadhgán added after a moment of thought. "In case you need assistance in handling her." Gods, he was sore. It had been years since he spent that long in the saddle. And she didn't look the least bit phased. *Damn witch.* He thought with a proud smile. He knew she was sore and tired. *You are a damn fine woman, and shaping up to be a fine warrior.* He wanted to rub the soreness from her shoulders that he knew had to be screaming after pulling on a bow all day. He remembered what it was like in the beginning for himself. Every muscle in his body hurt, for years, while he was in rigorous training. He'd had years to get where he was now, and Anene didn't. He couldn't help but to be in awe of her.

"That was my thought. Besides, if I can't control her, I intend to make good on my threat and expel her. Then make sure she can't go to another."

"Meaning if *you* can't handle her, then *no* witch can." He sounded rude and meant to.

"That's not what I meant." She could feel the irritation rise but smothered it down. She knew how she sounded and couldn't fault his interpretation. "But I know of no other witch in the surrounding areas more powerful than myself. And it's not like I can't put the power in a jar and wait for the next witch to come along." She stopped and rounded on him. "You must have a low opinion of me if you think I am so arrogant as to think that if I can't handle her no one can."

"On the contrary." His barb hit the mark as planned. She was a real beauty when she was lit up with her anger, not that she wasn't at any other time. He was always amazed at her ability to hold her anger to the point of not losing it, and never once grabbed for her fantastic power in anger. He wished she would use it when training. Other than when she lit the waster with Brigid's flames and then threw wind at him, she never reached for her powers in training. "I think very highly of you, and I agree with most of what you say. However, I don't think you will have difficulty in keeping the sentient in her place."

Well, that tripped her up. "Why?"

"You have already shown her once that you will not be her puppet. You have already shown her you have the strength required to overcome her." He smiled at the dumbfounded look on her face. "I happen to think you will do beautifully in making her come to heel, so to speak. But..." he hesitated.

"Go on." *God for heaven's sake don't stop now*, she thought.

"I don't have the best knowledge, it's true, when it comes to sentient powers. But remember that sentients join with another for several reasons. It is always, or should always be, their choice to do so. They have their own minds, and they are to be worked *with,* not controlled."

"I have to be able to control them or I could do—"

"You mistake my meaning." He interrupted gently. "Aye you've a need to be able to control what and how you handle them that is true. But they are not servants to do thy bidding."

"*To do thy bidding*?" Anene covered her mouth with her hand to keep the laughter in. "I cannot believe you just said that."

"My mode of speech does not diminish the words spoken, witch."

"Oh, Aye, I know, but, '*thy bidding*?'" She sobered but kept the smile. "I do understand what you were saying. We work as a team, but they are not to be taken advantage of. And I need to think of them as people who have minds, souls, and wills of their own."

"Aye, you're right." At the border of the circle Tadhgán waited for Anene to touch the outlying stone before going through, then followed suit. While in the center of the circle he gazed toward the village and had quite a shock. "Jaysus! What a sight." There at the base of the hill stood Miranda and twenty-three other men and women. "I had no idea the coven was so large."

"I wonder where the others are." Anene smiled. "There are twenty-six members, the other three must not be coming." Looking to see who was missing, Anene understood the absence. "The ones missing are the Elders of the coven. They only come for the dire issues or weddings." She opened her arms and welcomed the coven to her circle. "Welcome all of you. I don't know if our High Priestess has filled you in on what is happening here today." She waited to see that there were nods from some and shakes from others. She looked to her mother for confirmation.

"I didn't have time to fill the whole coven in on what has been going on. Besides, I wasn't sure what you would want told."

"Mother." Anene threw her hands up in exasperation. "The coven has a right to know what is happening. Hell, they bloody well need to know."

"What is it you need us to know then?" Colleen, the coven seer, stepped forward. One look and Anene could see that the seer had already been told about her. Whether it was by Miranda or a vision, Anene wasn't sure and decided it didn't matter.

"Before you enter the dance you need to be given all the information. After you have the facts, and you still want to be here, then by all means, you may enter the circle. However, if you feel this is too dangerous, please know that it is your choice, you may leave and return to your day. Nay," Anene could see fear on some of the newer faces. "This does not mean that you are to leave the coven or will be shunned by the members that stay." She wanted to reassure the new and older members. "This coven has always been one of choice and it will remain thus. However," looking to her mother. "I think the missing Elders should be able to make their decision as well. Mother, could you summon them to join us?"

When the absent Elders arrived, Anene told what her life's story was now. She included Miranda and the life she'd lead with and without Anene's father. She told about Tadhgán, where he was from and why he was there. She told about the sentient powers, the ones she had and that more were still sleeping. And finally, she spoke about what took place in her chamber with the newest addition. Anene explained she was going to allow the newest sentient to surface and wanted the coven as her backup in case things go wrong. At the end of the story Anene turned her back on the coven, walked back to Tadhgán who had stayed in the heart near the chamber entrance. He did not stand alone however, on either side of him stood Seamus and Scáth Chiaráin. Giving both dogs scratches behind the ears her eyes met Tadhgán's.

"How did I do?" she whispered.

"I'd say you did very well," his smile was enough to stop her heart. "Oh aye, very well indeed." He didn't watch the coven now. No, Tadhgán's eyes were on Anene. The uncertainty when she turned to face the coven, and the pride when she saw that every member was now standing inside the stone circle, waiting for her. She was magnificent. Her manner when speaking and laying out the facts to her coven, dealing with her staff, talking with the children in the village. Her training with him was becoming more strenuous than he thought it ever would have been. She could best him in the bow while on foot and riding. She was getting deadly with her swordsmanship; she's even managed to leave bruises on his body from hand to hand. But here and now seeing the simple disbelief and gratitude on her face, pushed him over the edge he was desperately trying to hold on to.

Tadhgán could no longer deny what he'd known since he first laid eyes on her at the old cottage. Mate, that single word he knew she wouldn't or couldn't understand. Aye, she was his mate, that much was true, and it was a fact he was mostly able to stamp down for the most part. However, over the weeks and months of being with her, seeing her, training her, finding reasons to touch her, and watching her with her coven. The coven where Miranda was still the High Priestess, even though there was no denying that Anene was the unofficial head. A fact that was made clear that night. Aye, she was his mate, but he could no longer deny that he was irrevocably in love with her. That knowledge filled him with warmth, pride, and scared the ever-loving shit out of him.

"Tadhgán," Anene called again. He just stood there with a stupefied look on his face. When calling his name didn't bring him round, she did the one thing that would. She walked over, balled up her fist and punched him in the gut.

"Bloody hell, witch!" Tadhgán's air was pushed from his diaphragm in a huff. It was a good punch, and he was caught unawares so he deserved the punch. "What is it that you want?"

"For YOU to pay attention." She smiled as she strolled back to her spot in the heart of the circle. The coven was stationed at the inside edges of the circle. It didn't go unnoticed that the warrior took the position at the center with her, Tadhgán stood at her back, the place of protection. "Stay close please." Her voice was almost too quiet to be heard, but he would always hear her. No matter where she stood or how quiet or loud she was. Tadhgán would always hear her.

"Always." That single word given, filled her with such heat, making both heart and stomach flutter in her throat. She wanted to reach back for him, but kept her hands loose at her sides.

"Let us begin." Anene closed her eyes, cleared her mind of all thoughts, and called to Brigid and Meili to be ready and on guard. "Alright you," speaking aloud for the benefit of those around her, she called the cold sentient. "You can come out now, but heed my warning, you try what you did, and you will be banished. Do you understand?"

I understand. Came the same cold ancient voice.

"Do you have issue with being heard by all around us?" Anene wanted to be clear she was in charge, but remembering Tadhgán's words before, Anene wanted to give the sentient some choices.

I have no issue.

"So be it." Anene then projected the conversation so all in the circle could hear and partake in the conversation if the need arose. "First, may I have your name?"

"Cailleach." Her ancient cold voice filled the circle. With it came cold that chilled the bones and filled the collective with a sense of fear. "I can feel the fear from your coven Anene."

"Can you blame them? You are named for the Goddess of Winter, and a powerful witch that is, at times, vengeful." Anene could feel the frigid cold that came with Cailleach in the whole of her body, and she didn't like it. "I will remind you to watch yourself Cailleach. I don't mind the winter, but the summer solstice is upon us, and I have no wish to feel the claws of winter yet."

"I have no wish to unleash the winter, but the cold follows where I go. If you do not wish to be afflicted with the temperature that is me, then you might want to ask Brigid for some assistance to counteract." There was a definite chill to her words, but Anene could find no malice in them.

"Fair point made. I've never used one of you with another." Anene's eyes scanned the circle. "But I guess there is no better time to try than now." Deep breath, "Brigid if you would please."

"It would be me pleasure Anene." Brigid's soft young lilt drifted on the winds. Thankfully, she filled Anene with enough warmth to keep her from freezing, but there was still some of the cold from Cailleach. "It is important that you feel us all. To take all the cold away will make Cailleach less effective." Came Brigid's soft lilty voice.

"I understand and I thank you for the warmth." Taking a moment to settle in the new state she was in, warm and chilly together was an odd sensation, but not totally unpleasant. Once settled, Anene shared the warmth with those in the circle. She refused to be comfortable while others froze. She smiled as the coven members all relaxed as the cold left their bones. "Cailleach, had we ever met before?"

"I came to you when you were but three years of age. During the one and only visit you made to Locbroalm." There was no mistaking the sorrow in her voice.

"I'm sorry, what?" Anene turned to face her mother. "I was taken to Locbroalm?"

"I didn't know about it until recently." Miranda sighed. She was still reeling from the information in the letter from Ciaran. Most she'd never be able to repeat, but thankfully, this was one of the few she could reveal. "While your father was here for a visit, a girl was taken from the village. I went with the coven and other members of the village to look for her and you stayed with Ciarán. I was gone for a week." She took a calming breath. When she thought about what Ciarán had done it made her so angry. "Ciarán decided to take you to the Palace while I was away so he could attend to a few matters."

"When you and the King arrived, he placed you in the nursery." Cailleach took over. "News must have gotten out that the King was in residence and had the heir. Soon there was a breech in the palace defenses and the room you were in was set on fire."

"My Goddess!" Siobhan whispered.

"Aye Siobhan," Cailleach addressed the secretive witch. "The intent was to burn the child while she slept in the nursery." The anger she felt in that act of attempted murder was felt by all.

"Easy there Cailleach," Anene reminded her. She waited while the sentient pulled back the anger. "I assume you came when the flames did to keep me safe."

"Aye. I did that." For the first time the voice took a wholly different tenor. Before she was hard, cold, and frankly pissed off. Now she was softer, smoother, and less chilly. "When the King saw the room smothered in flames, and his daughter in the middle of them. It took four guards to keep your father from running into the flames to get to you. Which I assume was the goal. Kill the King and the heir and the throne would be vacant. While the guards held the King back, the spellcaster, Fintan, showered the room with water to douse the flames."

"How did you save my daughter?" Miranda's voice was full of fear, for the child that was, and anger at the realm that has marked her for death.

"You had me covered in ice while Brigid kept me warm from within." Anene's eyes were glazed over as the past flitted through her like a movie. "What the hell is happening?" In her mind she could see a watery version of the scene Cailleach described. A devastatingly handsome man with silver hair cascading over broad shoulders. His shocking bright bright green eyes filled with rage and anguish as he struggled against a force that held him back. She couldn't see the others about or hear anything other than the man she now knew was her father, bellowing out her name.

"It comes from me." Cailleach answered. "You have the gift of sight; you can see what was and what has yet to come. Not as well as your seer or the young one she trains."

"I don't think I like that." Anene shivered as the vision closed and she was able to see the here and the now. She grabbed the sides of her head to keep them from exploding. She wobbled, but before she went down there was a pair of strong arms around her to keep her steady. Anene didn't need to see to know they were Tadhgán's.

"I have you, witch." His lips touched her ear. "Get your breath back." He whispered.

With his warmth at her back and his strength surrounding her, she was able to concentrate on removing the pain from her head. She had no doubt that without Tadhgán there to hold her up; to give her warmth and strength, she wouldn't have been able to do what was necessary. She pushed the pain from her head while holding on to the strong arms that surrounded her. She was distracted when she thought she felt his lips on the side of her head. *Wishful thinking you eejit.* She told herself.

"Focus Anene," Cailleach told her with a chuckle. "You're almost done."

"Meili, if you could help, that would be appreciated." Anene cringed as the pain came back.

"About time you asked." He scolded and took the pain and sent it away. Anene didn't know where and didn't really care at the moment. "Thank you." Not wanting to leave his arms yet she relaxed and leaned back resting her head on his chest with her eyes closed. "Is that what it's like for you when you have your visions?" Everyone knew who the question was for. As a collective unit all eyes fell on Colleen.

"It was in the beginning." Colleen who wasn't one who thrived on having all the attention on her shifted slightly. "But with some work and training you will be able to manage the pain and anticipate when the visions will come."

"Just what I need, more fecking training." She grumbled. She felt the soft rumble in his chest as Tadhgán chuckled. Knowing she couldn't stay as she was any longer, Anene reluctantly left the arms that encircled her. Turning to face him "Thank you."

"Always," he bowed his head. Before he backed away to give her space his auburn eyes held hers. He wanted to tell her then and there how he felt, but the words refused to surface. Instead, he called her the only endearment he could and hoped it would cover. "Witch."

With her back to him she smiled as he uttered the word that she no longer hated to hear from him. Now, whenever he called her *witch*, it made her insides warm, while her knees weakened slightly like jello.

"Cailleach, what I want to know is why my father had you sleep. You saved my life. I would've thought he would want you and I to have more time together."

"As grateful as he was to me, when you told the King my name he paled, and put me to sleep. I wasn't given the same as the others when they were asked, I was simply banished." Her words were icy and with them came the cold.

"Anene," Miranda warned when the circle's ground began to frost over.

"I know," Anene knew that she should hold back the sentient, but Cailleach was in pain, and she had legitimate anger. "Meili, take me somewhere where Cailleach can unleash her anger, and where there won't be any pitfalls."

"Ja, I think that would be a wise choice." Meili agreed.

"I'll go with you." Tadhgán stepped forward.

"Nay, you need to stay here. I have a feeling I need to do this alone." Anene told the warrior.

"This is not up for negotiation." He growled.

"You do not dictate what or how I run my life. *Or* use my magick. So, back off." Anene matched his anger.

"You have no choice." Countering her anger.

"Oh laddie, that was a mistake," Colleen chuckled. "Have you learned nothing since meeting Anene?"

"I have no choice?" She simply couldn't believe her ears.

"Here we go." Miranda along with the coven took a step back. "Tadhgán, do you remember what I told you in the beginning? Anene bends to know one."

"I have no choice, you say?" She held out her hand and her bow materialized in her hand. Drawing back the string a blue green flaming arrow appeared aimed at his chest. "You say I have no choice?"

"Going off on your own right now is a mistake and you know it." She was magnificent. Her stance with the bow was perfection. But it was that power she was wielding that made her thus. She was angry that was true and Tadhgán knew that her anger was warranted. But he was fairly certain that she would not let her arrow fly. As his eyes met hers, he became a little less certain that she would keep the arrow nocked.

"Are you suggesting I *can't* take care of myself?" There was a warning in her voice, and he knew he *shouldn't* take the bait.

"I am saying that going off without someone to watch your back might not be wise." He decided to take the bait, but he hoped it was at least more diplomatic.

"Eejit" came a male witch's voice from somewhere in the background.

"Tadhgán?" Anene said as sweetly as she could. "Fuck you." She released the arrow and rifted away.

The arrow lodged itself in the ground between his feet. "I was thinking, not too long ago, I wanted her to start using her powers while working with the weapons." He looked up from the arrow at Miranda and began to laugh. "This wasn't quite what I meant, but it will suffice."

"You baited her on purpose." Miranda grinned.

"Aye, but I need to get her to have the same effect without the anger." Tadhgán bent to pick up the flaming arrow, the flames tickled his hand but gave no heat. "Amazing." It was nothing but flame, yet it had shape, weight, and substance to it. She truly was a wonderous woman and a very powerful witch. "She is, in a word, fantastic."

"What do you mean you can't find the doorway?" Sitting up on the dais, Flann's black batlike wings twitched with agitation. He sighed, stood, and smiled as soldiers and advisors shrunk back in fear of his reaction. He thrived on the fear he instilled in those around him and the realm. Soon this Golden Realm would be nothing more than that of dark terror. As it was, the shining palace with its golden rooms and vibrant paintings were already dull, crumbling, and listless. "Tell me again how you've managed to lose Tadhgán Ultan." His smooth voice was likened to a snake that slithered in the grass. There was nothing more dangerous than when that voice was soft, as it was now.

"My lord, we had him in our sights, even when he went high in the clouds which is beyond us—"

"If that is the case, then pray tell, how is it, if it is beyond you, that you could see him in the clouds?" Flann's attention, no longer on the general, but instead on the trembling female fairy who was chained and collared next to the throne. The black haired, blue eyed, young fairy with pale luminous skin adorned with dragonfly wings was his latest plaything. He had no need for her name. She was no more than his toy, and like most toys, they had a short shelf life. Taking her hair in his hands he decided this toy was not long for the shelf.

"We have spellcasters who were able to spy him in the clouds, but he just disappeared as I told you before. After that we searched the mountain range he was in for the door. But it has been years, lord. Can you not let us have the..." he stumbled, "the prisoner?"

"No Tarken, you may not have the prisoner." He tired of this. "Soon the abomination will come for her father. I need him here in order to ensure that she comes." Flann turned to face the general. "You will continue to search for the doorway. And I will get word to our allies and see if they can move things a little faster." Flann's black eyes scanned the room of his courtiers.

He made sure that only the purest of blood were allowed in the palace. All the gray eyes looked back at him, at Flann, the ruler of Locbroalm. Not the blood traitor King who had been his prisoner these last few hundred years. He didn't care if the admiration they showed was false. It was the fear that was underneath that he loved, thrived on and ultimately, got off on. It also amused him, that not one fairy saw it coming. Certainly not from him.

Not from the small and fragile child that was Flann. As he grew older, his height allowed him to tower over most. Where others gained muscles and talents with weapons, he stayed slight and not fit for the title of warrior. He did however have a clever and fast mind. And because he was slight of build, lighter on his feet, and faster than most, Flann became quite formidable with the blade. Not the sword mind you, no, they were too heavy. So, he created a blade of his own. It was as long and strong as those wielded by the guards and the King's soldiers, but it was almost weightless. He named it Póg na Díoltas, Kiss of Revenge. Flann had so enjoyed using his blade for that very reason.

Looking down his thin nose he decided it was time to find a new toy, but first. "You may all leave." He told the hall, "Tarken, a word." Taking his time descending the steps from where the throne and the chained fairy sat. "I want you to bring me something new tonight." Flann didn't miss the quick look Tarken sent the black-haired female. She was a beauty when he brought her just two weeks before. Tall, slender, bright eyed. Now she was gaunt, pale, and praying for death. Tarken knew that her wish would be granted, but he was afraid it would not be a swift one. No Flann would take his time and make her last moments long and painful. She was in store for a most awful death.

"Have you tired of her this soon? It has only been a fortnight." Tarken had been the one fairy in Locbroalm who was able to question the ruler and not have to worry about the repercussions others suffered. Some imprisoned, others flogged, most, beheaded by Flann himself using his blade Póg na Díoltas.

"Heed me, bring me something new," Flann drew his dark brows together for a moment. Maybe he was being too hasty. Tarken was correct, it *had* only been a fortnight since the female was brought to him. "You're right. It can wait. This one might last a while longer." Turning, Flann glided across the floor stopping to take the chain of the female. She knew it would be worse for her if she fought back, so she, resigned to her fate, eased her battered body off the floor to follow. "Tarken?" Flann, never taking his eyes off the blue-eyed female.

"Aye lord?"

"Tomorrow night will be fine." Without another word Flann and the defeated fairy left the throne room for his chambers and ultimately to the room Flann created underneath.

Upon entering the rooms that had once belonged to the blood traitorous king and his false queen, Flann's thin lips smiled down at the frightened female. It gave him a thrill to take these rooms and turn them to his dark needs and deeds.

"You, wait here." He attached the end of her chain to the iron handle he put in the wall. "I will return shortly for you." Flann moved to the center of the room where the floor opened revealing a stone stair descending to his altar room, and to, as he liked to call it, the playroom. Turning left to the altar room, Flann stopped at the black door. While he readied himself Flann concentrated on the almost oil-like substance dripping from the door it's self. He tried not to let the stench of the dead sea phase him as he turned the handle and opened the black door. The room he entered was not in the palace, it wasn't even in Locbroalm. Flann followed the dark, dank path that was laid before him. While his footsteps made little to no noise on the wet stones, he tried to keep his eyes forward. Not that he was forbidden from looking about. It was the tunnel of water being held back by an unseen force that made him want to keep his eyes forward. It was the unfamiliar life swimming in that thick black water all around him, wanting nothing more than to rip him to pieces that kept his eyes trained ahead.

As Flann walked the seemingly endless tunnel, he thought about the fairy chained in his bed chamber and what he would like to accomplish with her before the night was finished. The finely made black breeches grew uncomfortable at the thoughts that ran through his mind. He knew to stop and adjust would be a mistake, so he turned his thoughts to the coming meeting. Finally, the door to his destination was in view. Flann smiled as it swung open for him to enter. In anticipation ,he lengthened his stride to pick up the pace. The door which opened on its own accord, allowing him to sail through, closed in the same manner. His ears caught the sound of the tunnel he'd just left, collapse on itself. It always made his heart stutter. What if that were to happen, while he was still in it? He wondered. Would he drown first or be eaten?

"Flann." Came a thick heavy voice from the bowels of the black blank space. "What have you come to tell me?"

"My people still have not found the doorway the false queen created." This was still a major source of anger for him. "I've told them to continue the search, but I think it might be time to hurry the abomination along. Might you be able to send something her way?" Flann wasn't sure what was worse, the tunnel of water, what swam in its depths, the possibility of collapse, and being crushed. Or, talking to a dark room, void of light, and knowing that the room and its occupant were just as, if not more, deadly than that of the dark water.

"Oh, little Flann." Answered a craggily dank chuckle. Flann moved his eyes to try and pinpoint where the voice originated from. As always, he was left with the feeling of blindness. For, that's just what he was once he crossed through the doorway. Blind. It was a feeling that both terrified and filled him with erotic euphoria. For he knew, he would enjoy bringing that same feeling to others. "I assure you, that the more deadly of the two, is where you are standing."

"I meant no offense." He knew better. For years he'd schooled himself to keep his mind blank while in this room. But there were times, like now, that the stray thought would sneak through.

"As for the doorway, I am not the least bit surprised. The witch who created it was very talented and powerful."

"Was?" Flann's heart skipped a beat. "Has the False Queen met her end?"

"Another witch has risen who has surpassed the power of her mother." The phantom occupant allowed that to sink into the blind fairy.

"The abomination is more powerful than the False Queen?" His blood ran cold. Flann had no love for the Queen, but had a healthy respect for the power she wielded.

"Indeed, and she has your missing warrior training her." The dark occupant watched as the fairy tried to rein in his anger at the latest news. His emotions were always so easy to manipulate to the occupants' needs. It didn't take much to work the fairy up.

"Do you think me afraid of Tadhgán Ultan?" Flann's hatred for The Right Hand was legendary. Flann had appealed to Ciarán himself soon after the coronation for the appointment. His keen mind was unmatched by anyone else in the realm, but the *King* had chosen that brute with the feathered wings over *him*.

"Careful, you are letting your emotions get in the way, Flann." Came the warning from the void. Flann could feel the hatred burning in him for Tadhgán and the rest of the realm dull, until there was nothing left but cold, hard, malice. "Much better. As to your request, we have already sent a message. One that was created a very long time ago. One that was in holding for the right moment." The air grew thick with the smell of death, and a soulless joy. "Let it never be said that we don't have patience." Joining the putrid smell, the sound of oily laughter made Flann's wings twitch. "Now if you wish us to send something else to hurry them along, what will you give us in return?" The voice turned silky, almost cooing in nature.

"What will you have of me?"

"We will want more years, I think three hundred years will do, and..." Suddenly Flann was no longer the only fairy in the room. Standing in her bright court dress stood the girl that Flann had planned on mating with. She would be crowned once the King and the heir were no longer an issue. She was, in Flann's opinion, the most attractive fairy in the realm. He might have loved her at one time, but that feeling had long since disappeared. He wasn't sure when it happened. But seeing her there, frightened, shaking from the cold a small niggle of the forgotten feeling began to resurface. Her violet eyes found his and a relief, a horrible relief filled her eyes.

"Flann!" She threw herself into his arms. Yes, the long-lost feeling of love filled him now as he wrapped his arms around her. "What is happening? I don't know how I got here." She sobbed against the soft velvet tunic he wore.

"Why is she here?" The steel that coated his voice was such that his own generals would shrink from. Yet, had no effect on the occupant of the dark space.

"You want us to hurry the witch in her quest, it will cost you another three hundred years and the girl in your arms."

"What was that!" In her fear she whipped around to see who else was in the room only to find it empty and filled with an endless black. "Flann what is happening?" She turned to look at the man that she had known all her life. She had watched him turn colder and colder over the years until she, at last, had to deny him. But as she stood there, she saw a little of the man she'd once known.

"Ellia," Flann whispered, cupping the sides of her face. "I..." he couldn't finish. "Fine, I accept. Take her."

"Oh, my dear boy, no." Came the wet menacing cooing. "We will not *take* her; *you* must give her."

"What does that mean, Flann?" Ellia's face was tear streaked, and her violet eyes bore into his black ones. "What has happened to you?" her fingers touched his cheeks.

Flann brought her lips to his own in a brief joining. With their eyes locked, Flann wrapped his long fingers around her delicate throat and squeezed. He watched as her eyes bulged in shock; her fingers scratched at his hands to try and dislodge herself. Her nails tore at the flesh until his hands bled. Flann watched as the lack of air began to make her thrashing less. Just before the last of her life left, there was betrayal and defiance in her eyes. Finally, the bright violet eyes that he had once loved, dimmed, and died out, along with that long-forgotten love. Instead, there with the dead fairy at his feet Flann straightened, pulled his shoulders back and held his head high. There was no feeling left in him.

The goal had been successful. As Flann turned and left, a figure, darker than the space it occupied, emerged. While the door opened, the hulking figure watched Flann disappear to the tunnel. The door closed as the figure looked down at the body of the fairy still on the ground and smiled. "You have done very well Ellia." The figure told her. Its voice was as dark and dank as the realm it hailed from. "You may rise now." He studied the fairy as she slowly got to her feet, brushed off the dress she wore and faced the dark figure.

"After all these years you still need to resort to the manipulation of my death." Her venom was unmistakable. And had she been anyone else, she would have been slaughtered on the spot. But over the years her talents have been quite useful.

"But I so enjoy watching you die." Wet foot falls sounded on the floor as the figure moved. "I must admit, you Púca, are an interesting creature." Now circling her. "While the rest of your kind stay in Quelocand making mischief and helping farmers prosper, you came to us, offering your services for our needs." The figure moved about the room, void of features, just the darkest of shadows in a dark room. "I have often wondered why you would do this?"

"I have bigger ambitions than that of my brethren. Let them do as they will in Quelocand, I prefer this." The Púca shifted from the fairy Ellia that

Flann had loved centuries before to a woman with brown hair and dressed in clothing from 1722. "I like to change my shape often." To prove the point, the next shape was that of the large black horse that, it is said, will take someone, who has been too much with drink, for a wild ride. Then another shift, and instead of the horse stood a small child of no more than six.

"Do you want me to move the witch and her warrior along?" Came the sing-song voice of the child form.

"No, I have others. Go and I will call when I have need of you." The figure disappeared and the Púca, knowing the room would disintegrate with her next shift, became the deadliest creature in the water.

The chained fairy watched as Flann emerged from the staircase in the floor. There was something different about him. He looked harder, darker, colder. His dark eyes were nothing more than soulless black pools of hatred. The fairy knew she was going to die and soon. her only hope was that it would be quick. She prayed to the Gods, as she had done all night, that the next fairy he took would find a way to kill the monster stalking toward her now, freeing themselves and the realm.

"I thought you had outlasted your usefulness," His voice slithered over her gaunt skin, "but I was mistaken. I have a job for you." Knowing her fate she closed her eyes and put her mind elsewhere.

The following morning the realm woke to a new gruesome sight above the palace gates. Three new pikes had been placed on full display. The first held the mangled body of a female fairy. Her body showed the weeks of abuse she had suffered. Bruises on top of bruises, cuts deep enough to see the organs trying to slip through. Instead of the pike stabbing the center of the torso, Flann had her impaled in the most sensitive part between her legs, along with the handle of a mace he had used to sodomise her during her last night alive. The next held the black-haired head that had been slowly ripped from her body. Blood and brain matter was seen dripping down the black metal pike. The last pike held the once beautiful dragonfly wings that had gloriously adorned her back.

Never had the realm of Locbroalm been subject to that kind of violence. And it did precisely what Flann knew it would. It told the realm that a new era had begun, and Flann was the leader.

Twenty-Three

Anene managed to make it home later that night. The feel of Cailleach's full power was a force to be reckoned with. Anene felt it was better to keep the sentient under a somewhat tight leash, however she would never again lock her away like her father had done. Even though now, she had a better understanding of why he had, at least with Cailleach. She was angry, no question, but not at Anene, or those among her coven. Amazingly enough she wasn't even really angry with her father. No, Cailleach's quarrel was with the long-ago rulers of the realms. When Anene asked about the cause of the anger, all Cailleach would say was that it was not time for that tale.

"As I have said before," Anene told Seamus as she filled his food bowl with dinner. "I am getting fecking tired of all the secrets, and 'it's not time to tell this tale' shite." She watched Seamus nibble at the kibble in his bowl and thought about how Cailleach made herself known while in the chamber. Her anger nearly froze Tadhgán and the dogs to death. "And what the bloody hell made you go all frozen ice queen in the chamber? What Tadhgán asked regarding the books I have in the chamber was a perfectly logical question. Why was the question so bad that you nearly killed all of us?" She asked while preparing small potatoes for boiling and two beef ribeyes for grilling. Thankfully, she'd pre-salted the meat before feeding Seamus and they were ready to be patted dry.

One of the books you have in the chamber is important. And before you ask, Nay, I can't tell you which one or why. Cailleach answered in her deep other world brogue. *I am sorry, lass, but there are rules that we must obey.*

"Which is why you can't tell me *why* I have sentients after, according to all of you, has not happened in an eon." Steaks buttered on all sides; it was time to move on to the seasonings. Onion powder, garlic powder, and black pepper. Simple and always hits the spot. Anene was thrilled that the hob she picked out had a grill in the middle. It was something in the beginning she wasn't sure she would use, but boy was she wrong. Especially in the winter months. With the solstice only a week away, the weather was perfect for outdoor grilling. But after the day she'd had, using the griller on the hob was easier. The small potatoes ready and drained, Anene added butter, minced garlic and dill to the bowl. After a few turns with the rubber spatula, she covered the bowl and moved back to the steaks. In the middle of turning the second ribeye she froze. "Why the hell am I cooking two pieces of meat?" A knock sounded on her kitchen door. Placing the streak back on the grill, Anene went to the door and wasn't as surprised as she should have been to see Tadhgán on the other side of it.

That's why. Brigid's soft lilt smoothed over Anene's conscience. *And might I say he is looking very nice.*

"Brigid," Anene had to laugh, "It's like having a teenager in my head."

"I don't understand what that means." Tadhgán scowled.

"You don't understand a lot of things," She laughed warmly. "But I'm sure the longer you're here you'll become more versed in the lingo." She rubbed her forehead, the headache she had earlier was getting worse. "What can I do for you?"

"I wanted to make sure you were back safe and in one piece." Now he'd laid eyes on her, he could calm down and relax. It was true, he had baited her with good results, but that didn't mean that he wanted her out of his sight.

"Have you eaten anything for dinner?" She was still irritated with him; more herself truth be told. It took longer than it should have, but it didn't take her long to figure out he set her up at the circle. She needed to have a word with him about that.

"I have not." He could see the headache behind her eyes and wanted to find a way to make it go away.

"I appear to have made too much for myself, so would you like to join me for steak and potatoes?" She stepped back from the doorway to give him entry. It was subtle, but Tadhgán understood the move. Dinner was not a request.

"I thank you." He smirked as he moved past her. Having never been in her home he took the opportunity to look about the kitchen. The size and basic layout was the same as Miranda's and the one in the old cottage, but the *feel* in hers was different. This was a room for someone who truly loved to cook. Sit at the table or in front of the fire to talk with friends and family or sit in the quiet and read. "I like this room." Even though his eyes were not on her, Tadhgán knew where she was in the room. Being in the same space with her was both a comfort and a torture. It soothed him around the edges to be in her presence, but his insides were jumping. He wanted to grab her, plant his lips on hers while his hands roamed... clearing his throat, and tried to think of anything that would calm his blood.

"Thank you," Her voice was soft and quiet, no doubt, due to the head pain. "Aye, this is my favorite room to be sure. What would you like to drink?" She turned to face him, instead of the cold empty hearth, he stood silhouetted with the fire at his back, wings still ghosted, in his full armor. Sword at his hip, bow in one hand and the other holding the hand of a small young girl. She had his hair and blue green eyes. On her back she carried wings that were like his and yet not. There was deep love and admiration in his eyes when he looked at her.

"Please, don't wait too long," the little girl's voice carried a mixture of Ireland and other to Anene's ears. "Please mama, don't wait too long, we need you."

Anene blinked her eyes to bring her back to the kitchen she was in. Back in focus it took her all of two seconds to realize she was now on the floor and in Tadhgán's arms. "I'm sorry. Did I faint?" Her head was splitting once again, like it did at the circle. "There has to be a way to do this without the splitting head pain."

"It is the price you pay for the visions." Tadhgán told her. He had at one time envied Fintan for his visions, but not the aftermath the fairy had to deal with. Sometimes the pain was so bad Fintan would sick up whatever was in his system. For that and some other things, Tadhgán no longer wanted the gift of sight. "Try to do what you did at the circle. Ask Meili to take the pain away."

"Nay, if he takes it away, then who is the poor sod that gets stuck with it?" She leaned fully into his chest and cradled her head in her hands. A bottle of water dropped in her lap. She cracked her eyes a bit to see that Seamus too, was there and wanted to help with the pain. "Thank you laddie." She reached up and tugged softly on his floppy ears. With a huff the Irish Dane lowered and rested his massive head on her lap. "In the press over the sink is a small gold metal box." She told Tadhgán. "If you would take a scoop of that mixture, add it to the kettle and set it to boil that would be helpful."

"What is the press?" Tadhgán whispered, not wanting to hurt her head.

"The press? Oh, the cupboard. The cabinet." She explained with a small smile.

"Oh Aye." Not wanting to leave her on the floor, Tadhgán gently picked her up, and placed her on the sofa. He wasn't surprised the dog followed and resumed his place at her side, his head in her lap.

The gold box was right where she said it would be, he followed her directions to make the brew. While the kettle sat on the flame, he opened every press door until finally he found the cups. Cup in hand he filled it with a strange tea-like mixture. Before going to her, he turned the grill off under the now burnt pieces of meat. "Here you go then." He held the cup until he was sure she had a proper grip on it. Satisfied he squatted down in front of her rather than sitting on the other side of her on the sofa. She took a sip and cringed.

"I should have told you not to boil the water with the mix in the water. Nay." Stopping him from taking the cup from her hands. "It only means the brew is stronger than it needs to be, but given the headache, maybe stronger is better." She took another sip and shivered. "It just tastes like holy shite." She smiled and gazed into his eyes, auburn with a hint of gold at the edges, that hadn't been there when she first met him. "Did...did I faint?"

"Nay, but your eyes clouded over like Fintan's does when he has a vision." If she were anything like Fintan, he figured she wouldn't remember what she spoke aloud while in the throws. "You wanted to know who she was and how long was too late." He told her. He wanted to tuck her hair behind her ear but resisted the urge. "Do you want to tell me what you saw?"

"You, here in your full armor with weapons, but you weren't alone." She had known the second she saw the child that she was Tadhgán's, and the child's eyes were unmistakably hers. But it wasn't until the girl spoke that Anene *knew* the child was theirs. Hers and his. Anene also knew that this was a glimpse of the future, her future, as long as she didn't wait too long. But what could she tell the man before her now? Should she tell him that the girl's hand he clutched was their child? It was in the moment that she finally understood why there were some things that needed to wait until it was time. Here she was with the man that she wanted. She had an inkling that he might want her, and knew she shouldn't tell him all that she gleaned. Knowing that if she did, she might get the man, but would it be true? Or if he knew before it was time, would she forfeit the child? So instead, she would tell him all, but that fact. "You had a little girl with you. She told me that I was needed and not to wait too long." *Goddess I hope I'm doing the right thing not telling him all.*

Only you can know that. Cailleach answered softly, not wanting to hurt her already splitting head. *But I think maybe you are going to have to make a stronger brew. Your visions aren't strong, but they are hard hitting.*

"Thank you, captain obvious." Anene grumbled.

I do not know the reference, but I understand the sarcasm well enough.

"Sorry, Cailleach." Anene smirked.

"I was here with a girl child?" Tadhgán's handsome face paled for a second but recovered quickly.

"I know it's strange." She took another sip of the tea, wincing. "This is bloody awful. Not your fault." She interjected before he could say a word. "I didn't tell you what to do properly, and besides, Cailleach says I'm going to have to make it stronger anyway."

"Your head, how is it now?" He stayed where he was squatting in front of her wanting to gather her in his arms to give what comfort he could.

"A little better." She sighed and sunk further into the sofa. With her head leaning against the back and eyes closed. "I imagine that the steaks are ruined."

"Aye, they were quite blackened." He smiled, naturally she would worry about the food and not the vision. He knew she was holding things back, for whatever reason. He couldn't begrudge her that though, for he himself was also holding back.

"Damit. Well Seamus will be happy with one of them, and I suppose I can give the other to Scáth Chiaráin tomorrow." *What the hell am I going to have for dinner now?* She wondered. "I don't suppose you can handle the hob?"

"The hob? Have you some sort of animal that is unknown to me?" He watched Anene pick up her head and look at him with amusement. Soon he was treated to a sound that he rarely got to hear. The laugh was husky and sexy as hell.

"Oh, don't make me laugh, it hurts." Bringing her hand to her head to try and keep throbbing down. "I keep forgetting where you're from." She took a deep breath, closed her eyes, and tried to move the pain from her head. It took a few minutes, but she was able to move it enough, so the tea had a better chance. "That's better." Eyes open and looking at Tadhgán. She felt the warmth that seemed to radiate from him and seep into her bones. She once again gazed at the ghosted wings on his back, wishing he would stop hiding them. "The *hob* is the stove." She explained.

"Why can't you just call the thing by its proper name?" he huffed.

"Who is to say what is proper? The hob for us, the stove for others, the bin for us, the trash cans for others." She shrugged her shoulders. "To each his own. Everyone is right no matter what they call it. Why do you call a witch a spellcaster?" When he didn't have an answer, only a perplexed look on his face, Anene had the satisfaction of knowing that she had stumped him. "See, it's all a matter of what you were raised with." She slugged the rest of the tea, "Gah!" she shivered. "That's fecking awful. If this is going to be a regular occurrence, I need to make this stronger and taste a hell of lot better." She started to uncurl her body to get up, she was impressed at how fast Tadhgán could move for such a large man. One second, he was crouched in front of her and before she blinked, he was standing, holding out his hand to her. "Thank you." Slipping her hand in his, allowing him to help her to her feet. However, once on her feet Anene was a little unsteady. Tadhgán took the cup from her and wrapped his other arm around her to keep her stable.

"Easy there, l...witch." He corrected. He needed to get things back on track, he needed to cover his feelings and fast. "When you're steady and fed we can go through the new training regimen I have devised." Clearing his throat, he stepped back from her. Satisfied she was steady he took the cup back to the kitchen, leaving her both dumbfounded, and a little pissed.

"New regimen?" With Seamus pressed to her side for support Anene moved slowly to the kitchen. "Do you have a training model?"

"Aye, and I think that it's time that you start working on the sword work."

"What the bloody hell is wrong with me swordsmanship?" Now she was really pissed. Anene knew there was nothing wrong with her work with the blade.

"Your footwork is sloppy, and you lose focus." *You're a bloody bastard.* He told himself.

"You fecking gobshite there is nothing wrong with—"

"You have yet to best me in the sparring ring." He cut her off. Tadhgán knew what he was doing, it was true she needed to work, and he wanted her to best him, but more importantly, if she was pissed off at him, she wasn't scrutinizing him with her knowing eyes. "Also, I want to start working on you merging your magick with the weapons. You proved that you could merge your flames, now you need to work on the others." He had gone from concerned and comforting to asshole trainer in less than a minute. Tadhgán leaned back on the counter, arms crossed over his chest. The color was back in her face as was the spark in her blue green eyes. "Before you shoot another arrow at me, think," he could see her calculating how to take him down.

"Why," Anene said, one hand on Seamus's back and the other on the back of the chair at the far end of the kitchen table. She had done what he asked and thought. And it didn't take long for her to gather the facts. Every time she had used her magick since her work with Tadhgán had begun, it was because he had done or said something that she felt she needed to prove a point. It was never in true anger, but she had been irritated. "Why have you been baiting me? First in the cellar after Brigid woke, then when we were sparing you got me to use Meili, --"

"I remember them." He interrupted.

"Then at the circle," She went on as if he hadn't spoken. "You baited me then. Do you have any idea how dangerous it was to bait a witch who does not have control over her powers?" No longer needing the support she stalked over and punched him in the shoulder. "You fecking eejit! I could have killed you."

"First, ow!" He was both proud and worried that she had the strength to hurt him. "Second, there was never any need to worry that you would cause me any real harm." He had enough smarts to know that he should move out of her reach.

"How the bloody hell could you have known that?"

"You have had these powers since you were a babe. Other than Cailleach, your father made sure, when a power manifested to give you the time to learn them before making them sleep. As for the others, the magick you received is of your mother. She has been training you all your life to respect what was running through your blood." He was now by the door of the kitchen. "You have amazing control of your anger, and I knew this every time. But playtime is over." With that he walked out the door leaving her with her mouth held agape.

Tadhgán walked a few yards away from the cottage before unleashing his wings and shooting up to the night sky. He spent the next few hours stretching his wings and making passes over the village. He knew they were all safe, but there was something nagging at him. Not knowing what or where the feeling was coming from, Tadhgán needed to patrol and start to push his training with Anene even harder.

Twenty-Four

The following morning Anene arrived to find Tadhgán out in the paddock with the horses. Staying clear of Cathal, which amused her, and giving Caoimhe, the expecting mare, some extra care in his brushing.

"There now," She heard his deep tenor soothing the uncomfortable mare as she kicked at her own belly. "You won't have long to wait there darlin." He gave her a few more treats, Anene watched as he moved to Tadgh then to Rí. Each one seemed to have taken a shine to him. But it seemed the jury was still out as far as Cathal was concerned. "You know I mean you or you mistress no harm you bloody beast. You might think about that the next time I come out to feed you." Tadhgán told the massive Shire. "Kick at me again and I won't give you your feed you fucking devil." Cathal kept his head held high as he pawed at the ground and snorted.

"The male posturing is truly amusing." Anene announced as she leaned against the fence of the paddock. Cathal, wanting to show where the fairy was in the pecking order, whinnied and pranced over to her for his daily nuzzle. "Hello me darlin." She kissed his soft nose. "Are you giving Tadhgán a tough time?" She laughed when the Shire's head bounced up and down in his answer. "Aye, I see." She held her hand out to the Irish Drought, the Connemara Pony and then the Gypsy Vanner. "How are you feeling there luv?" She ran her fingers through the mane Tadhgán had brushed out. "Aye I know, but I agree with himself." She told the mare as she groaned. "You've not long to wait yet."

"Are you ready to start?" Tadhgán asked as he closed the gate to the paddock.

"I guess." She sighed, kissed her favorite boy on the nose and followed Tadhgán back to the cottage and the training ground in the lower level. "By the way, don't, and I cannot emphasize this enough, don't provoke me into using my magick on you." She told him as she reached for the long sword on the rack. No longer working with the wooden training swords, but thankfully the blades had been spelled to harm none. Anene had yet to disarm him, so that was her goal. If she could disarm Tadhgán then she knew that she truly could hold her own in a fight.

"I promise nothing. But my hope is that I won't have to." Taking his sword. "You have up to this point trained like any other soldier, which is admirable I assure you. Yet is unwise."

"I wanted—"

"You wanted to prove that you could, and you have," he nodded. "However, you are not just any soldier."

"Yeah, I am the heir—"

"Aye, you are the heir to the throne, this is fact and can't be forgotten." He interrupted her for no other reason than he liked the fire in her eyes when it happened. "But you are also powerful. You have advantages that others do not, and it is time to start using them."

"That seems like cheating. The easy—"

"This will be war, and you will be in battles. There is no—"

"STOP interrupting me dammit!" Her sword gripped in her hand, but to Tadhgán's surprise there was not one flicker of flame on the sword or the witch. She had a nice handle on her temper now. "I know this will be a battle and that there will be a war. I know that I will be expected to lead, which is something that I have no idea how to do. All this is because I am the heir, and thank you for reminding me of that fact, yet again. Aye, I wanted to prove that I could train without the use of magick as an aide." She placed both hands on the hilt of her sword and took the stance. The muscles in her arms, shoulders and back showed the work that she had put in.

"Good stance." He moved around her, correcting her feet. "If you have your feet placed that way you will lose your balance." Approving of the adjustment. "You have become a good fighter. Now," Opposite her Tadhgán took his stance. "it's time to make you a formidable one. Use all you have, not just what you have learned from me."

Making the first move Tadhgán arced his blade down on hers. Their blades clashed against each other sending the dreadful song dancing around the room. He was much stronger, that was true, but Anene was faster. Thanks to all the training over the last few months her stamina, and endurance were almost a match for his. But he was still backing her into a corner. She knew she was about to lose another match. But now she had more to prove. She wanted to best him. He told her to use everything that she had, so it was time to do just that.

Tadhgán was about to bark at her for not using all she had, he was about to bring his sword in for another deafening clash against hers when she disappeared. The unexpected move surprised and unbalanced him enough that it sent him stumbling. Whipping around he found her standing in the middle of the room. "Not bad, next time don't wait for the opponent to turn to find you." He scolded as he stalked toward her sword ready to strike. But once again as he brought it down, she disappeared, only this time she rifted a few feet from him.

Anene, not waiting for him to attack, in one fast fluid movement sheathed her sword, took the sling from her belt, pulled back, aimed, and launched a small blue-green fireball, hitting him in the chest. With him temporarily distracted by the flames licking at his chin, Anene unsheathed her long sword and advanced on him. The moment she was in front of him, she doused the flames, at the same time her sword connected with his shoulder.

"Fuck!" Tadhgán bellowed as the blade dug into his shoulder, spelled or not, it still hurt. Not allowing him the time to recover, Anene advanced again and again until Tadhgán, not Anene, found himself in the corner. In such a tight space the long sword was useless, dropping the sword and taking out the short sword for the closer battles he tried for a blow to the stomach, but once again she rifted away. Only this time she appeared behind him in the corner and using Cailleach's wind she blew him across the room. Picking up his dropped sword Anene rifted to the side of him long enough to drop his lost weapon and to get another shot in on the other shoulder. This time, instead of just rifting, she combined Meili and Brigid. Tadhgán stood in shock as the woman disappeared in blue green flames and reappeared in the same glorious fashion. While he was confounded by the blaze, Anene struck, knocking the sword from his hands, swept his legs, sending him to the floor. Standing over him with the tip of the sword pressed to his throat, Anene's flames slowly died away until only the sword was aflame.

"Do you yield?" She mentally checked her footing, stance, and hands in case he should try regaining the upper hand. She was thrilled she'd in fact bested him in one on one but wouldn't let her guard down.

While Anene was checking herself, Tadhgán was sorting out his options. She had completely blown him away with the meshing of magickal and the physical attacks. In his current state he knew there was no way to get back the upper hand. If she had an unspelled weapon, any move she made would slit his throat. She'd done what almost no one had been able to do, beaten him.

"I yield." Opening his hands in surrender, the final realization of the win crossed over her face. Tadhgán knew in that moment there was nothing that could stop her. The fact that he was training her for battle clenched at his heart and filled him with such fear. "You have exceeded my expectations, witch." When she removed the tip of her sword from his throat, Tadhgán got to his feet. "You did very well." He told her as he took both swords to rehang them on the rack.

"Very well? Hell man! I fecking well beat you!" She shouted with pure joy and Tadhgán had the pleasure of watching her do what can only be described as a victory dance. He chuckled, then groaned as her hips swayed from side to side to the tune that played in her head. Whatever the tune, he was enjoying the display. "I bested the Great Tadhgán Ultan! Warrior of Locbroalm and Right Hand to the King!" She shouted while spinning in a slow circle. "Thank you," she faced him, as he was now leaning against the weapons rack, arms and long legs crossed. She bowed at the waist. "for your participation."

"Are you quite finished?" he was trying and failing to hide his amusement.

"Nay, I am not finished. I beat you." Standing in place, shoulders held back, head high with a regal look of command. "Admit it, I beat you and beat you well."

"Aye, I admit it, you beat me and as you say, you beat me well." He bowed at the waist. He admired the way she sauntered over to him.

"*Now,* play time is done." And with that she turned and sailed up the stairs leaving him looking after her, chuckling as his own words were flung back at him.

"Aye," he stood, placing his hand over his trumping heart. "Aye, Luv play time is finally over."

Twenty–Five

Over the next few days leading up to Samhradh, Anene's focus was split between perfecting her abilities to merge her magick with the weapons, trying to master, and failing, at producing the shield of protection Tadhgán had used against her. Not to mention the preparations for the celebrations of the summer solstice. Her cloud nine feeling after beating Tadhgán was short lived. There was no question she could now hold her own against him, however, she was warned not to be predictable in a fight. To prove the point on one occasion he dropped all the weapons and tackled her to the ground. Then brought a concealed dagger to her throat. Anene felt that the demonstration gained her knowledge on two fronts. First, she agreed she needed to work on the variety in which she used her magick as well as work more on her hand to hand. The other point this demonstration proved, was that she loved him on top of her. His weight, the feel of his muscular body pressed to hers. His auburn hair that was always pulled back during a session had come loose, curtaining her face in the unmatched color.

Anene was thrilled her memory brought his eyes to the forefront. Like his hair, there was no match for the color of his eyes. Auburn, with the tiniest hint of gold around the edges. His long almond eyes normally were assessing his opponent or engaging in a critical assessment. But there was the occasional sweetness when he was dealing with the local children who had come to love him. But in the moment, Anene only saw determination to prove his point and something that might have been heat. Goddess, she hoped that what she saw was heat in his eyes that day.

"Anene!" Miranda's sharp voice brought Anene out of her memories and back to the task at hand. What was the task she was meant to be doing now? She looked down at the table and she remembered. *Oh Aye, chopping and cooking.* Scolding herself, as she was holding one of her sharpest chopping knives and not paying attention.

"Sorry mother, I was in my head." She got her hands back to work. The chopping and slicing of the vegetables for various dishes were needed for the evening celebrations. She and the rest of the coven had already lit a small balefire that morning at her circle as well as the bonfire behind Miranda's cottage. When it became too risky to have a bonfire in the middle of the village, Miranda built a smaller stone circle on her property.

"I don't know what you have on your mind, but you should know better than to let it wander when you have a knife in your hands." Miranda scolded.

"Aye, I know." She smiled as her mother had rightly scolded her. "Mother, when we were living in the old cottage you also owned this place. I never asked before and I always wondered. Why have both properties?"

"Oh, I don't know, I guess you could call it intuition. After your father and I came together, we came back here for the Samhradh. I wanted to light the fires and pay homage to the gods and goddesses. On that first visit I fell in love with the lands that surrounded your circle. So, I bought it."

"What, you just bought the whole of the village? Just like that?" *How does one buy a village?* She wondered

"No, there were a lot of hoops and whatnot that we had to go through. I was a woman and not allowed to buy or even own land back then. So, Ciarán had to buy the land. Over the years, he bought more and more. Then as the laws changed, he would transfer the land deeds to me. As the village grew, we added the two cottages. First, the one you, your father and I lived in, but a few years later I added this one. It was then that I added the smaller circle."

"When was this? What year?" Anene had finally been able to come to terms with the news of her mother's age. And being able to talk to someone who had been through the ages, has been an eye opener for sure. It was fascinating, albeit not surprising the amount of things that history books got wrong or had misleading information.

"Well, we started to buy up the land the year after Ciarán and I came together in 1723. The old cottage was created in 1754 and this one was built in 1845 when the village and coven were created." They worked in silence for a little while. Anene focused on the food she was prepping for the celebration of the longest day of the year. "This solstice will be even more special with the strawberry moon rising." Miranda plated the veggie, meat, and cheese platters. It was the only thing her daughter would allow her to cook. She wasn't a bad cook, but there was no question she couldn't hold a candle to Anene's talent in the kitchen.

"Aye, it will be a spectacular sight tonight." Anene was simply tingling at the thought of being in her circle when the moon showed her face that night.

"You will be in the celebrations tonight." This was not a request; this was an order from The High Priestess and her mother. Anene wasn't sure which held more power over her. If she was going to be honest, it was probably her mother that held the bigger sway.

"Aye mother, I will be there as I always am. But..."

"I know, you need your time as well. Solitude, recharge, and cleanse. I know. You need that more than anyone else. But the coven needs to see you as does the village." She thought for a moment. "Tadhgán should also attend. He has become a staple in the village and the children simply love him."

"I'll ask him, but he might have his own ritual for the day and night."

"Be that as it may, he needs to be seen as much as you do. The coven is fully abreast of the facts, but there are some in the village who are not, and he needs to be seen."

"How has the research into the archives been going?" Anene slid the large ham in the hob and started on the beef tenderloin. Trimming the fat and silver skin. Making sure to keep all the trimmings for the gravy. She cut the loin in half, tied the two sections together, salted and placed them in the fridge for a few hours. as she grabbed the potatoes there was a knock on the kitchen door. "Well, perfect timing." Anene thrusts the basket of potatoes in Tadhgán's hands. "You can clean these while mother fills us in on the research and I work on to other things." Not waiting for a response, she turned and left him standing in the doorway holding the basket of potatoes.

"I came to see if there was anything that was needed for your rituals today?" He walked in, placing the basket on the table. "Why was I holding that?"

"So you could clean and slice them. Why else?" Anene's asked while pointing to the sink. Taking the basket to said sink and showing him what to do.

"I know how to clean a spud, witch." He grumbled as he snatched the brush and russet from her hand and began to scrub the dirt away.

"So, your research?" Anene giggled while looking at her mother.

"Well, we haven't come across much of anything yet. But I have a feeling that the answer will be in the oldest part of the archives."

"You mean in Ciaran's writings?" Tadhgán's voice wafted over from the sink.

"Maybe or might be in my own journals. I feel like I'm close, it just needs a little more time." Feeling more than slightly frustrated. She could feel the answer was literally at her fingertips yet, still out of reach. "Maybe after Samhradh I can devote more time to it." She smiled as Scáth Chiaráin leaned against her. She knew that the dog was a guardian and that the dog was not his true form, but that didn't stop her from treating him as such. It always amazed her that he was the guardian, and yet he bowed to Seamus, Anene's Irish Dane. "Tadhgán, I will need you to be present during the celebrations." Once again, not a request. "Do you have your own rituals that you want to follow today?" She asked after giving Anene's words some thought.

"Nay, we don't have the same as you, and what rituals we had have been forbidden under the rule of Flann." With the last potato finished and placed on the towel to dry Tadhgán turned to see both women staring at him with horrified expressions.

"He has forbidden the rituals to the Gods?" Miranda trembled in anger.

"Aye, he has." He shuffled under their eyes. Even before the usurper had forbidden the practice he hardly ever participated in the prayers, or offerings to the Gods. Now that it had to be done in secret, he never did. The risk, in his eyes, was not worth it. He was needed by his King, and would not risk being put to death because he made offerings to the Gods. Gods who took his mother from him and never saw fit to gift him with the name of his father. "I will make sure I am at the bonfire for the feasting." Wanting to change the subject for no other reason than to turn his thoughts to something else.

"Grand," Anene sensing his need, moved on. "Now, I need you to slice those nice and thin." She handed him the slicing knife. His fingers brushed hers, at her small intake of breath, their eyes snapped on each other's for a moment before Anene reluctantly broke the contact. Taking a steadying breath as her heart stuttered, cheeks slightly flushed, all the while tingling ran from her toes to the top of her head.

Am I sensing a change here? Brigid quipped with a giggle.

Seriously, how old are you? Anene questioned.

Old enough to know that you need to jump that fairy as soon as you can. Came Cailleach's older and more authoritative voice.

Women! Grumbled Meili.

"Oh, for the love of Pete." Anene began to roll with laughter. "All three of you please, go away from me. I need a day and a night of peace." *I love all of you, but I need my own counsel for a little while, please.*

Aye, have fun, Brigid chirped

Be well, and be safe. Cailleach mothered.

Ja, we will come back after a night and a day. But should you need us beforehand, all you need is to call out and we will return.

And just like that Anene felt alone for the first time in months. It was wonderful to be in her own skin alone. It was also strange and a little unsettling not to feel Brigid's young girlish laughter, Cailleach's wise counsel with an undercurrent of anger, or Meili's need to be indifferent and yet father-like.

"I thank you all, for the space." Anene turned and faced her mother and Tadhgán. "Did you know I would be able to do that? Ask them to go for a time?"

"Little is known about sentients. There hasn't been a joining in more years than I can count." Tadhgán remarked.

"That's information you're going to have to talk to them about. They'll know more about it. Provided that they are permitted to give you the information." Miranda grumbled while she looked at her watch. "We need to hurry."

Over the next few hours, the kitchen was bustling with activity. There was a swinging door of coven members. Picking up dishes, stopping to help with the prep, or just stopping to chat while the others worked. Tadhgán, as an outsider looking in, felt the dynamic was that of a large loving family.

"Are you alright there, luv?" Colleen asked while leaning against the counter next to him. She smiled at the slight startle and raised brow. "You're in Ireland, laddie. You need to get used to hearing the word. It doesn't have the same power here that it does for you."

"Aye, I have noticed." His eyes traveled the room until they found their mark. Anene's raven hair, piled on her head, the smile she gave the male witch made her features light up. He loved to see her smile and yet hated that it was given to anyone other than himself. The way she moved around the kitchen was pure magick. The sway of her hip was a dance that he wanted to join.

"Not to worry," Colleen smiled at his focus on the High Priestess's daughter. "I feel all will be well." She chuckled as Tadhgán whipped his focus from Anene and the male witch that he wanted to slice to bits, to the seer next to him. "Nay, I will not tell you what I've seen." she assured.

"Tadhgán!" Sonya squealed as she made a bee line for him with her not so little puppy bounding after her. She wrapped her arms around his leg and sent him a smile that could melt even the coldest of hearts. Unable to resist the young girl, he bent down and hoisted her up on his hip. She brought her lips close to his ear. "Can we go flying?" She whispered.

"Nay," he chuckled, "But I can cart you around for a bit." He glanced at the seer and saw that she not only heard the girl's plea but was not the least bit phased by it.

"I'm a seer, luv, not much gets hidden from me, or her."

"To which her are you referring?" He thought he knew but wanted to ask.

"Och, you're a smart lad, you'll figure it out soon enough." She smiled at the man and the girl in his grasp then went to help with the next task.

Anene watched as Tadhgán left with Sonya and her dog in tow. She moved so she could see when he was out of the house he settled the girl on his shoulders, bouncing her a few times to elicit the pure joy she felt in the laugh. Anene giggled when the other children saw the ride Sonya was receiving and began vying for the next spot. His laughter trickled through the breeze directly to her heart while watching him run, with Sonya still perched on his shoulders, begging her to protect him from the angry ogres at his heels. Rubbing her chest Anene tore her eyes from the scene and the man she wanted to join.

Twenty-Six

With the Solstice to a close, Anene was finally able to walked to her circle. She loved being with the coven during the celebrations, but she needed, as her mother said, to have her solitude and time to connect and recharge. Every summer, on the longest day of the year, people would come from all over the country. Visitors flocked to Suíochán an Ard-Shargert, wanting to watch the witches celebrate. It was wonderful for the purse strings, but could be hard on those who wanted and thrived on solitude. As the sun disappeared below the horizon, *this* was where she wanted to be: in the middle of her circle to watch the moon and stars rise. She was getting the feeling her time here was slowly coming to an end. There were things still to learn, but the feeling of foreboding was ever present. And it was that feeling that was giving her doubts.

She had every confidence in her power. For reasons she was unaware of—until recently, that is—her power was immeasurable. It was the battle training she'd been doing with Tadhgán she was unsure of. He was a skilled warrior and instructor; her own experiences were a testament to his skills. He was a beast when it came to training. She was stronger, her handling of the sword was exceptional, and her aim with the bow was unmatched. Because of this and Anene's skill with the blade, Tadhgán had difficulty disarming, especially when she imbued her weapons with her powers. There was no reason for her to doubt, but lately she was distracted beyond measure.

Anene stood, smiling, in the middle of the stone circle, watching the village as the celebrations continued below. Taking a deep, cleansing breath, she drew her eyes to the heavens and to the stars that would slowly awaken for their nighttime display. Soon the moon would light the sky, then the beauty would be complete. As the sun began its descent, the large golden moon showed her glorious face. This was her time. The time between night and day. She could feel her power humming, recharging, from the ground on which she stood. Raising her arms, Anene was able to draw from the moon as well as the earth.

That was how Tadhgán found her, rooted to the ground. Hands to the sky, with power running down her fingertips, and up from her feet only to meet in the middle with a shimmering explosion. She was absolutely stunning. When he first saw her months ago, strolling by the old cottage, he thought she was a pretty lass. She had a fit and trim body that he would've liked to get his hands on. Now, after the hard training he'd put her through, she was a woman who could drop any of his honed soldiers to the ground. Her leggings showed off her well-toned legs, along with the loose, billowy tank top she wore that allowed her well-defined arms to be seen. As he stood just outside the power-filled circle, Tadhgán drank in the sight of the woman before him. He had come to love her more deeply than he ever thought possible. It had been foretold that he would find his one true life mate and they would be stronger than any other before them, but he never imagined that it would be his King's daughter. This otherworldly creature before him, half witch, and half fairy, seemed to call out to his half fairy and whatever the other half may be.

His mother never told him who his father was, only that he was not of the fairy realm. Tadhgán knew he was different the moment his wings came in. The other Fae children had membranous wings of different shapes and sizes that always adorned their backs. However, his were large, black-feathered wings that he could bring out at will. Most often he wore his wings within himself. That was the form he took most of the time. Better to have the look of no wings than something no one else had. However, no matter what, some would look down on him with their intolerance of anything that was different from themselves.

As he stood, watching Anene pull the power from the earth and the moon into herself, he marveled at the magnitude of his feelings for her. He needed to tell her how he felt and beg her not to go after Flann. He couldn't lose her, not now that he'd finally found her.

"I know you're there." Her soft, lilty voice carried over to him. "Are you going to stand there or are you going to—"

"I think I'll wait here where it is safe, until you are finished, thank you." Tadhgán chuckled as he locked his hands behind his back. He loved watching her, no matter what she was doing, but when she was in her power, she was magnificent.

"I won't harm you; you know." Her laugh was like silk as she slid her eyes briefly in his direction, shook her head and smiled. "So be it." She stood for a few more minutes before she lowered her arms and turned toward him. There he was, just on the outside of the stone circle: his tall, muscular body clad in his jeans and t-shirt. Unfamiliar attire for him, but boy did he play it off well. His long auburn hair pulled back in one of her ties, while still concealing his pointed ears. The action made her uncomfortable. Why shouldn't he show his ears? She loved them. Just as she loved the way his body moved during training, so confident, so precise. Not one ounce of hesitation or uncertainty. The way his tall frame towered over her 5 feet 6 inches by an entire foot. His auburn eyes, which could in one look, melt or infuriate her. And the way he spoke to her, there was never any kowtowing or bowing she had come to see in the people of the village or those who would come to her wanting help. No, Tadhgán spoke to her like an equal, or at times like a soldier. There were times when she'd catch him looking at her in such a way; it could make any woman blush all over. If she was being honest with herself, it was those looks she loved the most. Anene had been all over the world, and never had a man look at her the way Tadhgán does when he thought she was unaware. "Ok I'm finished."

"What were you doing?" He always had questions when it came to her magick and how she wielded it. He'd become more and more comfortable with her magickal talents during his time in her realm.

"I was drawing from the moon to cleanse my body, the magick within, as well as drawing from the dance here to replenish from the day's exertion and to bring me to my center." Anene explained as she watched him move towards her, his eyes locked on hers. Her heart raced at the intensity radiating from him. As he stepped closer, her stomach began to flutter, and a flush roamed over her body. She only wished that he knew how he made her feel. But she knew Tadhgán only saw her as a warrior to save his realm, not as a woman he could love—no matter how much she wished it otherwise. Her heart skipped a beat when he stopped but a breath away from her.

"Hello there, witch." He smiled into her multi-colored eyes. Did she understand, he wondered, that his scorn of calling her *witch* had become a term of endearment for him? "Happy solstice," his deep voice all but purred, not knowing it made her knees turn to jelly. His hands longed to touch her long raven hair that, thanks to her father's blood, sparkled with silver throughout.

"Happy solstice." Anene' blood sang when he called her *witch*. She'd hated when he flung it at her in the beginning. It was amazing how he managed to make that one word sound sexy and delicious. Anene allowed herself to hope for more. "Is this your first solstice out of Locbroalm?"

"I don't want to talk to you about the solstice." Tadhgán took a chance she wouldn't turn him into a toad and reached out to touch the end of the braided hair draped over her shoulder.

"What then?" Her breath hitched at the small touch. *Has he ever touched me like this before?* she wondered. *No, it's always been to show me how to hold a bow, nock an arrow, or to guide my stance when working with the sword.*

"If you promise not to use magick on me, I would very much like to show you." Tadhgán had been trained at an incredibly early age to watch the subtleties in other Fae and those humans who live in Quelocand. To understand the subtleties, he could determine if there was a lie, truth, concealed pain, nerves, and so on. He'd tried using this training to help him navigate Anene. But he came to one disheartening conclusion; for all his training, it could not help him with this woman. He wasn't sure if it was because she was part human and part fairy. Or if it were because she was also a witch and could mask all the tells that would give her away. Or if it was because he was in love with her.

"Tadhgán's, so help me, if you're about to show me some other type of hand to hand—" She tried to walk away, but he gripped her upper arm to keep her in place. Anene looked down at the enormous hand clasped around her arm, then into the eyes of the man impeding her retreat. "Unless you want me to—"

"Turn me into a toad?" Tadhgán supplied a small smile. "I would rather you didn't, to be honest." He let go so she could turn her body to face him. He decided to take a different tack. "I wanted to show you this one move." Tadhgán could actually see the fire in her eyes and hoped this wasn't a huge mistake. "I want you to try and slap me." He nearly lost his composure at the expression on her face at the request.

"I'm sorry, what?" She couldn't have heard that right. "You want me to slap you?"

"Nay, I want you to *try* and slap me. No worries, you *won't* be able to." and with that small slight at her ability the fire had bloomed to an inferno.

"I have no idea what your game is here, laddie, but I want no part of it." When she turned once more to leave, Tadhgán again made a grab for her arm. She rounded on him, as expected, but instead of a slap, her hand was balled up in a fist. Thankfully, since he was expecting a move, he snatched her fist, whipped it behind her back, and hauled her into his body, putting their chests flush together. Knowing how scrappy she was, Tadhgán was wise enough to angle his lower body to the side, thus protecting his most sensitive parts. She had stunning eyes normally, with the deepest blue in the center and her father's bright iridescent green on the outside, but now in her fiery temper, the green of her eyes were glowing with power she kept at bay. It was something he'd admired from the beginning—she never reached for magick in anger.

"Let go of me." Anene ground out through her teeth. When he didn't, she tried to punch with her other hand. He subsequently disarmed her in the same fashion, with both arms now pinned behind her back. Being pressed to his hard body, filled her with such need for him to want more than a training exercise.

"You were meant to slap at me, Luv, not try to land your fist in my face," he realized too late that he'd slipped and used the endearment. Tadhgán watched her eyes widen as she stopped struggling against his hold.

Twenty-Seven

"What did you call me?" She couldn't have heard that right? Her memory flashed to the day he explained the use of the term Luv. How in her realm it was nothing more than a placeholder for a given name. Yet, in his realm 'Luv' was meant only for those whom you truly loved. "Tadhgán, what did you just call me?" she asked again.

"I think ye heard plain enough, Anene." Releasing one of her wrists from his grasp, he tucked a strand of loose raven hair behind her ear. He stilled when her free hand cupped his cheek, bringing his eyes back to her. "Anene, please—" He couldn't finish. He wanted to ask her to take him into her heart, to love him in return, to share his life. To beg her not to go to war where he might lose her before they had a chance to really be together. But he couldn't, *wouldn't*. The choice needed to come from her own heart and head.

"Tadhgán, say it again, please," she whispered. When he shook his head, she smiled. She knew he wouldn't. Her mother told her stories about how her father had declared his love. Just like now, it was a slip up and then the ball, as it were, was then in her mother's court. As it was now, in Anene's. "Okay, then I'll talk. But first, can you let go of my other wrist please?" When he arched his expressive brow, she chuckled. "I promise not to deck you." He released her then took three steps backwards. She already missed the warmth that radiated off him, but more, she missed the feel of his body against hers. She knew what he was doing. He wanted to give her all the space needed so she could come to her own decisions with no interference from him. What he didn't seem to realize was she'd already made her choice. She was his, and he was hers. No matter what. She took a deep breath and tried to settle her heart and nerves. "Are you aware that in my life I have had three relationships and one that was fairly serious?"

"How serious?" His voice was so quiet and guarded that she wasn't sure she really heard him.

"Enough that I'd agreed to marry him. However, I broke it off almost as soon as I said aye to the engagement. I realized I loved him, but I wasn't *in love* with him. He was a genuinely nice man, and I think . . . we could've had a good comfortable life. But, in the long run, I don't think I would've been happy. As it turns out, he wouldn't have been either." She paused for a moment to slow her heart before she went on. "And would you like to know why I wasn't in love with him?" When he made no answer, she continued. "I wasn't sure at the time. I thought maybe it was me and that I was broken somehow. That, for some reason, I was not built to have that kind of love in my life." She took a breath and noticed his fists clenched at his side. "Then, one day, I decided to walk past the old cottage after I'd closed the shop for the night and there you were. This mountain of a man dressed in leather armor, armed to the teeth, and large, black-feathered wings hidden within his body." His eyes widened, and his body tensed at the mention of the wings. Nodding her head she went on. "Aye, I could see your wings. Even though you hide them. My first thought when I saw you was 'Am I dreaming?' then I wondered why this man would hide such beautiful wings." Anene walked further into the circle and touched the King's stone. Most would feel cold, wet stone, but she could feel the warmth and the power that pulsed.

"Why have you never mentioned this before?" Tadhgán had broken his silence. "About my wings? Why have you never asked about my wings?"

"Because you have yet to bring them out for me to see. I can see them because of my powers, yet they are not on display for the naked eye. I didn't ask about them because you either weren't ready or didn't want me to know about them. I decided to wait and give you the privacy to tell me about them yourself." She smiled. "I guess I blew that out of the water. But I wanted you to know that if you were keeping them to yourself because of a misguided notion that I would be repulsed, I wanted you to know, I'm not. Although I have not seen them in the flesh, as it were, they are glorious." She nodded to make her point and continued. "Now you've distracted me, and I've lost track of what I was saying."

"You were talking about how we met," he answered quietly. Hearing her words about his hidden wings warmed his heart more than he thought possible. Tadhgán wanted to unleash them then and there, but knew if he did, she wouldn't get through what she wanted to say.

"Oh, aye, that's right. Here was this absolutely gorgeous man who looked every bit as dangerous as he did delectable. Then you opened your mouth!" She sighed and looked to the moon. "You were so exasperating! Overbearing and quite rude, come to think of it. And there were times when you were such an asshole that I contemplated turning you into any manner of things. But over time, I came to see past the rough warrior, to the man beneath. That was the man I wanted to see more of. So, I watched, and I was able to catch glimpses of him. He appeared when dealing with my mother, or with the village children who wanted to use him as a jungle gym. Who was willing to help a family he didn't know build a small house for a little girl's dog. The list goes on. Then there were times when I would catch him staring at me, and I would wish it meant something more than a trainer looking at his student. I wanted those looks to mean that he wanted me as I wanted him." By now, Anene was standing at arm's length from him. She wanted to be able to see him clearly as she told him what he needed to hear before they could go any further. "You told me once that the term 'Luv' may be casual here, but in Locbroalm it is saved for that precious one that you genuinely love—wholeheartedly love and plan to have your day start and stop with them. To breathe for, to live for." She stepped closer. Still not touching, but near enough she could feel the heat pumping from every inch of his 6-foot 6-inch frame. "I am going to give you words that I have never given to another man. They are words that are as precious to me as 'Luv' is to you, Mo ghrá amháin." Her voice hitched slightly on the words she gave him. "It means, my one and only love."

"Anene, please." Waiting to hear the word from her was torture.

"Tadhgán." She stepped so her front was pressed to his. Cupping his face in her hand. "I find you to be rough, hard, a pain in the ass most times, but gentle when you think it's needed, kind...and I love you with all my heart. So be gentle with my heart please, because you have the power to pulverize it to the point of no recovery."

"Anene." He took her hands from his face and brought them to his lips, kissing the palms before placing her hands over his heart and covering them with his own. "There is so much I want to say to you. First is that you are also a major pain in the ass." He smirked and gently squeezed her hands in his. "But you are one of the best warriors I have had the pleasure to train. Because of this and your own powers, you have become a formidable opponent for whomever steps in your path. This is a source of immense pride and terror for me." He took a deep breath to tell her things that he never spoke of. "I have been an outsider in my world because of my unknown heritage. My mother was Fae, but she has never talked of my father. The wings your magick allows you to see, they do not match those of my realm. Because of this I have been ostracized and left with the belief that I would never find my mate, despite what was foretold to me. Then I came through the doorway to Quelocand, you gave me hope that I might have at last found my true mate." He took a steadying breath, with one hand still cupped over hers. He took the other to cradle the side of her head, laying his forehead on hers. "I know the word 'mate' won't mean much to you, but where I hail from, it is everything. It means that you are my soulmate, that I will stand with you no matter what, I will cherish you till the breath leaves my body, then I will wait for you to return to me on the other side of the veil. I will protect you with my life and, most importantly, love you with every fiber I have wrapped in my being. I love you, witch." He smiled at her small chuckle. "Will you accept and become my mate?"

"Were you not paying attention to my words earlier? You are mine and I am yours. I love you. If a mate is what you want, then a mate you will have of me. Now for Goddess's sake, please kiss me."

It was all he needed to hear. With his hand on the side of her face, he wrapped his fingers around the back of her neck and gently brought her lips to meet his. When he was finally able to taste her, he all but growled with the need to deepen the meeting. Sensing his need, Anene wrapped her arms around his neck and angled her head. She shivered as he ran his hands down her sides to pull her even closer. Tadhgán ran his tongue along her lips at the same time as he pulled her in, causing her to gasp. She tasted better than he ever thought possible. A sultry mix of peach and honeysuckle. The heady combination nearly dropped him, as did the small moan that escaped her throat. He broke away from her devastating succulent mouth and ran his lips down her throat.

"Oh god, Tadhgán." Anene could feel her need for him build to a boiling point that, if not sated soon, would explode. She knew he would be a good kisser, but nothing prepared her for the talent he had with those lips. Lips that were now kissing, nipping, and sucking on spots that she didn't even know would make her feel this pent up. "If you don't stop that, I may cum right here and now."

"We can't have that, my Luv," he breathed on her neck, making her tremble with monstrous need. "We can stop here and now, and venture back to your home." He looked into her glowing blue eyes with the green rims, and it made his constricting jeans become almost painful. She stepped from his embrace slightly placing her hands on the side of his face and looked deep into his eyes.

"This is *my* choice, *my* land and most importantly, *my* dance. We stay here, but to ensure we have privacy." She moved further into the heart of the dance. Tadhgán beheld the wondrous creature before him, with her graceful arms above her head. Now that he was accustomed to her magicks, he could smell and feel the power she was going to wield. She was lit from within, whips of green and blue left the space around her and shimmered with the majesty that was her. As she swept her hands down, an opalescent dome materialized and covered the entire eighty stone dance. "Now, no one will see or hear us. In fact, anyone who gets too close will be turned away."

"You want to stay here, then?" Tadhgán met her in the center of the dance. When he touched her, a pulse of power sparked between them. "What, was that?" He nearly jumped back, but Anene tightened her grip on his hand to hold him in place.

"Have no fear, I have a feeling this was meant to happen, and this ground was meant for us." She ran her hands up his muscular chest, over the broad shoulders only to stop on the sides of his neck. "Unless you would *rather* go indoors?" She would leave the decision to him, but she felt very strongly that their first coupling was meant to be in the middle of her circle.

He leaned in and kissed her forehead, both eyelids, the tip of her nose, both cheeks then landing on her lips. A soft lingering sweet touch. "I want you here, in *your* place, at your center." He wrapped his arms around her middle, pulling her tight against him. He no longer cared that they were outside. All he cared about was the woman he didn't know he wanted, needed, and had been waiting for all his life, was finally in his arms, and she *loved* him.

Anene ran her hands down his chest only to have him catch her wrists, halting her from going any further. With wrists in hand, Tadhgán raised her arms above her own head.

"Keep them up." His voice's intensity had her shiver in anticipation. With her arms raised, he smoothed his hands down her body until he reached the hem of her shirt. With the billowing, gauze-like fabric in hand, Tadhgán began the slow process to pull her free of the covering. "Beautiful," he told her as the top slipped from his fingers and flitted in the breeze, her tanned skin, iridescent under the full moon's glow. As she lowered her arms, the red, lacy bra highlighted her breasts like perfect mounds on her chest. While the black leggings were a sharp contrast that made his mouth water.

"My turn." Anene's skin was burning under his gaze. She looked at the black t-shirt he was wearing, snapped her fingers, and the shirt disappeared. "Much better." She gave a wolf's grin as her leering eyes roamed over his torso. He had the palest skin she had ever seen—and she lived in Ireland—but although it was pale, there was an unmistakable luminescence that gave him a warm glow. The well-defined muscles of his stomach, chest, shoulders, and arms were akin to a sculpted statue. Anene could see hints of the wing tattoos curving over his shoulders, arms, and wrists. In all the time he had been training her, he'd never removed his shirt. So even though she could *see* his wings, she'd only ever caught glimpses of the tattoos that adorned his body.

She circled around to finally see the wings that were inked in his glowing skin. "My god," she breathed. The black ink covered his whole back, including the backs of his arms and, she rightly assumed, his legs. She saw him tense and knew immediately what he was thinking. "These are beautiful," she whispered, running fingers over the lines of the etched wings. "I could look at these for years and never tire of the masterful beauty they represent." Placing both hands on his lower back, Anene gently kissed the center of his back. "Please don't ever worry about the wings you have. You were given them for a reason, I love them, as should you."

Tadhgán slowly turned to face her. "I love you, witch," he said, running his hands down her back, cupping her hips, then picking her up. Anene wrapped her legs around his torso. "I am thankful for my wings, which have saved my life and the life of my King many times." He assured her. "I would like to know where they came from, but there is no way to know. My mother has gone through the veil and no one else in the realm knows who my father was."

"Would you . . ." she trailed off, not knowing if she should go on. He might not be ready to know the truth she had gleaned while touching the phantom wings on his back.

"What is it, Luv?" Tadhgán took a firmer grip on her so he could touch under her chin to bring her remarkable eyes to his.

"Would you like to know about your wings?" she asked quietly, while holding her breath.

"How—?" The wind seemed to leave his lungs. Gently, he placed her on the ground and settled his hands on her shoulders.

"When I touched the tattoos, I was given glimpses of your wings' origins." Unable to read his expression, she shook her head "I'm sorry, I shouldn't have invaded—" Her words were cut off as his mouth crushed against hers.

"Don't ever be sorry, my Luv," he said against her lips. "One day I would like you to tell me what you saw." He kissed her gently. "But for now—" He turned her and pressed her back to his front, running his lips down her neck while his hands palmed her breasts. "I have more important things to occupy my mind and body with." A smile spread across his lips as a quiet moan sounded from her mouth. He loved to hear it but couldn't wait to hear her lose the firm control she held on herself. While his one hand began playing with her nipples the other ventured down her body to the apex still covered in the tight legging material.

"Tadhgán." Even still mostly dressed, the sensations she had running through her was staggering. She could feel her core's blazing heat and wanted nothing more than to throw him down and mount him at once before she combusted. As he pressed his hand at her apex, she nearly lost her control then and there. Instead, she reached her hands behind her to grab him through his jeans. The sheer size of him, while still confined by clothing, was jaw dropping. While she squeezed and rubbed, he matched her in motion. She wanted him now. She didn't want to finish like this. She wanted him inside of her. As she thought it, the rest of their clothes disappeared in a blink. Finally, skin to skin, Anene nearly cried out.

"That really is handy." Tadhgán wrapped his one hand around her throat and tipped her chin to bring her lips to his, while the other finally dove into her core. "Not yet," he panted as she began to tremble.

"Ah, Goddess," she moaned as his fingers moved in and out of her in a divinely slow torturing motion. "Tadhgán, please, I...I can't." Her hands no longer around his length, were now gripping his arm to hold herself up.

"Are you ready for me, Luv?" He wasn't sure he could wait much longer himself. But, as always, he would yield to her.

"Please, I . . . need you, ah—" She was trembling with need as he withdrew his fingers and turned her to face him while simultaneously laying her in the grass. Once on her back, Tadhgán hips nestled between her legs, his arousal resting against the heat of her core. He began to move his hips slowly on the outside of her, slicking him all over. He might not be inside her yet, but he was hitting her in just the right spot. "Oh." She brought his mouth to hers. With her tongue tangling with his, Anene ran her hands down his sides, stopping at his perfect ass. Squeezing and pressing him closer and faster, she desperately wanted to cum. It was like their minds were linked.

"Not yet," he commanded. "I want that for when I am inside you. Filling you."

"Tadhgán, please." She placed her hands on either side of his face and kissed him deeply. "Bring them out. Bring out your wings."

"Brace yourself." He angled himself at her entrance as the tattoos came to life. As they exploded from his back, he drove himself inside her. Anene cried out in triumph.

"Gods, you're perfect," he growled down at her while watching the eyes of the woman he loved fill with tears. He raised himself on his forearms . "Why are you crying? Did I hurt you?"

"Goddess no, you didn't hurt me." She kissed him, then reached toward his wings. "They are more beautiful than I could imagine. I could see them before, but they were in a smoky haze." Tadhgán settled back down, laying on top of her. He lay motionless, still sheathed inside her while she reached to touch his black wings. "They are so...I have never seen a black this dark before." He brought one feathery wing down for her touch, something that he had never done. He'd never brought them out for any sexual encounter at all. The sensation of her fingers dancing over the crest of his wings forced a moan from his lips and a jerk of his hips. "Did that feel good?" She asked as ran her fingers down the other wing and watched him shutter. "Do you want me to stop?"

"Gods, no." He crushed his mouth to hers and began to move his hips. "Don't ever stop," Tadhgán growled out as he buried his face in the crook of her neck.

Anene was in ecstasy. The more he moved inside her, the harder it was for her to concentrate on his wings. She met him thrust for thrust. Crying out, she let go of his wings and drew her hands above her head meeting his. Hands clasped, eyes locked, there was nothing but the feel of each other and the bond that was forming.

"Tadh—" she couldn't finish his name as she exploded. Tadhgán felt her clench around him as he slowed to watch her come undone beneath him. She shimmered from head to toe, as if, once again, being lit from within. "Oh my god." She bucked as he began to move again. "Tadhgán, I can't go again, ahhh—" Arching her back, she could feel herself building again. "Go with me."

"Anene, look at me." She met his eyes. "Stay on me, Luv." He rolled his hips causing her eyes to roll back in pleasure. "On me, Luv," he growled and brought her focus back to his eyes. "There you are. You feel so good."

"I'm—" Her words were caught in her throat as Tadhgán captured her mouth. Her body tightened up and she could feel him tense. As a moan escaped her lips they broke the kiss. Tadhgán's auburn eyes glowed a new bright gold and a round, spiked glow encircled his head. "Is breá liom tú mo Rí," she told him in her language.

"I love you." His body tensed and he cried out as his climax matched hers with an intensity that seemed to shake the ground.

In that moment, neither took notice as a blue-green and gold flash erupted from them, covering the circle, spilling over the village and the surrounding villages. This protective barrier would keep the people safe, for now, from the coming war. The people that Anene and Tadhgán loved would not only be safe from a physical attack, but would also be untouched by a magickal one.

Twenty-Eight

"What was it you said?" Hours later, as the couple lay under the night sky in each other's arms, Tadhgán asked about the words Anene spoke. He knew that they were Irish, but he was unfamiliar with the language.

"Oh." She knew he wouldn't be ready for the words she spoke, at least not yet. So not wanting to be untruthful, she fudged the translation. "I love you, my warrior." She reached up and stroked his cheek and marveled at how warm she was under the covering of his wing. "We should get up and get dressed soon. The sun will rise in a little while."

"In that case," he rolled over to rest on top of her and slid himself home "let's cum with the sunrise." He slowly rolled his hips, choking out the chuckle in Anene's throat with a soft moan of pleasure.

Later with the sun low, covering the sky in the morning's colorful masterpiece, the pair emerged from the shower of Anene's little cottage. After the hot water had run cold, a meal was in order to refuel after the night and morning sexcapades. A quick knock sounded on the kitchen door and Miranda sailed in.

"Mornin, Mother." Anene smiled and kissed her mother's cheek. "You're up early." At the look of murder on her mother's face her smile died. The look was not aimed at her, but at Tadhgán. Anene glanced between the two and noticed three things. First, Tadhgán was standing at full attention. Second, his wings, which had been out since the night before, were pulled back into his body. That, infuriated her to no end. Last, the soft glow that had encircled his head after they first made love was gone. *When did that disappear?* she wondered.

"How *dare* you." Miranda's voice was dangerously quiet. And for the first time, Anene saw the Queen her mother had once been.

"Wait." Anene stepped between them and faced her mother. "What are you talking about?"

"How dare he—?" Miranda all but growled.

And then she knew. Her mother knew what they had become. "Hold it!" Anene demanded, throwing her hands in a global sign for stop. "What right do you have to come into *my* home and speak to me, or Tadhgán for that matter, in this manner?"

"He is my subj—"

"Not any more he's not!" The windows trembled under the bellow of Anene's anger. Her mother's eyes widened, there were times when she forgot just how powerful her daughter was. "You may have been his Queen when you were in Locbroalm, but not here! And sure, as *fuck, not* in my house!" In her anger and need to defend not only Tadhgán but herself, the blue-green aura of Brigid began to glow around her.

"Anene." Tadhgán placed his hands on her shoulders to try and calm her down. "You're glowing, my Luv." He met Miranda's eyes over her head. "I love her." In Locbroalm that would've been all that needed to be said. But because this was Miranda's and the King's daughter, he knew that wouldn't be enough.

"Have you any idea what this is going to do? What the implications of this will be?" Miranda whispered.

"What are you afraid of, mother? That it will cause a war?" Anene chuckled darkly. "Oh wait, there already is one."

"Yes, there is! And it was caused by the King of the Fairies choosing a human for his bride and making her his Queen!" The strain of the words spoken etched themselves on her face. "Then when there was a child in the wings . . ." she chose not to finish.

"You listen to me, both of you." Anene stepped away from Tadhgán and turned her body so she could address them at the same time. "I don't give a flying *fuck* what the fairies think of me. Or you for that matter." She directed to her mother. "This is the man that *I* chose! This is the man that chose me! And I will be *Goddamned* if I allow you or anyone to tell me we can't have each other! And you!" She rounded on the man who was beaming with pride in his woman. "Don't you *ever* hide your wings in shame again! They are magnificent and they deserve to be seen!"

"Easy, Luv," Tadhgán soothed. "It was a reflex, to hide them." He explained. "Not out of shame, but in deference to the Queen."

"Anene's right." Miranda sighed. "I'm not Queen here, and I have no right to question who you love." Taking a deep breath, "I never asked you to hide your wings. In Locbroalm or here."

"Fine, now that's settled." Anene took a breath, letting her shoulders drop. Stepping into Tadhgán's waiting arms, she beamed as the wings in question were back on proud display. She couldn't wait to see them in the sun. Mentally shaking her head at the errant thought, she turned her attention back to her mother. "So, why are you up so early?"

Sensing that the turmoil had ended Miranda pulled a mug from the press and made herself coffee before sitting at the table to explain. "Well, I came to tell you of the vision Colleen had last night." She took a slow satisfying sip of her coffee. "Why don't I tell you about it while you make us some breakfast." She smirked, knowing full well withholding the information was the best way to get her daughter to make breakfast.

"Sneaky witch." With eyes narrowed, Anene began to pull what she needed for the full fry that her growling stomach was begging for. "But you have to talk while I cook."

"Certainly." Miranda grinned in triumph while holding her mug in a salute. "Last night after you left, Colleen and Sandra came back to the cottage for tea and plan this year's solstice events. It wasn't long after we sat down that there was a flash of power coming from your circle." Miranda noted the knowing look on her daughter's face and blank look on Tadhgán's face. *Interesting. She knows something he doesn't. I'll ask her about it later when I have her alone,* Miranda decided. "That's when Colleen was taken by her vision. It was different from the visions she normally has. Scared the shit out of us let me tell you." She shivered at the memory.

"What do you mean it was different?" Tadhgán asked before Anene could open her mouth.

"When she has a vision, she goes into a quiet state. Then she tells what she saw. But this . . ." Miranda looked at her arm as the hairs stood on end, thinking about it. "Her eyes went white, and she spoke in a voice that was not her own. She sounded almost, I don't know, ethereal?"

"Was it threatening?" Anene slid the potatoes in the hob with the tomatoes to finish roasting, then started the bacon, black and white puddings, and toast before moving to the eggs.

"No," Miranda hedged. "It was more like a warning. Maybe an order." She watched as Tadhgán rose from his chair to butter the toast. Knowing that Anene wouldn't want more help than that, made her smile.

"What did she say?" Anene asked as she and Tadhgán moved seamlessly around each other.

"The time of the gathering is nearly at a close. The time of the fortification and conditioning is nigh. The union of The Celestial Fae and Danu Blessed

High Priestess will strengthen the people and bring the realms of human, Tuatha Dé Danann, and spellcasters as one. Prepare to travel to the world beyond."

Anene stood, frozen in place as her mother recounted the seer's words. She understood its general meaning and it terrified her. "Why didn't you come and tell us this last night?" Cast iron skillet in hand, she began to distribute the eggs and puddings.

"I *tried* to, but every time I came near your property line I *decided* to go in a different direction." Her mother's brow arched knowingly. "Besides—thank you," she said, as the eggs were piled on her plate, "what could you have done last night that you can't do today?"

"We have to leave for Locbroalm," Tadhgán supplied. He was glossing over the rest of the message, as he wasn't sure what it meant yet. Who or what was the Celestial Fae? He had a feeling the Danu Blessed High Priestess was Anene. And a union? When he felt Anene's fingertips brush his wings something clicked in him. He spun around and grasped her upper arms. "Where did the wings come from?" His auburn eyes were filled with such intensity that Anene's eyes stung.

"They came from your mother." Her voice was almost too quiet to hear. She placed both her hands over his racing heart.

"Nay, my mother was fairy with dragonfly wings?" He corrected, but deep down, he realized the stories he'd been told about his parentage were about to be shattered.

"The woman who raised you, was your adopted mother." She steadied herself, "Before your father died from wounds, he received in battle he and your mother went to the temple. It was there they gave you over to the priestess to raise as her own. When she agreed, you were placed in her arms. She loved you immensely. Your father died in the temple two days later. I don't know who he was, but your mother," Anene hesitated, but knew he needed to know the truth, at least what she was able to give him. "Your birth mother is The Mórrígan." She felt him stiffen at the name of his mother. "It's because of her you have the crow's wings and the ability to pull them into yourself. I believe the coupling of The Mórrígan, and your father was one of love. They took each other as mates my love. But..." *he needs to know,* she told herself. "The Mórrígan knew in mating with your father, it would bring forth a child of Fae and god. A child to aid in the foretold war that would change the course of the worlds we inhabit." She cupped his face in her hands and brought her lips to his. "You're God blessed, my love, and all the better for it. There is more—"

"Nay," he cupped the sides of her face and touched his forehead to hers. Eyes closed, "I don't want any more right now." He kissed her softly and gave her a small smile. "I think, for now, I have all I can manage," Taking a deep breath, he released her and turned to her mother and his Queen. "Do I have your blessing to handfast with your daughter?"

"What!" both women said in unison.

"Did you not understand all of the words spoken by your seer?" At their blank expressions he repeated the line. "*The union of The Celestial Fae and Danu Blessed High Priestess will strengthen the people and bring the realms of human, Tuatha Dé Danann, and Spellcasters as one. Prepare to travel to the world below.*" A light showed in Miranda's eyes as she understood the implication. "Aye, you have it, the *union*"—he looked back at Anene who had gone pale— "I will not force you into anything, Luv, please don't be afraid."

"I'm not afraid," she shook her head to clear her mind. "I am...I'm annoyed? Aye, I'm annoyed that the gods are telling us to get married. Kinda takes the romance out of it." she grumbled

"And the impending war just spices it right up?" Came Miranda's sarcastic voice from the table where the forgotten breakfast laid, stone cold.

"Sorry." Getting a glare from Anene. "Do you want or need my blessing?" she asked the couple.

"No!" The forcefulness of Anene's response caught them all off guard. "I don't need the blessing," she stated. "But before I agree I want to ask you," she looked back at Tadhgán. "Are you asking because the gods have deemed it so? Or are you asking because you want this?" Her breath whooshed from her lungs as she was pulled against him. His eyes were gold and fire in one. Without warning, he scooped her into his arms and marched out the door. "What the hell are you doing?"

"Hold on tight." Was all he said before vaulting into the air.

Miranda watched as he flew higher and higher with her daughter in his arms.

"Well boys," Looking back at Seamus who was whining and Scáth Chiaráin who was sitting like a statue with eyes on the disappearing couple. "I guess we should clean up the mess in there and head to the archives and do some more digging."

Twenty-Nine

Miranda and the dogs ventured down the stone stairs of the library to the archives. The curator who was behind her desk looked up to acknowledge the newcomer. Her crinkled eyes lit up when she saw Miranda and just as quickly clouded over with panic at the sight of her companions.

"High Priestess, you can't have dogs in here!" She whispered. The older woman stood wringing her hands, distressed at the sight of the dogs. Miranda, on the other hand, struggled to keep a straight face.

"Why ever not?" Miranda hoped her voice sounded sincere in asking the question. The last thing she wanted to do was offend the woman. It was true Stella was not a member of the coven, but she had almost more knowledge about the histories, spells, and grimoires than even Miranda. The coven had made her offers many times over the years to join, which she always declined. Stella is happiest in the bowels of the library, checking and rechecking to make sure all was in order and training the next in line for when she retires.

"Dogs carry fleas," her voice was small and meek, unless you mistreat the contents of her archives. *Nobody* wanted to be in her crosshairs then.

"Oh, well, they don't have fleas." Miranda assured.

"They have dirt," the curator squeaked, "dirt on their paws and coats."

"No dirt on the paws or the coats." Miranda smiled sweetly. She really loved this woman.

"They have," stumped for a second, "fur that flies when they move about." She nodded her head in triumph.

"Well, you have me there, they have fur." She rested her hand on Seamus's head and felt Scáth Chiaráin lean against her leg. "But you see, Stella, Seamus is missing Anene, and as for Scáth Chiaráin," She looked down at the smaller black dog. The Guardian summoned by her mate to protect her. "Well, he stays with me." There was an air of authority in her voice. "But, if you're so worried about the..." she tried desperately not to snicker, "the fur, I can spell them." Knowing Stella had a soft spot for animals, and would never want magick used on them, Miranda figured the offer would be rejected.

"Nay, that's not necessary." Stella eyed the two dogs and sighed. "No chewing, eating, or lifting of those legs my lads." She told them sternly, turned on her heel and walked back up to the main library.

"Thank you, Stella!" Miranda called. "Let's go, and remember what she said, no chewing, eating, or lifting of the leg in here. Do you suppose she should have added squatting?"

"Woof!" both said in unison, making Miranda laugh even harder.

As she started in on the journals, she thought about how her morning started. Mad as hell and worried that Tadhgán and Anene had mated. She had enormous respect for the lad and knew he would live or die for her daughter. That he would love her and cherish her. She had all that and more with Ciaran. But she also knew what it meant to love and mate with a fairy, how others would perceive the union. How her own coven reacted when they found out about herself and Ciarán. But if she were honest with herself, she was angrier with Ciaran. This little development was not in his letter. There was so much he had written to her, information that he knew she needed to know. But she wished to the Goddess she didn't, or that she now had to keep quiet. With everything he'd told her and all the things she knew he still held back, not one word was on those pages about their daughter mating with Tadhgán Ultan.

She remembered Ciarán told her when they met the first time, he knew instantly that she was his mate. The struggle he went through waiting for her feelings to match his was excruciating. He never worried about Locbroalm accepting her, as his realm was one of peace and love. Or so he thought. As her memories played out, there was an old buried past that had been beating on the recesses of her mind since the creature in Anene's shop. Miranda reached for the journal she kept while on her journey to Ireland in 1722. Flipping through the old thick pages to the entry she wanted.

1722, 3 June

The day was hot and one of idleness; Ciarán has been gone from me for a fortnight and I am longing for his return. The others have asked to go sea bathing; I, myself have no wish to, but saw no reason not to grant the request.

"Goddess the outfits we had to wear whenever a woman wanted to go take a dip in the ocean." She told the sleeping dogs. "Do you know why we had to hold onto ropes when we were in the water?" She asked the void, as the dogs had no interest in her monologue. "It was because the bathing costumes were so heavy that a woman could drown in them" Shaking her head she returned to the journal.

1722, 4 June

We have a new member of the coven, whilst down sea bathing there was a woman who knew who and what we were. Constance became fast friends with the others. That night back at the lodging house the whole of the coven wanted to add her as a new sister. Never had I experienced anything like this; I cautioned against it, citing that we had no knowledge of her and knew not whence she came, but I had been vehemently overruled. Me! Their High Priestess. I shall sleep on the situation and hopefully the Goddess will help me understand the new actions of my sisters.

1722, 6 June

Ciarán is back with me at last; I have so missed his grace, laugh, love, and touch. However, the joy I feel for his return has been overshadowed by the change in my sisters since the arrival of Constance; they have become intolerant and cruel which is not their nature. Constance met Ciarán this morning when we broke our fast; by nightfall my sisters were sighting whispers of the evils that come from the coupling of fairies and witches.

1722, 7 June

Last night when the moon was high in the sky I was awakened from my sleep; I can only guess by the Goddess herself. I knew not why it needed to be done, but I felt compelled to walk under the Moon Goddesses light. I found Constance performing dark spells near the wall of the lodging house; I was not certain of what I was seeing, but when her hands, slick and wet with the blood of the helpless animal she had slain, body hoisted to the moon, I had no choice but to freeze the witch in place. When I approached her, I felt the evil that was in her; she was not that of a witch. It was my fear that brought Ciarán to me in an instant and at that moment the imposter revealed her true self; a witch she was not, but that of a Púca. Come to make strife among the coven and my sisters.

Ciarán, using his own magick destroyed the Púca in the hopes that it would reverse the workings; It did not. As the Púca was destroyed my sisters emerged from their beds, only seeing Constance's warped warnings come to pass, in their eyes, her words had been proven. They would not be swayed or reasoned with, and the women that surrounded Ciarán and I under the descending moon were not my sisters any longer.

1722, 9 June

After a night and a day of deliberation the coven demanded the head of the fairy that killed their sister; of which I refused them. As I would not give them his head or leave his side I have been banished; I have been forbidden to return to my homeland and should I attempt to return to my native soil I shall be hunted and burned at the stake. I have been named as the killer of fellow witches, A Witch Hunter; what the Púca has done was done well and permanently. Nor I or Ciarán could reverse what was cast.

As the sun dipped on the horizon I watched from a distance as the woman who had once been my coven, my family, my sisters, board the ship to sail back to America on the morrow; the sadness I feel is paramount. I woke this night, with the moon on her last night of fullness, in the arms of my man and mate, I cannot stay sad for long. I sit now, at the window, and I know that I will never see my native land or its people again. I look over the land and at the man in my bed land I know that sadness may never completely leave me, but I am home; as my home is wherever my love is.

"Oh, my Goddess." Reading the journals brought it all back to her. She never thought she could forget the details of how she was severed from her first sisters. But there was one very important detail she had forgotten. The woman from the beach, Constance, the Púca. She had forgotten the look of her, the lines of her face, the sound of her voice. Miranda had even forgotten the details of the impact Constance had on the coven. As the veil on her memories lifted, Miranda could see the woman clearly. See the same woman who walked into Anene's shop. The same woman who Ciarán had destroyed that night, then Anene had destroyed in her shop.

"If Ciarán didn't kill her, who is to say that Anene did?" She remembered the strife that had gone through her sisters back then. "I have to warn the others." But as she rose there was something that took her to the book Ciarán had been working on before his capture. Flipping through, her eyes settled on the page. The air seemed to leave her body; she was chilled to the bone as if she were submerged in a bath filled with ice.

"Oh My God! No!" Hand over her mouth she bolted from the room.

Anene should've been scared shitless being in the air without the use of an airplane. Witches did *not* fly, no matter what the stories said. They kept their feet firmly on the ground, where the Goddess intended them to be, dammit. Yet, there she was, cradled in the arms of a man with God given wings to join the clouds in their merry dance across the sky.

"If you go any higher, my love, I might not be able to breathe." The air had already begun to thin. Tadhgán halted his flight and hovered in place while his opaque black wings flapped in slow motion. Anene took in their graceful movements, enjoying the slight flecks of iridescence filtering through the black feathers. A glint caught her attention. It looked like gold leaf had been brushed on the tips of his feathers. Had the gold always been there? Or was it the knowledge of his mother and the golden heritage that brought the gold out.

"You asked me if I wanted you," His voice brought her focus back to him. "Or if my hand was being pushed by the Gods." He looked into her eyes and then to the clouds that danced past then as he kept them in place.

"Well, actually what I asked was whether you wanted to *marry* me yourself, or were you being pushed by the Gods." Knowing he wouldn't drop her; she took one hand from the hold she had on his neck to touch his lips. "I know you want me as I want you. I know that you will never have another, as I won't either. We're it for each other. But marriage? That's a little different here, than where you hail from."

"I see." And he did. He brushed his lips over hers. "What you don't fully understand is, in my mind, and the minds of those in my realm, we are already one. Mated for life, and in the eyes of the King as well as the Gods, we are, to use your term, *married.*" He kissed her again, then rested his forehead on hers. "I asked for the handfasting because I know it is your custom, and I wanted you to have..." he stopped cold as tears ran down her cheeks.

"You wanted me to have the full experience of getting married," Anene finished, and she loved him all the more for thinking of it. "And the choice should I need it."

"Aye." He kissed her in the clouds and chuckled when a rare, White-tailed Sea Eagle came over to inspect the flying man. "Look," he whispered to Anene.

They watched as the largest bird of prey in Ireland circled them. The impressive wingspan was almost as large as Tadhgán's. With one final circle of the majestic bird, the Eagle bowed his graceful head to Tadhgán and flew off.

"Tadhgán," Anene drew his attention back to her. "I would love to have a Handfasting with you." She kissed his eyes, cheeks, nose, then finally his lips. "But we have to go down and do this now. We need to leave for Locbroalm before nightfall tomorrow." There was a feeling in the pit of her stomach, and a chill of foreboding walked her icy fingers up her spine.

"Why so soon?" He thought about the message again. He couldn't find anything in it that said they had to leave that soon.

"I'm not sure, it's a feeling I have. I can't explain it." She could feel something pushing at her, in her center and her back there was a tingling that seemed to say, *let me out!*

"You don't need to explain. Far be it for me to question the Danu Blessed High Priestess." He touched his lips to her. "This may be the last time we are alone for a while." He nipped at her bottom lip. Anene's quick intake of breath was all he needed to deepen the meeting. Savoring the flavor of her mouth, he could feel himself stiffen with a new hot need to have her. *I wonder if we could have each other in the air?* He wondered and quickly dismissed the thought.

"We will have time before we leave, but something is wrong. Let's go to the village center." She could feel her mother's fear. "Tadhgán, now, go now!"

Thirty

As Tadhgán flew closer, Miranda and the rest of the coven were gathered under the tree in the village center. Not worrying anymore about hiding his wings, Tadhgán flew to the center of the village landing on the green under the tree. The moment his feet hit the ground Anene made a beeline for her mother. The gathered coven members were wide eyed as they took in Tadhgán and the majesty of his wings. He fought the urge to pull them back into his body but knew that it would upset Anene. And it was time to see if this coven was better than Miranda's old one. Tadhgán walked the short distance to the bench where his mate and mother sat.

"Mother, what happened?" sitting next to her, Anene didn't like the pale grey wash of her mother. "What happened?" she asked the surrounding coven.

"She came to the archives to read," Stella stepped forward, hands wringing. "Not more than a half hour passed, did she shoot past me in a blaze."

"I was on my way to open the bakery when she came rushing out." Siobhan stayed in the back of the crowd, but all eyes were on her. "I caught her in a run. She was ashen and in a panic, so I brought her to the bench here. It wasn't long before Colleen was at her side with the rest."

"I didn't see what caused the flight, but I knew it was serious so sent out the alarm." Holding up her cell phone Colleen smiled weakly, "Thank the Goddess for technology."

"I know who she was." Miranda spoke quietly. Scáth Chiaráin stood at attention next to his charge scanning the people and surrounding area.

"Who?" Tadhgán came to kneel in front of Miranda, his long black wings lifting so as not to snag on the ground. "Miranda, whom are you speaking of?"

"The woman who came to the shop, the one that we couldn't save. I know who she is." Her eyes passed over the coven she had created. At first only sisters, then as the years passed, brothers were added. Miranda couldn't pinpoint when it happened. But one day she realized there were quite a few men in the coven, and they were the better for it. She'd known there were other covens that were either all men or women. But over the passage of time, she found that a well-balanced coven was a stronger one. She was proud of what she had created here. "This was put in motion the moment I was born." She told them all. "You all know my story,"

"Might I suggest that we go somewhere more private?" Colleen cut in. "I'm afraid we might be making a scene.

"Aye, you're right." Anene stood and looked about, it was early yet but the village was starting to fill with tourists. She glanced to Tadhgán and as much as she hated it Anene gave him a small nod. Understanding, he pulled his wings in so as not to attract attention of the tourists. "Those of you who have shops," looking about, "please make sure they're tended, then come to Coven Stead with the rest of us." Helping her mother to her feet, it was decided to have her walk so that there was less attention brought by the gathering of witches.

Coven Stead, an old stone barn that dated, as far as anyone could tell, from the 1700's at least. On that infamous trip to Ireland in 1722, Miranda fell in love with the old barn the moment she laid eyes on it. It wasn't known then how old the barn was, but it was in pristine condition. Soon it became a meeting place for her and Ciarán. It was where they made love for the first time. It was where they declared their love and became mates. After her coven had banished her, it was where she and Ciarán had made a home before going to Locbroalm. Whenever they came back to Quelocand the old stone barn was where they lived. It wasn't until Miranda built the village that the couple created the cottage that would hold the doorway to Locbroalm.

"This place is stunning." Tadhgán marveled as they walked through the oversized round topped door, with its iron strappings and braided iron pulls. "The stonework alone is masterful." He settled Miranda at the unofficial head of the round Irish Yew table. He watched as she placed her palms flat on the surface, a subtle wave of power trickled down to the center carving. The etching at the heart of the sacred table was the same as the village. The Shield of Protection with the sword piercing the top through the bottom on a bed of two crisscross arrows. "The table, the symbol in the center?"

"It's the same as the village layout." Miranda confirmed. "You're one of the few to have seen the village from the air. Who can and has seen the full layout."

"Where did the table come from?" He wondered aloud.

"Ciarán and I built it when we first lived here." She leaned back into the high-backed oak chair with its intricate carvings. "Then later I added the carving." She closed her eyes and tried to steal herself for the information she was going to give the coven.

Before Tadhgán could ask anything else the coven members began to trickle in and find seats. He took notice that the older members took the chairs surrounding the table, while the younger and newer members stood or took what chairs remained. It fascinated him that all this was done without a word. Anene wrapped her arms around his middle.

"My love." She whispered. Crooking his finger under her chin and bringing her lips to his. The soft swift joining was not nearly enough to satisfy him, but he knew that it would have to do for now.

"I have a need for you, witch." He whispered in her ear before nipping at her lobe. He felt her grip the hair that he had trailing down his back and tug. "Easy now." He smiled and laid his forehead to hers.

"I also have a need, my love," eyes closed, her whispered words sent shivers down his body. "But we must wait." Placing her hand on his heart she smiled as he covered her hand with his own.

"I see you two have finally stopped stepping around each other and got to stepping with each other instead." Edith, the oldest member, spoke with a warm chuckle. She would have said more but Miranda rose from her chair.

"Now that we are all assembled." Miranda, who seemed to have her feet back under her stood tall and strong. "I am sorry for the way this started. I was in shock before, but I am steady now." She reached out for her daughter's hand, giving it a quick squeeze. "First, you all know how I came to be here," She waited while her eyes roamed over the brothers and sisters that made up the coven she cherished. "There was some information, however, that I had not remembered." She shrugged. "I have no explanation how that is the case."

"It was a spell that robbed you of your full memories." Colleen's sweet voice carried from behind Edith. "Not the same as what was used on Anene, but just as powerful. With one caveat." Colleen hated that all eyes were trained on her. As the coven seer she had gotten used to the attention being on her, but she still hated it. "Anene's will lift in increments when she *truly* needs it to." Giving a pointed look at the witch in question.

"Aye I know, I have to be patient." She leaned more into Tadhgán. "It has never been my strong suit." She grumbled.

"Yours," Colleen continued with a snicker, "Miranda, was broken the moment you read your journal with an open and free mind."

"I don't know how open and free minded I was." She thought about her anger in the mating of her daughter and the warrior, and Ciarán not warning her it was going to happen. But once again she admitted that what she was really angry about was the latter of the two. Ciarán's silence on the subject. "Mm, you might have the right of it there Colleen." She nodded to the seer and to the coven as a whole. "You'll remember that there was a visitor at Cailleach's Nook. The creature took the form of a woman to deliver a message. *'We and our marionette will finally take back what is ours. Our victory will reign when the land has been rid of your stench. We will dance on the bones of your dead while the living shall be put back in the chains you once wore.'"*. She recounted the words spoken that day. "The woman seemed familiar, but I couldn't place her. With the help of many of you I have been in the archives looking for some insight."

"We never did find anything." A young witch recounted.

"And you wouldn't have. While you were in the lower section I was in the oldest part of the archives. I had a feeling the answer was there. Today I went through my earliest journals from when I first came to Ireland. It was then I began to remember," She huffed, "thanks to my own words." Miranda laid out what she had learned in her journal entries. It was painful to remember what happened to her coven of old. They had been her sisters, and because of the spell workings of a demented Púca, she'd lost her sisters and the land of her birth. But as hard as it was to remember what was, it was that much harder to share those stories with the brothers and sisters of now. Miranda felt like she was a failure for not seeing what was happening right in front of her nose. She knew that her feelings were misplaced. If she were meant to see what was happening, she would have. If she were meant to prevent the damage to her coven, she would have. All this she knew, and still it filled her with feelings of failing. Her daughter's voice thankfully pulled her from her inner self doubts.

"Wait the witch that caused you to be, what, excommunicated, wasn't a witch at all, but a Púca?" Anene asked, "Are you sure?" *That doesn't fit with the lore of Púca's.* She thought "They're mischievous, it's true, but they're not known to be evil. Or have the ability to wield that kind of power."

"It depends on what legend you read, Luv," Tadhgán laid a hand on her shoulder. But his intuition told him there was more to this than a Púca going bad. "What is the rest?"

"The woman, no, Púca was destroyed by Ciarán as I said. You know the end of that history." The collective nodded in agreement. "However, the woman who came into your shop?" Miranda's eyes now on Anene. "That was the same woman. As it turns out your father had not destroyed her as we thought. Instead, it came to the shop to deliver a message."

"That's why the dark magick she wove on your sisters wasn't broken with her death." Colleen added, "And why the distrust still lives on today. While the Púca lives, so does it's magick."

"So how do you kill a Púca?" A male witch asked.

"There is no known way. Until now, there has never been a reason to." MaryKate said absently as she thumbed through her spell book. She may have been the village Búistéir, and to some, a little scary, but she's also the best spell keeper in the coven. Every member had their own Book of Shadows, but hers was meticulous. Yet the coven's Book of Spells, that was always with Miranda, The High Priestess, was often added to by MaryKate.

"Well, you've got one now." Chimed Edith.

"There is more." Tadhgán had been watching Miranda and knew in his bones there was more than a malevolent Púca.

"Yes, there's more." Turning to face the warrior and give him her full attention as she laid out the rest. "The Púca was not acting alone. As I said this was set into motion the moment I was born." She wanted to pace the room as she told what she knew, but Miranda stayed rooted in her spot. "As my mother lay in the birthing bed giving me life, the long-awaited prophecy was finally read. It is still not known to me the exact wording of it, for it is kept with two races. The Tuatha de Danann have one as well as the ones for whom the Púca was, and is, still working with. It says that a union of a high priestess and the King of the fairies will bring forth a child that will lead the worlds and all her realms to a final battle to end all battles." Her heart broke as Tadhgán took a hold of Anene's arm and drew her closer to him in an act of protection. "A traitor would rise to power and the long-forgotten foe would be revealed." Miranda's eyes never left Tadhgán's. She saw the moment he realized what it all meant.

"No," It was a single word, but somehow that one word allowed the whole room to feel not only his terror, but his heartbreak. Anene's eyes bounded from her mother to her ghost pale mate. The look in his eyes filled her with a dread that she had no hope of fully comprehending.

"What is it?" She cupped her hands around his face to draw his sorrow filled eyes to hers. "My love?"

"He can't bring himself to say the names." Edith spoke from her seat. "But you must, laddie."

"Fomorians." The one name filled the room, some knew it and the danger that came with it. Others only knew it as a myth and didn't have the fear and worry they should.

Thirty-One

"Fuck me," Siobhan's voice carried over the table. "Are you telling me that one of your own is working with the rulers of pain, evil and destruction!" She vaulted from her seat and marched on Tadhgán. But her path was blocked by a glowering Anene.

"I may not understand the fight in your eyes Siobhan," her lilt took a softer yet dangerous tone, "but should you take one more step toward him with that look in your eyes, I can assure you, you will meet *my* wrath." She warned as blue and green flames began to lick at her skin. The witch heeded the warning and backed up a few steps. "Wise decision." Anene nodded. "Now, explain."

"The Fomorians or Fomori are enemy to the Tuatha Dé Danan." Tadhgán's deep voice was shaking as his anger was getting the better of him. "When we first came to the island the Fomori were there. As was the dark. There was never any sun, life, or love." He reached toward Anene who took his hand in hers. "We never had any real intent on war with them, such was not in our nature. Soon we saw that the island was not going to be enough for the death and destruction they thrived on."

"Meaning?" Asked a young female that Tadhgán had seen working Anene's shop but had not spoken to.

"The leader Balor had grown tired of the small island and was bent on destroying it, then moving to the next. His plan was total world domination." He told her. "It was then that we stepped in and went to war." Taking a deep breath "It was before my time, but the war was long and bloody. The Fomori were beaten back. They not only lost this island, but all others. With help from Witrotean," He sent a brief glance to Siobhan, "We were able to lock them in the sea in a realm from whence they could not leave."

"What is Witrotean?" MaryKate asked, "And why would you look to her?"

"Witrotean is another realm, the realm of witches. Witrotean means Ocean of the Witches." Sparing MaryKate a swift look of the eyes. "He looks to me when he says it because I am of that realm." Head held high; Siobhan waited for the outrage. But none came. Then she spied Miranda smiling. "Why do you smile High Priestess? Have I not just confessed to lying to you?"

"Because I knew there was something, but I couldn't figure what. It's nice to finally have the answer." Miranda walked to the witch and drew Siohban into her arms. "I care not where you came to us from. Only that you're here and true."

"Why have we never heard of Witrotean?" Anene wondered as she leaned into Tadhgán's chest; this has been a very long day, and there was no end in sight.

"After the battle and the Fomori were locked in their realm, their realm was broken." Siobhan bowed her head to Miranda, then wound her way back to her seat.

"What do you mean broken?" His wings twitched with the tension he was feeling. "Your brethren had plenty of power to kill the mighty Doran. He was King among the soldiers and was unmatched in battle. After the battle was won and the Fomori were sealed away, one of *your* witch sisters," his anger was truly something to be reckoned with. Anyone who had sense subconsciously moved back from him while he spoke. "snuck up and drove a cursed dagger into his middle."

"Lies!" Siobhan shouted "We were a peaceable realm; always have been. Only when we were called on for help did we enter the arena of war." There was sorrow in her voice and in her eyes. Yet in a flash, that sorrow disintegrated into hot rage. "It was *your* kind that set to slaughter any of us who dared step out of our realm again after the final battle."

"You are both wrong," Cailleach was once again speaking through Anene, "Be assured I have her consent to be here warrior." She told Tadhgán, who was poised to strike. "You, little queen, are also incorrect." Anene's white opaque eyes landed on Miranda before sliding back to the Fairy Warrior. It gave Tadhgán a chill to see the eyes that had appeared that day in the chamber of her circle. They were not the blue green of his mates, but white with swirling clouds that filled him with dread. "I will not harm her."

"Explain and give me my mate." If Cailleach was the essence of cold, then he was that of heat.

"It was not the Witroteanians who poisoned and killed Doran," She explained to Tadhgán. "nor was it Locbroalm who were killing your sisters," acknowledging Siobhan. "But alas, it was the same Púca who was playing a farse with both your realms. The goal, or course, was to cause unrest and malcontent amongst the realms that defeated the Fomorians."

"How is that possible?" Miranda took a small step forward. "This happened before humans walked in this realm" Miranda countered.

"It means," Anene's voice was her own once more, "that this was set in motion before there was a prophecy. Or at the very least, the one that is known, is not the true prophecy." She took her mother's hands in hers. "It means this was set in motion *before* your birth."

"That changes nothing," Edith was getting tired and wanted to go home. "There is a traitor in Locbroalm, and that is something that threatens us all. What is to be done?" She yawned. "And be quick, my bones are tired and long for the comfort of my chair and the shows on the telly."

"As always Edith, I can count on you to bring us back on task." Miranda sighed and eyed her daughter and her man.

"Tadhgán and I will leave for Locbroalm tomorrow before nightfall." Anene told the coven. "We have a few things to do together. One of which includes heading to the shop to fill in the rest of the staff and hand everything over." There was no denying, the action was going to put a hole in her heart, but Anene knew it was what was needed to be done. "For now, why don't you all head back to your shops and families." A sigh of relief could be heard from Edith.

"Finally," The older witch muttered as she and the coven shuffled out. "My old bones are no longer meant for this trek." Miranda, Anene and Tadhgán watched them make their way back to the village or their homes.

"We have some things to deal with." Without another word, Tadhgán scooped her up and vaulted to the sky.

"Oh, I bet you do." Miranda smiled, she remembered all too well what it was like when she and Ciarán first declared themselves. "Couldn't keep our hands off each other." She told the dogs who were once again her companions. "Well, I have my own things to tend to, don't I?"

Slamming on the ground, Tadhgán cradled his love so close she felt no more than a slight bump on the landing. Neither were in the mood for the soft lovemaking they have shared thus far. Tadhgán backed her to a large redwood tree, all the while she was unbuttoning his jeans. Getting frustrated, Anene once again, to save time, snapped their clothes away.

"Ye read me mind, Luv," he growled in her native lilt as he pinned her to the tree. "Wrap your legs around me and hold on." As soon as she was in position, he slammed into her. "Gods, you are already so ready for me." She was already squeezing him, and it was magnificent. He wanted to pound her but for fear of hurting her.

"You won't hurt me." She read the concern on his face. "Tadhgán, please, fuck me. Now!" She panted.

"As you wish." Getting a better grip on her, he drew himself out and slammed back into her, hitting that secret sensual spot she'd never experienced before.

"Oh yes, that's it." Anene braced her hands on his shoulders. "Don't stop." She could feel herself building as he sheathed himself to the hilt repeatedly in an almost painful pleasure. "I'm gonna cum," she cried out.

"Not yet." Tadhgán withdrew, denying her the release her body desperately craved. Dropping her feet to the ground, he turned her to face the tree. "Put your hands on the tree, Luv." She did as he bid, as he ran his hands down her back. In the back of his mind, he noticed something light, almost shimmering, marring her back. He would think about that later. Placing his hands on her hips, he brought her closer, causing Anene to bend more at the waist. Now at the angle he wanted, Tadhgán cupped her breast with one hand, rolling her nipple and running his other fingers up and down her already wet sex, causing a whimper to escape from her. Slowly he worked his fingers in her, the sound that tumbled out of her was more of a gargled groan than anything else.

"Tadhgán . . .Ah—Goddess please." Looking over her shoulder at him, Anene watched as he leaned down and kissed the center of her back. "I need to---,"

"Aye, Luv," he released her breast, angled himself at her swollen and ready sex and in one sudden powerful thrust he was sheathed to the hilt. She cried out as the denied orgasm was finally released. Not wanting to give her time to recover, he set a hard, almost brutal pace. "FUUUCK!" He reached up and took her hair in his fist, wrapping the length around his wrist to better hold her in place.

Anene was holding on to the tree for dear life. The release she had was barely sated before he began slamming into her again. The pleasure was almost more than she could endure. She could feel the building once more and wasn't sure she could manage what was coming.

"Tadhgán!" she screamed. "Goddess, yes!" Her fingers dug painfully into the trunk of the redwood tree, she prayed would hold. "Ah, Goddess! I'm cuming!"

"Don't hold back, Luv!" Tadhgán grunted as he was doing all he could to let her get there so they could fall together. "Go with me! Let me hear you!"

As one, the keening that was released from them was more than either one had ever experienced. Both collapsed to the forest floor, panting, and slicked with sweat. When Anene was able, her eyes roved over the man next to her. Once again, there was a golden spiked glow circling his head and another glow whose source she couldn't see. As they lay there, a hawk sounded in the distance, alerting them that their solitude was about to be disturbed. Anene snapped their clothes back in place and giggled at the arched brow of her man.

"We need to go," was all she said to him. Tadhgán, understanding, stood, scooped her in his arms, walked the edge of the forest, and vaulted to the sky. "We have to head to the shop," she told him. "I know we have to prepare, but I need to talk to them and explain. Especially to Sharon." and with that Tadhgán changed direction.

It took some doing, but before long Anene had calmed Sharon enough to listen to reason. Thankful to the coven members who already worked in the shop and a few others who stopped in to say that they would help out in the owners absence. Anene called all the vendors to let them know about the changes happening in the shop. It was the call to Deirdre that brought out Sharon's tears of relief. The Ardmore witch offered to come and help give the manager some assistance in the ordering of stock. After a few long hours Anene felt a little more settled about the handover, she and Tadhgán left the shop by the back door.

Feeling the press for time, Anene rifted them to the Old Cottage to prepare what they felt they needed for the journey to Locbroalm. While he was in the lower level Anene was drawn to her old bedroom on the second floor. Or more precisely, to the closet the room contained. Standing before the closed door filled her stomach with butterflies. Knowing the magickal block that once barred her had been lifted she opened the door to retrieve what her father had left for her. Before her sat a large black leather covered chest with golden fixtures.

Given the size, Anene expected a heavy beast she was going to have to drag, but to her surprise it weighed nothing at all. What didn't surprise her was the love she felt from a father to his daughter emanated from the chest. There was no question, it was created by her father, for her.

Placing the chest on her childhood bed, she examined it more closely, it was simply exquisite. It didn't escape her notice that it was the perfect marrying of her and her man. The black leather and gold trimmings, and the swirling blue green crystal at the lock, its heart. With shaking hands, she opened the lid to find three items nested in silk that mimicked that of the night sky.

A horse bow, with exquisite carvings along the limbs she didn't recognize. She was surprised at it's light weight, but remembering how her arms ached after her work with the bow she was relieved. A glint drew her eye back to the chest, placing the bow on the bed she reached for the sword next. She didn't know what to call it, for it wasn't long enough to be a long sword, but too long to be a short sword. Markings that matched that of the bow were etched down the center of the black blade. As her hands grasped the handle grip the etchings glowed in blues and greens. Once again, the sword was the perfect marrying of Anene and Tadhgán.

As her eyes committed the beauty of the sword to memory she could feel there was more to it, but the sword wasn't ready to reveal it's full self as of yet. Laying the black blade next to the bow she reached into the chest for the black leather armor. Not knowing much about armor in general, didn't take away from her noticing that it was finely crafted. Like the bow and sword the leather was light weight, yet she knew that it would protect.

When she touched the items she felt, power, love, and a consciousness. She wasn't ready to comprehend what it all meant, yet she understood that ,right now, she wasn't meant to. Anene knew she would need to have the chest and the gifts from her father with her, or more importantly, *on* her when she arrived in Locbroalm. Carefully replacing the items back in and closing the chest with a single tear slipping down her cheek she took a steadying breath.

"Thank you, father." She whispered. "I will do what I can to bring honor to this." Resting her hands on the latch she felt the urgency once more that she was needed. "I will be there as soon as I can." *And I will release you from the bounds of your prison.* Vowing silently felt safer somehow. Almost fearing to say the words aloud, would allow the wrong ears to hear them. Anene picked up the gifts from her father and rejoined her man.

"What have you there, Luv?" Tadhgán reached his hands out to free her of the burden she carried. When the leather covered chest touched his fingers, he knew what it was. "Is this from the closet then?" at her nod and went on. "From your father?" Another nod. "Do you want to tell me what is inside?"

"Not tonight." She rested her hand on his cheek. "For now let's just add this to the rest and head back to my cottage." She watched as he did as she wanted and smiled that he did so without question or comment. She met him at the front door of the old cottage, took his hand in hers, rose on her toe and pressed her lips to his. "Do you want to rift to my cottage or fly?" A squeak escaped her mouth as she was jerked to his chest, and his lips crushed hers in a scorching kiss full of need.

"I don't think I can fly us anywhere safely Luv." He growled against her neck. Her breath caught in her throat as he trailed hot kisses down. "You may have to rift us there."

"As you wish my love." And in an instant, they were gone to spend their last night in her home.

Waking in Tadhgán's arms should have felt strange to her, yet all she felt was the rightness of it. So, she knew that wasn't the reason for waking before dawn. There was somewhere she needed to be, but where? Careful not to wake him, Anene slipped from under Tadhgán's arms and padded to the window of her room. It shouldn't have been possible to, but as she cast her eyes over the horizon she spied Cathal in the paddock of the Old Cottage. Dressing quickly and quietly she rifted to see her boy once more.

Not wanting to spook the small herd, Anene appeared a few yards from the paddock and walked the rest of the way. As if he'd been expecting her, the black Shire stood at attention at the fence, waiting. Seeing him brought tears to her eyes. There were so many things she was having to give up and leave behind, her animals being the hardest. She knew that Colm would look after them and love them. But the knowledge of that didn't didn't matter as far as her heart was concerned.

"There you are my lad." Reaching her hands to his large head. The moment she touched his slick coat she had a flash of the pair of them in the fray of battle. Then another flash of them high in the clouds flying with great speed and urgency. "Oh, what have you been keeping from me young man?" She understood then, her Cathal would not be left behind and was so much more than he seemed. "I have no way of knowing how to bring you to Locbroalm," at his snort she smiled. "and I have a feeling it's something that I won't need to be worrying over. She watched as he turned his head and looked to the rest of the herd and most importantly to Caoimhe. His nicker and massive hooves pawed a the ground so show his agitation at leaving her behind. "Have no fear they will be looked after and very well cared for." She needed to call Colm to let him know he needed to come and bring the horses back to the farm. "Come here lovies." One by one Anene loved on her horses. "Don't you worry, I will be with you again." As the sun was starting to crest over the horizon Anene kissed her loves on the nose and rifted back to her cottage. She made the call to Colm and to him to pick up Rí, Caoimhe, and Tadhg, for she knew that Cathal somehow would not be in the paddock when Colm arrived.

Heart settled, Anene crawled back into bed with her still sleeping man. After morning lovemaking and a bite to eat, a knock sounded at the front door. Anene was not surprised to see her mother on the other side. It was the entire coven behind her that was a surprise to see.

"What's this?" She asked her mother.

"The coven is here to perform the handfasting for you at the circle." Miranda smiled knowingly. "If that is your wish?"

"Aye." Anene looked back over her shoulder to Tadhgán, and a warm glow filled her and settled in her heart. "That is my wish."

Thirty-Two

Anene, Tadhgán, and Miranda stood in the heart of the stone circle, while the rest of the coven surrounded them on the outside. The couple faced each other while her mother draped and wrapped the coven's gold, blue and green cords around their clasped hands.

"I, Miranda Wilkinson, come forward to complete the tying of Anene Wilkinson's and Tadhgán Ultan's hands. With this material, I bind thee, Anene and Tadhgán, to the vows you make to each other. The binding is not formed by this knot, but by your vows. You hold in your hands and hearts the making and breaking of this union." Miranda's words wobbled with feeling.

"With your hands and hearts now bound together as one," she continued, "I would like to share with you a blessing upon your union. May your mornings bring joy, and your evenings bring peace. May your troubles grow few as your blessings increase. Be no worse than the happiest day of your past. May you keep each other safe and may the children you bear be many times blessed as their parents are." She gave her daughter a knowing look that was not lost on Anene or Tadhgán.

A shimmering glow emanated from the cords wrapping the couple as one. They grew warm then vanished in a blinding light. It only lasted a few seconds, but in that moment Miranda was once again stuck by the figure who stood in a glow of light. Yet, unlike the day she, in her anger, was going to strike at Tadhgán, Miranda was able to see who was in the glow. It seemed so obvious now, a mother will always come to her child, whether he be in danger, or on the day he was to be married to his mate. The Mórrígan looked at her son then to Miranda, Goddess or no, no mother has dry eyes when their child commits themself to another. Miranda bowed her head then, like it never happened, The Mórrígan disappeared as did the glow. Anene, unaware of the Goddesses visit, looked back at hers and her now husband's wrists. The cords had not disappeared after all. They were now a shimmering, colorful tattoo on both their wrists. When they released their hands, Anene could see the handfasting cords were still tied together and just moved and stretched with them. A gasp brought her eyes from the new magickal cords to the coven's seer, Colleen.

Colleen's hand was covering her mouth as she looked at Tadhgán. The soft, golden spiked glow that had circled him was now a solid, shimmering crown hovering just above his head. There was no mistaking the meaning behind the royal piece. Here stood a King. But a King to whom was still unknown to all, but Anene.

"Anene?" Her mother's soft voice drew her from her thoughts. "Here." Miranda handed her a conjured mirror so she might see what the rest could see.

As Anene viewed herself in the temporary glass, above her head, much like Tadhgán's, hovered a golden crown with green and blue encrusted jewels. Once again, there was no mistaking its meaning. She stood in her stone circle, a Queen. Tadhgán's Queen. But once again a Queen for whom? Anene was not ready to answer the question before her. As the royal adornments began to fade, Anene felt a flutter and knew it was time to go through the doorway.

"There will come a time when I may call for aid," Anene addressed the coven. "Can I count on you?"

"You can count on us." The coven answered as one, to her shock, they all bowed to her and Tadhgán. Including her mother.

"Thank you." She looked to her husband, her mate, her one and only love. "Are you ready?" At his nod, she took Tadhgán's newly tattooed, corded hand in hers, readying herself to transport them both by way of rifting when she noticed her mother. She was dressed in fighting leathers and had weapons of her own.

"If you think you're going to Locbroalm without me, you are out of your fecking mind!" Miranda's mind was made up. "The man they have prisoner may be your father, but he is *my* mate and husband." She closed her eyes to ensure her anger and anguished heart stayed just below the surface. "I want him back." Her stance was unmistakable. There was no way they were leaving without her. Anene just held out her other hand and waited for her mother to take hold. "Thank you."

"As you said, he is your mate and husband. I would move mountains to get mine back if he were taken." She looked back to the coven. "Please, look after yourselves." Anene locked eyes with Colleen. "Keep a lookout for my call and look for more covens to converge. Be well brothers and sisters." And with that, the three of them rifted to the training area of the old cottage.

Silently, Anene opened her fathers chest and removed the gifts. One look at her mother told her Miranda had known about the chest and its contents. *Hell,* she thought while she pulled on the new black armor, *she might even know more about the sword,* but she wouldn't ask. She didn't want her mother to have to refuse her the information. While they strapped on their swords, quivers, and bows over their clothes Anene glanced over to Tadhgán who was once more back in the leather armor he arrived in. The scarred supple hunter green leather showed the years and years of wear. Anene decided, it was a damn fine look on him. Her's were similar to his, but the smaller shoulders and loss of the elbow pads allowed her better movement for her sword work and her archery. On her hip was the sword her father had left her, along with the bow on her back and sling shot on her upper thigh. Once dressed they moved to the older cellar, where the doorway had been placed all those years before.

Anene stood, and stared at a blank wall in the oldest part of the cellar. A wall, held the doorway created as a link between the two realms. Her mind wandered to times she'd passed the old cottage over the years. She never remembered there being a basement, let alone a doorway to another realm hidden in the walls.

"Are you ready, Luv?" Tadhgán asked, their corded hands linked while his other hovered over the blank wall before them. At her nod, he placed his hand on the cold stone wall, watched as it dissolved revealing a long, dark, stone covered tunnel, lit by torchlight. He took a deep breath, stepped through the doorway into the tunnel and then turned to wait for the women to join him. When the last foot left the mortal realm, the doorway closed, and a stone wall reappeared causing a dead end behind them.

"Anene!" Miranda's gasp had Tadhgán whipping back around to look at his mate. He was not prepared for what he saw.

There she was in her soft black leathers, with the sword from her father on her hip and the sling shot on her upper thigh. Nestled on her back was her quiver and bow, but it was the new adornments that took his breath away. Along with her weapons, she now carried large, brilliant wings. Wings that were not like the rest of the realm, or like Tadhgán's God given wings. He marveled at the perfect mix of the two. Anene's wings, like her eyes, carried a legion of dark blues and iridescent greens. They shimmered with hints of gold throughout, but it was their texture that was astonishing. Where Locbroalm had batlike wings, butterfly, and dragonfly wings, most Fae carried wings that consisted of a solid membranous layer in assorted colors, shapes, and sizes. Then, there were Tadhgán's black-feathered wings with a gold tinge at the tips. Anene's wings *looked* feathered like her mates, but were, upon closer inspection, hundreds of individual wings layered like feathers to form the greater wing. Her wings were nothing like that any realm had ever witnessed. The majesty of them gleamed with the magnitude of pure power that resided in their mistress. Her rounded human ears had elongated slightly at the tops to become more pointed while her already smooth skin had taken a porcelain look. If Tadhgán didn't know better, he would have thought she was a full-blooded fairy.

"What's happened to me?" Anene panicked. She could feel the changes being made to her body. She touched her face and felt the newly shaped ears, the texture of her skin. She looked over her shoulder at the wings that now jetted from her back. She pressed one hand to her abdomen and the other to her heart. Once again she felt the same flutter she felt in the stone circle after the handfasting. Eyes wide, she looked to her mate. "Tadhgán,"

"I know," he whispered and came to her side, drawing her in and placing his hands over hers. "I love you, witch." He kissed her lips. But before more could be said, a commotion at the other end of the tunnel drew their attention. Footsteps pounding on the stone floors, the clinking of metal armor and the swish and clang of swords being drawn could be heard running toward them.

"I think it's time to get the hell out of here," Miranda cautioned.

"Give me your hands." Anene latched on to her mother and mate. As the soldiers came around the bend, Anene closed her eyes and rifted them out of the tunnel.

When her eyes opened, she was greeted to a circle that was hers, but *not* hers. From its heart, Anene looked around and saw other Fae beyond the stones, silent, and very well armed. There, closer than the rest, stood a male with long white hair that spilled freely down his back. A small, red, intricate circlet decorated his head with the impressive knotwork forming a V on his mocha skin. His tall, lanky body was clad in black leather armor. Red, batlike wings fluttering behind him. On his hip was a longsword, but in his hands was a bow nocked with an arrow ready to fly.

"Well," the silky voice wafted over the distance between them. The sound of it made the hair on her arms and the back of her neck stand. A sliver of a smirk formed on the Fae's lips. Anene's new wings rustled in agitation. "We have been waiting for you."

To be Continued . . .

Anene and Tadhgán
will return in book 2
Locbroalm: The Golden Realm
June 20, 2026

About the Author

Cadmi Ó'Cléirigh Nora Weirich

Nora Weirich/Cadmi Ó'Cléirigh lives with her husband and four fur babies. Since 2007 she's been a Teachers Aide in her local school district. When not at school or in her office writing, you can find her in her favorite chair curled up with a blanket, a warm cup of coffee or tea with her nose in a book.

Over the years she has fallen in love with Romantasy books. When the opportunity arose, she took the plunge and tried her hand at the genre, for which she created the pen name Cadmi Ó'Cléirigh. She is currently working on book two of the Golden Realm Chronicles.

Other Works

Cadmi Ó'Cléirigh

The Golden Realm Chronicles
Quelocand: Land of the Queens
Locbroalm: The Golden Realm (Coming Soon)

Nora Weirich

Mackay Series
Mackay's Cliff House (Coming Soon)
Dunnegan's Cottage

Social Media

Cadmi Ó'Cléirigh

Nora Weirich